Thomas Heywood, John Addington Symonds, Arthur Wilson Verity

Thomas Heywood

Thomas Heywood, John Addington Symonds, Arthur Wilson Verity

Thomas Heywood

ISBN/EAN: 9783337396657

Printed in Europe, USA, Canada, Australia, Japan

Cover: Foto ©Raphael Reischuk / pixelio.de

More available books at **www.hansebooks.com**

THE BEST PLAYS OF THE OLD DRAMATISTS.

THOMAS HEYWOOD

EDITED BY A. WILSON VERITY:

WITH AN INTRODUCTION

BY J. ADDINGTON SYMONDS.

"I lie and dream of your full Mermaid wine."—*Beaumont.*

UNEXPURGATED EDITION.

LONDON:

VIZETELLY & CO., 16, *HENRIETTA STREET,*

COVENT GARDEN.

1888.

" What things have we seen
Done at the Mermaid ! heard words that have been
So nimble, and so full of subtle flame,
As if that every one from whence they came
Had meant to put his whole wit in a jest,
And had resolved to live a fool the rest
Of his dull life."

Master Francis Beaumont to Ben Jonson.

" Souls of Poets dead and gone,
What Elysium have ye known,
Happy field or mossy cavern,
Choicer than the Mermaid Tavern ? "

Keats.

CONTENTS.

The world's a theatre, the earth a stage, [1]
Which God and nature doth with actors fill :
Kings have their entrance in due equipage,
And some their parts play well, and others ill.
The best no better are (in this theátre),
Where every humour's fitted in his kind ;
This a true subject acts, and that a traitor,
The first applauded, and the last confined ;
This plays an honest man, and that a knave,
A gentle person this, and he a clown,
One man is ragged, and another brave :
All men have parts, and each one acts his own.
She a chaste lady acteth all her life ;
A wanton courtezan another plays ;
This covets marriage love, that nuptial strife :
Both in continual action spend their days :
Some citizens, some soldiers, born to adventer,
Shepherds, and sea-men.   Then our play's begun
When we are born, and to the world first enter,
And all find exits when their parts are done.
If then the world a theatre present,
As by the roundness it appears most fit,
Built with star-galleries of high ascent,
In which Jehove doth as spectator sit,
And chief determiner to applaud the best,
And their endeavours crown with more than merit ;
But by their evil actions dooms the rest
To end disgraced, whilst others praise inherit ;
He that denies then theatres should be,
He may as well deny a world to me.

THOMAS HEYWOOD. [2]

[1] "So compared by the Fathers," Heywood explains in the margin.

[2] Prefixed to his *Apology for Actors* (1612).

THOMAS HEYWOOD.

"IF I were to be consulted as to a reprint of our old English dramatists," says Charles Lamb, "I should advise to begin with the collected plays of Heywood. He was a fellow actor and fellow dramatist with Shakespeare. He possessed not the imagination of the latter, but in all those qualities which gained for Shakespeare the attribute of gentle, he was not inferior to him—generosity, courtesy, temperance in the depths of passion ; sweetness, in a word, and gentleness ; Christianism, and true hearty Anglicism of feelings, shaping that Christianism, shine throughout his beautiful writings in a manner more conspicuous than in those of Shakespeare ; but only more conspicuous, inasmuch as in Heywood these qualities are primary, in the other subordinate to poetry." In another note Lamb calls Heywood a "prose Shakespeare." Allowing for the exaggeration with which an enthusiastic love for our then

neglected minor dramatists charged the criticism of Charles Lamb, this verdict is in many points a just one. Heywood, while he lacks the poetry, philosophy, deep insight into nature, and consummate art of Shakespeare—those qualities, in a word, which render Shakespeare supreme among dramatic poets—has a sincerity, a tenderness of pathos, and an instinctive perception of nobility, that distinguish him among the playwrights of the seventeenth century. Like Dekker, he wins our confidence and love. We keep a place in our affection for his favourite characters; they speak to us across two centuries with the voices of friends; while the far more brilliant masterpieces of many contemporary dramatists stir only our aesthetic admiration.[1]

Heywood, unlike many of his contemporaries, and in this respect notably unlike Dekker, seems to have kept tolerably free from joint composition. Of twenty-four plays, only two, *The Late Lancashire Witches* and *Fortune by Land and Sea*, were produced by him in collaboration, the former with Brome, and the latter with W. Rowley. Of all the playwrights of that period he was the most prolific. In 1633 he owned to having " had either an entire

---

[1] Until recently, Heywood's plays were only accessible piecemeal and in parts. Dodsley's collection contained two; Dilke's contained three, and Baldwyn's two. Between 1842 and 1851, the Old Shakespeare Society produced altogether twelve; while Mr. Halliwell in 1853 printed the *Lancashire Witches* separately. At last, in 1874 Mr. John Pearson issued a complete edition in six volumes. Since that date another play in MS. by Heywood, *The Captives*, was discovered and printed by Mr. A. H. Bullen in the last volume of his *Old Plays* (1885).

hand or at least a main finger " in two hundred and
twenty dramas ; and after that date others were
printed, which may perhaps be reckoned in augmentation of this number. His literary fertility is proved
by his *Nine Books of Various History concerning
Women*, a folio of 466 pages, which appeared in
1624 with this memorandum :   " Opus excogitatum
inchoatum, explicitum, et typographo excusum inter
septemdecem septimanas."   Kirkman, the book-
seller, in his advertisement to the reader at the end
of the second edition of his catalogue of plays,
observes of Heywood that " he was very laborious ;
for he not only acted almost every day, but also
obliged himself to write a sheet every day for
several years together."   Besides composing
dramas, he delighted in the labour of compilation,
and had for some time on hand a Biographical
Dictionary of all the poets, from the most remote
period of the world's history down to his own time.
The loss of his MS. collections for this book is
greatly to be regretted, since there was no man of
that century better qualified by geniality and
honesty of purpose for the task than the old playwright, who put into the lips of Apuleius :—

> " Not only whatsoever's mine,
>   But all true poets' raptures are divine."

Even as it is, the few lines in Heywood's *Hierarchy
of Angels* on the nicknames of the poets of his day
are among the raciest scraps of information which
we possess about those dramatists.   The miscella-

neous nature of Heywood's literary labours justifies us in classing him, together with Robert Greene, among the earliest professional *littérateurs* of our language. His criticism is often quite as valuable as his dramatic poetry. The whole of the running dialogue between Apuleius and Midas in *Love's Mistress*, for example, contains a theory of the relation of poets to the public, while the prologues to *A Challenge for Beauty* and *The Royal King and Loyal Subject* are interesting as showing to what extent the dramatists of the Elizabethan age pursued their art with conscious purpose and comparison.

, We may notice how careless, in common with many of his contemporaries, Heywood was concerning the fate of his dramatic writings. Plays, and comedies in particular, were written, not to be read and studied, but to be acted. This we should never forget while passing judgment upon the unequal work of the Elizabethan playwrights. In the Address to the Reader, prefixed to the *English Traveller*, Heywood complains that this tragi-comedy had been published without his consent, and apologises for coming forward to father it before the world, adding, not without a sly poke at Jonson and his school :—

"True it is that my plays are not exposed unto the world in volumes, to bear the title of works (as others) ; one reason is, that many of them by shifting and change of companies had been negligently lost ; others of them are still retained in the hands of some actors, who think it against their peculiar profit to have them come in print ; and a third that it never was any great ambition in me to be in this kind voluminously read."

In the preface to the *Rape of Lucrece* he repeats his complaints against the clandestine and un-authorised publication of his plays, with this de-claration of his own habit of dealing with them : —

"It hath been no custom in ine of all other men (courteous readers) to commit my plays to the press ; the reason, though some may attribute to my own insufficiency, I had rather subscribe, in that, to their severe censure, than, by seeking to avoid the imputa-tion of weakness, to incur greater suspicion of honesty ; for though some have used a double sale of their labours, first to the stage, and after to the press ; for my own part I here proclaim myself ever faithful to the first, and never guilty of the last."

He then proceeds to show that the pirated editions of his plays in mangled copies have forced him to right himself before the public by superin-tending the issue of a certain number of his works. In the prologue to *If you Know not Me, you Know Nobody*, the same apology is reiterated in terms which throw a curious light upon the short-hand reporters of plays for the press, employed by piratical booksellers to the prejudice of authors and theatre managers :—

> " Some by stenography drew
> The plot ; put it in print (scarce one word true) :
> And in that lameness it hath limped so long,
> The author now to vindicate that wrong
> Hath took the pains, upright upon its feet
> To teach it walk, so please you sit, and see't."

Of the twenty-three plays in Mr. Pearson's collec-tion, four—namely, the two parts of *Edward IV.* and the two parts of *If you Know not Me, you Know Nobody*—are histories of the old-fashioned sort, rudely dramatised from English chronicles,

and seasoned with comic and pathetic episodes.
Of the two series, *Edward IV.* has in it more of
Heywood's special quality ; the interlude of the
Tanner of Tamworth and the romance of Mistress
Shore displaying his double power of dealing with
drollery and passion in the simplest and most
natural style. In truth, the second part of *Edward IV.*, which begins with a dull, confused
account of that king's wars in France, becomes a
romantic drama on the legend of Jane Shore.
This is chiefly remarkable for the way in which
Heywood sustains the character of Master Shore,
who is the very mirror of sound English middle-
class Christianity. The erring wife's portrait is
touched with striking, if somewhat sentimental,
appeals to natural sympathy. Both are excellent
examples of the dramatist's homely art and
honest humanity, though nothing can be balder
and more artless than the manner of their death
together on the stage. *If you Know not Me, you
Know Nobody* is a chronicle of the reign of Queen
Elizabeth, including her early dangers and the late
glories of the defeat of the Armada. The whole
series of scenes breathes the strongest English
patriotism and the most enthusiastic Protestant
feeling. It is a pity that, hastily and clumsily
pieced together, a drama so interesting in its
matter should almost be valueless as a work of art.
It was published as a companion to S. Rowley's
When you See Me, you Know Me, which has
been reprinted by Dr. Karl Elze.

The *Late Lancashire Witches* and the *Wise Woman of Hogsdon* are comedies of English life, without that element of romantic interest which Heywood usually added to the domestic drama. The plot of the latter play turns upon the quackeries and impostures of a professed fortune-teller ; but to mention it in the same breath with Jonson's *Alchemist* would be ridiculous. The *Lancashire Witches*, though it attempts, in one scene at least, to touch the deeper interest of witchcraft, deals for the most part only with the vulgar and farcical aspects of the subject. It has nothing in common with *The Witch of Edmonton* or Middleton's *Witch.* A household turned topsy-turvy, a coursing-match spoiled, a farm-servant changed into a gelding, and a bridegroom be-witched with a charmed codpiece-point upon his wedding night, are among its insipid drolleries. In *Fortune by Land and Sea, The English Tra-veller, The Fair Maid of the Exchange*, and both parts of *The Fair Maid of the West*, Heywood displays to better advantage his predilection for hómespun stories, dealing chiefly with the incidents of country life and the adventures of English captains on the high seas. Pure comedy and pure tragedy were neither of them suited to his genius. He required a subject in which the familiar events of English domestic life might be contrasted with the romantic episodes of sea-roving and of foreign travel. To interweave these motives with the addition of pathos and sentiment, was

just what he could do successfully. No dramatist
has painted more faithful *home* pictures. None
have thrown more natural light upon the pursuits
of English gentlemen in the first half of the seventeenth century. The merit of all these five plays is
considerable. It would have been impossible even
for Fletcher to realise a difficult scene with greater
ease and delicacy than are displayed in the interview between young Geraldine and Wincott's wife
in *The English Traveller*. A pair of lovers, who
have been parted, meet again and renew their old
vows in the bedroom of the girl just made a wife.
The calm strength and honourable feeling displayed by this Paolo and his Francesca in their
perilous interview are the result of unsuspecting
innocence and sweetness. If the situation is
almost unnatural and disagreeable, the-poet has
contrived to invest it with the air of purity, reality,
sincerity, and health. *Fortune by Land and Sea* is
richer in scenes which reveal Heywood at his best.
The opening of this play is one of his most
vigorous transcripts from contemporary English
country life. Frank Forrest, a daring and high-
blooded youngster, evades his careful father, and
flies off to a neighbouring tavern, less for the sake
of drinking than in order to meet spirited companions. One of them picks a quarrel with him
about his respect for his old father, and the boy is
killed. The grief of old Forrest, the challenge
given by the brother to Frank's murderer, the duel
that ensues, and young Forrest's escape, are all set

forth with photographic reality and force. Event
huddles upon event, and the whole proceeds with
the simplicity of truth. These scenes only form a
prelude to the play, which, like most of Heywood's, contains a double plot ; but at the same
time they are its salt. The *Fair Maid of the
West*, a romantic drama in two parts, sets forth
the adventures of the Devonshire Captain Spencer
and his love Bess Bridges, who is introduced to us
as the mistress of a Plymouth inn. It may be
said in passing, that few tavern-scenes in our Elizabethan drama, not even those of Dekker, are
better painted than those which form the introduction to Act I. Battles with pirates, slavery in
Fez, and adventures in Florence form the staple of
the drama, ·which must have presented many
attractions to an English audience of the age of
Stukeley, Sherley, and Drake. The *Fair Maid of
the Exchange* is another play belonging to what the
Germans style *das bürgerliche Drama*. To my
mind its sentiment is sickly, and its story, in spite
of many beautiful passages, disagreeable. Phillis
is the Fair Maid ; and the real hero of the piece is
a cripple, who saves her from a ruffianly assault,
and who falls in love with her. She returns his
love ; but Heywood had not the courage to
develop this situation. Therefore he makes the
cripple plead the cause of another suitor to the
Fair Maid, who at the end of the play transfers her
affections with a levity and a complacency that
would be offensive in real life. The charm of this

comedy consists in a certain air of April-morning freshness; it has, moreover, one of Heywood's most exquisite songs, a lyric that deserves to rank with Dekker's, and which is made for music : " Ye little birds that sit and sing."

The seven plays on English domestic subjects which I have now enumerated, are all of them eclipsed in their own kind by Heywood's master-piece, *A Woman Killed with Kindness.* Leaving that, the finest bourgeois tragedy of our Elizabethan literature, for future comment, we come to another group of Heywood's plays, which may perhaps be best described as romances. Of these, *The Four Prentices of London*, a juvenile performance of the poet, is both the least interesting, and by far the most extravagant. Guy, Eustace, Tancred, and Godfrey, the four sons of the Duke of Boulogne, and at the same time 'prentices in London shops, start off like Paladins, and win their laurels in the first Crusade. Whether this absurd play was intended, like Fletcher's *Knight of the Burning Pestle*, for a parody of chivalrous romances, or whether, as its dedication to "the Honest and High-spirited 'Prentices, the Readers" seems to imply, it was meant for a hyperbolical compliment to the courage of London counter-jumpers, is not a very important matter. The latter is the more probable supposition. The plot is a tissue of sanguinary and sentimental adventures, with a certain admixture of good-humoured sarcasm on the London cits, that may have gratified their 'prentice-lads. The

old quarto has for frontispiece a curious woodcut
of the four knightly shop-boys. *The Royal King
and Loyal Subject* is a drama with an ideal inten-.
tion. Pretending to be founded upon English
history, it really sets forth the contest of generosity
between a monarch and one of his great nobles.
In the course of this play Heywood has used some
of the motives that add pathos to *Patient Grissil ;*
the King of England exposes the Lord Marshal to
a series of humiliations and studied insults before,
as a climax to the favour he intends to heap upon
him, he unites his own family and that of his subject by a triple bond of marriage. The whole situation is better in conception than in execution. I
take it to be one of Heywood's earlier dramatic
essays. *A Challenge for Beauty* tells the tale of a
proud Portuguese Queen, who thinks herself the
fairest woman of the world, but who is brought at
the end of the play to admit that she is vanquished
as much in beauty by an English lady as her
husband's captains are surpassed in courage and
courtesy by English gentlemen. The most interesting portion of the drama is subordinate to the
subject which supplies the title. The contest of
generosity between a noble Spaniard, Valladaura,
and an English captain, Montferrers, who has been
sold into slavery together with a friend that he
dearly loved, displays all that innate gentleness
and chivalry which Lamb recognized as the fairest
of Heywood's characteristics. Valladaura finds his
old enemy Montferrers in the slave-market, pays

down his price, and sets him free. Montferrers
cannot accept freedom while his friend remains a
slave. Valladaura buys them both, taking Montferrers with him to remain, an honoured guest, in
his own house. Now begins the duel of courtesy
between the two men. Valladaura loves a lady,
Petrocella, and beseeches the Englishman to plead
his suit with her. Montferrers executes the task,
though he also loves Petrocella, and discovers in the
course of his wooing that she returns his passion. The
use he makes of her avowal is to bind her over to
accept the Spaniard's suit. But Valladaura is no whit
less chivalrous. He resigns the lady to the man
who has deserved her best. Those who have not
studied the working out of such strained situations .
in the *Lustspiele* of Heywood or of Fletcher, can
hardly imagine what flesh and blood reality these
poets gave to almost inconceivable improbabilities.
The vigorous and natural play of passions under
strange disguises and painful conditions — the
hesitations of divided allegiance—confusions of sex
—contradictory emotions, pleased our play-going
ancestors ; and the dramatists had the skill to display the truth of human nature beneath the mask
and garb of romantic fantasies. Under other hands,
or in an age of less directness, such motives would
have been ridiculous or offensive. *A Maidenhead
well Lost*, is a romance of this type with Italian
characters. While challenging comparison with
similar comedies by Fletcher, Ford, Massinger, and
others, it is but a tasteless and feeble production.

Heywood was so thorough an Englishman that, for the full exercise of his poetic faculty, he needed a subject smacking of his native soil.

Having now described Heywood's Histories, Domestic Dramas, and Romances, it remains for me to speak of the fourth group into which his plays may be divided. At the same time, I should observe that these divisions are, after all, but incomplete and artificial. Many of those which I have classified as Domestic Dramas, for example, borrow largely from the element of romance, while two of them are virtually comedies of farcical intrigue. The *Golden, Silver, Brazen,* and *Iron Ages* form a series of four plays, in which Heywood has dramatised antique legends, following principally Homer and Ovid in the selection of his material. Though there are many passages of graceful poetry and of humorous burlesque in these long-winded mythologies, they cannot be said to have much value either as dramas or as descriptive poems. That Heywood felt a natural predilection for this kind of composition may be seen in the rhyming versions he has made of Lucian's Dialogues. Some of these, especially the conversations of Jupiter with Ganymede, and of Juno with Jupiter, deserve attention for their plain, straightforward rendering into racy English of the witty Greek. *Love's Mistress,* which is a dramatic translation of Apuleius's tale of Cupid and Psyche, is written in the same mood. It takes the form of a long allegorical masque ; and here the poetry is sustained throughout at a higher level. Last of all these classic dramas in my list comes the *Rape of Lucrece*. Here Heywood quits the epical or allegorical treatment of classical subject-matter for the domain of tragedy. Yet he has given to this episode of ancient Roman history more the form of a chronicle-play than of the legitimate drama.

It cannot be denied that the effects of negligence in composition and over-strained fertility are traceable in all that Heywood wrote. He has produced no masterpiece, no thoroughly sustained flight of fancy, no play perfect in form, and very few absolutely self-consistent characters. His finest passages seem to flow from him by accident, as the result of a temporary exaltation of his talent, rather than of settled purpose. His best scenes are improvised. Nor is it possible to evade the conclusion, quaintly phrased by Kirkman, that "many of his plays being composed loosely in taverns, occasions them to be so mean." These defects, indeed, Heywood shared in common with his contemporaries. Not many dramatic compositions of the seventeenth century can boast of classical finish or of artistic unity. Yet there is in the best works of such men as Marlowe, Webster, Ford, and Fletcher, a natural completeness, an unstudied singleness of effect, which Heywood almost invariably misses. With all our affection for him, we are forced to admire his poetry in fragments and with reservations. Perhaps he shows to best advantage in the extracts made by Lamb.

No dramatist ever used less artifice. The subjects which he chose are either taken straight from real life, or else adopted crudely from the legends of ancient Greece and Rome. In each case Heywood's manner and method are the same. He uses simple, easy English, and sets forth unaffected feeling. The scenes have no elaborate connexion. They cohere by juxtaposition. The language is never high-flown or bombastic ; rarely rising to the height of poetical diction, and attaining to intensity only when the passion of the moment is overwhelming, it owes its occasional force to its sincerity.

His means of reaching the heart are of the simplest ; yet they are often deep and effectual. He depends for his tragic effects upon no Até, no midnight horrors, no sarcastic knave. Yet his use of some mere name—*Nan, Nan!*—and his allusions to Christ and our religion, go straight to the very soul. His men are all gentlemen ; and it may be said in passing that he had more understanding of men, especially high-spirited young men, than of women. Nothing could be finer than the bearing, for example, of young Forrest when he challenges Rainsford, or of Valladaura and Montferrers, or again of Frankford and Sir Charles Mountford in *A Woman Killed with Kindness*. Now and then he touches the spring of true poetic language, as in these phrases :—

> "Oh, speak no more !
> For more than this I know and have recorded
> Within the red-leaved table of my heart.".

Or again :—

> " My friend and I
> Like two chain bullets side by side will fly
> Thorough the jaws of death."

Or yet again :—

> " Astonishment,
> Fear, and amazement beat upon my heart,
> Even as a madman beats upon a drum."

The last line of this quotation is a splendid instance of the way in which the old dramatists heightened horror by connecting one terrific image with another of a different sort, yet no less terrible. The fury of a lunatic hideously rattling his drum with fantastic gestures rushes across our mind without distracting our attention from the anguish of the man who speaks the words. The simile does but add force to his bewilderment.

Though not a lyrist in any high sense of the word, Heywood at times produced songs remarkable for purity and freshness. To one of these in the *Fair Maid of the Exchange* I have already called attention. Not less beautiful is a morning ditty, which begins " Pack, clouds away," in the *Rape of Lucrece*. The patriotic war-song in the First Part of *King Edward IV.*, " Agincourt, Agincourt, know ye not Agincourt ? " is full of fire ; while a humorous catch, " The Spaniard loves his ancient slop," must have been a favourite with the groundlings, since it occurs in both *The Rape of Lucrece* and *A Challenge for Beauty.* ' There is plenty of proof that Heywood could write good words for-street melodies. That his English style is generally free, flowing, and vernacular admits of no question; yet such were the contradictions of the age in which he lived, that he must needs at intervals display his erudition by the pedantic coinage of new phrases. Such words as " trifulk," to " diapason," " sonance," " cathedral state," " tenébrous," " mœchal," " monomachy," " obdure " for " obdurate," all of which occur in *The Rape of Lucrece*, demand for their inventor the emetic which Jonson in *The Poetaster* administered to Marston, and prove conspicuously how a little learning on the lips of an honest playwright is a dangerous thing.

The Rape of Lucrece, as I have before hinted, is nothing but the narrative of Livy divided into tableaux with no artistic consistency. It contains the whole story of Tullia's ambition and the death of Servius, the journey of Brutus to Delphi, the fulfilment of the oracle, the betrayal of Gabii, the camp at Ardea, the crime of Tarquin, the rising of the Roman nobles, the war with Porsena, and the stories of Horatius and Scevola. The characters are devoid of personal reality. Lucrece herself is more a type of innocence than a true woman. Of the minor characters which fill out the play, by far the most original is Valerius. His part must have been a favourite with the London audience, for on the title-page we read : " with the several songs in their apt places by Valerius, the merry lord among the Roman peers." Instead of fooling, sulking, or gaming, as the other nobles do beneath the Tarquin

tyranny, he does nothing but sing. It is impossible
to extract from him a word of sense in sober prose.
But love songs, loose songs, drinking songs, dirges,
street cries, a Scotch song, a Dutch song, and pas-
toral ditties, with rhymes on the names of public
houses, public women, ale, wine, and so forth, flow
from him in and out of season.   He is the most
striking instance of the licence with which the
poets of the time were forced to treat their subjects
for the sake of the gallery.   Some of his verses are
full of exquisite feeling ; others are grossly coarse ;
some are comical, and others melancholy ; but all
are English.   When Valerius first hears of the outrage offered to Lucrece, he breaks out into a catch
of the most questionable kind, together with
Horatius Cocles and a Clown.   The whole matter
is turned to ridicule, and it is difficult after this
musical breakdown to read the tragedy except as
a burlesque.

   Love's Mistress is a Masque in five acts rather
than a play proper.   In its day it enjoyed great
popularity, for it was represented before James I.
and his queen three times within the space of eight
days.   Its three prologues and one epilogue are
remarkable even among the productions of that
age for their fulsome flattery.   The story of Cupid
and Psyche, on which the Masque is founded,
could not have failed to yield some beauties even
to a far inferior craftsman than Heywood ; and
there are many passages of delicate and tender
poetry scattered up and down the piece.   Indeed,

the whole is treated with an airy grace that has peculiar charm, while its abrupt contrasts and frequent changes must have made it a rare spectacle under the wise conduct of

"that admirable artist, Mr. Inigo Jones, master-surveyor of the king's work, &c., who to every act, nay, almost to every scene, by his excellent inventions gave such an extraordinary lustre—upon every occasion changing the stage, to the admiration of all the spectators—that, as I must ingenuously confess, it was above my apprehension to conceive."

Still, even in *Love's Mistress*, Heywood betrays that lack of the highest artistic instinct, which we discover in almost all his work. He cannot manage the Court pageant with that exquisite tact which distinguishes the *Endimion* and the *Sapho* of Lyly. The whole play has a running commentary of criticism and exposition, conveyed in a dialogue between Apuleius, the author of the legend, and Midas, who personates stupidity. Apuleius explains the allegory as the action proceeds ; Midas remains to the end the dull unappreciative boor, who " stands for ignorance," and only cares for dancing clowns, or the coarse jests of buffoons. Apuleius is the type of the enthusiastic poet, whose wit is " aimed at inscrutable things beyond the moon." Midas is the gross conceited groundling, who, turning everything he touches to dross, prefers Pan's fool to Apollo's chorus, and drives the god of light indignantly away. Both of them wear asses' heads : Midas, because he grovels on the earth ; Apuleius, because all human intellect proves foolish if it flies too far. There is much

good-humoured irony in this putting of donkey's
ears on the poet's head. This contrast between
art and ignorance is paralleled by a series of subtle
antitheses that pervade the play. Immortal Erôs
finds a balance in the stupid clown, who boasts that
Apollo has given him music, Cupid love, and
Psyche beauty ; but who remains untunable, unlov-
able, and hideous to the end. The juxtaposition
of heaven and hell within our souls, the aspirations
and the downfalls of our spirit, the nobility and the
vileness of men around us, the perpetual contradiction between the region toward which we soar
in our best moments, and the dull ground over
which we have to plod in daily life : such are the
metaphysical conceptions which underlie the shifting scenes and many-twinkling action of the
masque. It would be unfair to institute any comparison between *Love's Mistress* considered as a
poem, and the delicate version of the legend in the
Earthly Paradise. Yet there are touches of true
poetry here and there throughout the play. The
haunted house of Love which receives Psyche and
where Echo and Zephyrus are her attendants, the
visit of her three sisters, and the midnight awaking
of wrathful Cupid, are all conceived with light and
airy fancy. Cupid in his anger utters this curse on
women :—

> " You shall be still rebellious, like the sea,
>   And, like the winds, inconstant ; things forbid
>   You most shall covet, loathe what you would like
>   You shall be wise in wishes, but, enjoying,
>   Shall venture heaven's loss for a little toying."

There is another aspect under which *Love's Mis-tress* may be viewed—as a very early attempt at classical burlesque. Cupid, for example, is the naughty boy of Olympus. He describes Juno's anger against Ganymede :—

> "The boy by chance upon her fan had spilled
> A cup of nectar : oh, how Juno swore !
> I told my aunt I'd give her a new fan
> To let Jove's page be Cupid's serving-man."

Vulcan appears at his forge with more orders than he knows how to deal with :—

> "There's half a hundred thunder-bolts bespoke ;
> Neptune hath broke his mace ; and Juno's coach
> Must be new-mended, and the hindmost wheels
> Must have two spokes set in."

He thinks of making Venus "turn she-smith," but

> "She'd spend me more
> In nectar and sweet balls to scour her cheeks,
> Smudged and besmeared with coal-dust and with smoke,
> Than all her work would come to."

This is, of course, very simple fooling. Yet it contains the germ of those more thorough-going parodies in which the present age delights.

The play in which Heywood showed for once that he was not unable to produce a masterpiece is *A Woman Killed with Kindness.* All his powers of direct painting from the English life he knew so well, his faculty for lifting prose to the border-ground of poetry by the intensity of the emotion which he communicates, his simple art of laying bare the very nerves of passion, are here exhibited in perfection. This domestic tragedy touches one like truth. Its scenes are of everyday life. Common talk is used, and the pathos is homely; not like Webster's, brought from far. Tastes may differ as to the morality or the wholesomeness of the sentiment evolved in the last act. None, however, can resist its artless claim upon our sympathies. The story may be briefly told. Mr. Frankford, a country gentleman of good fortune, marries the sister of Sir Francis Acton, and receives into his house an agreeable gentleman of broken means called Wendoll. They live together happily till Wendoll, trusted to the full by Frankford, takes advantage of his absence to seduce his wife. Nicholas, a servant, who, with the instinct of a faithful dog, has always suspected the stranger, discovers and informs Frankford of his dishonour. Frankford obtains ocular proof of his wife's guilt, and punishes her by sending her to live alone, but at ease, in a manor that belongs to him. There she pines away and dies at last, after a reconciliation with her injured husband.[1]

In the *genre* Heywood had predecessors, but none of his rivals surpassed him. The chief in-

---

[1] With this main-plot Heywood has interwoven a subordinate and independent story. To dwell upon this under-plot would be superfluous. Yet I may point out that it is borrowed from an Italian Novella by Illicini, the incidents of which Heywood carefully transferred to English scenes. In like manner *The Captive*, consists of a main-plot borrowed from the *Mostellaria* of Plautus and an under-plot adapted from a novella of the Neapolitan, *Masuccio*. See my *Shakspere's Predecessors* (p. 462), and a letter written by me to the *Academy* (Dec. 12, 1885).

terest of the play centres in the pure, confiding, tender-hearted character of Frankford. His blithe contentment during the first months of marriage, and the generosity with which he opens his doors to Wendoll, form a touching prelude to the suspicions, indignantly repelled at first, which grow upon him after he has weighed the tale of his wife's infidelity related by Nicholas. He resolves to learn the truth, if possible, by actual experience. Here is interposed an admirable scene, in which Frankford and his wife, with Wendoll and another gentleman, play cards. The dialogue is a long *double entendre*, skilfully revealing the tortures of a jealous husband's mind and his suspicious misinterpretation of each casual word. When they rise from the card-table, Frankford instructs Nicholas to get him duplicate keys for all his rooms. Then he causes a message to be delivered to him on a dark and stormy evening, and sets off with his servant, intending to return at midnight unnoticed and unexpected. His hesitation on the threshold of his wife's chamber is one of the finest turning-points of the dramatic action. At last he summons courage to enter, but returns immediately :—

> " O me unhappy ! I have found them lying
> Close in each other's arms and fast asleep.
> But that I would not damn two precious souls,
> Bought with my Saviour's blood, and send them, laden
> With all their scarlet sins upon their backs,
> Unto a fearful judgment, their two lives
> Had met upon my rapier."

Then, with a passionate stretching forth of his

desire toward the impossible, which reveals the whole depth of his tenderness, he cries :—

> " O God ! O God ! that it were possible
> To undo things done ; to call back yesterday !
> That Time could turn up his swift sandy glass,
> To untell the days, and to redeem these hours !
> Or that the sun
> Could, rising from the west, draw his coach backward,
> Take from the account of time so many minutes,
> Till he had all these seasons called again,
> Those minutes, and those actions done in them,
> Even from her first offence ; that I might take her
> As spotless as an angel in my arms !
> But oh ! I talk of things impossible,
> And cast beyond the moon.   God give me patience .!
> For I will in and wake them. "

The following scene, in which Frankford pleads with his guilty and conscience-stricken wife, is full of pathos.   Its passion is simple and homefelt.   Each question asked by Frankford is such as a wronged husband has the right to ask.   Each answer given by the wife is broken in mere monosyllables more eloquent than protestation.   We feel the whole, because not a word is strained or far-fetched, because the tenderness of Frankford is not merely sentimental, because he does not rave or tear his passion to tatters ; finally, because in the profundity of his grief he still can call his wife by her pet name.

Mrs. Frankford is no Guinevere, nor, again, like Alice in *Arden of Feversham*, is she steeled and blinded by an overwhelming passion.   Heywood fails to realise her character completely, producing, as elsewhere in his portraits of women, a weak and vacillating picture.   She changes quite suddenly

from love for her newly-wedded lord to light longing for Wendoll, and then back again to the
remorse which eats her life away. Wendoll is
drawn more powerfully. We see the combat in
his soul between the sense of duty to his benefactor
and the love which invades him like an ocean,
drowning all the landmarks he had raised to warn
him from the perilous ground. Adultery has been
three times treated by Heywood. In *The English
Traveller* Mrs. Wincott sins with the same limp and
unexplained facility as Mrs. Frankford. In *Edward
IV.* Jane Shore is meant to raise the same sentimental pity as Mrs. Frankford on her death-bed.

Thomas Heywood was a Lincolnshire man, pre-
sumably of good family, though I cannot find that
the Visitations of that county record any pedigree
of his name. No poet of his age showed a more
intimate acquaintance with the habits of country
gentlemen, and none was more imbued with the
spirit of true gentleness. He was a Fellow of
Peter House, Cambridge, where he probably acquired that learning which sat upon him so lightly.
He began to write for the stage as early as 1596,
and in 1598 we find him engaged as an actor and
a sharer in Henslowe's company. Little else is
known about his life, and, though it is certain that
he lived to a ripe age, we are ignorant of the date
of his death. Like many authors of his period,
he adopted a motto for his works, to which he ad-
hered, placing on his title-pages, *Aut prodesse solent
aut delectare.* We may still say, with truth, that

what he has written almost invariably succeeds in both these aims. His plays are defiled with very few unpardonably coarse scenes, those to be found in *A Royal King and Loyal Subject* being an exception to prove the rule. While concluding these introductory remarks, I can only express my regret that the editor has not been able to include more pieces of Heywood in the Mermaid Series ; for Heywood is essentially an author whom we love the better the more we read of him. It is impossible to rise from the perusal of his plays without being refreshed and invigorated. May the five here presented, out of the twenty-four which bear his name, induce students to carry their researches further. They will, I feel confident, discover that three other sets of five plays are no less worthy of perusal than the five here chosen for their recreation.

JOHN ADDINGTON SYMONDS.

. The text of four of the plays contained in this volume is substantially that of Pearson's reprint (1874) ; the exception is *The Fair Maid of the West*, reprinted from the edition by Collier, though I have felt it necessary to dissent from Collier's readings in several places. For the convenience of the reader I have attempted to indicate the changes of scene in the whole of the plays, marking also the probable locality of each scene, and altering the rather vague and unsatisfactory stage directions of the old copies. My thanks are due to Mr. S. W. Orson for many valuable suggestions.   A. W. V.

THE RED BULL THEATRE.

EYWOOD'S PLAYS were frequently acted on the stage of the Red Bull Theatre, of which Kirkman supplied an illustration in his collection of *Drolls and Farces*. This illustration has been reproduced as a front-piece to the present volume. The theatre was one of the oldest in London; originally·it was, as the name indicates, an inn yard, converted into a regular theatre during Elizabeth's reign, and, like several contemporary playhouses, often used for other amusements; it was never considered a high-class theatre, but it was very popular. Its site was on a plot of ground, between the upper end of St. John Street and Clerkenwell Green, during the eighteenth century still called Red Bull Yard, and named Woodbridge Street at the beginning of the present century. In 1819 a writer who carefully investigated the matter could find no trace of the theatre; though he indicated a field of search by suggesting that its exact position might perhaps be set forth in existing leases.

Various companies played at the Red Bull at different times. In 1623 the Queen's company (under the jurisdiction of the "now Earl of Leicester, then Lord Chamberlain of the Household of the said late Queen Anne of Denmark") gave place to the Prince's, so called after Prince Charles. In 1629, women actors (who also appeared at other theatres) played at the Red Bull. In 1639 the Red Bull Company got into trouble. A complaint was made to the king "that the stage-players of the ·Red Bull have lately, for many days together, acted a scandalous and libellous play, wherein they have audaciously reproached, and in a libellous manner traduced and personated, not only some of the Aldermen of the City of London and other persons of quality, but also scandalised and defamed the whole profession of Proctors belonging to the Court of Civil Law, and reflected upon the Government." For this they received "exemplary punishment." In the following year the company which had been playing at the Fortune Theatre changed to the Red Bull.

Heywood.

This was the only theatre that lived on until Restoration times, though not without many difficulties. Such items of information as the following (1655) are not uncommon :—"At the playhouse this week many were put to the rout by the soldiers." "The actors, too," Kirkman writes, " were commonly not only stripped, but many times imprisoned, till they paid such ransom as the soldiers should impose upon them." Although the Red Bull survived the Commonwealth it succumbed soon after the Restoration. In 1660 Charles II. issued an order (not very rigorously carried out) for their suppression, as a concession to civic authorities. In 1661 Pepys wrote that " the clothes are very poor, and the actors but common fellows." Better and more modern theatres arose, and in 1663 Davenant declared that "the Red Bull stands empty for fencers : there are no tenants in it but spiders."

A WOMAN KILLED WITH KINDNESS.

ROM two entries in Henslowe's Diary the date when *A Woman Killed with Kindness* was written can be fixed with remarkable certainty. One entry runs :—" Paid, at the appointment of the Company, the 6th of March, 1603, unto Thomas Heywood, in full payment for his play, called *A Woman Killed with Kindness,* the sum of . . . £3 ;" and the other—" Paid, at the appointment of Thomas Blackwood, the 7th of March, 1603, unto the tailor which made the black satin suit for the *Woman Killed with Kindness* the sum of . . . . 10s." The earliest printed notice of the piece occurs in Middleton's *The Blacke Booke,* 1604, where it is coupled with the *Merry Devil of Edmonton :*—" And being set out of the shop, ... she, by thy instructions, shall turn the honest simple fellow off at the next turning, and give him leave to see the *Merry Devil of Edmonton,* or *A Woman Killed with Kindness,* when his mistress is going herself to the same murder." In 1607 the play was published, and a third edition appeared in 1617. It may be worth while to note that the title of the piece was a proverbial expression : compare, for instance, *The Taming of the Shrew* (to which Professor Dowden assigns the date 1597), iv. 1. 221 :

" This is a way to kill a wife with kindness."

Professor Ward (*English Dramatic Literature,* ii. 114) refers also to Fletcher's *The Woman's Prize,* iii. 4 :—

" Some few,
For those are rarest, they are said to kill,
With kindness and fair usage."

An interesting point in the history of this drama is the fact that it was quite recently revived by the Society of Dramatic Students, and revived, I believe, with signal success. Perhaps the only weak element in the five acts is the readiness with which the wife falls. I may add that the division of the play into acts and scenes is here attempted for the first time, at least in any edition of the piece.

THE PROLOGUE

I COME but like a harbinger, being sent
   To tell you what these preparations mean :
Look for no glorious state ; our Muse is bent
   Upon a barren subject, a bare scene.
We could afford this twig a timber tree,
   Whose strength might boldly on your favours build ;
Our russet, tissue ; drone, a honey-bee ;
   Our barren plot, a large and spacious field ;
Our coarse fare, banquets ; our thin water, wine ;
   Our brook, a sea ; our bat's eyes, eagle's sight ;
Our poet's dull and earthy Muse, divine ;
   Our ravens, doves ; our crow's black feathers, white :
But gentle thoughts, when they may give the foil,
Save them that yield, and spare where they may spoi'.

DRAMATIS PERSONÆ.

Sir FRANCIS ACTON, Brother of Mistress FRANKFORD.
Sir CHARLES MOUNTFORD.
Master FRANKFORD.
Master WENDOLL, Friend to FRANKFORD.
Master MALBY, Friend to Sir FRANCIS.
Master CRANWELL.
SHAFTON, a False Friend to Sir CHARLES.
OLD MOUNTFORD, Uncle to Sir CHARLES.
TIDY, Cousin to Sir CHARLES.
SANDY.
RODER.
NICHOLAS,
JENKIN,
ROGER BRICKBAT,   Servants to FRANKFORD.
JACK SLIME,
SPIGOT, a Butler,
Sheriff.
A Serjeant, a Keeper, Officers, Falconers, Huntsmen, a
    Coachman, Carters, Servants, Musicians.

Mistress FRANKFORD.
SUSAN, Sister of Sir CHARLES.
CICELY, Maid to Mistress FRANKFORD.
Women Servants.

SCENE—THE NORTH OF ENGLAND.

A WOMAN KILLED WITH KINDNESS.

—·⁙·—

ACT THE FIRST.

SCENE I.—*A Room in* FRANKFORD'S *House.*

Enter Master FRANKFORD, Mistress FRANKFORD, Sir FRANCIS ACTON, Sir CHARLES MOUNTFORD, Master MALBY, Master WENDOLL, *and* Master CRANWELL.

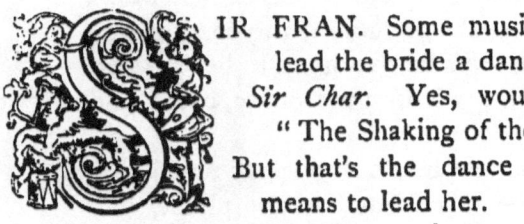IR FRAN. Some music there : none lead the bride a dance ?

Sir Char. Yes, would she dance " The Shaking of the Sheets ; "[1]
But that's the dance her husband means to lead her.   ·

Wen. That's not the dance that every man must dance,
According to the ballad.

Sir Fran. Music, ho !
By your leave, sister ;—by your husband's leave,
I should have said : the hand that but this day

---

[1] A popular tune to which many ballads were set.   Here a *double entente* is intended.

Was given you in the church I'il borrow : sound !
This marriage music hoists me from the ground.
   Frank. Ay, you may caper, you are light and free :
Marriage hath yoked my heels; pray then pardon me.
   Sir Fran. I'll have you dance too, brother.
   Sir Char. Master Frankford,
You are a happy man, sir ; and much joy
Succeed your marriage mirth ! you have a wife
So qualified, and with such ornaments
Both of the mind and body. First, her birth
Is noble, and her education such
As might become the daughter of a prince :
Her own tongue speaks all tongues, and her own hand
Can teach all strings to speak in their best grace,
From the shrillest treble to the hoarsest base.
To end her many praises in one word,
She's beauty and perfection's eldest daughter,
Only found by yours, though many a heart hath sought
   her.
   Frank. But that I know your virtues and chaste
   thoughts,
I should be jealous of your praise, Sir Charles.
   Cran. He speaks no more than you approve.
   Mal. Nor flatters he that gives to her her due.
   Mis. Frank. I would your praise could find a fitter
   theme
Than my imperfect beauties to speak on :
Such as they be, if they my husband please,
They suffice me now I am married :
His sweet content is like a flattering glass,
. To make my face seem fairer to mine eye ;
But the least wrinkle from his stormy brow
Will blast the roses in my cheeks that grow.
   Sir Fran. A perfect wife already, meek and patient :
How strangely the word " husband " fits your mouth,
Not married three hours since ! Sister, 'tis good ;
You, that begin betimes thus, must needs prove

Pliant and duteous in your husband's love.—
Gramercies, brother, wrought her to't already ;
Sweet husband, and a curtsey, the first day !
Mark this, mark this, you that are bachelors,
And never took the grace of honest man ;
Mark this, against you marry, this one phrase :
" In a good time that man both wins and woos,
That takes his wife down in her wedding shoes." [1]

   Frank. Your sister takes not after you, Sir Francis ;
All his wild blood your father spent on you :
He got her in his age, when he grew civil :
All his mad tricks were to his land entailed,
And you are heir to all ; your sister, she
Hath to her dower her mother's modesty.

   Sir Char. Lord, sir, in what a happy state live you !
This morning, which to many seems a burden
Too heavy to bear, is unto you a pleasure.
This lady is no clog, as many are :
She doth become you like a well-made suit,
In which the tailor hath used all his art ;
Not like a thick coat of unseasoned frieze,
Forced on your back in summer. She's no chain
To tie your neck, and curb you to the yoke ;
But she's a chain of gold to adorn your neck.
You both adorn each other, and your hands,
Methinks, are matches : there's equality
In this fair combination ; you are both
Scholars, both young, both being descended nobly.
There's music in this sympathy ; it carries
Consort, and expectation of much joy,
Which God bestow on you, from this first day
Until your dissolution ; that's for aye.

   Sir Fran. We keep you here too long, good brother
      Frankford.
Into the hall ; away ! go cheer your guests.
What, bride and bridegroom both withdrawn at once ?

      [1] A proverbial saying.

If you be missed, the guests will doubt their welcome,
And charge you with unkindness.
　Frank. To prevent it,
I'll leave you here, to see the dance within.
　Mis. Frank. And so will I.
　　　　[*Exeunt* FRANKFORD *and* Mistress FRANKFORD.
　Sir Fran. To part you, it were sin.
Now, gallants, while the town-musicians
Finger their frets [1] within ; and the mad lads
And country-lasses, every mother's child,
With nosegays and bridelaces in their hats,
Dance all their country measures, rounds, and jigs, ·
What shall we do ?　Hark, they are all on the hoigh ; [2]
They toil like mill-horses, and turn as round,—
Marry, not on the toe.　Ay, and they caper,
Not without cutting ; you shall see, to-morrow,
The hall-floor pecked and dinted like a mill-stone,
Made with their high shoes : though their skill be small,
Yet they tread heavy where their hob-nails fall.
　Sir Char. Well, leave them to their sports.　Sir
　　　Francis Acton,
I'll make a match with you ; meet to-morrow
At Chevy-chase, I'll fly my hawk with yours.
　Sir Fran. For what ?　For what?
　Sir Char. Why, for a hundred pound.
　Sir Fran. Pawn me some gold of that:
　Sir Char. Here are ten angels ; [3]
I'll make them good a hundred pound to-morrow
Upon my hawk's wing.
　Sir Fran. 'Tis a match, 'tis done.
Another hundred pound upon your dogs ;
Dare ye, Sir Charles ?
　Sir Char. I dare : were I sure to lose,
I durst do more than that : here is my hand,

---

[1] The points at which a string is to be stopped in a lute or guitar.—*Halliwell.*
[2] Out of all bounds.　　　　　　[3] Gold coins.

The first course for a hundred pound.

Sir Fran. A match.

Wen. Ten angels on Sir Francis Acton's hawk ;
As much upon his dogs.

Cran. I am for Sir Charles Mountford ; I have seen
His hawk and dog both tried.   What, clap you hands?
Or is't no bargain?

Wen. Yes, and stake them down :
Were they five hundred, they were all my own.

Sir Fran. Be stirring early with the lark to-morrow ; [1]
I'll rise into my saddle ere the sun
Rise from his bed.

Sir Char. If there you miss me, say
I am no gentleman : I'll hold my day.

Sir Fran. It holds on all sides.   Come, to-night let's
      dance,
Early to-morrow let's prepare to ride ;
We had need be three hours up before the bride.

                                   [*Exeunt.*

SCENE II.—*A Yard.*

Enter NICHOLAS, JENKIN, JACK SLIME, *and* ROGER
  BRICKBAT, *with* Country Wenches, *and two or three*
  Musicians.

Jenk. Come, Nick, take you Joan Miniver to trace
withal; Jack Slime, traverse you with Cicely Milk-pail :
I will take Jane Trubkin, and Roger Brickbat shall have
Isbel Motley ; and now that they are busy in the parlour,
come, strike up; we'll have a crash [2] here in the yard.

Nic. My humour is not compendious ; dancing I
possess not, though I can foot it ; yet, since I am fallen
into the hands of Cicely Milk-pail, I consent.

---

[1] Did Heywood remember Shakespeare's " Stir with the lark to-
morrow, gentle Norfolk "?

[2] A merry bout.

Slime. Truly Nick, though we were never brought up like serving courtiers, yet we have been brought up with serving creatures, ay, and God's creatures too; for we have been brought up to serve sheep, oxen, horses, hogs, and such like : and, though we be but country fellows, it may be in the way of dancing we can do the horse-trick as well as serving-men.

Brick. Ay, and the cross-point too.

Jenk. O Slime, O Brickbat, do not you know that comparisons are odious? now we are odious ourselves too, therefore there are no comparisons to be made betwixt us.

Nic. I am sudden, and not superfluous;
I am quarrelsome, and not seditious;
I am peaceable, and not contentious;
I am brief, and not compendious.

Slime. Foot it quickly : if the music overcome not my melancholy, I shall quarrel; and if they do not suddenly strike up, I shall presently strike them down.

Jenk. No quarrelling, for God's sake : truly, if you do, I shall set a knave between ye.

Slime. I come to dance, not to quarrel. Come, what shall it be? " Rogero? "[1]

Jenk. " Rogero ! " no; we will dance " The Beginning of the World."

Cicely. I love no dance so well as " John come kiss me now."

Nic. I, that have ere now deserved a cushion, call for the " Cushion-dance."

Brick. For my part, I like nothing so well as " Tom Tyler."

Jenk. No ; we'll have " The Hunting of the Fox."

Slime. " The Hay," " The Hay ;" there's nothing like " The Hay."

Nic. I have said, I do say, and I will say again—

---

[1] The tunes here mentioned are all more or less familiar from other passages in the old dramatists.

Jenk. Every man agree to have it as Nick says.

All. Content.

Nic. It hath been, it now is, and it shall be—

Cicely. What, Master Nicholas, what?

Nic. " Put on your smock a' Monday."

Jenk. So the dance will come cleanly off. Come, for God's sake agree of something : if you like not that, put it to the musicians ; or let me speak for all, and we'll have " Sellenger's round."

All. That, that, that.

Nic. No, I am resolved, thus it shall be :

First take hands, then take ye to your heels.

Jenk. Why, would ye have us run away?

Nic. No ; but I would have you shake your heels.

Music, strike up !

> [*They dance.* NICHOLAS *whilst dancing speaks* · *stately and scurvily, the rest after the country fashion.*

Jenk. Hey ! lively, my lasses ! here's a turn for thee !

> [*Exeunt.*

SCENE III.—*The Open Country.*

Horns wind. *Enter* Sir CHARLES MOUNTFORD, Sir FRANCIS ACTON, MALBY, CRANWELL, WENDOLL, Falconers, *and* Huntsmen.

Sir Char. So ; well cast off : aloft, aloft ! well flown ! Oh, now she takes her at the sowse,[1] and strikes her Down to the earth, like a swift thunder-clap.

Wen. She hath struck ten angels out of my way.

Sir Fran. A hundred pound from me.

Sir Char. What, falconer !

---

[1] We have here a number of not very intelligible terms borrowed from falconry. " At the sowse " was said of a bird when the hawk swooped straight down upon it.

Fal. At hand, sir.

Sir Char. Now she hath seized the fowl, and 'gins to
    plume her,
Rebeck her not : rather stand still and check her.
So, seize her gets,[1] her jesses,[2] and her bells :
Away!

Sir Fran. My hawk killed too.

Sir Char. Ay, but 'twas at the querre,[3]
Not at the mount, like mine.

Sir Fran. Judgment, my masters.

Cran. Yours missed her at the ferre.

Wen. Ay, but our merlin [4] first had plumed the fowl,
And twice renewed her from the river too ;
Her bells, Sir Francis, had not both one weight,
Nor was one semi-tune above the other :
Methinks these Milan bells do sound too full,
And spoil the mounting of your hawk.

Sir Char. 'Tis lost.

Sir Fran. I grant it not.   Mine likewise seized a fowl
Within her talons ; and you saw her paws
Full of the feathers : both her petty singles,
And her long singles gripped her more than other ;
The terrials of her legs were stained with blood :
Not of the fowl only, she did discomfit
Some of her feathers ; but she brake away. '
Come, come, your hawk is but a rifler.

Sir Char. How !

Sir Fran. Ay, and your dogs are trindle-tails and
    curs.

Sir Char. You stir my blood.
You keep not one good hound in all your kennel,
Nor one good hawk upon your perch.

Sir Fran. How, knight !

Sir Char. So, knight : you will not swagger, sir?

[1] Booty.
[2] The short leather straps round the hawk's legs.
[3] Perhaps from the German *quer* = oblique.
[4] A small species of hawk.

Sir Fran. Why, say I did?

Sir Char. Why, sir,   .
I say you would gain as much by swaggering,
As you have got by wagers on your dogs :
You will come short in all things.

Sir Fran. Not in this :
Now I'll strike home.

'*Sir Char.* Thou shalt to thy long home,
Or I will want my will.

Sir Fran. All they that love Sir Francis, follow me.

Sir Char. All that affect Sir Charles, draw on my part.

Cran. On this side heaves my hand.

Wen. Here goes my heart.

> [*They divide themselves.* Sir CHARLES MOUNT-
> FORD, CRANWELL, Falconer, *and* Hunts-
> man, *fight against* Sir FRANCIS ACTON,
> WENDOLL, *his* Falconer, *and* Huntsman ;
> *and* Sir CHARLES'S *side gets the better, beat-
> ing the others away, and killing both of* Sir
> FRANCIS'S *men.   Exeunt all except* Sir
> CHARLES.

Sir Char. My God ! what have I done? what have I
      done ?
My rage hath plunged into a sea of blood,
In which my soul lies drowned.   Poor innocents,
For whom we are to answer !   Well, 'tis done,
And I remain the victor.   A great conquest,
When I would give this right hand, nay, this head,
To breathe in them new life whom I have slain !
Forgive me, God ! 'twas in the heat of blood,
And anger quite removes me from myself :
It was not I, but rage, did this vile murder ;
Yet I, and not my rage, must answer it.
Sir Francis Acton he is fled the field ;
With him all those that did partake his quarrel,
And I am left alone with sorrow dumb,
And in my height of conquest overcome.

Enter SUSAN.

Susan. O God! my brother wounded 'mong the
    dead!
Unhappy jest, that in such earnest ends:
The rumour of this fear stretched to my ears,
And I am come to know if you be wounded.
    Sir Char. Oh! sister, sister, wounded at the heart.
    Susan. My God forbid!
    Sir Char. In doing that thing which He forbad,
I am wounded, sister.
    Susan. I hope not at the heart.
    Sir Char. Yes, at the heart.
    Susan. O God! a surgeon there!
    Sir Char. Call me a surgeon, sister, for my soul;
The sin of murder it hath pierced my heart,
And made a wide wound there: but for these scratches,
They are nothing, nothing.
    Susan. Charles, what have you done?
Sir Francis hath great friends, and will pursue you
Unto the utmost danger of the law.
    Sir Char. My conscience is become mine enemy,
And will pursue me more than Acton can.
    Susan. Oh, fly, sweet brother.
    Sir Char. Shall I fly from thee?
Why, Sue, art weary of my company?
    Susan. Fly from your foe.
    Sir Char. You, sister, are my friend;
And, flying you, I shall pursue my end.
    Susan. Your company is as my eye-ball dear;
Being far from you, no comfort can be near;
Yet fly to save your life: what would I care
To spend my future age in black despair,
So you were safe? and yet to live one week
Without my brother Charles, through every cheek
My streaming tears would downwards run so rank,
Till they could set on either side a bank,

And in the midst a channel; so my face
For two salt-water brooks shall still find place.
   Sir Char. Thou shalt not weep so much, for I will
    stay
In spite of danger's teeth ; I'll live with thee,
Or I'll not live at all.   I will not sell
My country and my father's patrimony,
Nor thy sweet sight, for a vain hope of life.

Enter Sheriff, *with* Officers.

   Sher. Sir Charles, I am made the unwilling instru-
    ment
Of your attach [1] and apprehension :
I'm sorry that the blood of innocent men
Should be of you exacted.   It was told me
That you were guarded with a troop of friends.
And therefore I come thus armed.
   Sir Char. O, Master Sheriff,
I came into the field with many friends,
But see, they all have left me : only one
Clings to my sad misfortune, my dear sister.
I know you for an honest gentleman ;
I yield my weapons, and submit to you ;
Convey me where you please.
   Sher. To prison then,
To answer for the lives of these dead men
   Susan. O God ! O God !
   Sir Char. Sweet sister, every strain
Of sorrow from your heart augments my pain ;
Your grief abounds, and hits against my breast.
   Sher. Sir, will you go ?
   Sir Char. Even where it likes you best.   [*Exeunt.*

[1] Arrest.

ACT THE SECOND.

SCENE I.—FRANKFORD'S *Study*.

Enter FRANKFORD.

RANK. How happy am I amongst other men,
That in my mean estate embrace content !
I am a gentleman, and by my birth,
Companion with a king ; a king's no
I am possessed of many fair revenues,   [more.
Sufficient to maintain a gentleman.
Touching my mind, I am studied in all arts ;
The riches of my thoughts, and of my time,
Have been a good proficient ; but the chief
Of all the sweet felicities on earth,
I have a fair, a chaste, and loving wife ;
Perfection all, all truth, all ornament:
If man on earth may truly happy be,
Of these at once possessed, sure I am he.

Enter NICHOLAS.

Nic. Sir, there's a gentleman attends without
To speak with you.
Frank. On horseback?
Nic. Yes, on horseback.
Frank. Entreat him to alight, I will attend him.
Know'st thou him, Nick?
Nic. Know him ! yes, his name's Wendoll :

It seems he comes in haste : his horse is booted
Up to the flank in mire, himself all spotted
And stained with plashing. Sure he rid in fear,
Or for a wager : horse and man both sweat ;
I ne'er saw two in such a smoking heat.
    Frank. Entreat him in : about it instantly.
[*Exit* NICHOLAS.

This Wendoll I have noted, and his carriage
Hath pleased me much : by observation
I have noted many good deserts in him :
He's affable, and seen [1] in many things,
Discourses well, a good companion ;
And though of small means, yet a gentleman
Of a good house, though somewhat pressed by want :
I have preferred him to a second place
In my opinion, and my best regard.

   Enter WENDOLL, Mistress FRANKFORD, *and* NICHOLAS.

    Mis. Frank. O Master Frankford, Master Wendoll
    here
Brings you the strangest news that e'er you heard.
    Frank. What news, sweet wife? What news, good
    Master Wendoll?
    Wen. You knew the match made 'twixt Sir Francis
    Acton
And Sir Charles Mountford.
    Frank. True, with their hounds and hawks.
    Wen. The matches were both played.
    Frank. Ha ! and which won?
    Wen. Sir Francis, your wife's brother, had the worst,
And lost the wager.
    Frank. Why, the worse his chance :
Perhaps the fortune of some other day
Will change his luck.
    Mis. Frank. Oh, but you hear not all.
Sir Francis lost, and yet was loth to yield :

[1] Versed.

Heywood.   C

At length the two knights grew to difference,
From words to blows, and so to banding sides;
Where valorous Sir Charles slew in his spleen
Two of your brother's men; his falconer,
And his good huntsman, whom he loved so well:
More men were wounded, no more slain outright.

Frank. Now, trust me, I am sorry for the knight;
But is my brother safe?

Wen. All whole and sound, .
His body not being blemished with one wound:
But poor Sir Charles is to the prison led,
To answer at the assize for them that's dead.

Frank. I thank your pains, sir; had the news been
better .
Your will was to have brought it, Master Wendoll.
Sir Charles will find hard friends; his case is heinous,
And will be most severely censured on [1]:
I'm sorry for him. Sir, a word with you;
I know you, sir, to be a gentleman .
In all things; your possibilities but mean :
Please you to use my table and my purse,
They are yours. '

Wen. O Lord, sir, I shall never deserve it.

Frank. O sir, disparage not your worth too much :
You are full of quality and fair desert :
Choose of my men which shall attend on you,
And he is yours. I will allow you, sir,
Your man, your gelding, and your table, all
At my own charge; be my companion.

Wen. Master Frankford, I have oft been bound to
you
By many favours; this exceeds them all,
That I shall never merit your least favour :
But, when your last remembrance I forget,
Heaven at my soul exact that weighty debt !

Frank. There needs no protestation; for I know you

---

[1] To censure, in legal language, means to pass judgment on.

Virtuous, and therefore grateful. Pr'ythee, Nan,
Use him with all thy loving'st courtesy.
Mis. Frank. As far as modesty may well extend,
It is my duty to receive your friend.
Frank. To dinner, come, sir; from this present day,
Welcome to me for ever : come, away.
      [*Exeunt* FRANKFORD, Mistress FRANKFORD,
          and WENDOLL.
Nic. I do not like this fellow by no means :
I never see him but my heart still yearns :
Zounds! I could fight with him, yet know not why :
The devil and he are all one in my eye.

Enter JENKIN.

Jen. O Nick, what gentleman is that comes to lie at
our house? my master allows him one to wait on him,
and I believe it will fall to thy lot.
Nic. I love my master ; by these hilts I do !
But rather than I'll ever come to serve him,
I'll turn away my master.

Enter CICELY.

Cicely. Nich'las, where are you, Nich'las? you must
come in, Nich'las, and help the young gentleman off with
his boots.
Nic. If I pluck off his boots, I'll eat the spurs,
And they shall stick fast in my throat like burs.
Cicely. Then, Jenkin, come you.
Jen. Nay, 'tis no boot for me to deny it. My master
hath given me a coat here, but he takes pains himself to
brush it once or twice a day with a holly-wand.
Cicely. Come, come, make haste, that you may wash
your hands again, and help to serve in dinner.
Jen. You may see, my masters, though it be afternoon
with you, 'tis but early days with us, for we have not
dined yet : stay a little, I'll but go in and help to bear up
the first course, and come to you again presently. [*Exeunt.*
                          C 2

SCENE II.—*A Room in the Gaol.*

Enter MALBY *and* CRANWELL.

Mal. This is the sessions-day; pray can you tell me
How young Sir Charles hath sped?   Is he acquit,
Or must he try the law's strict penalty ?
    Cran. He's cleared of all, spite of his enemies,
Whose earnest labour was to take his life :
But in this suit of pardon he hath spent
All the revenues that his father left him ;
And he is now turned a plain countryman,
Reformed in all things.   See, sir, here he comes.

Enter Sir CHARLES *and* Keeper.

    Keep. Discharge your fees, and you are then at
        freedom.
    Sir Char. Here, Master Keeper, take the poor re-
        mainder
Of all the wealth I have : my heavy foes
Have made my purse light ; but, alas ! to me
'Tis wealth enough that you have set me free.
    Mal. God give you joy of your delivery !
I am glad to see you abroad, Sir Charles.
    Sir Char. The poorest knight in England, Master
        Malby :
My life hath cost me all my patrimony ~
My father left his son : well, God forgive them
That are the authors of my penury.

Enter SHAFTON.

    Shaf. Sir Charles ! a hand, a hand ! at liberty?
Now, by the faith I owe, I am glad to see it.
What want you ? wherein may I pleasure you ?
    Sir Char. O me ! O most unhappy gentleman !
I am not worthy to have friends stirred up,
Whose hands may help me in this plunge of want.

I would I were in Heaven, to inherit there
The immortal birth-right which my Saviour keeps,
And by no unthrift can be bought and sold;
For here on earth what pleasures should we trust?

Shaf. To rid you from these contemplations,
Three hundred pounds you shall receive of me;
Nay, five for fail. Come, sir; the sight of gold
Is the most sweet receipt for melancholy,
And will revive your spirits : you shall hold law
With your proud adversaries. Tush, let Frank Acton
Wage with his knighthood like expense with me,
And he will sink, he will. Nay, good Sir Charles,
Applaud your fortune, and your fair escape
From all these perils.

Sir Char. O sir, they have undone me.
Two thousand and five hundred pound a year
My father, at his death, possessed me of;
All which the envious Acton made me spend.
And, notwithstanding all this large expense,
I had much ado to gain my liberty :
And I have only now a house of pleasure,
With some five hundred pounds, reserved
Both to maintain me and my loving sister.

Shaft. [*Aside.*] That must I have, it lies convenient
_ for me :
If I can fasten but one finger on him,
With my full hand I'll gripe him to the heart.
'Tis not for love I proffered him this coin,
But for my gain and pleasure. [*Aloud.*] Come, Sir
      Charles,
I know you have need of money ; take my offer.

Sir Char. Sir, I accept it, and remain indebted .
Even to the best of my unable power.
Come, gentlemen, and see it tendered down.   [*Exeunt.*

SCENE III.—*A Room in* FRANKFORD'S *House.*

Enter WENDOLL *melancholy.*

Wen. I am a villain if I apprehend
But such a thought : then, to attempt the deed,—
Slave, thou art damned without redemption.
I'll drive away this passion with a song.
A song ! ha, ha : a song ! as if, fond man,
Thy eyes could swim in laughter, when thy soul
Lies drenched and drownèd in red tears of blood.
I'll pray, and see if God within my heart
Plant better thoughts.   Why, prayers are meditations ;
And when I meditate (O God, forgive me !)
It is on her divine perfections.
I will forget her ; I will arm myself
Not to entertain a thought of love to her :
And, when I come by chance into her presence,
I'll hale these balls until my eye-strings crack,
From being pulled and drawn to look that way.

Enter over the stage, FRANKFORD, Mistress FRANKFORD,
and NICHOLAS.[1]

O God ! O God ! with what a violence
I'm hurried to mine own destruction.
There goest thou, the most perfectest man
That ever England bred a gentleman ;
And shall I wrong his bed ? Thou God of thunder !
Stay in thy thoughts of vengeance and of wrath,
Thy great, almighty, and all-judging hand
From speedy execution on a villain :
A villain, and a traitor to his friend.

Enter JENKIN.

Jenk. Did your worship call ?
Wen. He doth maintain me, he allows me largely
Money to spend——

---

[1] They evidently pass through the gallery above and leave the
stage to Wendoll.

Jenk. By my faith, so do not you me; I cannot get a cross of you.

Wen. My gelding, and my man——

Jenk. That's Sorrell and I.

Wen. This kindness grows of no alliance 'twixt us——

Jenk. Nor is my service of any great acquaintance.

Wen. I never bound him to me by desert :
Of a mere stranger, a poor gentleman,
A man by whom in no kind he could gain,
He hath placed me in the height of all his thoughts,
Made me companion with the best and chiefest
In Yorkshire. He cannot eat without me,
Nor laugh without me : I am to his body
As necessary as his digestion,
And equally do make him whole or sick :
And shall I wrong this man ? Base man ! ingrate !
Hast thou the power straight with thy gory hands
To rip thy image from his bleeding heart ?
To scratch thy name from out the holy book
Of his remembrance ; and to wound his name
That holds thy name so dear ? or rend his heart
To whom thy heart was knit and joined together ?
And yet I must : then, Wendoll, be content ;
Thus villains, when they would, cannot repent.

Jenk. What a strange humour is my new master in !
pray God he be not mad : if he should be so, I should
never have any mind to serve him in Bedlam. It may
be he's mad for missing of me.

Wen. [*Seeing* JENKIN.] What, Jenkin, where's your
	mistress ?

Jenk. Is your worship married ?

Wen. Why dost thou ask ?

Jenk. Because you are my master ; and if I have a
mistress, I would be glad, like a good servant, to do my
duty to her.

Wen. I mean Mistress Frankford.

Jenk. Marry, sir, her husband is riding out of town,

and she went very lovingly to bring him on his way to
horse.[1]   Do you see, sir? here she comes, and here I go.
   Wen. Vanish.   [*Exit* JENKIN.

Re-enter MISTRESS FRANKFORD.

   Mis. Frank. You are well met, sir; now, in troth, my
   ، husband,
Before he took horse, had a great desire
To speak with you : we sought about the house,
Hollaed into the fields, sent every way,
But could not meet you : therefore he enjoined me
To do unto you his most kind commends.
Nay, more ; he wills you, as you prize his love,
Or hold in estimation his kind friendship,
To make bold in his absence, and command
Even as himself were present in the house :
For you must keep his table, use his servants,
And be a present Frankford in his absence.
   Wen. I thank him for his love.—
Give me a name, you whose infectious tongues
Are tipped with gall and poison : as you would
Think on a man that had your father slain,
Murdered   your   children,   made   your   wives   base
         strumpets,
So call me, call me so : print in my face
The most stigmatic title of a villain,
For hatching treason to so true a friend.   [*Aside.*
   Mis. Frank. Sir, you are much beholding[2] to my
         husband ;
You are a man most dear in his regard.
   Wen. [*Aside.*] I am bound unto your husband, and
         you too.
I will not speak to wrong a gentleman
Of that good estimation, my kind friend :
I will not ; zounds ! I will not.   I may choose,

----

[1] *i.e.* To accompany him.   [2] Beholden.

And I will choose.   Shall I be so misled?
Or shall I purchase to my father's crest
The motto of a villain?   If I say
I will not do it, what thing can enforce me?
What can compel me?   What sad destiny
Hath such command upon my yielding thoughts?
I will not—Ha! some fury pricks me on,
The swift Fates drag me at their chariot-wheel,
And hurry me to mischief.   Speak I must;
Injure myself, wrong her, deceive his trust.
    Mis. Frank. Are you not well, sir, that you seem thus
      troubled?
There is sedition in your countenance.
    Wen. And in my heart, fair angel, chaste and wise.
I love you: start not, speak not, answer not.
I love you: nay, let me speak the rest:
Bid me to swear, and I will call to record
The host of Heaven.
    Mis. Frank. The host of Heaven forbid
Wendoll should hatch such a disloyal thought!
    Wen. Such is my fate; to this suit I was born,
To wear rich pleasure's crown, or fortune's scorn.
    Mis. Frank. My husband loves you.
    Wen. I know it.
    Mis. Frank. He esteems you
Even as his brain, his eye-ball, or his heart.
    Wen. I have tried it.
    Mis. Frank. His purse is your exchequer, and his
      table
Doth freely serve you.
    Wen. So I have found it.
    Mis. Frank. O! with what face of brass, what brow of
      steel,
Can you, unblushing, speak this to the face
Of the espoused wife of so dear a friend?
It is my husband that maintains your state;
Will you dishonour him that in your power

Hath left his whole affairs? I am his wife,
It is to me you speak.

Wen. O speak no more!
For more than this I know, and have recorded
Within the red-leaved table of my heart.
Fair, and of all beloved, I was not fearful
Bluntly to give my life into your hand,
And at one hazard all my earthly means.
Go, tell your husband; he will turn me off,
And I am then undone. I care not, I;
'Twas for your sake. Perchance in rage he'll kill me:
I care not, 'twas for you. Say I incur
The general name of villain through the world,
Of traitor to my friend; I care not, I.
Beggary, shame, death, scandal, and reproach,
For you I'll hazard all: why, what care I?
For you I'll live, and in your love I'll die.

Mis. Frank. You move me, sir, to passion and to pity.
The love I bear my husband is as precious
As my soul's health.

Wen. I love your husband too,
And for his love I will engage my life:
Mistake me not, the augmentation
Of my sincere affection borne to you
Doth no whit lessen my regard of him.
I will be secret, lady, close as night;
And not the light of one small glorious star
Shall shine here in my forehead, to bewray
That act of night.

Mis. Frank. What shall I say?
My soul is wandering, and hath lost her way.
Oh, Master Wendoll! Oh!

Wen. Sigh not, sweet saint;
For every sigh you breathe draws from my heart
A drop of blood.

Mis. Frank. I ne'er offended yet:
My fault, I fear, will in my brow be writ.

Women that fall, not quite bereft of grace,
Have their offences noted in their face.
I blush and am ashamed.   Oh, Master Wendoll,
Pray God I be not born to curse your tongue,
That hath enchanted me !   This maze I am in
I fear will prove the labyrinth of sin.

Re-enter NICHOLAS *behind.*

Wen. The path of pleasure, and the gate to bliss,
Which on your lips I knock at with a kiss.
    Nic. [*Aside.*] I'll kill the rogue.
    Wen. Your husband is from home, your bed's no blab.
Nay, look not down and blush.
                [*Exeunt* WENDOLL *and* Mistress FRANKFORD.
    Nic. Zounds ! I'll stab.
Ay, Nick, was it thy chance to come just in the nick ?
I love my master, and I hate that slave :
I love my mistress, but these tricks I like not.
My master shall not pocket up this wrong ;
I'll eat my fingers first.   Whay say'st thou, metal ?
Does not the rascal Wendoll go on legs
That thou must cut off ?   Hath he not ham strings
That thou must hough ?   Nay, metal, thou shalt stand
To all I say.   I'll henceforth turn a spy,
And watch them in their close conveyances.
I never looked for better of that rascal,
Since he came miching [1] first into our house :
It is that Satan hath corrupted her,
For she was fair and chaste.   I'll have an eye
In all their gestures.   Thus I think of them,
If they proceed as they have done before :
Wendoll's a knave, my mistress is a——-   [*Exit.*

                [1] Sneaking or stealing into.

ACT THE THIRD.

SCENE I.—*A Room in* SIR CHARLES MOUNTFORD'S
House.

Enter Sir CHARLES MOUNTFORD *and* SUSAN.

SIR CHAR. Sister, you see we are driven
to hard shift
To keep this poor house we have left
unsold;
I am now enforced to follow husbandry,
And you to milk; and do we not live
well?
Well, I thank God.

Susan. O brother, here's a change,
Since old Sir Charles died, in our father's house!

Sir Char. All things on earth thus change, some up,
some down;
Content's a kingdom, and I wear that crown.

Enter SHAFTON *with a* Serjeant.

Shaf. Good morrow, morrow, Sir Charles : what, with
your sister,
Plying your husbandry?—Serjeant, stand off.—
You have a pretty house here, and a garden,
And goodly ground about it. Since it lies
So near a lordship that I lately bought,
I would fain buy it of you. I will give you——

Sir Char. O, pardon me : this house successively
Hath 'longed to me and my progenitors
Three hundred years. My great-great-grandfather,

He in whom first our gentle style began,
Dwelt here; and in this ground, increased this mole-hill
Unto that mountain which my father left me.
Where he the first of all our house began,
I now the last will end, and keep this house,
This virgin title, never yet deflowered
By any unthrift of the Mountfords' line.
In brief, I will not sell it for more gold
Than you could hide or pave the ground withal.

   Shaf. Ha, ha! a proud mind and a beggar's purse!
Where's my three hundred pounds, besides the use?
I have brought it to an execution
By course of law : what, is my moneys ready?

   Sir Char. An execution, sir, and never tell me
You put my bond in suit! you deal extremely.

   Shaf. Sell me the land, and I'll acquit you straight.

   Sir Char. Alas, alas! 'tis all trouble hath left me
To cherish me and my poor sister's life.
If this were sold, our names should then be quite
Razed from the bed-roll[1] of gentility.
You see what hard shift we have made to keep it
Allied still to our own name.   This palm, you see,
Labour hath glowed within : her silver brow,
That never tasted a rough winter's blast
Without a mask or fan, doth with a grace
Defy cold winter, and his storms outface.

   Susan. Sir, we feed sparing, and we labour hard,
We lie uneasy, to reserve to us
And our succession this small plot of ground.

   Sir Char. I have so bent my thoughts to husbandry,
That I protest I scarcely can remember
What a new fashion is; how silk or satin
Feels in my hand : why, pride is grown to us
A mere, mere stranger.   I have quite forgot
The names of all that ever waited on me;
I cannot name ye any of my hounds,

            [1] *i.e.* Bead roll

Once from whose echoing mouths I heard all music
That e'er my heart desired.   What should I say?
To keep this place I have changed myself away.
 Shaf. [*To the* Serjeant.]   Arrest him   at   my   suit.
 Actions and actions
Shall keep thee in perpetual bondage fast :
Nay, more, I'll sue thee by a late appeal,
And call thy former life in question.
The keeper is my friend, thou shalt have irons,
And usage such as I'll deny to dogs :
Away with him !
 Sir Char. [*To* SUSAN.]   You are   too   timorous :
But trouble is my master,
· And I will serve him truly.—My kind sister,.
Thy tears are of no force to mollify
This flinty man.   Go to my father's brother,
My kinsmen and allies ; entreat them for me,
To ransom me from this injurious man,
That seeks my ruin.
 Shaf. Come, irons, irons ! come away ;
I'll see thee lodged far from the sight of day.
  [*Exeunt* SHAFTON *and* Serjeant *with* Sir CHARLES.
 Susan. My heart's so hardened with the frost of grief,.
Death cannot pierce it through.   Tyrant too fell !
So lead the fiends condemnèd souls to hell.

   Enter Sir FRANCIS ACTON *and* MALBY.

 Sir Fran. Again to prison ! Malby, hast thou seen
A poor slave better tortured ?   Shall we hear
The music of his voice cry from the grate,[1]   ,
" Meat for the Lord's sake " ?   No, no, yet I am not
Throughly revenged.   They say he hath a pretty wench
Unto his sister : shall I, in mercy-sake
To him and to his kindred, bribe the fool
To shame herself by lewd dishonest lust ?

---

 [1] Alluding obviously to the debtors' prisons ; the lines remind us
at once of *Pickwick*.

I'll proffer largely ; but, the deed being done,
I'll smile to see her base confusion.

   Mal. Methinks, Sir Francis, you are full revenged
For greater wrongs than he can proffer you.
See where the poor sad gentlewoman stands.   '

   Sir Fran. Ha, ha ! now will I flout her poverty,
Deride her fortunes, scoff her base estate ;
My very soul the name of Mountford hates.
But stay, my heart ! oh, what a look did fly
To strike my soul through with thy piercing eye !   '
I am enchanted ; all my spirits are fled,
And with one glance my envious spleen struck dead.

   Susan. Acton ! that seeks our blood.   [*Runs away*,

   Sir Fran. O chaste and fair !

   Mal. Sir Francis, why, Sir Francis, zounds ! in a trance ?
Sir Francis, what cheer, man ?   Come, come, how is't ?

   Sir Fran. Was she not fair ?   Or else this judging eye
Cannot distinguish beauty.

   Mal. She was fair.   /

   Sir Fran. She was an angel in a mortal's shape,
And ne'er descended from old Mountford's line.
But soft, soft, let me call my wits together.
A poor, poor wench, to my great adversary
Sister, whose very souls denounce stern war,
One against other.   How now, Frank ? turned fool
Or madman, whether ? But no ; master of
My perfect senses and directest wits.
Then why should I be in this violent humour
Of passion and of love ; and with a person
So different every way, and so opposed
In all contractions, and still-warring actions ?
Fie, fie ; how I dispute against my soul !
Come, come ; I'll gain her, or in her fair quest
Purchase my soul free and immortal rest.   [*Exeunt.*

'SCENE II.—*A Sitting-Room in* FRANKFORD'S *House.*

Enter Serving-Men, *one with a voider and a wooden knife*[1] *to take away; another with the salt and bread; another with the table-cloth and napkins; another with the carpet:*[2] JENKIN *follows them with two lights.*

Jenk. So, march in order, and retire in battle array. My master and the guests have supped already, all's taken away : here, now spread for the serving-men in the hall.   Butler, it belongs to your office.

But. I know it, Jenkin.   What d'ye call the gentleman that supped there to-night ?

Jenk. Who, my master ?

But. No, no ; Master Wendoll, he's a daily guest : I mean the gentleman that came but this afternoon.

Jenk. His name's Master Cranwell.   God's light, hark, within there, my master calls to lay more billets upon the fire.   Come, come ! Lord, how we that are in office here in the house are troubled !   One spread the carpet in the parlour, and stand ready to snuff the lights ; the rest be ready to prepare their stomachs.   More lights in the hall there.   Come, Nich'las.   [*Exeunt all but* NICHOLAS.

Nic. I cannot eat, but had I Wendoll's heart
I would eat that ; the rogue grows impudent.
Oh, I have seen such vile notorious tricks,
Ready to make my eyes dart from my head.
I'll tell my master, by this air I will !
Fall what may fall, I'll tell him.   Here he comes.

Enter FRANKFORD, *brushing the crumbs from his clothes with a napkin, as newly risen from supper.*

Frank. Nicholas, what make you here? why are not you
At supper in the hall among your fellows ?

---

[1] With which the scraps were swept into the voider or basket.
[2] *i.e.* Table-cover.

Nic. Master, I stayed your rising from the board,
To speak with you.

Frank. Be brief, then, gentle Nicholas ;
My wife and guests attend me in the parlour.
Why dost thou pause ?   Now, Nicholas, you want money,
And, unthrift-like, would eat into your wages
Ere you have earned it : here, sir,'s half a crown ;
Play the good husband,[1] and away to supper.

Nic. By this hand, an honourable gentleman ! I will
not see him wronged.—Sir, I have served you long ; you
entertained me seven years before your beard.[2] You
knew me, sir, before you knew my mistress.

Frank. What of this, good Nicholas ?

Nic. I never was a make-bate [3] or a knave ;
I have no fault but one : I'm given to quarrel,
But not with women.   I will tell you, master,
That which will make your heart leap from your breast,
Your hair to startle from your head, your ears to tingle.

Frank. What preparation's this to dismal news ?

Nic. 'Sblood, sir ! I love you better than your wife ;
I'll make it good.

Frank. You are a knave, and I have much ado
With wonted patience to contain my rage,
And not to break thy pate.   Thou art a knave :
I'll turn you, with your base comparisons,
Out of my doors.

Nic. Do, do : there is not room
For Wendoll and for me both in one house.
Oh master, master, that Wendoll is a villain.

Frank. Ay, saucy !

Nic. Strike, strike ; do, strike ; yet hear me : I am no fool,
I know a villain, when I see him act
Deeds of a villain.   Master, master, that base slave
Enjoys my mistress, and dishonours you.

[1] *i.e.* Be frugal.
[2] *i.e.* Before you had a beard.
[3] Promoter of quarrels.

Frank. Thou hast killed me with a weapon whose
　　sharp point
Hath pricked quite through and through my shivering
　　heart :
Drops of cold sweat sit dangling on my hairs,
Like morning's dew upon the golden flowers,
And I am plunged into strange agonies.
What didst thou say? If any word that touched
His credit or her reputation, ·
It is as hard to enter my belief
As Dives into heaven.
　　Nic. I can gain nothing ;
They are two that never wronged me. I knew before
T'was but a thankless office, and perhaps
As much as is my service, or my life
Is worth. All this I know ; but this and more,
More by a thousand dangers, could not hire me
To smother such a heinous wrong from you.
I saw, and I have said.
　　Frank. [*Aside.*] 'Tis probable ; though blunt, yet he
　　is honest :
Though I durst pawn my life, and on their faith
Hazard the dear salvation of my soul,
Yet in my trust I may be too secure.
May this be true? O, may it, can it be?
Is it by any wonder possible?
Man, woman, what thing mortal may we trust,
When friends and bosom wives prove so unjust?—
To NICHOLAS.] What instance hast thou of this strange
　　report?
　　·*Nic.* Eyes, eyes.
　　Frank. Thy eyes may be deceived, I tell thee :
For, should an angel from the heavens drop down,
And preach this to me that thyself hast told,
He should have much ado to win belief ;
In both their loves I am so confident.
　　Nic. Shall I discourse the same by circumstance?

Frank. No more! to supper, and command your fellows
To attend us and the strangers. Not a word,
I charge thee on thy life : be secret then,
For I know nothing.

    Nic. I am dumb; and, now that I have eased my
       stomach,
I will go fill my stomach.

    Frank. Away ; be gone.   [*Exit* NICHOLAS.
She is well born, descended nobly ;
Virtuous her education, her repute
Is in the general voice of all the country
Honest and fair ; her carriage, her demeanour,
In all her actions that concern the love
To me her husband, modest, chaste, and godly.
Is all this seeming gold plain copper ?
But he, that Judas that hath borne my purse,
And sold me for a sin !—O God ! O God !
Shall I put up these wrongs? No. Shall I trust
The bare report of this suspicious groom,
Before the double-gilt, the well-hatched ore
Of their two hearts ? No, I will lose these thoughts :
Distraction I will banish from my brow,
And from my looks exile sad discontent,
Their wonted favours in my tongue shall flow ; .
Till I know all, I'll nothing seem to know.
Lights and a table there ! Wife, Master Wendoll,
And gentle Master Cranwell.

Enter Mistress FRANKFORD, WENDOLL, CRANWELL,
NICHOLAS, *and* JENKIN, *with cards, carpets, stools,
and other necessaries.*

    Frank. O Master Cranwell, you are a stranger here,
And often baulk my house : faith, y'are a churl :
Now we have supped, a table, and to cards.

    Jenk. A pair of cards,[1] Nicholas, and a carpet to cover
the table. Where's Cicely with her counters and her

---

    ¹ *j*   c of cards.

              I 2

box? Candles and candlesticks there! Fie, we have such a household of serving creatures! unless it be Nick and I, there's not one amongst them all can say bo to a goose. Well said,[1] Nick.

    [*They spread a carpet, set down lights and cards.*

Mis. Frank. Come, Master Frankford, who shall take my part?

Frank. Marry, that will I, sweet wife.

Wen. No, by my faith, sir; when you are together I sit out: it must be Mistress Frankford and I, or else it is no match.

Frank. I do not like that match.

Nic. [*Aside*] You have no reason, marry, knowing all.

Frank. 'Tis no great matter neither. Come, Master Cranwell, shall you and I take them up?

Cran. At your pleasure, sir.

Frank. I must look to you, Master Wendoll, for you will be playing false; nay, so will my wife too.

Nic. [*Aside.*] Ay, I will be sworn she will.

Mis. Frank. Let them that are taken playing false, forfeit the set.

Frank. Content; it shall go hard but I'll take you.

Cran. Gentlemen, what shall our game be?

Wen. Master Frankford, you play best at noddy.[2]

Frank. You shall not find it so; indeed you shall not.

Mis. Frank. I can play at nothing so well as double ruff.

Frank. If Master Wendoll and my wife be together, there's no playing against them at double hand.

Nic. I can tell you, sir, the game that Master Wendoll is best at.

Wen. What game is that, Nick?

Nic. Marry, sir, knave out of doors.

Wen. She and I will take you at lodam.

---

[1] *i.e.* Well done.

[2] Said to have been something like cribbage; of the other games mentioned accounts are easily accessible, while it would be superfluous to comment on the various quibbles.

Mis. Frank. Husband, shall we play at saint?

Frank. My saint's turned devil.   No, we'll none of
. saint :
You are best at new-cut, wife ; you'll play at that.

Wen. If you play at new-cut, I am soonest hitter of any
here, for a wager.

Frank. 'Tis me they play on.   Well, you may draw
out.
For all your cunning, 'twill be to your shame ;
I'll teach you, at your new-cut, a new game.
Come, come.

Cran. If you cannot agree upon the game, to post and
pair.

Wen. We shall be soonest pairs ; and my good host,
When he comes late home, he must kiss the post.

Frank. Whoever wins, it shall be thy cost.

Cran. Faith, let it be vide-ruff, and let's make honours.

Frank. If you make honours, one thing let me crave :
Honour the king and queen ; except the knave.

Wen. Well, as you please for that.   Lift who shall
deal.

Mis. Frank. The least in sight : what are you, Master
Wendoll ?

Wen. I am a knave.

Nic. [*Aside.*] I'll swear it.

Mis. Frank. I a queen.

Frank. [*Aside.*] A quean[1] thou shouldst say.   [*Aloud.*]
Well, the cards are mine ;
They are the grossest pair that e'er I felt.

Mis. Frank. Shuffle, I'll cut : would I had never dealt.

Frank. I have lost my dealing.

Wen. Sir, the fault's in me :
This queen I have more than mine own, you see.
Give me the stock.

Frank. My mind's not on my game.
Many a deal I have lost ; the more's your shame.

---

[1] In the now obsolete sense of a whore.

You have served me a bad trick, Master Wendoll.

Wen. Sir, you must take your lot.   To end this strife,
I know I have dealt better with your wife.

Frank. Thou hast dealt falsely, then.

Mis. Frank. What's trumps?

Wen. Hearts: partner, I rub.

Frank. [*Aside.*] Thou robb'st me of my soul, of her
   chaste love;
In thy false dealing thou hast robbed my heart.
[*Aloud.*] Booty you play; I like a loser stand,
Having no heart, or here or in my hand.
I will give o'er the set; I am not well.
Come, who will hold my cards?

Mis. Frank. Not well, sweet Master Frankford!
Alas, what ail you?   'Tis some sudden qualm.

Wen. How long have you been so, Master Frankford?

Fran. Sir, I was lusty, and I had my health,
But I grew ill when you began to deal.
Take hence this table. Gentle Master Cranwell,
You are welcome; see your chamber at your pleasure.
I'm sorry that this meagrim takes me so,
I cannot sit and bear you company.
Jenkin, some lights, and show him to his chamber.
                    [*Exeunt* CRANWELL *and* JENKIN.

Mis. Frank. A night-gown for my husband; quickly
   there:
It is some rheum or cold.

Wen. Now, in good faith, this illness you have got
By sitting late without your gown.

Frank. I know it, Master Wendoll.
Go, go to bed, lest you complain like me.
Wife, prythee, wife, into my bed-chamber;
The night is raw and cold, and rheumatic:
Leave me my gown and light; I'll walk away my fit.

Wen. Sweet sir, good night.

Frank. Myself, good night.   [*Exit* WENDOLL.

Mis. Frank. Shall I attend you, husband?

Frank. No, gentle wife, thou'lt catch cold in thy head;
Prythee, be gone, sweet; I'll make haste to bed.

Mis. Frank. No sleep will fasten on mine eyes, you
    know,
Until you come.

Frank. Sweet Nan, I prythee go.—

                    [*Exit* Mistress FRANKFORD.

I have bethought me : get me, by degrees,
The keys of all my doors, which I will mould
In wax, and take their fair impression,
To have by them new keys. This being compassed,
At a set hour a letter shall be brought me,
And, when they think they may securely play,
They nearest are to danger. Nick, I must rely
Upon thy trust and faithful secrecy.

Nic. Build on my faith.

Frank. To bed then, not to rest :
Care lodges in my brain, grief in my breast.   [*Exeunt.*

ACT THE FOURTH.

SCENE I.—*A Room in* Old MOUNTFORD's *House.*

Enter SUSAN, Old MOUNTFORD, SANDY, RODER, *and*
TIDY.

 MOUNT. You say my nephew is in
great distress :
Who brought it to him, but his own
lewd life ?
I cannot spare a cross.[1] I must
confess   [what then ?
He was my brother's son : why, niece,
This is no world in which to pity men.

Susan. I was not born a beggar, though his extremes
Enforce this language from me : I protest
No fortune of mine own could lead my tongue
To this base key. I do beseech you, uncle,
For the name's sake, for Christianity,
Nay, for God's sake, to pity his distress :
He is denied the freedom of the prison,
And in the hole is laid with men condemned ;
Plenty he hath of nothing but of irons,
And it remains in you to free him thence.

O. Mount. Money I cannot spare; men should take
heed ;
He 'lost my kindred when he fell to need.   [*Exit.*

Susan. Gold is but earth, thou earth enough shalt have,

---

[1] Piece of money.

When thou hast once took measure of thy grave.
You know me, Master Sandy, and my suit.
Sandy. I knew you, lady, when the old man lived;
I knew you ere your brother sold his land;
Then you sung well, played sweetly on the lute;
But now I neither know you nor your suit.   [*Exit.*
Susan. You, Master Roder, was my brother's tenant,
Rent free he placed you in that wealthy farm,
Of which you are possessed.
Roder. True, he did;
And have I not there dwelt still for his sake?
I have some business now; but, without doubt,
They that have hurled him in will help him out.   [*Exit.*
Susan. Cold comfort still : what say you, cousin Tidy?
Tidy. I say this comes of roysting, swaggering.
Call me not cousin : each man for himself.
Some men are born to mirth, and some to sorrow.
I am no cousin unto them that borrow.   [*Exit.*
Susan. O charity ! why art thou fled to heaven,
And left all things upon this earth uneven?
Their scoffing answers I will ne'er return;
But to myself his grief in silence mourn.

Enter Sir FRANCIS ACTON *and* MALBY.

Sir Francis. She is poor, I'll therefore tempt her with
   this gold.
Go, Malby, in my name deliver it,
And I will stay thy answer.
Malby. Fair mistress, as I understand, your grief
Doth grow from want, so I have here in store
A means to furnish you, a bag of gold,
Which to your hands I freely tender you.
Susan. I thank you, Heavens ! I thank you, gentle sir :
God make me able to requite this favour !
Mal. This gold Sir Francis Acton sends by me,
And prays you——
Susan. Acton ! O God ! that name I am born to curse :

Hence, bawd ! hence, broker ! see, I spurn his gold ;
My honour never shall for gain be sold.
Sir Fran. Stay, lady, stay.
Susan. From you I'll posting hie,
Even as the doves from feathered eagles fly.   [*Exit.*
Sir Fran. She hates my name, my face : how should I
    woo ?
I am disgraced in every thing I do.
The more she hates me, and disdains my love,
The more I am rapt in admiration
Of her divine and chaste perfections.
Woo her with gifts I cannot, for all gifts
Sent in my name she spurns : with looks I cannot,
For she abhors my sight ; nor yet with letters,
For none she will receive.   How then, how then ?
Well, I will fasten such a kindness on her
As shall o'ercome her hate and conquer it.
Sir Charles, her brother, lies in execution
For a great sum of money ; and, besides,
The appeal is sued still for my huntsman's death,
Which only I have power to reverse :
In her I'll bury all my hate of him.
Go seek the keeper, Malby, bring him to me :
To save his body, I his debts will pay ;
To save his life, I his appeal will stay.   [*Exeunt.*

SCENE II.—*A Prison Cell.*

Enter Sir CHARLES MOUNTFORD, *with irons, his feet bare,*
    his garments all ragged and torn.

Sir Char. Of all on the earth's face most miserable,
Breathe in this hellish dungeon thy laments,
Thus like a slave ragged, like a felon gyved.
What hurls thee headlong to this base estate?

O unkind uncle ! O my friends ingrate !
Unthankful kinsmen ! Mountford's all too base,
To let thy name be fettered in disgrace !
A thousand deaths here in this grave I die ;
Fear, hunger, sorrow, cold, all threat my death,
And join together to deprive my breath.
But that which most torments me, my dear sister
Hath left to visit me, and from my friends
Hath brought no hopeful answer : therefore I
Divine they will not help my misery.
If it be so, shame, scandal, and contempt
Attend their covetous thoughts ; need make their graves !
Usurers they live, and may they die like slaves !

Enter Keeper.

Keep. Knight, be of comfort, for I bring thee freedom
From all thy troubles.
Sir Char. Then I am doomed to die ;
Death is the end of all calamity.
Keep. Live : your appeal is stayed ; the execution
Of all your debts discharged ; your creditors
Even to the utmost penny satisfied.
In sign whereof, your shackles I knock off ;
You are not left so much indebted to us
As for your fees ; all is discharged, all paid.
Go freely to your house, or where you please ;
After long miseries, embrace your ease.
Sir Char. Thou grumblest out the sweetest music
      to me
That ever organ played. Is this a dream ?
Or do my waking senses apprehend
The pleasing taste of these applausive news ?
Slave that I was, to wrong such honest friends,
My loving kinsmen, and my near allies.
Tongue, I will bite thee for the scandal breathed
Against such faithful kinsmen : they are all
Composed of pity and compassion,

Of melting charity, and of moving ruth.
That which I spake before was in my rage ;
They are my friends, the mirrors of this age,
Bounteous and free. The noble Mountford's race,
Ne'er bred a covetous thought, or humour base.

Enter SUSAN.

Susan. I can no longer stay from visiting
My woful brother : while I could, I kept
My hapless tidings from his hopeful ear.
Sir Char. Sister, how much am I indebted to thee,
And to thy travel !
Susan. What, at liberty ?
Sir Char. Thou seest I am, thanks to thy industry :
Oh ! unto which of all my courteous friends
Am I thus bound ? My uncle Mountford, he
Even of an infant loved me : was it he ?
So did my cousin Tidy ; was it he ?
So Master Roder, Master Sandy too :
Which of all these did this high kindness do ?
Susan. Charles, can you mock me in your poverty,
Knowing your friends deride your misery ?
Now, I protest I stand so much amazed
To see your bonds free, and your irons knocked off,
That I am rapt into a maze of wonder :
The rather for I know not by what means
This happiness hath chanced.
Sir Char. Why, by my uncle,
My cousins, and my friends : who else, I pray,
Would take upon them all my debts to pay ?
Susan. O brother, they are men all of flint,
Pictures of marble, and as void of pity
As chased bears. I begged, I sued, I kneeled,
Laid open all your griefs and miseries,
Which they derided ; more than that, denied us
A part in their alliance ; but, in pride,
Said that our kindred with our plenty died.

Sir Char. Drudges too much—what did they? oh,
    known evil !
Rich fly the poor, as good men shun the devil.
Whence should my freedom come? of whom alive,
Saving of those, have I deserved so well?
Guess, sister, call to mind, remember [1] me :
These I have raised ; they follow the world's guise ;
Whom rich in honour, they in woe despise.
    Susan. My wits have lost themselves, let's ask the keeper.
    Sir Char. Gaoler !
    Keep. At hand, sir.
    Sir Char. Of courtesy resolve me one demand.
What was he took the burthen of my debts
From off my back, stayed my appeal to death,
Discharged my fees, and brought me liberty?
    Keep. A courteous knight, one called Sir Francis Acton.
    Sir Char. Ha! Acton ! O me, more distressed in this
Than all my troubles ! hale me back,
Double my irons, and my sparing meals
Put into halves, and lodge me in a dungeon
More deep, more dark, more cold, more comfortless.
By Acton freed ! not all thy manacles
Could fetter so my heels as this one word
Hath thralled my heart ; and it must now lie bound
In more strict prison than thy stony gaol.
I am not free ; I go but under bail.
    Keep. My charge is done, sir, now I have my fees ;
As we get little, we will nothing leese.[2]   [*Exit.*
    Sir Char. By Acton freed, my dangerous opposite !
Why, to what end? on what occasion? ha !
Let me forget the name of enemy,
And with indifference balance this high favour :
Ha!
    Susan. [*Aside.*] His love to me? upon my soul 'tis so :
That is the root from whence these strange things grow.
    Sir Char. Had this proceeded from my father, he

    [1] *i.e.* Remind.   [2] Or lese, *i.e.* lose.

That by the law of nature is most bound
In offices of love, it had deserved
My best employment to requite that grace :
Had it proceeded from my friends or him,
From them this action had deserved my life :
And from a stranger more ; because from such
There is less expectation [1] of good deeds.
But he, nor father, nor ally, nor friend,   /
More than a stranger, both remote in blood
And in his heart opposed my enemy,—
That this high bounty should proceed from him,—
Oh, there I lose myself ! What should I say,
What think, what do, his bounty to repay?

Susan. You, wonder, I am sure, whence this strange
Proceeds in Acton.   I will tell you, brother :   [kindness
He dotes on me, and oft hath sent me gifts,
Letters and tokens : I refused them all.

Sir Char. I have enough, though poor ; my heart is set,
In one rich gift to pay back all my debt.   [*Exeunt.*

·∕SCENE III.—*A Room in* FRANKFORD'S *House.*

Enter FRANKFORD, *and* NICHOLAS *with keys.*

Frank. This is the night that I must play my part
To try two seeming angels.   Where's my keys?

Nic. They are made according to your mould in wax :
I bade the smith be secret, gave him money,
And here they are.   The letter, sir.

Frank. True, take it, there it is ;   [*Gives him letter.*
And when thou seest me in my pleasant'st vein,
Ready to sit to supper, bring it me.

Nic. I'll do't, make no more question but I'll do't.
      [*Exit.*

[1] " Execution " in the early eds.

Enter Mistress FRANKFORD, CRANWELL, WENDOLL, *and*
JENKIN.

Mis. Frank. Sirrah, 'tis six o'clock already struck !
Go bid them spread the cloth and serve in supper.

Jenk. It shall be done, forsooth, mistress.   Where's
Spigot, the butler, to give us out salt and trenchers ?

[*Exit.*

Wen. We that have been a-hunting all the day
Come with preparèd stomachs.   Master Frankford,
We wished you at our sport.

Frank. My heart was with you, and my mind was on
        you.
Fie, Master Cranwell ! you are still thus sad ?
A stool, a stool.   Where's Jenkin, and where's Nick ?
'Tis supper-time at least an hour ago.
What's the best news abroad ?

Wen. I know none good.

Frank. But I know too much bad.   [*Aside.*

Enter JENKIN *and* Butler *with a table-cloth, bread,
    trenchers, and salt.*

Cran. Methinks, sir, you might have that interest
In your wife's brother, to be more remiss
In his hard dealing against poor Sir Charles,
Who, as I hear, lies in York Castle, needy,
And in great want.   [*Exeunt* JENKIN *and* Butler.

Frank. Did not more weighty business of my own
Hold me away, I would have laboured peace
Betwixt them, with all care ; indeed I would, sir.

Mis. Frank. I'll write unto my brother earnestly
In that behalf.

Wen. A charitable deed,
And will beget the good opinion
Of all your friends that love you, Mistress Frankford.

Frank. That's you for one ;   I know you love Sir
        Charles,
And my wife too, well.

Wen. He deserves the love
Of all true gentlemen ; be yourselves judge.
    Frank. But supper, ho!   Now as thou lov'st me,
        Wendoll,
Which I am sure thou dost, be merry, pleasant,
And frolic it to-night.   Sweet Master Cranwell,
Do you the like.   Wife, I protest my heart
Was ne'er more bent on sweet alacrity.
Where be those lazy knaves to serve in supper?

Re-enter NICHOLAS.

    Nic. Here's a letter, sir.
    Frank. Whence comes it? and who brought it?
    Nic. A stripling that below attends your answer,
And, as he tells me, it is sent from York.
    Frank. Have him into the cellar; let him taste
A cup of our March beer : go, make him drink.
                        [*Reads the letter.*
    Nic. I'll make him drunk, if he be a Trojan.
    Frank. My boots and spurs! where's Jenkin? God
        forgive me,
How I neglect my business!   Wife, look here ;
I have a matter to be tried to-morrow
By eight o'clock, and my attorney writes me,
I must be there betimes with evidence,
Or it will go against me.   Where's my boots?

Re-enter JENKIN *with boots and spurs.*

    Mis. Frank. I hope your business craves no such
That you must ride to-night.   [despatch
    Wen. [*Aside.*]   I hope it doth.
    Frank. God's me! no such despatch!
Jenkin, my boots.   Where's Nick?. Saddle my roan,
And the grey dapple for himself.   Content ye,
It much concerns me.   Gentle Master Cranwell,
And Master Wendoll, in my absence use
The very ripest pleasures of my house.

Wen. Lord! Master Frankford, will you ride to-night?
The ways are dangerous.

Frank. Therefore will I ride
Appointed well; and so shall Nick my man.

Mis. Frank. I'll call you up by five o'clock to-morrow.

Frank. No, by my faith, wife, I'll not trust to that;
'Tis not such easy rising in a morning
From one I love so dearly : no, by my faith,
I shall not leave so sweet a bedfellow,
But with much pain.   You have made me a sluggard
Since I first knew you.

Mis. Frank. Then, if you needs will go
This dangerous evening, Master Wendoll,
Let me entreat you bear him company.

Wen. With all my heart, sweet mistress. My boots there!

Frank. Fie, fie, that for my private business
I should disease[1] my friend, and be a trouble
To the whole house !   Nick !

Nic. Anon, sir.

Frank. Bring forth my gelding.—[*Exit* NICHOLAS.]—
        As you love, me sir,
Use no more words : a hand, good Master Cranwell.

Cran. Sir, God be your good speed !

Frank. Good night, sweet Nan ; nay, nay, a kiss and
        part.
[*Aside.*] Dissembling lips, you suit not with my heart.
                                                [*Exit.*

Wen. How business, time, and hours, all gracious
        prove,
And are the furtherers to my new-born love !
I am husband now in Master Frankford's place,
And must command the house.   My pleasure is
We will not sup abroad so publicly,
But in your private chamber, Mistress Frankford.

Mis. Frank. O, sir, you are too public in your love,
And Master Frankford's wife——

---
[1] Inconvenience.

Heywood.   E.

Cran. Might I crave favour,
I would entreat you I might see my chamber ;
I am on the sudden grown exceeding ill,
And would be spared from supper.
    Wen. Light there, ho!
See you want nothing, sir ; for, if you do,
You injure that good man, and wrong me too.
    Cran. I will make bold : good night.   [*Exit.*
    Wen. How all conspire
To make our bosom sweet, and full entire !
Come, Nan, I pr'ythee let us sup within.
    Mis. Frank. Oh, what a clog unto the soul is sin !
We pale offenders are still full of fear ;
Every suspicious eye brings danger near,
When they whose clear hearts from offence are free
Despise report, base scandals do outface,
And stand at mere defiance with disgrace.
    Wen. Fie, fie ! you talk too like a puritan.
    Mis. Frank. You have tempted me to mischief, Master
    Wendoll :
I have done I know not what. Well, you plead custom ;
That which for want of wit I granted erst,
I now must yield through fear. Come, come, let's in ;
Once o'er shoes, we are straight o'er head in sin.
    Wen. My jocund soul is joyful above measure ;
I'll be profuse in Frankford's richest treasure.   [*Exeunt.*

SCENE IV.--*Another part of the House.*

Enter CICELY, JENKIN, *and* Butler.

Jenk. My mistress and Master Wendoll, my master,
sup in her chamber to-night. Cicely, you are preferred
from being the cook to be chambermaid : of all the loves
betwixt thee and me, tell me what thou thinkest of this ?

Cicely. Mum; there's an old proverb,—when the cat's away, the mouse may play. .

Jenk. Now you talk of a cat, Cicely, I smell a rat.

Cicely. Good words, Jenkin, lest you be called to answer them.

Jenk. Why, God make my mistress an honest woman! are not these good words? Pray God my new master play not the knave with my old master! is there any hurt in this? God send no villainy intended! and, if they do sup together, pray God they do not lie together! God make my mistress chaste, and make us all His servants! what harm is there in all this? Nay, more; here is my hand, thou shalt never have my heart unless thou say Amen.

Cicely. Amen, I pray God, I say.

Enter Serving-man.

Serv. My mistress sends that you should make less noise, to lock up the doors, and see the household all got to bed: you, Jenkin, for this night are made the porter to see the gates shut in.

Jenk. Thus, by little and little, I creep into office. Come, to kennel, my masters, to kennel; tis eleven o'clock, already.

Serv. When you have locked the gates in, you must send up the keys to my mistress.

Cicely. Quickly, for God's sake, Jenkin, for I must carry them. I am neither pillow nor bolster, but I know more than both.

Jenk. To bed, good Spigot; to bed, good honest serving-creatures; and let us sleep as snug as pigs in pease-straw.   [*Exeunt.*

SCENE V.—*Outside* FRANKFORD'S *House.*

Enter FRANKFORD *and* NICHOLAS.

Frank. Soft, soft ; we have tied our geldings to a tree,
Two flight-shot [1] off, lest by their thundering hoofs
They blab our coming back.   Hear'st thou no noise ?
Nic. Hear ! I hear nothing but the owl and you.
Frank. So ; now my watch's hand points upon twelve,
And it is dead midnight.   Where are my keys ?
Nic. Here, sir.
Frank. This is the key that opes my outward gate ;
This is the hall-door ; this the withdrawing chamber ;
But this, that door that's bawd unto my shame,
Fountain and spring of all my bleeding thoughts,
Where the most hallowed order and true knot
Of nuptial sanctity hath been profaned ;
It leads to my polluted bed-chamber,
Once my terrestrial heaven, now my earth's hell,
The place where sins in all their ripeness dwell.
But I forget myself : now to my gate.
Nic. It must ope with far less noise than Cripple-gate,
or your plot's dashed.
Frank. So, reach me my dark lanthorn to the rest ;
Tread softly, softly.
Nic. I will walk on eggs this pace.
Frank. A general silence hath surprised the house,
And this is the last door.   Astonishment,
Fear, and amazement play against my heart,
Even as a madman beats upon a drum.
Oh, keep my eyes, you Heavens, before I enter,
From any sight that may transfix my soul ;
Or, if there be so black a spectacle,
Oh, strike mine eyes stark blind ; or, if not so,
Lend me such patience to digest my grief
That I may keep this white and virgin hand
From any violent outrage or red murder !
And with that prayer I enter.   [*Exeunt.*

---

[1] *i.e.* Two bow-shots.

SCENE VI.—*The Hall of* FRANKFORD'S *House.*

NICHOLAS *discovered.*

Nic. Here's a circumstance.
A man be made cuckold in the time
That he's about it. An the case were mine,
As 'tis my master's,—'sblood that he makes me swear!—
I would have placed his action, entered there ;
I would, I would

Enter FRANKFORD.

Frank. Oh! oh !
Nic. Master, 'sblood! master ! master !
Frank. O me unhappy ! I have found them lying
Close in each other's arms, and fast asleep.
But that I would not damn two precious souls,
Bought with my Saviour's blood, and send them, laden
With all their scarlet sins upon their backs,
Unto a fearful judgment, their two lives
Had met upon my rapier.
Nic. 'Sblood, master, what, have you left them sleeping
still ? let me go wake them.
Frank. Stay, let me pause a while.
O God ! O God ! that it were possible
To undo things done ; to call back yesterday !
That Time could turn up his swift sandy glass,
To untell the days, and to redeem these hours !
Or that the sun
Could, rising from the west, draw his coach backward,
Take from the account of time so many minutes,
Till he had all these seasons called again,
Those minutes, and those actions done in them,
Even from her first offence ; that I might take her
As spotless as an angel in my arms !
But, oh ! I talk of things impossible,
And cast beyond the moon.[1] God give me patience !
For I will in and wake them.   [*Exit.*

---

[1] A proverbial expression for anything extravagant or out of reach.

Nic. Here's patience perforce;[1]
He needs must trot afoot that tires his horse.

Enter WENDOLL, *running over the stage in a night-gown,*
FRANKFORD *after him with a sword drawn; a* Maid-
servant *in her smock stays his hand, and clasps hold
on him.* FRANKFORD *pauses for a while.*

Frank. I thank thee, maid; thou, like the angel's hand,
Hast stayed me from a bloody sacrifice.[2] [*Exit* Maid-ser-
Go, villain, and my wrongs sit on thy soul   [vant.
As heavy as this grief doth upon mine!
When thou record'st my many courtesies,
And shalt compare them with thy treacherous heart,
Lay them together, weigh them equally,
'Twill be revenge enough. Go, to thy friend
A Judas: pray, pray, lest I live to see
Thee, Judas-like, hanged on an elder-tree.

Enter Mistress FRANKFORD *in her night attire.*

Mis. Frank. Oh, by what word, what title, or what name,
Shall I entreat your pardon? Pardon! oh!
I am as far from hoping such sweet grace
As Lucifer from heaven. To call you husband—
O me, most wretched! I have lost that name,
I am no more your wife.

Nic. 'Sblood, sir, she swoons.

Frank. Spare thou thy tears, for I will weep for thee:
And keep thy countenance, for I'll blush for thee.
Now, I protest, I think 'tis I am tainted,
For I am most ashamed; and 'tis more hard
For me to look upon thy guilty face,
Than on the sun's clear brow. What wouldst thou speak?

Mis. Frank. I would I had no tongue, no ears, no eyes,
No apprehension, no capacity.
When do you spurn me like a dog? when tread me

---

[1] " Patience perforce," a phrase when some evil must be endured.
—*Halliwell.*   [2] Alluding to Gen. xxii. 10, 11.

Under your feet? when drag me by the hair?
Though I deserve a thousand thousand fold
More than you can inflict: yet, once my husband,
For womanhood, to which I am a shame,
Though once an ornament—even for His sake
That hath redeemed our souls, mark not my face,
Nor hack me with your sword ; but let me go
Perfect and undeformèd to my tomb.
I am not worthy that I should prevail
In the least suit; no, not to speak to you,
Nor look on you, nor to be in your presence.
Yet, as an abject, this one suit I crave ;
This granted, I am ready for my grave.   [*Kneels.*
    Frank. My God, with patience arm me! Rise; nay, rise,
And I'll debate with thee.   Was it for want
Thou playedst the strumpet?   Wast thou not supplied
With every pleasure, fashion, and new toy,
Nay, even beyond my calling?
    Mis. Frank. I was.
    Frank. Was it then disability in me ;
Or in thine eye seemed he a properer man ?
    Mis. Frank. Oh, no.
    Frank. Did not I lodge thee in my bosom ?
Wear thee here in my heart ?
    Mis. Frank. You did.
    Frank. I did, indeed ; witness my tears I did.
Go, bring my infants hither.

           Enter Servant *with two* Children.

                    O Nan ! O Nan !
If neither fear of shame, regard of honour,
The blemish of my house, nor my dear love
Could have withheld thee from so lewd a fact,
Yet for these infants, these young harmless souls,
On whose white brows thy shame is charactered,
And grows in greatness as they wax in years,—
Look but on them, and melt away in tears.

Away with them ! lest, as her spotted body
Hath stained their names with stripe of bastardy,
So her adulterous breath may blast their spirits
With her infectious thoughts.   Away with them !
                    [*Exeunt* Servant *and* Children.
Mis. Frank. In this one life I die ten thousand deaths.
Frank. Stand up, stand up ; I will do nothing rashly;
I will retire a while into my study,   '
And thou shalt hear thy sentence presently.   [*Exit.*
    Mis. Frank. 'Tis welcome, be it death.   O. me, base
        strumpet,
That, having such a husband, such sweet children,
Must enjoy neither ! Oh, to redeem my honour,
I would have this hand cut off, these my breasts seared,
Be racked, strappadoed, put to any torment :
Nay, to whip but this scandal out, I would hazard
The rich and dear redemption of my soul.
He cannot be so base as to forgive me ;
Nor I so shameless to accept his pardon.
O women, women, you that yet have kept
Your holy matrimonial vow unstained,
Make me your instance : when you tread awry,
Your sins, like mine, will on your conscience lie.

    Enter CICELY, JENKIN, *and all the serving-men as
        newly come out of bed.*   '
    All. O mistress, mistress, what have you done, mistress ?
    Nic. 'Sblood, what a caterwauling keep you here !
    Jenk. O Lord, mistress, how comes this to pass ? My
master is run away in his shirt, and never so much as
called me to bring his clothes after him.
    Mis. Frank. See what guilt is ! here stand I in this place,
Ashamed to look my servants in the face.

    Enter FRANKFORD *and* CRANWELL, *whom seeing she
        falls on her knees.*
    Frank. My words are registered in Heaven already,

With patience hear me. I'll not martyr thee,
Nor mark thee for a strumpet ; but with usage
Of more humility torment thy soul,
And kill thee even with kindness.

    Cran. Master Frankford——

    Frank. Good Master Cranwell. Woman, hear thy
Go make thee ready in thy best attire ;   [judgment.
Take with thee all thy gowns, all thy apparel ;
Leave nothing that did ever call thee mistress,
Or by whose sight, being left here in the house,
I may remember such a woman by.
Choose thee a bed and hangings for thy chamber ;
Take with thee every thing that, hath thy mark,
And get thee to my manor seven mile off,
Where live ; 'tis thine ; I freely give it thee.
My tenants by shall furnish thee with wains
To carry all thy stuff, within two hours,—
No longer will I limit thee my sight.
Choose which of all my servants thou likest best,
And they are thine to attend thee.

    Mis. Frank. A mild sentence.

    Frank. But, as thou hopest for Heaven, as thou
Thy name's recorded in the book of life,   [believest
I charge thee never, after this sad day,
To see me, or to meet me, or to send
By word or writing, gift, or otherwise,
To move me, by thyself, or by thy friends ;
Nor challenge any part in my two children.
So, farewell, Nan ! for we will henceforth be
As we had never seen, ne'er more shall see.

    Mis. Frank. How full my heart is, in mine eyes
What wants in words, I will supply in tears.   [appears ;

    Frank. Come, take your coach, your stuff; all must
Servants and all, make ready ; all be gone.   [along ;
It was thy hand cut two hearts out of one.   [*Exeunt.*

ACT THE FIFTH.

SCENE I.—*The Entrance to* Sir FRANCIS ACTON'S *House.*

Enter Sir CHARLES MOUNTFORD, *and* SUSAN, *both
well dressed.*

USAN. Brother, why have you tricked
me like a bride,
Bought me this gay attire, these
ornaments?
Forget you our estate, our poverty?
    Sir Char. Call me not brother,
but imagine me
Some barbarous outlaw, or uncivil kern;[1]
For if thou shutt'st thy eye, and only hearest
The words that I shall·utter, thou shalt judge me
Some staring ruffian, not thy brother Charles.
O sister!——
    Susan. O brother, what doth this strange language
mean?
    Sir Char. Dost love me, sister? wouldst thou see
me live
A bankrupt beggar in the world's disgrace,
And die indebted to my enemies?
Wouldst thou behold me stand like a huge beam
In the world's eye, a bye-word and a scorn?
It lies in thee of these to acquit me free,
And all my debt I may out-strip by thee.
    Susan. By me! why, I have nothing, nothing left;

---

[1] " Kern " signified in general any uncivilised person : used especially of the Irish.

I owe even for the clothes upon my back;
I am not worth——
    Sir Char. O sister, say not so;
It lies in you my downcast state to raise,
To make me stand on even points with the world.
Come, sister, you are rich; indeed you are;
And in your power you have, without delay,
Acton's five hundred pound back to repay.
    Susan. Till now I had thought you had loved me. By
      my honour
(Which I have kept as spotless as the moon),
I ne'er was mistress of that single doit
Which I reserved not to supply your wants;
And do you think that I would hoard from you?
Now, by my hopes in Heaven, knew I the means
To buy you from the slavery of your debts
(Especially from Acton, whom I hate),
I would redeem it with my life or blood.
    Sir Char. I challenge it; and, kindred set apart,
Thus, ruffian-like, I lay siege to your heart.
What do I owe to Acton?
    Susan. Why some five hundred pounds; towards
      which, I swear,
In all the world I have not one denier.[1]
    Sir Char. It will not prove so. Sister, now resolve[2]
      me:
What do you think (and speak your conscience)
Would Acton give, might he enjoy your bed?
    Susan. He would not shrink to spend a thousand
      pound,
To give the Mountfords' name so deep a wound.
    Sir Char. A thousand pound! I but five hundred
      owe;
Grant him your bed, he's paid with interest so.
    Susan. O brother!
    Sir Char. O sister! only this one way,

---

[1] A penny.   [2] Satisfy.

With that rich jewel you my debts may pay.
In speaking this my cold heart shakes with shame ;
Nor do I woo you in a brother's name,
But in a stranger's.   Shall I die in debt
To Acton, my grand foe, and you still wear
The precious jewel that he holds so dear?
   Susan. My honour I esteem as dear and precious
As my redemption.
   Sir Char. I esteem you, sister,
As dear, for so dear prizing it.
   Susan. Will Charles
Have me cut off my hands, and send them Acton ?
Rip up my breast, and with my bleeding heart
Present him as a token ?
   Sir Char. Neither, sister :
But hear me in my strange assertion.
Thy honour and my soul are equal in my regard ;
Nor will thy brother Charles survive thy shame.
His kindness, like a burthen hath surcharged me,
And under his good deeds I stooping go,
Not with an upright soul.   Had I remained
In prison still, there doubtless I had died :
Then, unto him that freed me from that prison,
Still do I owe this life.   What moved my foe
To enfranchise me ?   'Twas, sister, for your love.
With full five hundred pounds he bought your love,
And shall he not enjoy it?   Shall the weight
Of all this heavy burthen lean on me,
And will not you bear part ?   You did partake
The joy of my release ; will you not stand
In joint-bond bound to satisfy the debt?
Shall I be only charged ?
   Susan. But that I know
These arguments come from an honoured mind,
As in your most extremity of need
Scorning to stand in debt to one you hate,—
Nay, rather would engage your unstained honour

Than to be held ingrate,—I should condemn you.
I see your resolution, and assent ;
So Charles will have me, and I am content.
    Sir Char. For this I tricked you up.
    Susan. But here's a knife,
To save mine honour, shall slice out my life.
    Sir Char. Ay! know thou pleasest me a thousand
      times
More in that resolution than thy grant.—
Observe her love ; to soothe it to my suit,
Her honour she will hazard, though not lose :
To bring me out of debt, her rigorous hand
Will pierce her heart. O wonder ! that will choose,
Rather than stain her blood, her life to lose.—
Come, you sad sister to a woful brother,
This is the gate : I'll bear him such a present,
Such an acquittance for the knight to seal,
As will amaze his senses, and surprise
With admiration all his fantasies.
    Susan. Before his unchaste thoughts shall seize on me,
'Tis here shall my imprisoned soul set free.

      Enter Sir FRANCIS ACTON *and* MALBY.

    Sir Fran. How ! Mountford with his sister, hand in
      hand !
What miracle's afoot?
    Mal. It is a sight
Begets in me much admiration.
    Sir Char. Stand not amazed to see me thus attended :
Acton, I owe thee money, and being unable
To bring thee the full sum in ready coin,
Lo ! for thy more assurance, here's a pawn,—
My sister, my dear sister, whose chaste honour
I prize above a million : here, nay, take her ;
She's worth your money, man ; do not forsake her.
    Sir Fran. I would he were in earnest !
    Susan. Impute it not to my immodesty :

My brother being rich in nothing else
But in his interest that he hath in me,
According to his poverty hath brought you
Me, all his store ; whom howsoe'er you prize
As forfeit to your hand, he values highly,
And would not sell, but to acquit your debt,
For any emperor's ransom.
    Sir Fran. Stern heart, relent ;
Thy former cruelty at length repent.
Was ever known, in any former age,
Such honourable wrested courtesy ?
Lands, honours, life, and all the world forego,
Rather than stand engaged to such a foe.   [*Aside.*
    Sir Char. Acton, she is too poor to be thy bride,
And I too much opposed to be thy brother.
There, take her to thee : if thou hast the heart
To seize her as a rape, or lustful prey ;
To blur our house, that never yet was stained ;
To murder her that never meant thee harm ;
To kill me now, whom once thou savedst from death,
Do them at once : on her all these rely,
And perish with her spotted chastity.
    Sir Fran. You overcome me in your love, Sir
        Charles ;
I cannot be so cruel to a lady
I love so dearly.   Since you have not spared
To engage your reputation to the world,
Your sister's honour, which you prize so dear,
Nay, all the comforts which you hold on earth,
To grow out of my debt, being your foe,
Your honoured thoughts, lo ! thus I recompense :
Your metamorphosed foe receives your gift
In satisfaction of all former wrongs.
This jewel I will wear here in my heart ;
And, where before I thought her for her wants
Too base to be my bride, to end all strife,
I seal you my dear brother, her my wife.

Susan. You still exceed us : I will yield to fate,
And learn to love, where I till now did hate.
    Sir Char. With that enchantment you have charmed
        my soul,
And made me rich even in those very words :
I pay no debt, but am indebted more ;
Rich in your love, I never can be poor.
    Sir Fran. All's mine is yours ; we are alike in state,
Let's knit in love what was opposed in hate.
Come ! for our nuptials we will straight provide,
Blest only in our brother and fair bride.   [*Exeunt.*

SCENE II.—*A Room in* FRANKFORD'S *House.*

Enter CRANWELL, FRANKFORD, *and* NICHOLAS.

    Cran. Why do you search each room about your
        house,
Now that you have despatched your wife away ?
    Frank. O sir, to see that nothing may be left
That ever was my wife's. I loved her dearly,
And when I do but think of her unkindness,
My thoughts are all in hell ; to avoid which torment,
I would not have a bodkin or a cuff,
A bracelet, necklace, or rebato [1] wire ;
Nor any thing that ever was called hers,
Left me, by which I might remember her.
Seek round about.
    Nic. 'Sblood, master! here's her lute flung in a corner.
    Frank. Her lute ! O God ! upon this instrument
Her fingers have run quick division,
Sweeter than that which now divides our hearts.
These frets have made me pleasant, that have now

---

[1] A species of ruff for the neck : the wire would be used to
stiffen it.

Frets of my heart-strings made. O Master Cranwell,
Oft hath she made this melancholy wood,
Now mute and dumb for her disastrous chance,
Speak sweetly many a note, sound many a strain
To her own ravishing voice, which being well strung,
What pleasant strange airs have they jointly rung!
Post with it after her. Now nothing's left;
Of her and hers, I am at once bereft.

    Nic. I'll ride and overtake her; do my message,
And come back again.   [*Exit.*

    Cran. Mean time, sir, if you please,
I'll to Sir Francis Acton, and inform him
Of what hath passed betwixt you and his sister.

    Frank. Do as you please. How ill am I bested,
To be a widower ere my wife be dead!   [*Exeunt.*

SCENE III.—*A Country Road.*

Enter Mistress FRANKFORD, *with* JENKIN, CICELY, *a*
Coachman, *and three* Carters.

    Mis. Frank. Bid my coach stay: why should I ride in state,
Being hurled so low down by the hand of fate?
A seat like to my fortunes let me have;
Earth for my chair, and for my bed a grave.

    Jenk. Comfort, good mistress; you have watered your
coach with tears already: you have but two mile now to
go to your manor. A man cannot say by my old master
Frankford as he may say by me, that he wants manors;[1]
for he hath three or four, of which this is one that we are
going to now.

    Cicely. Good mistress, be of good cheer; sorrow, you
see, hurts you, but helps you not: we all mourn to see
you so sad.

---

[1] A quibble on "manners" and "manors."

Carter. Mistress, I spy one of my landlord's men
Come riding post : 'tis like he brings some news.
    Mis. Frank. Comes he from Master Frankford, he is
    welcome ;
So are his news because they come from him.

Enter NICHOLAS.

Nic. [*Presenting lute.*] There.
Mis. Frank. I know the lute ; oft have I sung to thee :
We both are out of tune, both out of time.
    Nic. Would that had been the worst instrument that
e'er you played on. My master commends him to ye ;
there's all he can find that was ever yours : he hath
nothing left that ever you could lay claim to but his
own heart, and he could afford you that. All that I
have to deliver you is this : he prays you to forget him,
and so he bids you farewell.
    Mis. Frank. I thank him : he is kind, and ever was.
All you that have true feeling of my grief,
That know my loss, and have relenting hearts,
Gird me about, and help me with your tears
To wash my spotted sins : my lute shall groan ;
It cannot weep, but shall lament my moan.

Enter WENDOLL.

Wen.[1] Pursued with horror of a guilty soul,
And with the sharp scourge of repentance lashed,
I fly from my own shadow. O my stars !
What have my parents in their lives deserved,
That you should lay this penance on their son ?
When I but think of Master Frankford's love,
And lay it to my treason, or compare
My murdering him for his relieving me,
It strikes a terror like a lightning's flash
To scorch my blood up. Thus I, like the owl,

[1] During this and some following speeches Wendoll evidently
remains unseen.

Ashamed of day, live in these shadowy woods,
Afraid of every leaf or murmuring blast,
Yet longing to receive some perfect knowledge
How he hath dealt with her. [*Sees* Mistress FRANKFORD.]
    O my sad fate!
Here, and so far from home, and thus attended!
O God! I have divorced the truest turtles
That ever lived together; and, being divided
In several places, make their several moan;
She in the fields laments, and he at home.
So poets write that Orpheus made the trees
And stones to dance to his melodious harp,
Meaning the rustic and the barbarous hinds,
That had no understanding part in them:
So she from these rude carters tears extracts,
Making their flinty hearts with grief to rise,
And draw down rivers from their rocky eyes.
    Mis. Frank. [*To* NICHOLAS.] If you return unto your
      master, say
(Though not from me; for I am all unworthy
To blast his name so with a strumpet's tongue)
That you have seen me weep, wish myself dead:
Nay, you may say too, for my vow is passed,
Last night you saw me eat and drink my last.
This to your master you may say and swear;
For it is writ in Heaven, and decreed here.
    Nic. I'll say you wept: I'll swear you made me sad.
Why how now, eyes? what now? what's here to do?
I'm gone, or I shall straight turn baby too.
    Wen. I cannot weep, my heart is all on fire:
Curst be the fruits of my unchaste desire!
    Mis. Frank. Go, break this lute upon my coach's
      wheel,
As the last music that I e'er shall make;
Not as my husband's gift, but my farewell
To all earth's joy; and so your master tell.
    Nic. If I can for crying.

Wen. Grief, have done,
Or like a madman I shall frantic run.
   Mis. Frank. You have beheld the wofullest wretch on
     earth;
A woman made of tears: would you had words
To express but what you see! My inward grief
No tongue can utter; yet unto your power
You may describe my sorrow, and disclose
To thy sad master my abundant woes.
   Nic. I'll do your commendations.
   Mis. Frank. Oh no:
I dare not so presume; nor to my children:
I am disclaimed in both; alas, I am.
Oh, never teach them, when they come to speak,
To name the name of mother; chide their tongue,
If they by chance light on that hated word;
Tell them 'tis naught; for, when that word they name,
Poor pretty souls! they harp on their own shame.
   Wen. To recompense her wrongs, what canst thou
     do?
Thou hast made her husbandless and childless too.
   Mis. Frank. I have no more to say. Speak not for
     me;
Yet you may tell your master what you see.
   Nic. I'll do't.   [*Exit.*
   Wen. I'll speak to her, and comfort her in grief.
Oh! but her wound cannot be cured with words.
No matter though, I'll do my best good-will
To work a cure on her whom I did kill.
   Mis. Frank. So, now unto my coach, then to my
     home,
So to my death-bed; for from this sad hour
I never will nor eat, nor drink, nor taste
Of any cates that may preserve my life:
I never will nor smile, nor sleep, nor rest;
But when my tears have washed my black soul white,
Sweet Saviour, to Thy hands I yield my sprite.

Wen. O Mistress Frankford—

Mis. Frank. Oh, for God's sake fly!
The devil doth come to tempt me ere I die.
My coach! this fiend, that with an angel's face
Conjured mine honour, till he sought my wrack,
In my repentant eyes seems ugly black.

[*Exeunt all, except* WENDOLL *and* JENKIN; *the*
Carters *whistling.*

Jenk. What, my young master that fled in his shirt!
How come you by your clothes again? You have made
our house in a sweet pickle, ha' ye not, think you? What,
shall I serve you still, or cleave to the old house?

Wen. Hence, slave! away with thy unseasoned mirth!
Unless thou canst shed tears, and sigh, and howl,
Curse thy sad fortunes, and exclaim on fate,
Thou art not for my turn.

Jenk. Marry, an you will not, another will: farewell,
and be hanged! Would you had never come to have
kept this coil[1] within our doors; we shall ha' you run
away like a sprite again.   [*Exit.*

Wen. She's gone to death; I live to want and woe;
Her life, her sins, and all upon my head.
And I must now go wander, like a Cain,
In foreign countries and remoted climes,
Where the report of my ingratitude
Cannot be heard. I'll over first to France,
And so to Germany and Italy;
Where when I have recovered, and by travel
Gotten those perfect tongues,[2] and that these rumours
May in their height abate, I will return:
And I divine (however now dejected)
My worth and parts being by some great man praised,
At my return I may in court be raised.   [*Exit.*

---

[1] *i.e.* Made this trouble.
[2] *i.e.* Acquired those tongues perfectly (French, German and
Italian).

SCENE IV.— *Before the Manor.*

Enter Sir FRANCIS ACTON, SUSAN, Sir CHARLES MOUNT-
FORD, CRANWELL, *and* MALBY.

Sir Fran. Brother, and now my wife, I think these
troubles
Fall on my head by justice of the Heavens,
For being so strict to you in your extremities :
But we are now atoned.[1]   I would my sister
Could with like happiness o'ercome her griefs,
As we have ours.

Susan. You tell us, Master Cranwell, wondrous
things,
Touching the patience of that gentleman,
With what strange virtue he demeans his grief.

Cran. I told you what I was a witness of ;
It was my fortune to lodge there that night.

Sir Fran. O that same villain Wendoll ! 'twas his
tongue
That did corrupt her ; she was of herself
Chaste, and devoted well.   Is this the house ?

Cran. Yes, sir, I take it here your sister lies.

Sir Fran. My brother Frankford showed too mild a
spirit
In the revenge of such a loathèd crime ;
Less than he did, no man of spirit could do :
I am so far from blaming his revenge,
That I commend it.   Had it been my case,
Their souls at once had from their breasts been freed :
Death to such deeds of shame is the due meed.

[*They enter the house.*

---

[1] Reconciled.

SCENE V.—*A Room in the Manor.*

Enter Sir FRANCIS ACTON, SUSAN, Sir CHARLES MOUNT-
FORD, CRANWELL, *and* MALBY ; JENKIN *and* CICELY
following them.

Jenk. O my mistress, my mistress, my poor mistress.

Cicely. Alas that ever I was born ! what shall I do
for my poor mistress?

Sir Char. Why, what of her ?

Jenk. O Lord, sir, she no sooner heard that her brother
and his friends were come to see how she did, but she,
for very shame of her guilty conscience, fell into such a
swoon, that we had much ado to get life into her.

Susan. Alas that she should bear so hard a fate !
Pity it is repentance comes too late.

Sir Fran. Is she so weak in body?

Jenk. O sir, I can assure you there's no hope of life in
her, for she will take no sustenance : she hath plainly
starved herself, and now she is as lean as a lath. She
ever looks for the good hour. Many gentlemen and
gentlewomen of the country are come to comfort her.

[*Exeunt.*

SCENE VI.—Mistress FRANKFORD'S *Bedchamber.*

Mistress FRANKFORD *in bed; enter* Sir CHARLES
MOUNTFORD, Sir FRANCIS ACTON, MALBY, CRAN-
WELL, *and* SUSAN.

Mal. How fare you, Mistress Frankford?

Mis. Frank. Sick, sick, oh, sick. Give me some air,
I pray you.
Tell me, oh, tell me where is Master Frankford ?
Will not he deign to see me ere I die ?

Mal. Yes, Mistress Frankford : divers gentlemen,
Your loving neighbours, with that just request

Have moved, and told him of your weak estate :
Who, though with much ado to get belief,
Examining of the general circumstance,
Seeing your sorrow and your penitence,
And hearing therewithal the great desire
You have to see him ere you left the world,
He gave to us his faith to follow us,
And sure he will be here immediately.
 Mis. Frank. You have half revived me with those
  pleasing news :
Raise me a little higher in my bed.
Blush I not, brother Acton ? Blush I not, Sir Charles ?
Can you not read my fault writ in my cheek ?
Is not my crime there ? tell me, gentlemen.
 Sir Char. Alas! good mistress, sickness hath not left you
Blood in your face enough to make you blush.
 Mis. Frank. Then sickness, like a friend, my fault
Is my husband come ? My soul but tarries [would hide.
His arrive, then I am fit for Heaven.
 Sir Fran. I came to chide you ; but my words of hate
Are turned to pity and compassionate grief.
I came to rate you ; but my brawls, you see,
Melt into tears, and I must weep by thee.
Here's Master Frankford now.

   Enter FRANKFORD.

 Frank. Good-morrow, brother ; morrow, gentlemen :
God, that hath laid this cross upon our heads,
Might (had He pleased) have made our cause of meeting
On a more fair and more contented ground ;
But He that made us, made us to this woe.
 Mis. Frank. And is he come? Methinks that voice I
 Frank. How do you, woman ?   . [know.
 Mis. Frank. Well, Master Frankford, well; but shall
I hope, within this hour. Will you vouchsafe, [be better,
Out of your grace and your humanity,   .
To take a spotted strumpet by the hand ?

Frank. This hand once held my heart in faster bonds
Than now 'tis gripped by me.   God pardon them
That made us first break hold !

Mis. Frank. Amen, amen.
Out of my zeal to Heaven, whither I'm now bound,
I was so impudent to wish you here;
And once more beg your pardon.   O good man,
And father to my children, pardon me,
Pardon, oh, pardon me ! My fault so heinous is,
That if you in this world forgive it not,
Heaven will not clear it in the world to come.
Faintness hath so usurped upon my knees
That kneel I cannot, but on my heart's knees
My prostrate soul lies thrown down at your feet
To beg your gracious pardon.   Pardon, oh, pardon me !

Frank. As freely, from the low depth of my soul,
As my Redeemer hath forgiven His death,
I pardon thee. I will shed tears for thee, pray with thee;
And, in mere pity of thy weak estate,
I'll wish to die with thee.

All. So do we all.

Nic. So will not I ;
I'll sigh and sob, but, by my faith, not die.

Sir Fran. O Master Frankford, all the near alliance
I lose by her shall be supplied in thee :
You are my brother by the nearest way ;
Her kindred hath fallen off, but yours doth stay.

Frank. Even as I hope for pardon at that day
When the great Judge of Heaven in scarlet sits,
So be thou pardoned.   Though thy rash offence
Divorced our bodies, thy repentant tears
Unite our souls.

Sir Char. Then comfort, Mistress Frankford ;
You see your husband hath forgiven your fall ;
Then rouse your spirits, and cheer your fainting soul.

Susan. How is it with you ?

Sir Fran. How do ye feel yourself?

Mis. Frank. Not of this world.

Frank. I see you are not, and I weep to see it.
My wife, the mother to my pretty babes !
Both those lost names I do restore thee back,
And with this kiss I wed thee once again :
Though thou art wounded in thy honoured name,
And with that grief upon thy death-bed liest,
Honest in heart, upon my soul, thou diest.　　[art free.

Mis. Frank. Pardoned on earth, soul, thou in Heaven
Once more :[1] thy wife dies thus embracing thee. [*Dies.*

Frank. New married, and new widowed.　Oh ! she's
　　dead,
And a cold grave must be her nuptial bed.　　·[sorrow

Sir Char. Sir, be of good comfort ; and your heavy
Part equally amongst us : storms divided
Abate their force, and with less rage are guided.

Cran. Do, Master Frankford : he that hath least part
Will find enough to drown one troubled heart.

Sir Fran. Peace with thee, Nan.　Brothers, and gentle-
All we that can plead interest in her grief,　　[men,
Bestow upon her body funeral tears.
Brother, had you with threats and usage bad
Punished her sin, the grief of her offence
Had not with such true sorrow touched her heart.

Frank. I see it had not : therefore on her grave
Will I bestow this funeral epitaph,
Which on her marble tomb shall be engraved.
In golden letters shall these words be filled,[2]
" Here lies she whom her husband's kindness killed."

[1] Meaning probably ' Kiss me once more.'
[2] ' Filled ' is equivalent perhaps to ' filled in,' *i.e.* on the tomb.

EPILOGUE

An honest crew, disposèd to be merry,
  Come to a tavern by, and called for wine:
The drawer brought it, smiling like a cherry,
  And told them it was pleasant, neat, and fine.
" Taste it," quoth one. He did so. " Fie ! " quoth he ;
" This wine was good ; now't runs too near the lee."

Another sipped, to give the wine his due,
  And said unto the rest it drunk too flat ;
The third said, it was old ; the fourth, too new ;
  Nay, quoth the fifth, the sharpness likes me not.
Thus, gentlemen, you see how, in one hour,
The wine was new, old, flat, sharp, sweet, and sour.

Unto this wine we do allude our play ;
  Which some will judge too trivial, some too grave :
You as our guests we entertain this day,
  And bid you welcome to the best we have.
Excuse us, then : good wine may be disgraced,
When every several mouth hath sundry taste.

THE FAIR MAID OF
THE WEST.

PART I.

HE *Fair Maid of the West, or a Girl worth Gold*, "as it was lately acted before the king and queen with approved liking," was first published (both parts) in 1631 : it had been acted as early as 1617, and from the title-page we may conclude that it held the stage for some time. It probably represents the dramatisation of some already-existent story-book or ballad. "We should be sorry," remarks Mr. Saintsbury,[1] " to lose *The Fair Maid of the West*, with its picture of Devonshire sailors, foreign merchants, kings of Fez, bashaws of various parts, Italian dukes, and what not. The two parts make anything but a good play, but they are decidedly interesting." Only the first has here been given, as it is complete in itself, and the second part is of less value.

I have marked the changes of scene, and in one or two places have made trifling corrections in the text. For instance, in scene iv. of the first act, by reading "your hopes deceased," and changing the punctuation, we get a very fair sense where Collier (who edited the play for the Shakespeare Society) was inclined to think that a line had dropped out.

[1] *Elizabethan Literature*, p. 284.

To the much worthy and my most respected
JOHN OTHOW, Esquire,
Counsellor at Law, in the noble Society of Gray's Inn.

SIR,

XCUSE this my boldness, I entreat you, and let it pass under the title of my love and respect, long devoted unto you ; of which, if I endeavour to present the world with a due acknowledgement, without the sordid expectation of reward or servile imputation of flattery, I hope it will be the rather accepted. I must ingenuously acknowledge, a weightier argument would have better suited with·your grave employment ; but there are retirements necessarily belonging to all the labours of the body and brain. If in any such cessation you will deign to cast an eye upon this weak and unpolished poem, I shall receive it as a courtesy from you, much exceeding any merit in me, my good meaning only excepted. Thus wishing you healthful ability in body, untroubled content in mind, with the happy fruition of both the temporal felicities of the world present, and the eternal blessedness of the life future, I still remain as ever, Yours, most affectionately devoted,

THOMAS HEYWOOD.

To the READER.

 OURTEOUS Reader, my plays have not been exposed to the public view of the world in numerous sheets and a large volume, but singly, as thou seest, with great modesty and small noise. These comedies, bearing the title of *The Fair Maid of the West*, if they prove but as gracious in thy private reading as they were plausible in the public acting, I shall not much doubt of their success. Nor need they, I hope, much fear a rugged and censorious brow from thee, on whom the greatest and best in the kingdom have vouchsafed to smile. I hold it no necessity to trouble thee with the argument of the story, the matter itself lying so plainly before thee in acts and scenes, without any deviations or winding indents.

Peruse it through, and thou mayst find in it
Some mirth, some matter, and, perhaps, some wit.

He that would study thy content,

T.H.

PROLOGUE.[1]

AMONGST the Grecians there were annual feasts,
To which none were invited, as chief guests,
Save princes and their wives.   Amongst the men,
There was no argument disputed then,
But who best governed ; and, as't did appear,
He was esteemed sole sovereign for that year.
The queens and ladies argued at that time
For virtue and for beauty which was prime,
And she had the high honour.   Two here be,
For beauty one, the other majesty,
Most worthy (did that custom still persever)
Not for one year, but to be sovereigns ever.

[1] Only spoken at court-performances of the play.

SPENCER,
CARROL, } Gentlemen.
FAWCETT,
Captain GOODLACK, SPENCER'S Friend.
ROUGHMAN,[1] a swaggering Gentleman.
CLEM, a Vintner's Apprentice.
Two Captains.
The Mayor of Foy.
An Alderman.
MULLISHEG, King of Fez.
Bashaw ALCADE.
Bashaw JOFFER.
A Spanish Captain.
An English Merchant.
A French Merchant.
An Italian Merchant.
A Surgeon.
A Preacher.
Drawers, Sailors, Spaniards, Moors.
Servants, Chorus.

BESS BRIDGES, the Fair Maid of the West.
A Kitchenmaid.

The EARL OF ESSEX,
The Mayor of Plymouth, } Mutes personated.[2]
Petitioners,

SCENE—ENGLAND, THE AZORES, MOROCCO.

---

[1] "Ruffman" in the old edition, in which, also, "Fawcett" is spelled "Forset."
[2] i.e. Mutæ personæ.

THE

FAIR MAID OF THE WEST.

——•᛭᛭᛭•——

ACT THE FIRST.

SCENE I.—*A Street in Plymouth.*

Enter CARROL *and two* Captains.

IRST CAPT. When puts my lord[1] to
    sea?
    2nd Capt. When the wind's fair.
    Car. Resolve me, I entreat; can you
    not guess
    The purpose of this voyage?
  1st Capt. Most men think
The fleet's bound for the Islands.[2]
  Car. Nay, 'tis like.
The great success at Cales,[3] under the conduct
Of such a noble general, hath put heart
Into the English : they are all on fire
To purchase from the Spaniard. If their carracks[4]
Come deeply laden, we shall tug with them
For golden spoil.

[1] The Earl of Essex.
[2] The so-called " Island Voyage " (1597) was against the Azores
and Spanish East and West Indies.   [3] Cadiz.
  [4] Large vessels : the word is of Spanish etymology.

Heywood.   G

2nd Capt. Oh, were it come to that!

1st Capt. How Plymouth swells with gallants; how the
Glister with gold !   You cannot meet a man   [streets
But tricked in scarf and feather, that it seems
As if the pride of England's gallantry
Were harboured here.   It doth appear, methinks,   .
A very court of soldiers.

Car. It doth so.   .
Where shall we dine to-day?

2nd Capt. At the next tavern by ; there's the best wine.

1st Capt. And the best wench, Bess Bridges ; she's the
Of Plymouth held : the Castle needs no bush,[1]   [flower
Her beauty draws to them more gallant customers
Than all the signs i' the town else.

2nd Capt. A sweet lass,
If I have any judgment.

1st Capt. Now, in troth,
I think she's honest.

Car. Honest, and live there !
What, in a public tavern, where's such confluence
Of lusty and brave gallants !   Honest, said you ?

2nd Capt. I vow she is, for me.

1st Capt. For all, I think.
I'm sure she's wondrous modest.

Car. But withal
Exceeding affable.

2nd Capt. An argument
That she's not proud.

Car. No ; were she proud, she'd fall.

1st Capt. Well, she's a most attractive adamant :[2]
Her very beauty hath upheld that house,
And gained her master much.

Car. That adamant
Shall for this time draw me too : we'll dine there.

2nd Capt. No better motion. Come to the Castle
        then.   [*Exeunt.*

[1] *i.e.* The ivy-bush, hung up outside taverns.   [2] Magnet.

SCENE II.— *In front of the Castle Tavern.*

Enter SPENCER *and* Captain GOODLACK.

Good. What, to the old house still?

Spen. Canst blame me, captain?
Believe me, I was never surprised till now,
Or catched upon the sudden.

Good. Pray resolve me;
Why, being a gentleman of fortunes, means,
And well revenued, will you adventure thus
A doubtful voyage, when only such as I,
Born to no other fortunes than my sword,
Should seek abroad for pillage?

Spen. Pillage, captain!
No, 'tis for honour; and the brave society
Of all these shining gallants, that attend
The great lord-general, drew me hither first,
No hope of gain or spoil.

Good. Ay, but what draws you to this house so oft?

Spen. As if thou knew'st it not.

Good. What, Bess?

Spen. Even she.

Good. Come, I must tell you, you forget yourself,
One of your birth and breeding thus to dote
Upon a tanner's daughter! why, her father
Sold hides in Somersetshire, and, being trade-fallen,
Sent her to service.

Spen. Prithee speak no more;
Thou tell'st me that which I would fain forget,
Or wish I had not known. If thou wilt humour me,
Tell me she's fair and honest.

Good. Yes, and loves you.

Spen. To forget that were to exclude the rest:
All saving that were nothing. Come, let's enter. [*Exeunt.*

SCENE III.—*A Room in the Castle Tavern.*

Enter SPENCER, Captain GOOLACK, *and two* Drawers.

.1st Draw. You are welcome, gentlemen.—Show them into the next room there.

2nd Draw. Look out a towel, and some rolls, a salt and trenchers.

Spen. No, sir, we will not dine.

2nd Draw. I am sure ye would, if you had my stomach.   What wine drink ye, sack or claret?

Spen. Where's Bess?

2nd Draw. Marry, above, with three or four gentlemen.

Spen. Go call her.

2nd Draw. I'll draw you a cup of the neatest wine in Plymouth.

Spen. I'll taste none of your drawing.   Go call Bess.

2nd Draw. There's nothing in the mouths of these gallants but " Bess, Bess."

Spen. What say y', sir?

2nd Draw. Nothing, sir, but I'll go and call her presently.

Spen. Tell her who's here.

2nd Draw. The devil rid her out of the house, for me !

Spen. Say y', sir?

2nd Draw. Nothing but anon, anon, sir.

Enter BESS BRIDGES.

Spen. See, she's come !·

Bess. Sweet Master Spencer, y'are a stranger grown. Where have you been these three days?

Spen. The last night
I sat up late at game.   Here, take this bag,
And lay't up till I call for't.

Bess. Sir, I shall.

Spen. Bring me some wine.

Bess. I know your taste,
And I shall please your palate.   [*Exit.*

Good. Troth, 'tis a pretty soul !

Spen. To thee I will unbosom all my thoughts :
Were her low birth but equal with her beauty,
Here would I fix my thoughts.

Good. You are not mad, sir ?
You say you love her.

Spen. Never question that.

Good. Then put her to't ; win Opportunity,
She's the best bawd. If, as you say, she loves you,
She can deny you nothing.

Spen. I have proved her
Unto the utmost test ; examined her,
Even to a modest force ; but all in vain :
She'll laugh, confer, keep company, discourse,
And something more, kiss ; but beyond that compass
She no way can be drawn.

Good. 'Tis a virtue
But seldom found in taverns.

Re-enter BESS, *with wine.*

Bess. 'Tis of the best Graves wine,[1] sir.

Spen. Gramercy, girl : come sit.

Bess. Pray pardon, sir, I dare not.

Spen. I'll ha' it so.

Bess. My fellows love me not, and will complain
Of such a saucy boldness.

Spen. Pox on your fellows !
I'll try whether their pottle-pots or heads
Be harder, if I do but hear them grumble.
Sit : now, Bess, drink to me.

Bess. To your good voyage !   [*Drinks.*

Re-enter 2nd Drawer.

2nd Draw. Did you call, sir ?

Spen. Yes, sir, to have your absence. Captain, this health.

---

[1] *i.e.* From the Graves district of Gascony, so called from the
pebbly character of the soil, and to-day celebrated for its red, but
more especially for its white wines.

Good. Let it come, sir.

2nd Draw. Must you be set, and we wait, with a —— !

Spen. What say you, sir ?

2nd Draw. Anon, anon : I come there.   [*Exit.*

Spen. What will you venture, Bess, to sea with me ?

Bess. What I love best, my heart : for I could wish
I had been born to equal you in fortune,
Or you so low, to have been ranked with me ;
I could have then presumed boldly to say,
I love none but my Spencer.

Spen. Bess, I thank thee.
Keep still that hundred pound till my return
From the Islands with my lord : if never, wench,
Take it ; it is thine own.

Bess. You bind me to you.

Re-enter 1st Drawer.

1st Draw. Bess, you must fill some wine into the Portcullis ; the gentlemen there will drink none but of your
drawing.

Spen. She shall not rise, sir. Go, let your master
    snick-up.[1]

1st Draw. And that should be cousin-german to the
    hick-up.

Re-enter 2nd Drawer.

2nd Draw. Bess, you must needs come. The gentlemen fling pots, pottles, drawers, and all down stairs.
The whole house is in an uproar.

Bess. Pray pardon, sir ; I needs must be gone.

2nd Draw. The gentlemen swear if she come not up
to them, they will come down to her.

Spen. If they come in peace,
Like civil gentlemen, they may be welcome :
If otherwise, let them usurp their pleasures.
We stand prepared for both.

---

[1] A term of contempt, as much as to say, " Go and be hanged."

Enter CARROL *and the two* Captains.

Car. Save you, gallants ! We are somewhat bold, to press
Into your company : it may be held scarce manners ;
Therefore, 'tis fit that we should crave your pardon.

Spen. Sir, you are welcome ; so are your friends.

1st Capt. Some wine !

Bess. Pray give me leave to fill it.

Spen. You shall not stir. So, please you, we'll join company.—
Drawer, more stools.

Car. I take't that's a she drawer. Are you of the house?

Bess. I am, sir.

Car. In what place ?

Bess. I draw.

Car. Beer, do you not ? You are some tapstress.

Spen. Sir, the worst character you can bestow
Upon the maid is to draw wine.

Car. She would draw none to us.
Perhaps she keeps a rundlet for your taste,
Which none but you must pierce.

2nd Cap. I pray be civil.

Spen. I know not, gentlemen, what your intents be,
Nor do I fear, or care. This is my room ;
And if you bear you, as you seem in show,
Like gentlemen, sit and be sociable.

Car. We will.— [*to* BESS.] Minx, by your leave.
Remove, I say.

Spen. She shall not stir.

Car. How, sir ?

Spen. No, sir. Could you outface the devil,
We do not fear your roaring.[1]

Car. Though you may be companion with a drudge,
It is not fit she should have place by us.—
About your business, housewife.

___
[1] Blustering.

Spen. She is worthy
The place as the best here, and she shall keep't.
    Car. You lie.
                    [*They draw and justle :* CARROL *is slain.*
Good. The gentleman's slain : away!
Bess. O, Heaven ! what have you done ?
Good. Undone thyself, and me too. Come away.
                    [*Exeunt* GOODLACK *and* SPENCER.
Bess. Oh, sad misfortune ! I shall lose him ever.
What ! are you men, or milksops ? Stand you still,
Senseless as stones, and see your friend in danger
To expire his last ?
    1st Capt. Tush ! all our help's in vain.
    2nd Capt. This is the fruit of whores ;
This mischief came through thee.
    Bess. It grew first from your incivility.
    1st Capt. Lend me a hand, to lift his body hence.
It was a fatal business.
                    [*Exeunt the* Captains, *bearing the body.*

        Re-enter the two Drawers.

    1st Draw. One call my master, another fetch the con-
stable.   Here's a man killed in the room.
    2nd Draw. How! a man killed, say'st thou? Is all paid?
    1st Draw. How fell they out, canst thou tell ?
    2nd Draw. Sure, about this bold Bettrice.[1] 'Tis not
so much for the death of the man, but how shall we
come by our reckoning ?   [*Exeunt* Drawers.
    Bess. What shall become of me ? Of all lost creatures,
The most infortunate !   My innocence
Hath been the cause of blood, and I am now
Purpled with murder, though not within compass
Of the law's severe censure : but, which most
Adds unto my affliction, I by this
Have lost so worthy and approved a friend,

        ───────────
        [1] The name, _erhaps, of some ballad heroine.

Whom to redeem from exile, I would give
All that's without and in me.

Enter FAWCETT.

Faw. Your name's Bess Bridges?
Bess. An unfortunate maid,
Known by that name too well in Plymouth, here.
Your business, sir, with me?
Faw. Know you this ring?
Bess. I do: it is my Spencer's.
I know, withal, you are his trusty friend,
To whom he would commit it. Speak: how fares he?
Is he in freedom, know ye?
Faw. He's in health
Of body, though in mind somewhat perplexed
For this late mischief happened.
Bess. Is he fled,
And freed from danger?
Faw. Neither. By this token
He lovingly commends him to you, Bess,
And prays you, when 'tis dark, meet him o' th' Hoe,
Near to the new-made fort, where he'll attend you,
Before he flies, to take a kind farewell.
There's only Goodlack in his company:
He entreats you not to fail him.
Bess. Tell him from me, I'll come, I'll run, I'll fly,
Stand death before me; were I sure to die.   [*Exeunt.*

SCENE IV.—*The Hoe.*

Enter SPENCER *and* Captain GOODLACK.

Good. You are too full of passion.
To have the guilt of murder burden me;
And next, my life in hazard to a death
So ignominious; last, to lose a love.

Spen. Canst thou blame me,
So sweet, so fair, so amorous, and so chaste,
And all these at an instant! Art thou sure
Carrol is dead?
Good. I can believe no less.
You hit him in the very speeding place.
Spen. Oh! but the last of these sits near'st my heart.
Good. Sir, be advised by me :
Try her, before you trust her.   She, perchance,
May take the advantage of your hopeful fortunes ;
But when she finds you subject to distress
And casualty, her flattering love may die,
Your hopes deceased.
Spen. Thou counsell'st well.
I'll put her to the test and utmost trial,
Before I trust her further.   Here she comes.

Enter FAWCETT, *and* BESS *with a bag.*

Faw. I have done my message, sir.
Bess. Fear not, sweet Spencer; we are now alone,
And thou art sanctuarèd in these mine arms.
Good. While these confer, we'll sentinel their safety.
This place I'll guard.
Faw. I this.
Bess. Are you not hurt,
Or your skin rased with his offensive steel ?
How is it with you ?
Spen. Bess, all my afflictions
Are that I must leave thee : thou know'st, withal,
My extreme necessity, and that the fear
Of a most scandalous death doth force me hence.
I am not near my country ; and to stay
For new supply from thence might deeply engage
      me
To desperate hazard.
Bess. Is it coin you want ?
Here is the hundred pound you gave me late :

Use that, beside what I have stored and saved,
Which makes it fifty more.   Were it ten thousand,
Nay, a whole million, Spencer, all were thine.
    Spen. No; what thou hast, keep still; 'tis all thine
      own.
Here be my keys : my trunks take to thy charge :
Such gold fit for transportage as I have,
I'll bear along : the rest are freely thine.
Money, apparel, and what else thou find'st,
Perhaps worth my bequest and thy receiving,
I make thee mistress of.
    Bess. Before, I doted ;
But now you strive to have me ecstasied.
What would you have me do, in which to express
My zeal to you ?
    Spen. I enjoin thee to keep
Ever my picture, which in my chamber hangs ;
For when thou part'st with that, thou losest me.
    Bess. My soul may from my body be divorced,
But never that from me.
    Spen. I have a house in Foy, a tavern called
The Windmill; that I freely give thee, too ;
And thither, if I live, I'll send to thee.
    Bess. So soon as I have cast my reckonings up,
And made even with my master, I'll not fail
To visit Foy, in Cornwall.   Is there else
Aught that you will enjoin me ?
    Spen. Thou art fair :
Join to thy beauty virtue.   Many suitors
I know will tempt thee : beauty's a shrewd bait,
But unto that if thou add'st chastity,
Thou shalt o'ercome all scandal.   Time calls hence ;
We now must part.
    Bess. Oh, that I had the power to make Time
      lame,
To stay the stars, or make the moon stand still,
That future day might never haste thy flight !

I could dwell here for ever in thine arms,
And wish it always night.
  Spen. We trifle hours.   Farewell !
  Bess. First take this ring :
'Twas the first token of my constant love
That passed betwixt us.   When I see this next,
And not my Spencer, I shall think thee dead ;
For, till death part thy body from thy soul,
I know thou wilt not part with it.
  Spen. Swear for me, Bess ; for thou mayst safely do't.
Once more, farewell : at Foy thou shalt hear from me.
  Bess. There's not a word that hath a parting sound
Which through mine ears shrills not immediate death.
I shall not live to lose thee.
  Faw. Best be gone ;
For hark, I hear some tread.
  Spen. A thousand farewells are in one contracted.
Captain, away !   [*Exeunt* SPENCER *and* GOODLACK.
  Bess. Oh ! I shall die.
  Faw. What mean you, Bess ? will you betray your
        friend,
Or call my name in question ? Sweet, look up.
  Bess. Ha, is my Spencer gone ?
  Faw. With speed towards Foy,
There to take ship for Fayal.
  Bess. Let me recollect myself,
And what he left in charge—virtue and chastity ;
Next, with all sudden expedition
Prepare for Foy : all these will I conserve,
And keep them strictly, as I would my life.
Plymouth, farewell : in Cornwall I will prove
A second fortune, and for ever mourn,
Until I see my Spencer's safe return.   [*Exeunt.*

SCENE V.—*The same.*

Hautboys. A dumb show.[1] Enter General, Captains and *the* Mayor *of* Plymouth. *At the other side petitioners with papers ; amongst these the* Drawers. *The* General *gives them bags of money. All go off, saving the two* Drawers.

1st Draw. 'Tis well that we have gotten all the money due to my master. It is the commonest thing that can be, for these captains to score and to score ; but when the scores are to be paid, *non est inventus.*

2nd Draw. 'Tis ordinary amongst gallants, now-a-days, who had rather swear forty oaths than only this one oath—"God, let me never be trusted !"

1st Draw. But if the captains would follow the noble mind of the general, before night there would not be one score owing in Plymouth.

2nd Draw. Little knows Bess that my master hath got in these desperate debts. But she hath cast up her account, and is gone.

1st Draw. Whither, canst thou tell?

2nd Draw. They say, to keep a tavern in Foy, and that Master Spencer hath given her a stock, to set up for herself. Well, howsoever, I am glad, though he killed the man, we have got our money.   [*Exeunt.*

---

[1] "Intended to denote the departure of the General (the Earl of Essex) and his followers."—*Collier.*

ACT THE SECOND.

SCENE I.—*Foy. The Windmill Tavern.*

Enter FAWCETT *and* ROUGHMAN.

AW. In your time have you seen a sweeter creature?

Rough. Some week, or thereabouts.

Faw. And in that time she hath almost undone all the other taverns : the gallants make no rendezvous now but at the Windmill.

Rough. Spite of them, I'll have her. It shall cost me the setting on, but I'll have her.

Faw. Why, do you think she is so easily won?

Rough. Easily or not, I'll bid as fair and far as any man within twenty miles of my head, but I will put her to the squeak.

Faw. They say there are knights' sons already come as suitors to her.

Rough. 'Tis like enough, some younger brothers, and so I intend to make them.

Faw. If these doings hold, she will grow rich in short time.

Rough. There shall be doings that shall make this Windmill my grand seat, my mansion, my palace, and my Constantinople.

Enter BESS BRIDGES *and* CLEM.

Faw. Here she comes. Observe how modestly she bears herself.

Rough. I must know of what burden this vessel is. I shall not bear with her till she bear with me ; and till then I cannot report her for a woman of good carriage.

[ROUGHMAN *and* FAWCETT *move aside.*

Bess. Your old master, that dwelt here before my coming, hath turned over your years[1] to me.

Clem. Right, forsooth : before he was a vintner, he was a shoemaker, and left two or three turnovers more besides myself.

Bess. How long hast thou to serve?

Clem. But eleven years, next grass, and then I am in hope of my freedom ; for by that time I shall be at full age.

Bess. How old art thou now?

Clem. Forsooth, newly come into my teens. I have scraped trenchers this two years, and the next vintage I hope to be bar-boy.

Bess. What's thy name?

Clem. My name is Clem : my father was a baker ; and, by the report of his neighbours, as honest a man as ever lived by bread.

Bess. And where dwelt he?

Clem. Below here, in the next crooked street, at the sign of the Leg. He was nothing so tall as I ; but a little wee man, and somewhat huck-backed.

Bess. He was once constable?

Clem. He was, indeed ; and in that one year of his reign, I have heard them say, he bolted and sifted out more business than others in that office in many years before him.

Bess. How long is't since he died?

Clem. Marry, the last dear year ; for when corn grew to be at a high rate,[2] my father never doughed after.

---

[1] *i.e.* Term of apprenticeship.

[2] We learn from Stow that in 1596 wheat was six, seven, and eight shillings per bushel ; the dearth continued and increased in 1597.—*Collier.*

Bess. I think I have heard of him.

Clem. Then I am sure you have heard he was an honest neighbour, and one that never loved to be meal-mouthed.

Bess. Well, sirrah, prove an honest servant, and you shall find me your good mistress.   What company is in the Mermaid ? [1]

Clem. There be four sea-captains.   I believe they be little better than pirates, they be so flush of their ruddocks.[2]

Bess. No matter ; we will take no note of them :
Here they vent many brave commodities,
By which some gain accrues.   They're my good cus-
        tomers,
And still return me profit.

Clem. Wot you what, mistress, how the two sailors would have served me, that called for the pound and a half of cheese ?

Bess. How was it, Clem ?

Clem. When I brought them a reckoning, they would have had me to have scored it up.   They took me for a simple gull, indeed, that would have had me to have taken chalk for cheese.

Bess. Well, go wait upon the captains : see them want no wine.

Clem. Nor reckoning neither, take my word, mistress.

Rough. She's now at leisure ; I'll to her.—
                    [*Coming forward.*
Lady, what gentlemen are those above ?

Bess. Sir, they are such as please to be my guests,
And they are kindly welcome.

Rough. Give me their names.

Bess. You may go search the church-book where they
        were christened :
There you perhaps may learn them.

Rough. Minion, how !

---

¹ A room in the tavern.   ² Gold coins.

Faw. Fie, fie ! you are too rude with this fair crea-
That no way seeks to offend you.   [ture,
   Bess. Pray, hands off !
   Rough. I tell thee, maid, wife, or whate'er thou beest,
No man shall enter here but by my leave.
Come, let's be more familiar.
   Bess. 'Las, good man !
   Rough. Why, know'st thou whom thou slightest ? I am
        Roughman,
The only approved gallant of these parts,
A man of whom the roarers stand in awe,
And must not be put off.
   Bess. I never yet heard man so praise himself,
But proved in the end a coward.
   Rough. Coward, Bess !
You will offend me, raise in me that fury
Your beauty cannot calm. Go to ; no more :
Your language is too harsh and peremptory ;
Pray let me hear no more on't.   I tell thee
That quiet day scarce passed me these seven years
I have not cracked a weapon in some fray,
And will you move my spleen ?
   Faw.   What, threat a woman ?
   Bess. Sir, if you thus persist to wrong my house,
Disturb my guests, and nightly domineer,
To put my friends from patience, I'll complain
And right myself before the magistrate.
Can we not live in compass of the law,
But must be swaggered out on't ?
   Rough. Go to, wench :
I wish thee well ; think on't, there's good for thee
Stored in my breast ; and when I come in place,
I must have no man to offend mine eye :
My love can brook no rivals. For this time
I am content your captains shall have peace,
But must not be used to it.
   Bess. Sir, if you come

Heywood.   H

Like other free and civil gentlemen,
You're welcome; otherwise my doors are barred you.
  Rough. That's my good girl.
I have fortunes laid up for thee : what I have,
Command it as thine own.   Go to ; be wise.
  Bess. Well, I shall study for't.
  Rough. Consider on't.   Farewell.
                    [*Exeunt* ROUGHMAN *and* FAWCETT.
  Bess. My mind suggests me that this prating fellow
Is some notorious coward.   If he persist,
I have a trick to try what metal's in him.

                    Re-enter CLEM.
What news with you ?
  Clem. I am now going to carry the captains a reckon-
  Bess. And what's the sum ?   [ing.
  Clem. Let me see—eight shillings and sixpence.
  Bess. How can you make that good ?   Write them a
    bill.
  Clem. I'll watch them for that ; 'tis no time of night
to use our bills.   The gentlemen are no dwarfs ; and
with one word of my mouth I can tell them what is to
be-tall.[1]
  Bess. How comes it to so much ?
  Clem. Imprimis, six quarts of wine, at sevenpence the
quart, seven sixpences.
  Bess. Why dost thou reckon it so ?
  Clem. Because, as they came in by hab nab, so I will
bring them in a reckoning at six and at sevens.
  Bess. Well, wine, three shillings and sixpence.
  Clem. And what wants that of ten groats ?
  Bess. 'Tis twopence over.
  Clem. Then put sixpence more to it, and make it four
shillings wine, though you bate it them in their meat.
  Bess. Why so, I prithee ?
  Clem. Because of the old proverb, " What they want

---

[1] A quibble on the German *bezahlen*, to pay.

in meat, let them take out in drink." Then, for twelve
pennyworth of anchoves, eighteenpence.

Bess. How can that be?

Clem. Marry, very well, mistress: twelvepence anchoves, and sixpence oil and vinegar. Nay, they shall
have a saucy reckoning.

Bess. And what for the other half-crown?

Clem. Bread, beer, salt, napkins, trenchers, one thing
with another; so the *summa totalis* is eight shillings and
sixpence.

Bess. Well, take the reckoning from the bar.

Clem. What needs that, forsooth? The gentlemen
seem to be high-flown already. Send them in but
another pottle of sack, and they will cast up the reckoning of themselves. Yes, I'll about it.   [*Exit.*

Bess. Were I not with so many suitors pestered,
And might I enjoy my Spencer, what a sweet,
Contented life were this! for money flows,
And my gain's great. But to my Roughman next.
I have a trick to try what spirit's in him.
It shall be my next business; in this passion
For my dear Spencer, I propose me this:
'Mongst many sorrows, some mirth's not amiss.   [*Exit.*

SCENE II.—*Fayal.*[1]

Enter SPENCER *and* Captain GOODLACK.

Good. What were you thinking, sir?

Spen. Troth, of the world: what any man should see
in't to be in love with it.

Good. The reason of your meditation?

Spen. To imagine that in the same instant that one
forfeits all his estate, another enters upon a rich posses-

---

[1] In the Azores.

sion. As one goes to the church to be married, another
is hurried to the gallows to be hanged; the last having
no feeling of the first man's joy, nor the first of the last
man's misery. At the same time that one lies tortured
upon the rack, another lies tumbling with his mistress
over head and ears in down and feathers. This when I
truly consider, I cannot but wonder why any fortune
should make a man ecstasied.

Good. You give yourself too much to melancholy.

Spen. These are my maxims; and were they as faithfully practised by others as truly apprehended by me, we
should have less oppression, and more charity.

Enter the two Captains.

1st Capt. Make good thy words.

2nd Capt. I say, thou hast injured me.

1st Capt. Tell me wherein.

2nd Capt. When we assaulted Fayal,
And I had, by the general's command,
The onset, and with danger of my person
Enforced the Spaniard to a swift retreat,
And beat them from their fort, thou, when thou saw'st
All fear and danger past, madest up with me,
To share that honour which was sole mine own,
And never ventured shot for't, or e'er came
Where bullet grazed.

Spen. See, captain, a fray towards;
Let's, if we can, atone [1] this difference.

Good. Content.

1st Capt. I'll prove it with my sword,
That though thou hadst the foremost place in field,
And I the second, yet my company
Was equal in the entry of the fort.
My sword was that day drawn as soon as thine,
And that poor honour which I won that day
Was but my merit.

---
[1] Reconcile.

2nd Capt. Wrong me palpably,
And justify the same !
Spen. You shall not fight.
1st Capt. Why, sir, who made you first a justicer,
And taught you that word " shall ? " You are no general ;
Or, if you be, pray show us your commission.
Spen. Sir, I have no commission but my counsel,
And that I'll show you freely.
2nd Capt. 'Tis some chaplain.
1st Capt. I do not like his text.
Good. Let's beat their weapons down.
1st Capt. I'll aim at him that offers to divide us !
                                            [*They fight.*
2nd Capt. Pox of these part-frays ! see, I am wounded,
By beating down my weapon.
Good. How fares my friend ?
Spen. You sought for blood, and, gentlemen, you
      have it.
Let mine appease you : I am hurt to death.
1st Capt. My rage converts to pity, that this gentleman
Shall suffer for his goodness.
Good. Noble friend,
I will revenge thy death.
Spen. He is no friend
That murmurs such a thought.—Oh, gentlemen,
I killed a man in Plymouth, and by you
Am slain in Fayal. Carrol fell by me,
And I fall by a Spencer. Heaven is just,
And will not suffer murder unrevenged.
Heaven pardon me, as I forgive you both !
Shift for yourselves : away !
2nd Capt. We saw him die,
But grieve you should so perish.
Spen. Note Heaven's justice,
And henceforth make that use on't—I shall faint.
1st Capt. Short farewells now must serve. If thou
      survivest,

Live to thine honour; but if thou expirest
Heaven take thy soul to mercy !   [*Exeunt* Captains.
   Spen. I bleed much;
I must go seek a surgeon.
   Good. Sir, how cheer you ?
   Spen. Like one that's bound upon a new adventure
To the other world; yet thus much, worthy friend,
Let me entreat you : since I understand
The fleet is bound for England, take your occasion
To ship yourself, and when you come to Foy,
Kindly commend me to my dearest Bess :
Thou shalt receive a will, in which I have
Possessed her of five hundred pounds a year.
   Good. A noble legacy.
   Spen. The rest I have bestowed amongst my friends,
Only reserving a bare hundred pounds,
To see me honestly and well interred.
   Good. I shall perform your trust as carefully
As to my father, breathed he.
   Spen. Mark me, captain ;
Her legacy I give with this proviso :
If, at thy arrival where my Bess remains,
Thou find'st her well reported, free from scandal,
My will stands firm ; but if thou hear'st her branded
For loose behaviour, or immodest life,
What she should have, I here bestow on thee ;
It is thine own : but, as thou lovest thy soul,
Deal faithfully betwixt my Bess and me.
   Good. Else let me die a prodigy.
   Spen. This ring was hers ; that, be she loose or chaste,
Being her own, restore her: she will know it ;
And doubtless she deserves it.   O my memory !
What had I quite forgot ?   She hath my picture.
   Good. And what of that ?
   Spen. If she be ranked among the loose and lewd,
Take it away : I hold it much indecent
A whore should ha't in keeping : but if constant,

Let her enjoy it.   This my will perform,
As thou art just and honest.

Good. Sense else forsake me.

Spen. Now lead me to my chamber.   All's made even—
My peace with earth, and my atone with Heaven.

[*Exeunt.*

SCENE III.—*A Field near Foy.*

Enter BESS BRIDGES, *like a* Page, *with a sword; and*
CLEM.

Bess. But that I know my mother to be chaste,
I'd swear some soldier got me.

Clem. It may be many a soldier's buff jerkin came out
of your father's tan-vat.

Bess. Methinks I have a manly spirit in me,
In this man's habit.

Clem. Now, am not I of many men's minds ; for, if
you should do me wrong, I should not kill you, though
I took you pissing against a wall.

Bess. Methinks I could be valiant on the sudden,
And meet a man i' the field.
I could do all that I have heard discoursed
Of Mary Ambree,[1] or Westminster's Long Meg.

Clem. What Mary Ambree was I cannot tell ; but
unless you were taller, you will come short of Long Meg.

Bess. Of all thy fellows, thee I only trust,
And charge thee to be secret.

Clem. I am bound in my indentures to keep my
master's secrets ; and should I find a man in bed with
you, I would not tell.

Bess. Begone, sir ; but no words, as you esteem my
favour.

---

[1] A famous English heroine, with whom Long Meg is sometimes
associated.

Clem. But, mistress, I could wish you to look to your long seams; fights are dangerous. But am not I in a sweet taking, think you?

Bess. I prithee, why?

Clem. Why, if you should swagger and kill anybody, I, being a vintner, should be called to the bar. [*Exit.*

Bess. Let none condemn me of immodesty,
Because I try the courage of a man,
Who on my soul's a coward, beats my servants,
Cuffs them, and, as they pass by him, kicks my maids;
Nay, domineers over me, making himself
Lord o'er my house and household. Yesternight
I heard him make appointment on some business
To pass alone this way. I'll venture fair,
But I will try what's in him.

Enter ROUGHMAN *and* FAWCETT.

Faw. Sir, I can now no farther; weighty business
Calls me away.

Rough. Why, at your pleasure, then.
Yet I could wish that ere I passed this field
That I could meet some Hector, so your eyes
Might witness what myself have oft repeated,
Namely, that I am valiant.

Faw. Sir, no doubt;
But now I am in haste. Farewell. [*Exit.*

Rough. How many times brave words bear out a
        man!
For if he can but make a noise, he's feared.
To talk of frays, although he ne'er had heart
To face a man in field, that's a brave fellow.
I have been valiant, I must needs confess,
In street and tavern, where there have been men
Ready to part the fray; but for the fields,
They are too cold to fight in.

Bess. You are a villain, a coward; and you lie.
                              [*Strikes him.*

Rough. You wrong me, I protest. Sweet, courteous
    gentleman,
I never did you wrong.
    Bess. Wilt· tell me that?
Draw forth thy coward sword, and suddenly,
Or, as I am a man, I'll run thee through,
And leave thee dead i' the field.
    Rough. Hold! as you are a gentleman.
I have ta'en an oath I will not fight to-day.
    Bess. Th'ast took a blow already, and the lie :
Will not both these enrage thee?
    Rough. No ; would you give the bastinado too,
I will not break mine oath.
    Bess. Oh! your name's Roughman :
No day doth pass you, but you hurt or kill !
Is this out of your calendar?
    Rough. I ! you are deceived.
I ne'er drew sword in anger, I protest,
Unless it were upon some poor, weak fellow,
That ne'er wore steel about him.
    Bess. Throw your sword.
    Rough. Here, sweet young sir ;   [*Gives up his sword.*
    but, as you are a gentleman,
Do not impair mine honour.
    Bess. Tie that shoe.
    Rough. I shall, sir.
    Bess. Untruss that point.[1]
    Rough. Any thing, this day, to save mine oath.
    Bess. Enough ;—yet not enough. Lie down,
Till I stride o'er thee.
    Rough. Sweet sir, any thing.
    Bess. Rise, thou hast leave. Now, Roughman, thou
    art blest :
This day thy life is saved ; look to the rest.
Take back thy sword.

[1] Untie that lace.

Rough. Oh! you are generous : honour me so much
As let me know to whom I owe my life.

Bess. I am Bess Bridges' brother.

Rough. Still methought
That you were something like her.

Bess. And I have heard
You domineer and revel in her house,
Control her servants, and abuse her guests,
Which if I ever shall hereafter hear,
Thou art but a dead man.

Rough. She never told me of a brother living ;
But you have power to sway me.

Bess. But for I see you are a gentleman,
I am content this once to let you pass ;
But if I find you fall into relapse,
The second's far more dangerous.

Rough. I shall fear it.
Sir, will you take the wine ?

Bess. I am for London,
And for these two terms cannot make return ;
But if you see my sister, you may say
I was in health.

Rough. Too well : the devil take you !   [*Aside.*

Bess. Pray, use her well, and at my coming back
I'll ask for your acquaintance. Now, farewell.   [*Exit.*

Rough. None saw't : he's gone for London ; I am
          unhurt ;
Then who shall publish this disgrace abroad ?
One man's no slander, should he speak his worst.
My tongue's as loud as his ; but in this country
Both of more fame and credit. Should we contest,
I can outface the proudest. This is, then,
My comfort. Roughman, thou art still the same,
For a disgrace not seen is held no shame.   [*Exit.*

SCENE IV.—*Fayal.*

Enter two Sailors.

1st Sail. Aboard, aboard! the wind stands fair for
The ships have all weighed anchor.   [England ;
2nd Sail. A stiff gale
Blows from the shore.

Enter Captain GOODLACK.

Good. The sailors call aboard, and I am forced
To leave my friend now at the point of death,
And cannot close his eyes.   Here is the will.
Now may I find yon tanner's daughter turned
Unchaste or wanton, I shall gain by it
Five hundred pounds a year.   Here is good evidence.
1st Sail. Sir, will you take the long-boat and aboard ?

Enter a third Sailor.

Good. With all my heart.
3rd Sail. What, are you ready, mates ?
1st Sail. We stayed for you.   Thou canst not tell
The great bell rung out now.   [who's dead ?
3rd Sail. They say 'twas for one Spencer, who this night
Died of a mortal wound.
Good. My worthy friend :
Unhappy man, that cannot stay behind,
To do him his last rites !—Was his name Spencer ?
3rd Sail. Yes, sir; a gentleman of good account,
And well known in the navy.
Good. This is the end of all mortality.   '
It will be news unpleasing to his Bess.
I cannot fare amiss, but long to see
Whether these lands belong to her or me.   ,

Enter SPENCER *and* Surgeon.

Sur. Nay, fear not, sir : now you have scaped this
My life for yours.   [dressing,
Spen. I thank thee, honest friend.

Sur. Sir, I can tell you news.

Spen. What is't, I prithee?

Sur. There is a gentleman, one of your name,
That died within this hour.   [died he?

Spen. My name! What was he? Of what sickness

Sur. No sickness, but a slight hurt in the body,
Which showed at first no danger, but, being searched,
He died at the third dressing.

Spen. At my third search I am in hope of life.
The Heavens are merciful.

Sur. Sir, doubt not your recovery.

Spen. That hundred pound I had prepared to expend
Upon mine own expected funeral,
I for name-sake will now bestow on his.

Sur. A noble resolution.

Spen. What ships are bound for England? I would gladly
Venture to sea, though weak.

Sur. All bound that way are under sail already.

Spen. Here's no security;
For when the beaten Spaniards shall return,
They'll spoil whom they can find.

Sur. We have a ship,
Of which I am surgeon, that belongs unto
A London merchant, now bound for Mamorah,
A town in Barbary; please you to use that,
You shall command free passage: ten months hence,
We hope to visit England.

Spen. Friend, I thank thee.

Sur. I'll bring you to the master, who I know
Will entertain you gladly.

Spen. When I have seen the funeral rites performed
To the dead body of my countryman
And 'kinsman, I will take your courteous offer.
England, no doubt, will hear news of my death;
How Bess will take it is to me unknown.
On her behaviour I will build my fate,
There raise my love, or thence erect my hate.   [*Exeunt.*

ACT THE THIRD.

SCENE I.—*Foy. A Street outside the Windmill Tavern.*

Enter ROUGHMAN *and* FAWCETT.

OUGH. Oh! you're well met.   Just as I
      prophesied,
   So it fell out.
      Faw. As how, I pray?
      Rough. Had you but stayed the cross-
      ing of one field,
You had beheld a Hector, the boldest Trojan
That ever Roughman met with.
   Faw. Pray, what was he?
   Rough. You talk of Little Davy, Cutting Dick,[1]
And divers such; but tush! this hath no fellow.
   Faw. Of what stature and years was he?
   Rough. Indeed, I must confess he was no giant,
Nor above fifty; but he did bestir him—
Was here, and there, and everywhere, at once,
That I was ne'er so put to't since the midwife
First wrapped my head in linen.   Let's to Bess:
I'll tell her the whole project.
   Faw. Here's the house:
We'll enter, if you please.   [*Exeunt.*

[1] Contemporary bravos of note.

SCENE II.—*A Room in the Tavern.*

Enter ROUGHMAN *and* FAWCETT.

Rough. Where be these drawers—rascals, I should say—
That will give no attendance?

Enter CLEM.

Clem. Anon, anon, sir : please you see a room? What,
you here, again ! Now we shall have such roaring !
Rough. You, sirrah, call your mistress.
Clem. Yes, sir, I know it is my duty to call her
mistress.
Rough. See an the slave will stir !
Clem. Yes, I do stir.
Rough. Shall we have humours, sauce-box? You have
    ears ;
I'll teach you prick-song.[1]
Clem. But you have now a wrong sow by the ear. I
will call her.
Rough. Do, sir; you had best.
Clem. If you were twenty Roughmans, if you lug me
by the ears again, I'll draw.
Rough. Ha ! what will you draw?
Clem. The best wine in the house for your worship ;
and I would call her, but I can assure you that she is
either not stirring, or else not in case.
Rough. How not in case?
Clem. I think she hath not her smock on ; for I think
I saw it lie at her bed's head.
Rough. What ! drawers grow capricious?[2]
Clem. Help ! help !

Enter BESS BRIDGES.

Bess. What uproar's this? Shall we be never rid
From these disturbances?

---

[1] Music noted down   [2] Witty.

Rough. Why, how now, Bess?
Is this your housewifery? When you are mine,
I'll have you rise as early as the lark.
Look to the bar yourself; these lazy rascals
Will bring your state behindhand.
   Clem. You lie, sir.
   Rough. How ! lie !
   Clem. Yes, sir, at the Raven in the High Street.   I
was at your lodging this morning for a pottle-pot.
   Rough. You will about your business : must you here
Stand gaping and idle?   [*Strikes him.*
   Bess. You wrong me, sir,
And tyrannize too much over my servants.
I will have no man touch them but myself.
   Clem. If I do not put ratsbane into his wine, instead
of sugar, say I am no true baker.   [*Exit.*
   Rough. What ! rise at noon?
A man may fight a tall fray in a morning,   [mangled,
And one of your best friends, too, be hacked and
And almost cut to pieces, and you fast,
Close in your bed, ne'er dream on't.
   Bess. Fought you this day?
   Rough. And ne'er was better put to't in my days.
   Bess. I pray, how was't?
   Rough. Thus.   As I passed yon fields——

                Enter Kitchenmaid.

   Maid. I pray, forsooth, what shall I reckon for the
jowl of ling [1] in the Portcullis?
   Rough. A pox upon your jowls, you kitchen-stuff !
Go, scour your skillets,[2] pots, and dripping-pans,
And interrupt not us.   [*Kicks at her.*
   Maid. The devil take your ox-heels, you foul cod's-
head ! must you be kicking?
   Rough. Minion ! dare you scold?

   [1] The fish so-called, which had been served to the guests in the
Portcullis.
   [2] Small metal pots.

Maid. Yes, sir ; and lay my ladle over your coxcomb.
                                                    [*Exit.*
Bess. I do not think that thou darest strike a man,
That swagger'st thus o'er women.
Rough. How now, Bess ?
Bess. Shall we be never quiet ?
Faw. You are too rude.
Rough. Now I profess all patience.
Bess. Then proceed.
Rough. Rising up early, minion, whilst you slept,
To cross yon field, I had but newly parted
With this my friend, but that I soon espied
A gallant fellow, and most strongly armed :
In the mid-field we met, and, both being resolute,
We justled for the wall.
Bess. Why, did there stand a wall in the mid-field ?
Rough. I meant, strove for the way.
Two such brave spirits meeting, straight both drew.

Re-enter CLEM.

Clem. The maid, forsooth, sent me to know whether
you would have the shoulder of mutton roasted or sod.[1]
Rough. A mischief on your shoulders ! [*Strikes him.*
Clem. That's the way to make me never prove good
porter.
Bess. You still heap wrongs on wrongs.
Rough. I was in fury,
To think upon the violence of that fight,
And could not stay my rage.
Faw. Once more proceed.
Rough. Oh ! had you seen two tilting meteors justle
In the mid-region, with like fear and fury
We too encountered. Not Briareus
Could with his hundred hands have struck more thick :
Blows came about my head,—I took them still ;
Thrusts by my sides, 'twixt body and my arms,—
Yet still I put them by.

[1] Boiled.

Bess. When they were past, he put them by.—Go on.
But in this fury, what became of him?
   Rough. I think I paid him home: he's soundly
   mauled.
I bosomed him at every second thrust.
   Bess. Scaped he with life?
   Rough. Ay, that's my fear. If he recover this,
I'll never trust my sword more.
   Bess. Why fly you not, if he be in such danger?
   Rough. Because a witch once told me
I ne'er should die for murder.
   Bess. I believe thee.
But tell me, pray, was not this gallant fellow
A pretty, fair, young youth, about my years?
   Rough. Even thereabout.
   Clem. He was not fifty, then.
   Bess. Much of my stature?
   Rough. Much about your pitch.[1]
   Clem. He was no giant, then.
   Bess. And wore a suit like this?
   Rough. I half suspect.
   Bess. That gallant fellow,
So wounded and so mangled, was myself.
You base, white-livered slave! it was this shoe
That thou stooped to untie; untrussed those points;
And, like a beastly coward, lay along
Till I strid over thee. Speak; was't not so?
   Rough. It cannot be denied.
   Bess. Hare-hearted fellow! milksop! Dost not blush?
Give me that rapier: I will make thee swear
Thou shalt redeem this scorn thou hast incurred,
Or in this woman shape I'll cudgel thee,
And beat thee through the streets. As I am Bess, I'll do't.
   Rough. Hold, hold! I swear.
   Bess. Dare not to enter at my door till then.
   Rough. Shame confounds me quite.

[1] Height: properly a hawking term.

Bess. That shame redeem, perhaps we'll do thee grace ;
I love the valiant, but despise the base.   [*Exit*

Clem. Will you be kicked, sir?

Rough. She hath wakened me,
And kindled that dead fire of courage in me
Which all this while hath slept.   To spare my flesh
And wound my fame, what is't?   I will not rest,
Till by some valiant deed I have made good
All my disgraces past.   I'll cross the street,
And strike the next brave fellow that I meet.

Faw. I am bound to see the end on't.

Rough. Are you, sir?   [*Beats off* FAWCETT.   *Exeunt.*

SCENE III.--*A Street in Foy.*

Enter the Mayor of Foy, *an* Alderman, *and* Servant.

Mayor. Believe me, sir, she bears herself so well,
No man can justly blame her ; and I wonder,
Being a single woman as she is,
And living in a house of such resort,
She is no more distasted.

Ald. The best gentlemen
The country yields become her daily guests.
Sure, sir, I think she's rich.

Mayor. Thus much I know: would I could buy her
state,
Were't for a brace of thousands !   [*A shot within.*

Ald. 'Twas said a ship is now put into harbour :
Know whence she is.

Serv. I'll bring news from the quay.   [*Exit.*

Mayor. To tell you true, sir, I could wish a match
Betwixt her and mine own and only son ;
And stretch my purse, too, upon that condition.

Ald. Please you, I'll motion [1] it.

___
[1] Propose.

Re-enter Servant.

Serv. One of the ships is new come from the Islands ;
The greatest man of note's one Captain Goodlack.
It is but a small vessel.

Enter Captain GOODLACK *and* Sailors.

Good. I'll meet you straight at the Windmill.
Not one word of my name.

1st Sail. We understand you.

Mayor. Sir, 'tis told us you came late from the Islands.

Good. I did so.

Mayor. Pray, sir, the news from thence ?

Good. The best is, that the general is in health,
And Fayal won from the Spaniards ; but the fleet,
By reason of so many dangerous tempests,
Extremely weather-beaten. You, sir, I take it,
Are mayor o' the town.

Mayor. I am the king's[1] lieutenant.

Good. I have some letters of import from one,
A gentleman of very good account,
That died late in the Islands, to a maid
That keeps a tavern here.

Mayor. Her name Bess Bridges ?

Good. The same. I was desired to make inquiry
What fame she bears, and what report she's of.
Now, you, sir, being here chief magistrate,
Can best resolve me.

Mayor. To our understanding
She's without stain or blemish, well reputed ;
And, by her modesty and fair demeanour,
Hath won the love of all.

Good. The worse for me.   [*Aside.*

Ald. I can assure you, many narrow eyes
Have looked on her and her condition ;
But those that with most envy have endeavoured
To entrap her, have returned, won by her virtues.

───

[1] More properly, queen's lieutenant.

Good. So all that I inquire of make report.
I am glad to hear't.   Sir, I have now some business,
And I of force must leave you.
    Mayor. I entreat you
To sup with me to-night.
    Good. Sir, I may trouble you.—
                   [*Exeunt* Mayor *and* Alderman.
Five hundred pound a year out of my way.
Is there no flaw that I can tax her with,
To forfeit this revenue ?   Is she such a saint,
None can missay her ?   Why, then, I myself
Will undertake it.   If in her demeanour
I can but find one blemish, stain, or spot,
It is five hundred pound a year well got.   [*Exeunt.*

SCENE IV.—*The Windmill Tavern.*

Enter CLEM *and* Sailors *on one side : on the other,* ROUGH-
MAN, *who draws and beats them off ; then re-enter*
CLEM, *and the* Sailors, *with* BESS.

    Bess. But did he fight it bravely ?
    Clem. I assure you, mistress, most dissolutely :[1]   he
hath run this sailor three times through the body, and yet
never touched his skin.
    Bess. How can that be ?
    Clem. Through the body of his doublet, I meant.
    Bess. How shame, base imputation, and disgrace,
Can make a coward valiant !   Sirrah, you
Look to the bar.
    Clem. I'll hold up my hand there presently.   [*Exit.*
    Bess. I understand you came now from the Islands?
    1st Sail. We did so.

    [1] He means " resolutely." Slender makes the same blunder (*Mer.*
Wives, i., 1).

Bess. If you can tell me tidings of one gentleman,
I shall requite you largely.

1st Sail. Of what name?

Bess. One Spencer.

1st Sail. We both saw and knew the man.

Bess. Only for that, call for what wine you please.
Pray tell me where you left him.

2nd Sail. In Fayal.

Bess. Was he in health? How did he fare?

2nd Sail. Why, well.

Bess. For that good news, spend, revel, and carouse;
Your reckoning's paid beforehand.—I am ecstasied,
And my delight's unbounded.

1st Sail. Did you love him?

Bess. Next to my hopes in Heaven.

1st Sail. Then change your mirth.

Bess. Why, as I take it, you told me he was well;
And shall I not rejoice?

1st Sail. He's well, in Heaven; for, mistress, he is dead.

Bess. Ha! dead! Was't so you said? Th' hast given
    me, friend,
But one wound yet: speak but that word again,
And kill me outright.

2nd Sail. He lives not.

Bess. And shall I?—Wilt thou not break, heart?
Are these my ribs wrought out of brass or steel,
Thou canst not craze [1] their bars?

1st Sail. Mistress, use patience,
Which conquers all despair.

Bess. You advise well.
I did but jest with sorrow: you may see
I am now in gentle temper.

2nd Sail. True; we see't.

Bess. Pray take the best room in the house, and there
Call for what wine best tastes you: at my leisure,
I'll visit you myself.

[1] Burst.

1st Sail. I'll use your kindness.   [*Exeunt* Sailors.
Bess. That it should be my fate!   Poor, poor sweet-
     heart !
I do but think how thou becom'st thy grave,
In which would I lay by thee.   What's my wealth,
To enjoy't without my Spencer ?   I will now
Study to die, that I may live with him.

             Enter Captain GOODLACK.

  Good. [*Aside.*] The further I inquire, the more I hear
To my discomfort.   If my discontinuance
And change at sea disguise me from her knowledge,
I shall have scope enough to prove her fully.
This sadness argues she hath heard some news
Of my friend's death.
  Bess. [*Aside.*] It cannot, sure, be true
That he is dead ; Death could not be so envious,
To snatch him in his prime.   I study to forget
That e'er was such a man.
  Good. [*Aside.*] If not impeach her,
My purpose is to seek to marry her.
If she deny me, I'll conceal the will,
Or, at the least, make her compound for half —
Save you, [*To* BESS] fair gentlewoman.
  Bess. You are welcome, sir.
  Good. I hear say there's a whore here, that draws wine.
I am sharp set, and newly come from sea,
And I would see the trash.
  Bess. Sure, you mistake, sir.
If you desire attendance, and some wine,
I can command you both.—Where be these boys ?
  Good. Are you the mistress ?
  Bess. I command the house.
  Good. Of what birth are you, pray ?
  Bess. A tanner's daughter.
  Good. Where born ?
  Bess. In Somersetshire.

Good. A trade-fallen tanner's daughter go so brave ! [1]
Oh ! you have tricks to compass these gay clothes.

Bess. None, sir, but what are honest.

Good. What's your name ?

Bess. Bess Bridges most men call me.

Good. Y'are a whore.

Bess. Sir, I will fetch you wine, to wash your mouth ;
It is so foul, I fear't may fester, else :
There may be danger in't.

Good. [*Aside.*] Not all this move her patience !

Bess. Good, sir, at this time I am scarce myself,
By reason of a great and weighty loss
That troubles me.—[*Notices the ring given to him by*
Spencer]—But I should know that ring.

Good. How ! this, you baggage ? It was never made
To grace a strumpet's finger.

Bess. Pardon, sir ;
I both must and will leave you. [*Exit.*

Good. Did not this well ? This will stick in my stomach.
I could repent my wrongs done to this maid ;
But I'll not leave her thus : if she still love him,
I'll break her heart-strings with some false report
Of his unkindness.

Re-enter CLEM.

Clem. You are welcome, gentleman. What wine will
you drink ? Claret, metheglin, or muscadine ? Cider, or
perry, to make you merry ? Aragoosa,[2] or peter-see-me [3] ?
Canary, or charnico [4] ? But, by your nose, sir, you
should love a cup of malmsey : you shall have a cup of
the best in Cornwall.

Good. Here's a brave drawer, will quarrel with his wine.

Clem. But if you prefer the Frenchman before the

---

[1] Fine.
[2] Query "Saragossa," which produces a large quantity of common
wine.
[3] A sweet Spanish wine from the Pedro Ximenes grape.
[4] A sweet wine grown in the neighbourhood of Lisbon.

Spaniard, you shall have either here of the deep red grape, or the pallid white.   You are a pretty tall gentleman; you should love high country wine: none but clerks and sextons love Graves wine.   Or, are you a married man, I'll furnish you with bastard,[1] white or brown, according to the complexion of your bedfellow.

Good. You rogue, how many years of your prenticeship have you spent in studying this set speech?

Clem. The first line of my part was " Anon, anon, sir;" and the first question I answered to, was loggerhead, or blockhead—I know not whether.

Good. Speak : where's your mistress?

Clem. Gone up to her chamber.

Good. Set a pottle of sack in the fire, and carry it into the next room.   [*Exit.*

Clem. Score a pottle of sack in the Crown, and see at the bar for some rotten eggs, to burn it : we must have one trick or other, to vent away our bad commodities.

[*Exit.*

SCENE V.—*A Bedroom in the Tavern.*

Enter BESS, *with* SPENCER'S *Picture.*

Bess. To die, and not vouchsafe some few commends
Before his death, was most unkindly done.
This picture is more courteous : 't will not shrink
For twenty thousand kisses; no, nor blush :
Then thou shalt be my husband ; and I vow
Never to marry other.

                    Enter Captain GOODLACK.

Good. Where's this harlot?

Bess. You are immodest, sir, to press thus rudely
Into my private chamber.

---

[1] Bastard was the name of a sweet Mediterranean wine : a time-honoured joke.

Good. Pox of modesty,
When punks[1] must have it mincing in their mouths !—
And have I found thee? thou shalt hence with me.
                         [*Seizes the picture.*
Bess. Rob me not of the chiefest wealth I have.
Search all my trunks ; take the best jewels there ;
Deprive me not that treasure : I'll redeem it
With plate, and all the little coin I have,
So I may keep that still.
Good. Think'st thou that bribes
Can make me leave my friend's will unperformed?
Bess. What was that friend?
Good. One Spencer, dead i' the Islands,
Whose very last words, uttered at his death,
Were these : " If ever thou shalt come to Foy,
Take thence my picture, and deface it quite ;
For let it not be said, my portraiture
Shall grace a strumpet's chamber."
Bess. 'Twas not so :
You lie ! you are a villain ! 'twas not so.
'Tis more than sin thus to belie the dead.
He knew, if ever I would have transgressed,
'T had been with him : he durst have sworn me chaste,
And died in that belief.
Good. Are you so brief?
Nay, I'll not trouble you.   God be wi' you !
Bess. Yet leave me still that picture, and I'll swear
You are a gentleman, and cannot lie.
Good. I am inexorable.
Bess. Are you a Christian ?
Have you any name that ever good man gave you ?
'Twas no saint you were called after.   What's thy name?
Good. My name is Captain Thomas Good——
Bess. I can see no good in thee :' rase that syllable
Out of thy name.
Good. Goodlack's my name.

                    [1] Prostitutes.

Bess. I cry you mercy, sir : I now remember you ;
You were my Spencer's friend ; and I am sorry,
Because he loved you, I have been so harsh :
For whose sake I entreat, ere you take't hence,
I may but take my leave on't.
  Good. You'll return it ?
  Bess. As I am chaste, I will.
  Good. For once I'll trust you.   [*Returns the picture.*
  Bess. O thou, the perfect semblance of my love,
And all that's left of him, take one sweet kiss,
As my last farewell !   Thou resemblest him
For whose sweet safety I was every morning
Down on my knees, and with the lark's sweet tunes
I did begin my prayers ; and when sad sleep
Had charmed all eyes, when none save the bright
      stars
Were up and waking, I remembered thee ;
But all, all to no purpose.
  Good. [*Aside.*] Sure, most sure,
This cannot be dissembled.
  Bess. To thee I have been constant in thine absence ;
And, when I looked upon this painted piece,
Remembered thy last rules and principles ;
For thee I have given alms, visited prisons,
To gentlemen and passengers lent coin,
That, if they ever had ability,
They might repay't to Spencer ; yet for this,
All this, and more, I cannot have so much
As this poor table.[1]
  Good. [*Aside.*] I should question truth,
If I should wrong this creature.
  Bess. I am resolved.—
See, sir, this picture I restore you back ;
Which since it was his will you should take hence,
I will not wrong the dead.
  Good. God be wi' you !

      [1] Picture.

Bess. One word more.
Spencer, you say, was so unkind in death.
Good. I tell you true.
Bess. I do entreat you, even for goodness' sake,
Since you were one that he entirely loved,
If you some few days hence hear me expired,
You will, 'mongst other good men, and poor people
That haply may miss Bess, grace me so much
As follow me to the grave. This if you promise,
You shall not be the least of all my friends
Remembered in my will. Now, fare you well !
Good. [*Aside.*] Had I had heart of flint or adamant,
It would relent at this.—[*Aloud.*] My Mistress Bess,
I have better tidings for you.
Bess. You will restore
My picture ? Will you ?
Good. Yes, and more than that :
This ring from my friend's finger, sent to you
With infinite commends.
Bess. You change my blood.
Good. These writings are the evidence of lands :
Five hundred pound a year's bequeathed to you,
Of which I here possess you : all is yours.
Bess. This surplusage of love hath made my loss,
That was but great before, now infinite.—
It may be compassed ; there's in this my purpose
No impossibility. [*Aside.*
Good. What study you ?
Bess. Four thousand pound, besides this legacy,
In jewels, gold, and silver, I can make,
And every man discharged. I am resolved
To be a pattern to all maids hereafter
Of constancy in love.
Good. Sweet Mistress Bess, will you command my
service ?
If to succeed your Spencer in his love,
I would expose me wholly to your wishes.

Bess. Alas ! my love sleeps with him in his grave,
And cannot thence be wakened : yet for his sake
I will impart a secret to your trust,
Which, saving you, no mortal should partake.
　　Good. Both for his love and yours, command my
　　　　service.
　　Bess. There's a prize
Brought into Falmouth road, a good tight vessel ;
The bottom will but cost eight hundred pound ;
You shall have money : buy it.
　　Good. To what end ?
　　Bess. That you shall know hereafter.   Furnish her
With all provision needful : spare no cost ;
And join with you a ging [1] of lusty lads,
Such as will bravely man her.   All the charge
I will commit to you ; and when she's fitted,
Captain, she is thine own.
　　Good. I sound it not.[2]
　　Bess. Spare me the rest.—This voyage I intend,
Though some may blame, all lovers will commend.
　　　　　　　　　　　　　　　　　[*Exeunt.*

[1] The old form of "gang."
[2] *i.e.,* I cannot fathom your meaning.

ACT THE FOURTH.

SCENE I.—*On Board a Spanish Vessel.*

After an alarum, enter a Spanish Captain, *with* Sailors, *bringing in an* English Merchant, SPENCER, *and the* Surgeon, *prisoners.*

CAPT. For Fayal's loss and spoil, by
  the English done,
We are in part revenged.   There's not
  a vessel
That bears upon her top St. George's
  cross,
But for that act shall suffer.
  Merch. Insult not, Spaniard,
Nor be too proud, that thou by odds of ships,
Provision, men, and powder, madest us yield.
Had you come one to one, or made assault
With reasonable advantage, we by this
Had made the carcase of your ship your graves,
Low sunk to the sea's bottom.
  S. Capt. Englishman, thy ship shall yield us pillage.
These prisoners we will keep in strongest hold,
To pay no other ransom than their lives.
  Spen. Degenerate Spaniard, there's no nobless in thee,
To threaten men unarmed and miserable.
Thou mightst as well tread o'er a field of slaughter,
And kill them o'er that are already slain,
And brag thy manhood.

S. Capt. Sirrah, what are you?

Spen. Thy equal, as I am a prisoner;
But once, to stay a better man than thou,
A gentleman in my country.

S. Capt. Wert thou not so, we have strappados, bolts,
And engines,[1] to the mainmast fastenèd,
Can make you gentle.

Spen. Spaniard, do thy worst :
Thou canst not act more tortures than my courage
Is able to endure.

S. Capt. These Englishmen,
Nothing can daunt them.   Even in misery,
They'll not regard their masters.

Spen. Masters !   Insulting, bragging Thrasos ![2]

S. Capt. His sauciness we'll punish 'bove the rest ;
About their censures[3] we will next devise.
And now towards Spain, with our brave English prize.

[Flourish.   Exeunt.

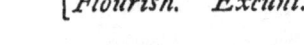

SCENE II. — *The Windmill Tavern.*

Enter BESS, *the* Mayor of Foy, Alderman, *and* CLEM.

Bess. A table and some stools !

Clem. I shall give you occasion to ease your tails,
presently.   [*Tables and stools set out.*

Bess. Will't please you sit ?

Mayor. With all our hearts, and thank you.

Bess. Fetch me that parchment in my closet window.

Clem. The three sheepskins with the wrong side outward ?

Bess. That with the seal.

---

[1] All instruments of torture.
[2] *i.e.* Boasters, Thraso being a braggart in one of Terence's
plays.   [3] Sentenc. s.

Clem. I hope it is my indenture, and now she means
to give me my time.   [*Exit.*

Ald. And now you are alone, fair Mistress Elzabeth,
I think it good to taste [1] you with a motion
That no way can displease you.

Bess. Pray, speak on.

Ald. 'T hath pleased here Master Mayor so far to look
Into your fair demeanour, that he thinks you
A fit match for his son.

Re-enter CLEM, *with the parchment.*

Clem. Here's the parchment; but if it be the lease of
your house, I can assure you 'tis out.

Bess. The years are not expired.

Clem. No; but it is out of your closet.

Bess. About your business.

Clem. Here's even Susannah betwixt the two wicked
      elders.   [*Exit.*

Ald. What think you, Mistress Elzabeth?

Bess. Sir, I thank you;
And how much I esteem this goodness from you,
The trust I shall commit unto your charge
Will truly witness. Marry, gentle sir!
'Las, I have sadder business now in hand
Than sprightly marriage; witness these my tears.
Pray read there.

Mayor. [*Reads.*] " The last will and testament of
Elzabeth Bridges; to be committed to the trust of the
mayor and aldermen of Foy, and their successors for
ever.

To set up young beginners in their trade, a thousand
      pound.

To relieve such as have had loss by sea, five hundred
      pound.

To every maid that's married out of Foy, whose name's
      Elzabeth, ten pound.

---

[1] Test.

To relieve maimed soldiers, by the year, ten pound.
To Captain Goodlack, if he shall perform the business
    he's employed in, five hundred pound.
The legacies for Spencer thus to stand :
To number all the poorest of his kin,
And to bestow on them—Item, to——"
    Bess. Enough ! You see, sir, I am now too poor
To bring a dowry with me fit for your son.
    Mayor. You want a precedent, you so abound
In charity and goodness.
    Bess. All my servants
I leave at your discretions to dispose ;
Not one but I have left some legacy.
What shall become of me, or what I purpose ;
Spare further to inquire.
    Mayor. We'll take our leaves,
And prove to you faithful executors
In this bequest.
    Ald. Let never such despair,
As, dying rich, shall make the poor their heir.
              [*Exeunt* Mayor *and* Alderman.
    Bess. Why, what is all the wealth the world contains,
Without my Spencer ?

       Enter ROUGHMAN *and* FAWCETT.

    Rough. Where's my sweet Bess ?
Shall I become a welcome suitor, now
That I have changed my copy ?[1]
    Bess. I joy to hear it.
I'll find employment for you.

    Enter Captain GOODLACK, Sailors, *and* CLEM.

    Good. A gallant ship, and wondrous proudly trimmed ;
Well caulked, well tackled, every way prepared.
    Bess. Here, then, our mourning for a season end.

---

[1] Made a complete change.

Rough. Bess, shall I strike that captain? Say the word,
I'll have him by the ears.
Bess. Not for the world.
Good. What saith that fellow?
Bess. He desires your love,
Good captain: let him ha' it.
Good. Then change a hand.
Bess. Resolve me all. I am bound upon a voyage :
Will you, in this adventure, take such part
As I myself shall do?
Rough. With my fair Bess,
To the world's end.
Bess. Then, captain and lieutenant both join hands;
Such are your places now.
Good. We two are friends.
Bess. I next must swear you two, with all your ging,[1]
True to some articles you must observe,
Reserving to myself a prime command,
Whilst I enjoin nothing unreasonable.
Good. All this is granted.
Bess. Then, first you said your ship was trim and gay:
I'll have her pitched all o'er ; no spot of white,
No colour to be seen ; no sail but black ;
No flag but sable.
Good. 'Twill be ominous,
And bode disastrous fortune.
Bess. I will ha't so.
Good. Why, then, she shall be pitched black as the
        devil.
Bess. She shall be called the Negro. When you know
My conceit,[2] captain, you will thank me for't.
Rough. But whither are we bound?
Bess. Pardon me that :
When we are out at sea, I'll tell you all.
For mine own wearing I have rich apparel,
For man or woman, as occasion serves.

---

[1] Gang.   [2] Idea.

Clem. But, mistress, if you be going to sea, what shall become of me a-land?

Bess. I'll give thee thy full time.

Clem. And shall I take time, when time is, and let my mistress slip away? No; it shall be seen that my teeth are as strong to grind biscuit as the best sailor of them all, and my stomach as able to digest powdered beef and poor-john.[1] Shall I stay here to score a pudding in the Half-moon, and see my mistress at the mainyard, with her sails up and spread? No; it shall be seen that I, who have been brought up to draw wine, will see what water the ship draws, or I'll bewray the voyage.

Bess. If thou hast so much courage, the captain shall accept thee.

Clem. If I have so much courage! When did you see a black beard with a white liver, or a little fellow without a tall stomach? I doubt not but to prove an honour to all the drawers in Cornwall.

Good. What now remains?

Faw. To make myself associate
In this bold enterprise.

Good. Most gladly, sir.
And now our number's full, what's to be done?

Bess. First, at my charge, I'll feast the town of Foy;
Then set the cellars ope, that these my mates
May quaff unto the health of our boon voyage,
Our needful things being once conveyed aboard;·
Then, casting up our caps, in sign of joy,
Our purpose is to bid farewell to Foy.

[*Exeunt. Hautboys long.*[2]

---

[1] Salt-fish.
[2] *i.e.* They are to play for some time so as to admit of fresh stage arrangements for the coming scenes.

SCENE III.—*Morocco. The Court.*

Enter MULLISHEG, Bashaw ALCADE, *and* Bashaw
JOFFER, *with other* Attendants.

Mull. Out of these bloody and intestine broils
We have at length attained a fortunate peace,
And now at last established in the throne
Of our great ancestors, and reign as King
Of Fez and great Morocco.
  Alc. Mighty Mullisheg,
Pride of our age and glory of the Moors,
By whose victorious hand all Barbary
Is conquered, awed, and swayed, behold thy vassals
With loud applauses greet thy victory. [*Shout; flourish.*
  Mull. Upon the slaughtered bodies of our foes
We mount our high tribunal ; and being sole,
Without competitor, we now have leisure
To stablish laws, first for our kingdom's safety,
The enriching of our public treasury,
And last our state and pleasure ; then give order
That all such Christian merchants as have traffic
And freedom in our country, that conceal
The least part of our custom due to us,
Shall forfeit ship and goods.
  Joff. There are appointed
Unto that purpose careful officers.
  Mull. Those forfeitures must help to furnish up
The exhausted treasure that our wars consumed :
Part of such profits as accrue that way
We have already tasted.
  Alc. 'Tis most fit
Those Christians that reap profit by our land
Should contribute unto so great a loss.
  Mull. Alcade, they shall.—But what's the style of king,
Without his pleasure ? Find us concubines,
The fairest Christian damsels you can hire,
Or buy for gold ; the loveliest of the Moors

We can command, and negroes everywhere;
Italians, French, and Dutch, choice Turkish girls,
Must fill our Alkedavy, the great palace
Where Mullisheg now deigns to keep his court.
    Joff. Who else are worthy to be libertines
But such as bear the sword?
    Mull. Joffer, thou pleasest us.
If kings on earth be térmèd demigods,
Why should we not make here terrestrial Heaven?
We can, we will: our God shall be our pleasure;
For so our Meccan prophet warrants us.
And now the music of the drums surcease;
We'll learn to dance to the soft tunes of peace.
                    [*Hautboys. Exeunt.*

SCENE IV.—*On Board an English Ship.*

Enter BESS *as a* Sea-captain, Captain GOODLACK,
    ROUGHMAN, *and others.*

    Bess. Good morrow, captain. Oh, this last sea-fight
Was gallantly performed! It did me good
To see the Spanish carvel[1] vail[2] her top
Unto my maiden flag. . Where ride we now?
    Good. Among the Islands.
    Bess. What coast is this we now descry from far?
    Good. Yon fort's called Fayal.
    Bess. Is that the place where Spencer's body lies?
    Good. Yes; in yon church he's buried.
    Bess. Then know, to this place was my voyage bound,
To fetch the body of my Spencer thence;
In his own country to erect a tomb
And lasting monument, where, when I die,
In the same bed of earth my bones may lie.
Then, all that love me, arm and make for shore:
Yours be the spoil, he mine; I crave no more.

---

[1] Or caravel, a small light ship.   [2] Lower.

Rough. May that man die derided and accursed
That will not follow where a woman leads.

Good. Roughman, you are too rash, and counsel ill.
Have not the Spaniards fortified the town?
In all our ging we are but sixty-five.

Rough. Come, I'll make one.

Good. Attend me, good lieutenant;
And, sweet Bess, listen what I have devised.
With ten tall fellows I have manned our boat,
To see what straggling Spaniards they can take.
And see where Fawcett is returned with prisoners.

Enter FAWCETT, *with two* Spaniards.

Faw. These Spaniards we by break of day surprised,
As they were ready to take boat for fishing.

Good. Spaniards, upon your lives, resolve us truly,
How strong's the town and fort?

1st Span. Since English Raleigh won and spoiled it
    first,
The town's re-edified, and fort new built,
And four field-pieces in the block-house lie,
To keep the harbour's mouth.

Good. And what's one ship to these?

Bess. Was there not, in the time of their abode,
A gentleman called Spencer buried there,
Within the church, whom some report was slain,
Or perished by a wound?

1st Span. Indeed, there was,
And o'er him raised a goodly monument;
But when the English navy were sailed thence,
And that the Spaniards did possess the town,
Because they held him for a heretic,
They straight removed his body from the church.

Bess. And would the tyrants be so uncharitable
To wrong the dead! Where did they then bestow him?

1st Span. They buried him i' the fields.

Bess. Oh, still more cruel!

1st Span. The man that ought [1] the field, doubtful his
  corn
Would never prosper whilst a heretic's body ·
Lay there, he made petition to the church
To ha' it digged up and burnt ; and so it was.
  Bess. What's he, that loves me, would persuade me
    live,
Not rather leap o'er hatches into the sea?
Yet, ere I die, I hope to be revenged
Upon some Spaniards, for my Spencer's wrong.
  Rough. Let's first begin with these.
  Bess. 'Las, these poor slaves ! Besides their par-
    doned lives,
One give them money.—And, Spaniards, where you
    come,
Pray for Bess Bridges, and speak well o' the English.
  1st & 2nd Span. We shall.
  Bess. Our mourning we will turn into revenge,
And since the church hath censured so my Spencer,
Bestow upon the church some few cast pieces.—
Command the gunner do't.
  Good. And, if he can,
To batter it to the earth.   [*A gun is discharged.*

Enter CLEM, *falling through haste.*

  Clem. A sail ! a sail !
  Bess. From whence ?
  Clem. A pox upon yon gunner ! Could he not give
warning, before he had shot ?
  Rough. Why, I prithee ?
  Clem. Why? I was sent to the top-mast, to watch,
and there I fell fast asleep. Bounce ! quoth the guns ;
down tumbles Clem ; and, if by chance my feet had not
hung in the tackles, you must have sent to England for
a bone-setter, for my neck had been in a pitiful taking.
  Rough. Thou told'st us of a sail.

_____
[1] Owned.

Enter Sailor, *above.*

Sail. Arm, gentlemen ! a gallant ship of war
Makes with her full sails this way ; who, it seems,
Hath took a bark of England.
    Bess. Which we'll rescue,
Or perish in the adventure.   You have sworn
That, howsoe'er we conquer or miscarry,
Not to reveal my sex.
    All. We have.
    Bess. Then, for your country's honour, my revenge,
For your own fame, and hope of golden spoil,
Stand bravely to't.—The manage of the fight
We leave to you.
    Good. Then, now up with your fights,[1] and let your
        ensigns,
Blest with St. George's cross, play with the winds.—
Fair Bess, keep you your cabin.
    Bess. Captain, you wrong me : I will face the fight ;
And where the bullets sing loud'st 'bout mine ears,
There shall you find me cheering up my men.
    Rough. This wench would of a coward make a
        Hercules.
    Bess. Trumpets, a charge ! and with your whistles
        shrill,
Sound, boatswains, an alarum to your mates.
With music cheer up their astonished souls,
The whilst the thundering ordnance bear the bass.
    Good. To fight against the Spaniards we desire.
Alarum, trumpets !   [*Alarum.*
    Rough. Gunners, straight give fire !   [*A shot is fired.*
                        [*Exeunt* GOODLACK, BESS, *&c.*

Re-enter Captain GOODLACK, *wounded*, BESS, ROUGHMAN,
        FAWCETT, *and* CLEM.

    Good. I am shot, and can no longer man the deck :
Yet let not my wound daunt your courage, mates.

---

[1] Defences placed round a vessel to protect the combatants.

Bess. For every drop of blood that thou hast shed,
I'll have a Spaniard's life.—Advance your targets,
And now cry all, "Board ! board ! Amain for England!"
[*Alarum. Exeunt* GOODLACK, BESS, &c.

Re-enter BESS, ROUGHMAN, FAWCETT, CLEM, &c.,
victorious. The Spaniards *prisoners.*

Bess. How is it with the captain ?
Rough. Nothing dangerous ;
But, being shot i' the thigh, he keeps his cabin,
And cannot rise to greet your victory.
Bess. He stood it bravely out, whilst he could stand.
Clem. But for these Spaniards : now, you Don Diegos,
You that made Paul's to stink.[1]
Rough. Before we further censure them, let's know
What English prisoners they have here aboard.   [*Exit.*
1st Span. You may command them all.   We that were
    now
Lords over them, fortune hath made your slaves.—
Release our prisoners.
Bess. Had my captain died,
Not one proud Spaniard had escaped with life.
Your ship is forfeit to us, and your goods :
So live.—Give him his long boat : him and his
Set safe ashore ; and pray for English Bess.
1st Span. I know not whom you mean ; but be't your
    queen,
Famous Elizabeth, I shall report
She and her subjects both are merciful. [*Exeunt* Spaniards.

Re-enter ROUGHMAN, *with a* Merchant, SPENCER *and*
    English Prisoners.

Bess. Whence are you, sir, and whither were you
    bound ?

---

[1] An allusion to the unsavoury exploit of a Spaniard, often re-
ferred to at this period.

Merch. I am a London merchant, bound for Barbary;
But by this Spanish man-of-war surprised,
Pillaged and captived.

Bess. We much pity you.
What loss you have sustained, this Spanish prey
Shall make good to you, to the utmost farthing.

Merch. Our lives, and all our fortunes whatsoever,
Are wholly at your service.

Bess. These gentlemen have been dejected long.
Let me peruse [1] them all, and give them money
To drink our health. And pray forget not, sirs,
To pray for——[*She sees* SPENCER.] Hold! support me,
   or I faint.

Rough. What sudden, unexpected ecstasy
Disturbs your conquest?

Bess. Interrupt me not;
But give me way, for Heaven's sake!

· *Spen.* I have seen
A face, ere now, like that young gentleman,
But not remember where.

Bess. But he was slain;
Lay buried in yon church; and thence removed,
Denied all Christian rites, and, like an infidel,
Confined unto the fields; and thence digged up,
His body, after death, had martyrdom.
All these assure me 'tis his shadow dogs me,
For some most just revenge, thus far to sea.—
Is it because the Spaniards scaped with life,
That were to thee so cruel after death,
Thou haunt'st me thus? Sweet ghost, thy rage forbear;
I will revenge thee on the next we seize.
I am amazed; this sight I'll not endure.
Sleep, sleep, fair ghost, for thy revenge is sure.

Rough. Fawcett, convey the owner to his cabin.
                    [*Exit* FAWCETT *with* BESS.

Spen. I pray, sir, what young gentleman is that?

[1] Examine.

Rough. He's both the owner of the ship and goods,
That for some reasons hath his name concealed.

Spen. Methinks he looks like Bess ; for in his eyes
Lives the first love that did my heart surprise.

Rough. Come, gentlemen, first make your losses good,
Out of this Spanish prize.   Let's then divide
Both several ways, and Heavens be our guide.

Merch. We towards Mamorah.

Rough. We where the Fates do please,
Till we have tracked a wilderness of seas.

         [*Flourish. Exeunt.*

Enter Chorus.

Our stage so lamely can express a sea,
That we are forced by Chorus to discourse
What should have been in action.   Now, imagine
Her passion o'er, and Goodlack well recovered ;
Who, had he not been wounded, and seen Spencer,
Had sure descried him.   Much prize they have ta'en :
The French and Dutch she spares ; only makes spoil
Of the rich Spaniard and the barbarous Turk.
And now her fame grows great in all these seas.
Suppose her rich, and forced, for want of water,
To put into Mamorah, in Barbary,
Where, wearied with the habit of a man,
She was discovered by the Moors aboard,
Which told it to the amorous King of Fez,
That ne'er before had English lady seen.
He sends for her on shore.   How he receives her,
How she and Spencer meet, must next succeed.
Sit patient, then : when these are fully told,
Some may hap say, " Ay, there's a girl worth gold."

            [*Exit.*

ACT THE FIFTH.

SCENE I.—*Morocco. The Court.*

Enter MULLISHEG, Bashaw ALCADE, Bashaw JOFFER, Attendants, &c.

Mull. But was she of such presence?

   Alc. To describe her
Were to make eloquence dumb.

   Mull. Well habited?[1]

   Alc. I ne'er beheld a beauty more complete.

   Mull. Thou hast inflamed our spirits.
In England born?

   Alc. The captain so reported.

   Mull. How her ship?

   Alc. I never saw a braver vessel sail.
And she is called the Negro.

   Mull. Ominous,
Perhaps, to our good fate : she in a Negro
Hath sailed thus far, to bosom with a Moor.
But for the motion made to come ashore,
How did she relish that?

   Alc. I promised to the captain large reward,
To win him to it, and this day he hath promised
To bring me her free answer.

   Mull. When he comes,
Give him the entertainment of a prince.

---

[1] Dressed.

Enter a Moor.

The news with thee?

Moor. The captain of the Negro craves admittance
Unto your highness' presence.

Mull. A guard attend him, and our noblest bashaws
Conduct him safe where we will parley him.   [*Flourish.*

Enter Captain GOODLACK *and* ROUGHMAN.

Good. Long live the high and mighty King of Fez!

Mull. If thou bring'st her, then dost thou bring me life.
Say, will she come?

Good. She will, my lord; but yet conditionally,
She may be free from violence.

Mull. Now, by the mighty prophet we adore,
She shall live lady of her free desires:
'Tis love, not force, must quench our amorous fires.

Rough. We will conduct her to your presence straight.
                [*Exeunt* ROUGHMAN *and* GOODLACK.

Mull. We will have banquets, revels, and what not,
To entertain this stranger.   [*Hautboys.*

Re-enter Captain GOODLACK *and* ROUGHMAN, *with* BESS
BRIDGES, *veiled,* FAWCETT, *and* Moors.

A goodly presence!—Why's that beauty veiled?

Bess. Long live the King of Fez.

Mull. I am amazed!
This is no mortal creature I behold,
But some bright angel, that is dropped from Heaven,
Sent by our prophet.—Captain, let me thus
Embrace thee in my arms.—Load him with gold,
For this great favour.

Bess. Captain, touch it not.—
Know, King of Fez, my followers want no gold.
I only came to see thee for my pleasure,
And show thee, what these say thou never saw'st,
A woman born in England.

Mull. That English earth may well be termed a Heaven,
That breeds such divine beauties.   Make me sure
That thou art mortal by one friendly touch.

Bess. Keep off : for, till thou swear'st to my demands,
I will have no commèrce [1] with Mullisheg,
But leave thee as I came.

Mull. Were't half my kingdom,
That, beauteous English virgin, thou shalt have.

Bess. [*Hands* GOODLACK *a paper.*] Captain, read.

Good. [*Reads.*] " First, liberty for her and hers to leave
the land at her pleasure.   Next, safe-conduct to and from
her ship, at her own discretion.   Thirdly, to be free from
all violence, either by the king or any of his people.
Fourthly, to allow her mariners fresh victuals aboard.
Fifthly, to offer no further violence to her person than
what he seeks by kindly usage and free entreaty."

Mull. To these I vow and seal.

Bess. These being assured,
Your courtship's free, and henceforth we secured.

Mull. Say, gentlemen of England, what's your fashion
And garb of entertainment ?

Good. Our first greeting
Begins still on the lips.

Mull. Fair creature, shall I be immortalized
With that high favour ?

Bess. 'Tis no immodest thing
You ask, nor shame for Bess to kiss a king. [*Kisses him.*

Mull. This kiss hath all my vitals ecstasied.

Rough. Captain,
This king is mightily in love.   Well, let her
Do as she list, I'll make use of his bounty.

Good. We should be madmen else.

Mull. Grace me so much as take your seat by me.

Bess. I'll be so far commanded.

Mull. Sweet, your age ?

Bess. Not fully yet seventeen.

[1] Intercourse.

Mull. But how your birth? How came you to this
To have such gentlemen at your command, [wealth,
And what your cause of travel? .

Bess. Mighty prince,
If you desire to see me beat my breast,
Pour forth a river of increasing tears,
Then you may urge me to that sad discourse.

Mull. Not for Mamorah's wealth, nor all the gold
Coined in rich Barbary. Nay, sweet, arise,
And ask of me, be't half this kingdom's treasure,
And thou art lady on't.

Bess. If I shall ask, 't must be, you will not give.
Our country breeds no beggars; for our hearts
Are of more noble temper.

Mull. Sweet, your name?

Bess. Elizabeth.

Mull. There's virtue in that name.
The virgin queen, so famous through the world,
The mighty empress of the maiden isle,
Whose predecessors have o'errun great France,
Whose powerful hand doth still support the Dutch,
And keeps the potent king of Spain in awe,
Is not she titled so?

Bess. She is.

Mull. Hath she herself a face so fair as yours,
When she appears for wonder?

Bess. Mighty Fez,
You cast a blush upon my maiden cheek,
To pattern me with her. Why, England's queen,
She is the only phœnix of her age,
The pride and glory of the Western Isles.
Had I a thousand tongues, they all would tire,
And fail me in her true description.

Mull. Grant me this:
To-morrow we supply our judgment seat,
And sentence causes; sit with us in state,
And let your presence beautify our throne.

Bess. In that I am your servant.

Mull. And we thine.
Set on in state, attendants and full train.
But find to ask, we vow thou shalt obtain.

[*Exeunt all except* GOODLACK.

Enter CLEM.

Clem. It is not now as when Andrea lived, or rather
Andrew, our elder journeyman.   What, drawers become
courtiers! Now may I speak with the old ghost in
Jeronimo—
When this eternal substance of my soul
Did live imprisoned in this wanton flesh,
I was a courtier in the court of Fez.[1]

Good. Oh, well done, Clem! It is your mistress'
    pleasure,
None come ashore that's not well habited.

Clem. Nay; for mine own part, I hold myself as good
a Christian in these clothes, as the proudest infidel of
them all.

Re-enter ALCADE *and* JOFFER.

Alc. Sir, by your leave, you're of the English train?

Clem. I am so, thou great monarch of the Mau-
ritanians.

Joff. Then, 'tis the king's command we give you all
attendance.

Clem. Great Signior of the Saracens, I thank thee.

Alc. Will you walk in to banquet?

Clem. I will make bold to march in towards your
banquet, and there comfit myself, and cast all caraways
down my throat, the best way I have to conserve myself
in health; and for your country's sake, which is called
Barbary, I will love all barbers and barberries the better.
And for you Moors, thus much I mean to say,
I'll see if more I eat, the more I may.

---

[1] From Kyd's oft-referred-to *Spanish Tragedy.*

Enter two Merchants.

1st Merch. I pray, sir, are you of the English train?

Clem. Why, what art thou, my friend?

1st Merch. Sir, a French merchant, run into relapse,
And forfeit of the law.   Here's for you, sir,
Forty good Barbary pieces, to deliver
Your lady this petition, who, I hear,
Can all things with the king.

Clem. Your gold doth bind me to you.—You may see
what it is to be a sudden courtier : I no sooner put my
nose into the court, but my hand itches for a bribe
already.—What's your business, my friend?

2nd Merch. Some of my men, for a little outrage done,
Are sentenced to the galleys.

Clem. To the gallows?

2nd Merch. No ; to the galleys.   Now, could your
      lady purchase
Their pardon from the king, here's twenty angels.[1]

Clem. What are you, sir?

2nd Merch. A Florentine merchant.

Clem. Then you are, as they say, a Christian?

2nd Merch. Heaven forbid, else !

Clem. I should not have the faith to take your gold,
Attend on me : I'll speak in your behalf.—   [else.
Where be my bashaws?   Usher us in state :
And when we sit to banquet, see you wait.

                                    [*Flourish.   Exeunt.*

SCENE II.—*The same.*

Enter SPENCER.

Spen. This day the king ascends his royal throne.
The honest merchant, in whose ship I came,
Hath, by a cunning quiddit[2] in the law,

---

[1] *i.e.* Coins.   [2] Subtle point.

Both ship and goods made forfeit to the king,
To whom I will petition. But no more ;
He's now upon his entrance. [*Hautboys.*

Enter MULLISHEG, BESS, Captain GOODLACK, ROUGH-
MAN, ALCADE, JOFFER, *with all the other train.*

Mull. Here seat thee, maid of England, like a queen—
The style we'll give thee, wilt thou deign us love.
Bess. Bless me, you holy angels !
Mull. What is't offends you, sweet ?
Spen. I am amazed, and know not what to think on't.
Bess. Captain, dost not see ? Is not that Spencer's
Good. I see, and, like you, I am ecstasied. [ghost ?
Spen. If mine eyes mistake not,
That should be Captain Goodlack, and that Bess.
But oh ! I cannot be so happy.
Good. 'Tis he, and I'll salute him.
Bess. Captain, stay.
You shall be swayed by me.
Spen. Him I well know ; but how should she come
Mull. What is't that troubles you ? [hither ?
Bess. Most mighty king,
Spare me no longer time but to bestow
My captain on a message.
Mull. Thou shalt command my silence, and his ear.
·*Bess.* [*To* GOODLACK.] Go wind about, and when you
  see least eyes
Are fixed on you, single him out, and see
If we mistake not. If he be the man,
Give me some private note.
Good. This. [*Making a sign.*
Bess. Enough.—What said your highness ?
Mull. Hark what I proffer thee. Continue here,
And grant me full fruition of thy love.——
Bess. Good.
Mull. Thou shalt have all my peers to honour thee,
Next our great prophet.

Heywood. L

Bess. Well.

Mull. And when thou'rt weary of our sun-burnt clime,
Thy Negro shall be ballast home with gold.

Bess. I am eternized ever!
Now, all you sad disasters, dare your worst ;
I neither care nor fear : my Spencer lives !

Mull. You mind me not, sweet virgin.

Bess. You talk of love :
My lord, I'll tell you more of that hereafter ;
But now to your state-business.—Bid him do thus
No more, and not to be seen till then.

Good. Enough.—Come, sir, you must along with me.

[*Exeunt* GOODLACK *and* SPENCER.

Bess. Now, stood a thousand deaths before my face,
I would not change my cheer, since Spencer's safe.

Enter CLEM *with the French and Italian* Merchants ;
and a Preacher.

Clem. By your leave, my masters ; room for generosity.[1]

1*st Merch.* Pray, sir, remember me.

2*nd Merch.* Good sir, my suit.

Clem. I am perfect in both your parts, without prompt-
ing.   Mistress, here are two Christen friends of mine
have forfeited ships and men to the black-a-morian king :
now, one sweet word from your lips might get their
release.   I have had a feeling of the business already.

Mull. For dealing in commodities forbid,
You're fined a thousand ducats.

Bess. Cast off the burden of your heavy doom :
A follower of my train petitions for him.

Mull. One of thy train, sweet Bess ?

Clem. And no worse man than myself, sir.

Mull. Well, sirrah, for your lady's sake
His ship and goods shall be restored again.

1*st Merch.* Long live the King of Fez !

Clem. Mayst thou never want sweet water to wash

---

[1] *i.e.* People well-born.

thy black face in, most mighty monarch of Morocco.—
Mistress, another friend ; ay, and paid beforehand.

Mull. Sirrah, your men, for outrage and contempt,
Are doomed unto the gallies.

Bess. A censure too severe for Christians.
Great king, I'll pay their ransom.

Mull. Thou, my Bess!
Thy word shall be their ransom : they're discharged.
What grave old man is that?

Joff. A Christian preacher ; one that would convert
Your Moors, and turn them to a new belief.

Mull. Then he shall die, as we are king of Fez.

Bess. For these I only spake ; for him I kneel,
If I have any grace with mighty Fez.

Mull. We can deny thee nothing, beauteous maid.
A kiss shall be his pardon.

Bess. Thus I pay't.

Clem. Must your black face be smouching my mistress'
white lips with a moorian![1] I would you had kissed
her a—

Alc. Hah ! how is that, sir?

Clem. I know what I say, sir ; I would he had kissed
her a—

Alc. A—what?

Clem. A thousand times, to have done him a pleasure !

Re-enter SPENCER *and* Captain GOODLACK.

Mull. That kiss was worth the ransom of a king.—
What's he, of that brave presence?

Bess. A gentleman of England, and my friend.
Do him some grace, for my sake.

Mull. For thy sake what would not I perform?
He shall have grace and honour.—Joffer, go
And see him gelded to attend on us :
He shall be our chief eunuch.

---

[1] Negro : perhaps a play on the word "murrain" is intended.

Bess. Not for ten worlds! Behold, great king, I stand
Betwixt him and all danger.—Have I found thee?—
Seize what I have; take both my ship and goods;
Leave nought that's mine unrifled: spare me him.—
And have I found my Spencer?

Clem. Please your majesty, I see all men are not capable of honour: what he refuseth, may it please you to bestow on me.

Mull. With all my heart. Go, bear him hence, Alcade,
Into our Alkedavy: honour him,
And let him taste the razor.

Clem. There's honour for me!

Alc. Come, follow.

Clem. No, sir; I'll go before you, for mine honour.

[*Exeunt* CLEM *and* ALCADE.

Spen. Oh! show yourself, renownèd king, the same
Fame blazons you. Bestow this maid on me:
'Tis such a gift as kingdoms cannot buy.
She is a precedent of all true love,
And shall be registered to after-times,
That ne'er shall pattern her.

Good. Heard you the story of their constant love,
'Twould move in you compassion.

Rough. Let not intemperate love sway you 'bove pity.
That foreign nation, that ne'er heard your name,
May chronicle your virtues.

Mull. You have wakened in me an heroic spirit:
Lust shall not conquer virtue.—Till this hour,
We graced thee for thy beauty, English woman;
But now we wonder at thy constancy.

Bess. Oh! were you of our faith, I'd swear great Mullisheg
To be a god on earth.—And lives my Spencer?
In troth I thought thee dead.

Spen. In hope of thee,
I lived to gain both life and liberty.

Re-enter CLEM, *running.*

Clem. No more of your honour, if you love me ! Is this
your Moorish preferment, to rob a man of his best jewels?

Mull. Hast thou seen our Alkedavy?

Clem. Davy do you call him? he may be called shavy;
I am sure he hath tickled my current commodity. No
more of your cutting honour, if you love me.

Mull. [*To* SPENCER.] All your strange fortunes we will
      hear discoursed,
And after that your fair espousals grace,
If you can find·a man of your belief
To do that grateful office.

Spen. None more fit
Than this religious and brave gentleman,
Late rescued from death's sentence.

Preach. None more proud
To do you that poor service.

Mull. Noble Englishman,
I cannot fasten bounty to my will
Worthy thy merit : move some suit to us.

Spen. To make you more renowned, great king, and us
The more indebted, there's an Englishman
Hath forfeited his ship for goods uncustomed.—

Mull. Thy suit is granted ere it be half begged :
Dispose them at thy pleasure.

Spen. Mighty king,
We are your highness' servants.

Mull. Come, beauteous maid ; we'll see thee crowned
      a bride.
At all our pompous banquets these shall wait.
Thy followers and thy servants press with gold ;
And not the mean'st that to thy train belongs,
But shall approve our bounty. Lead in state,
And, wheresoe'er thy fame shall be enrolled,
The world report thou art a Girl worth Gold. [*Exeunt.*

THE
ENGLISH TRAVELLER.

HE *English Traveller* was first printed in 1633, and from the preface it would seem that the publication of the play was an accident; the date of its production (at the Cockpit in Drury Lane) we do not know. The bye-plot of the prodigal Lionel and his servant is borrowed from Plautus' *Mostellaria*, which a century or more later was laid under contribution by Fielding in his *Intriguing Chambermaid*. Heywood may have known Plautus' comedy in the original or in one of the Italian versions. The character of Young Geraldine deserves study: "he is," says Professor Ward, "one of the truest gentlemen of Elizabethan comedy." Mr. Saintsbury (*Elizabethan Literature*, p. 284) ranks *The English Traveller* with *A Woman Killed with Kindness* as Heywood's best plays.

In the old editions the scenes are only partially indicated.

To the Right Worshipful

SIR HENRY APPLETON, KNIGHT BARONET, ETC.

Noble Sir,

 OR many reasons I am induced to present this Poem to your favourable acceptance ; and not the least of them that alternate love and those frequent courtesies which interchangeably passed betwixt yourself and that good old gentleman, mine uncle (Master Edmund Heywood), whom you pleased to grace by the title of father. I must confess I had altogether slept (my weakliness and bashfulness discouraging me) had they not been wakened and animated by that worthy gentleman your friend and my countryman, Sir William Elvish, whom (who for his unmerited love many ways extended towards me,) I much honour ; neither, sir, need you to think it any undervaluing of your worth to undertake the patronage of a poem in this nature, since the like hath been done by Roman Lælius, Scipio, Mæcenas, and many other mighty princes and captains ; nay, even by Augustus Cæsar himself, concerning whom Ovid is thus read (*De Tristi*, lib. 2)

Inspice ludorum sumptus, Auguste, tuorum :
Empta tibi magno talia multa leges.
Hæc tu spectasti, spectandaque sæpe dedisti.
Majestas adeo comis ubique tua est.

So highly were they respected in the most flourishing estate of the Roman Empire ; and if they have been vilified of late by any separistical humorist (as in the now questioned *Histrio-Mastix*),[1] I hope by the next term (Minerva assistente) to give such satisfaction to the world, by vindicating many

---

[1] By William Prynne : published in 1633. The full title of this bitter Puritan treatise was *Histrio-Mastix, the Player's Scourge, or Actor's Tragædie.*

particulars in that work maliciously exploded and condemned, as that no gentleman of quality and judgment but
shall therein receive a reasonable satisfaction.   I am loth by
tediousness to grow troublesome, therefore conclude with a
grateful remembrance of my service, intermixed with myriads
of zealous wishes for your health of body and peace of mind,
with superabundance of earth's blessings and Heaven's
graces, ever remaining,

Yours most observant,

THOMAS HEYWOOD.

TO THE READER.

 F, Reader, thou hast of this play been an
auditor, there is less apology to be used
by entreating thy patience. This tragi-
comedy (being one reserved amongst two
hundred and twenty in which I have had
either an entire hand, or at the least a main
finger) coming accidentally to the press,
and I having intelligence thereof, thought it
not fit that it should pass as *filius populi*, a bastard without a
father to acknowledge it.   True it is, that my plays are not
exposed unto the world in volumes, to bear the title of works,
(as others) ; one reason is, that many of them by shifting
and change of companies have been negligently lost ; others
of them are still retained in the hands of some actors, who
think it against their peculiar profit to have them come in
print ; and a third, that it never was any great ambition in
me, to be in this kind voluminously read.   All that I have
further to say at this time is only this : censure[1] I entreat as
favourably as it is exposed to thy view freely.   Ever

Studious of thy pleasure and profit,

THOMAS HEYWOOD.

[1] Judge.

PROLOGUE.

A STRANGE play you are like to have, for know,
We use no drum, nor trumpet, nor dumb show ;
No combat, marriage, not so much to-day
As song, dance, masque, to bombast out a play ;
Yet these all good, and still in frequent use
With our best poets ; nor is this excuse
Made by our author, as if want of skill
Caused this defect ; it's rather his self will.
Will you the reason know? There have so many
Been in that kind, that he desires not any
At this time in his scene, no help, no strain,
Or flash that's borrowed from another's brain ;
Nor speaks he this that he would have you fear it,
He only tries if once bare lines will bear it :
Yet may't afford, so please you silent sit,
Some mirth, some matter, and perhaps some wit.

DRAMATIS PERSONÆ.

GERALDINE, } Two young Gentlemen.
DELAVIL, }
Old WINCOTT.
Young LIONEL, a riotous Citizen.
Old GERALDINE, Father of Young GERALDINE.
Old LIONEL, a Merchant, Father of Young LIONEL.
REIGNALD, a parasitical Serving-man.
ROBIN, an old country Serving-man.
ROGER the Clown, Servant to Old WINCOTT.
RIOTER, a Spendthrift.
Two Gallants, his Companions.
Master RICOTT, a Merchant.
A Gentleman, Companion to DELAVIL.
A Usurer and his Man.
The Owner of the House, supposed to be possessed.
A Tavern Drawer.
Servants.

WINCOTT's Wife, a young Gentlewoman.
PRUDENTILLA, her Sister.
BLANDA, a Whore.
SCAPHA, a Bawd.
Two Wenches, Companions to BLANDA.
BESS, Chambermaid to Mistress WINCOTT.

SCENE—LONDON and BARNET.

THE

ENGLISH TRAVELLER.

SCENE I.—*A Room in* Old WINCOTT'S *House.*

Enter Young GERALDINE *and* DELAVIL.

EL. Oh, friend, that I to mine own notion
Had joined but your experience ! I have
The theoric, but you the practic.
    Y. Ger. I
Perhaps have seen what you have only
    Del. There's your happiness. [read of.
A scholar in his study knows the stars,
Their motion and their influence, which are fixed
And which are wandering, can decipher seas,
And give each several land his proper bounds ;
But set him to the compass, he's to seek,
When a plain pilot can direct his course
From hence unto both the Indies ; can bring back
His ship and charge, with profits quintuple.
I have read Jerusalem, and studied Rome,
Can tell in what degree each city stands,
Describe the distance of this place from that—
All this the scale in every map can teach ;
Nay, for a need could punctually recite

The monuments in either ; but what I
Have by relation only, knowledge by travel,
Which still makes up a complete gentleman,
Proves eminent in you.

Y. Ger. I must confess
I have seen Jerusalem and Rome, have brought
Mark from the one, from the other testimony,
Known Spain, and France, and from their airs have sucked
A breath of every language : but no more
Of this discourse, since we draw near the place
Of them we go to visit.

Enter Clown.

Clown. Noble Master Geraldine, worshipful Master
Delavil !

Del. I see thou still rememberest us.

Clown. Remember you ! I have had so many memo-
randums from the multiplicities of your bounties, that
not to remember you were to forgot myself; you are
both most ingeniously and nobly welcome.

Y. Ger. And why ingeniously and nobly ?

Clown. Because had I given your welcomes other
attributes than I have done, the one being a soldier, and
the other seeming a scholar, I should have lied in the
first, and showed myself a kind of blockhead in the last.

Y. Ger. I see your wit is nimble as your tongue ;
But how doth all at home ?

Clown. Small doings at home, sir, in regard that the
age of my master corresponds not with the youth of my
mistress, and you know cold January and lusty May
seldom meet in conjunction.

Del. I do not think but this fellow in time may for his
wit and understanding make almanacks.

Clown. Not so, sir, you being more judicious than I, I'll
give you the pre-eminence in that, because I see by proof
you have such judgment in times and seasons.

Del. And why in times and seasons?

Clown. Because you have so seasonably made choice
to come so just at dinner-time. You are welcome,
gentlemen; I'll go tell my master of your coming.

[*Exit* Clown.

Del. A pleasant knave.

Y. Ger. This fellow I perceive
Is well acquainted with his master's mind.
Oh 'tis a good old man.

Del. And she a lady
For beauty and for virtue unparalleled,
Nor can you name that thing to grace a woman
She has not in a full perfection.
Though in their years might seem disparity,
And therefore at the first a match unfit,
Imagine but his age and government,
Withal her modesty and chaste respect;
Betwixt them there's so sweet a sympathy
As crowns a noble marriage.

Y. Ger. 'Tis acknowledged;
But to the worthy gentleman himself
I am so bound in many courtesies,
That not the least, by all the expression
My labour or my industry can show,
I will know how to cancel.

Del. Oh, you are modest.

Y. Ger. He studies to engross me to himself,
And is so wedded to my company,
He makes me stranger to my father's house,
Although so near a neighbour.

Del. This approves you
To be most nobly propertied, that from one
So exquisite in judgment, can attract
So affectionate an eye.

Y. Ger. Your character
I must bestow on his unmerited love,
As one that know I have it, and yet ignorant
Which way I should deserve it: here both come.

Enter Old WINCOTT, *his* Wife, *and* PRUDENTILLA.

Win. Gentlemen, welcome; but what need I use
A word so common, unto such to whom
My house was never private ? I expect
You should not look for such a needless phrase,
Especially you, Master Geraldine ;
Your father is my neighbour, and I know you
Even from the cradle ; then I loved your infancy,
And since your riper growth bettered by travel :
My wife and you in youth were play-fellows,
And must not now be strangers ; as I take it,
Not above two years different in your age.
    Wife. So much he hath outstripped me.
    Win. I would have you
Think this your home, free as your father's house,
And to command it, as the master on't ;
Call boldly here, and entertain your friends,
As in your own possessions : when I see't,
I'll say you love me truly, not till then ;
Oh, what a happiness your father hath,
Far above me !—one to inherit after him,
Where I (Heaven knows) am childless.
    Y. Ger. That defect
Heaven hath supplied in this your virtuous wife,
Both fair, and full of all accomplishments ;
My father is a widower, and herein
Your happiness transcends him.
    Wife. Oh, Master Geraldine,
Flattery in men's an adjunct of their sex,
This country breeds it, and for that, so far
You needed not to have travelled.
    Y. Ger. Truth's a word
That should in every language relish well,
Nor have I that exceeded.
    Wife. Sir, my husband
Hath took much pleasure in your strange discourse

About Jerusalem and the Holy Land :
How the new city differs from the old,
What ruins of the Temple yet remain,
And whether Sion, and those hills about,
With the adjacent towns and villages,
Keep that proportioned distance as we read ;
And then in Rome, of that great pyramis
Reared in the front, on four lions mounted ;
How many of those idol temples stand,
First dedicated to their heathen gods,
Which ruined, which to better use repaired ;
Of their Pantheon, and their Capitol,—
What structures are demolished, what remain.

 Win. And what more pleasure to an old man's ear,
That never drew save his own country's air,
Than hear such things related?   I do exceed him
In years, I must confess, yet he much older
Than I in his experience.

 Pru. Master Geraldine,
May I be bold to ask you but one question,
The which I'd be resolved in ?

 Y. Ger. Anything
That lies within my knowledge.

 Win. Put him to't.
Do, sister, you shall find him, make no doubt,
Most pregnant in his answer.

 Pru. In your travels
Through France, through Savoy, and through Italy, ·
Spain, and the Empire, Greece and Palestine,
Which breeds the choicest beauties ?

 Y. Ger. In troth, lady,
I never cast on any in those parts
A curious eye of censure,[1] since my travel
Was only aimed at language, and to know ;
These passed me but as common objects did—
Seen, but not much regarded.

[1] Judgment.

Heywood.   M

Pru. Oh, you strive
To express a most unheard-of modesty,
And seldom found in any traveller,
Especially of our country, thereby seeking
To make yourself peculiar.
   Y. Ger. I should be loth
Profess in outward show to be one man,
And prove myself another.
   Pru. One thing more :
Were you to marry, you that know these climes,
Their states and their conditions, out of which
Of all these countries would you choose your wife ?
   Y. Ger. I'll answer you in brief: as I observe,
Each several clime, for object, fare, or use,
Affords within itself for all of these
What is most pleasing to the man there born :
Spain, that yields scant of food, affords the nation
A parsimonious stomach, where [1] our appetites
Are not content but with the large excess
Of a full table ; where the pleasing'st fruits
Are found most frequent, there they best content;
Where plenty flows, it asks abundant feasts ;
For so hath provident Nature dealt with all.
So in the choice of women : the Greek wantons,
Compelled beneath the Turkish slavery,
Vassal themselves to all men, and such best
Please the voluptuous that delight in change ;
The French is of one humour, Spain another,
The hot Italian has a strain from both,
All pleased with their own nations—even the Moor,
He thinks the blackest the most beautiful ;
And, lady, since you so far tax my choice,
I'll thus resolve you : being an Englishman,
'Mongst all these nations I have seen or tried,
To please me best, here would I choose my bride.
   Pru. And happy were that lady, in my thoughts,

[1] *i.e.* Whereas.

Whom you would deign that grace to.

Wife. How now, sister !

This is a fashion that's but late come up.

For maids to court their husbands.

Win. I would, wife,

It were no worse, upon condition

They had my helping hand and purse to boot,

With both in ample measure. Oh, this gentleman

I love, nay almost dote on.

Wife. You've my leave

To give it full expression.

Win. In these arms, then.

Oh, had my youth been blest with such a son,

To have made my estate to my name hereditary,

I should have gone contented to my grave,

As to my bed; to death, as to my sleep ;

But Heaven hath will in all things.   Once more
        welcome ;

And you, sir, for your friend's sake.

Del. Would I had in me

That which he hath, to have claimed it for mine own ;

However, I much thank you.

Enter Clown.

Win. Now, sir, the news with you ?

Clown. Dancing news, sir ; for the meat stands piping
hot upon the dresser, the kitchen's in a heat, and the
cook hath so bestirred himself that he's in a sweat.   The
jack [1] plays music, and the spits turn round to't.

Win. This fellow's my best clock,

He still strikes true to dinner.

Clown. And to supper too, sir : I know not how the
day goes with you, but my stomach hath struck twelve, I
can assure you that.

Win. You take us unprovided, gentlemen ;

Yet something you shall find, and we would rather

---

[1] Which made the spit turn ; it had been recently introduced.

Give you the entertain of household guests
Than compliment of strangers.   I pray enter.
[*Exeunt all but* Clown.

Clown. I'll stand to't, that in good hospitality there
can be nothing found that's ill : he that's a good housekeeper keeps a good table, a good table is never without
good stools, good stools seldom without good guests, good
guests never without good cheer, good cheer cannot
be without good stomachs, good stomachs without good
digestion, good digestion keeps men in good health; and
therefore, all good people that bear good minds, as you
love goodness, be sure to keep good meat and drink
in your houses, and so you shall be called good men, and
nothing can come on't but good, I warrant you.   [*Exit.*

SCENE II.—*A Room in* Old LIONEL'S *House.*

Enter REIGNALD *and* ROBIN, *two* Serving-men.

Reig. Away, you Corydon !
Rob. Shall I be beat out of my master's house thus ?
Reig. Thy master ! we are lords amongst ourselves,
And here we live and reign.   Two years already
Are past of our great empire, and we now
Write *anno tertio.*
Rob. But the old man lives
That shortly will depose you.
Reig. I' the meantime,
I, as the mighty lord and seneschal
Of this great house and castle, banish thee
The very smell o' the kitchen ; be it death
To appear before the dresser.
Rob. And why so ?
Reig. Because thou stink'st of garlick. Is that breath
Agreeing with our palace, where each room

Smells with musk, civet, and rich ambergris,
Aloes, cassia, aromatic gums,
Perfumes, and powders?   One whose very garments
Scent of the fowls and stables !   Oh, fie, fie !
What a base nasty rogue 'tis !
 Rob. Yet your fellow.
 Reig. Then let us put a cart-horse in rich trappings,
And bring him to the tilt-yard.
 Rob. Prank it, do ;
Waste, riot, and consume, misspend your hours
In drunken surfeits, lose your days in sleep,
And burn the nights in revels, drink and drab,
Keep Christmas all year long, and blot lean Lent
Out of the calendar; all that mass of wealth
Got by my master's sweat and thrifty care,
Havoc in prodigal uses ; make all fly,
Pour't down your oily throats, or send it smoking
Out at the tops of chimneys.   At his departure,
Was it the old man's charge to have his windows
Glister all night with stars? his modest house
Turned to a common stews? his beds to pallets
Of lusts and prostitutions? his buttery hatch [1]
Now made more common than a tavern's bar?
His stools, that welcomed none but civil guests,
Now only free for pandars, whores and bawds,
Strumpets, and such?
 Reig. I suffer thee too long.
What is to me thy country; or to thee
The pleasure of our city? thou hast cows,
Cattle, and beeves to feed, oves and boves ;
These that I keep, and in this pasture graze,
Are dainty damosellas, bonny girls.
If thou be'st born to hedge, ditch, thresh, and plough,
And I to revel, banquet and carouse ;
Thou, peasant, to the spade and pickaxe, I

---

[1] A term still used in the Universities.

The battoon and stiletto, think it only
Thy ill, my good; our several lots are cast,
And both must be contented.
    Rob. But when both
Our services are questioned—
    Reig. Look thou to one,
My answer is provided.

Enter Young LIONEL.

    Rob. Farewell, musk-cat!   [*Exit.*
    Reig. Adieu, good cheese and onions; stuff thy guts
With speck and barley-pudding for digestion;
Drink whig[1] and sour milk, whilst I rinse my throat
With Bordeaux and canary.
    Y. Lio. What was he?
    Reig. A spy, sir;
One of their hinds o' the country, that came prying
To see what dainty fare our kitchen yields,
What guests we harbour, and what rule we keep,
And threats to tell the old man when he comes;
I think I sent him packing.
    Y. Lio. It was well done.
    Reig. A whoreson-jackanapes, a base baboon,
To insinuate in our secrets.
    Y. Lio. Let such keep
The country, where their charge is.
    Reig. So I said, sir.
    Y. Lio. And visit us when we command them thence,
Not search into our counsels.
    Reig. 'Twere not fit.
    Y. Lio. Who in my father's absence should command,
Save I his only son?
    Reig. It is but justice.
    Y. Lio. For am not I now lord?

---

[1] A species of inferior drink, made from whey, and drunk by the lower classes in place of small beer. The exact nature of "speck" is unknown.

Reig. Dominus-fac-totum.
And am not I your steward ?
Y. Lio. Well remembered.
This night I have a purpose to be merry,
Jovial and frolic.   How doth our cash hold out ?
Reig. The bag's still heavy.
Y. Lio. Then my heart's still light.
Reig. I can assure you, yet 'tis pretty deep
Though scarce a mile to the bottom.
Y. Lio. Let me have
To supper, let me see, a duck—
Reig. Sweet rogue !
Y. Lio. A capon—
Reig. Geld the rascal !
Y. Lio. Then a turkey —
Reig. Now spit him, for an infidel !
Y. Lio. Green plover, snipe,
Partridge, lark, cock, and pheasant.
Reig. Ne'er a widgeon ?
Y. Lio. Yes ; wait thyself at table.
Reig. Where I hope
Yourself will not be absent.
Y. Lio. Nor my friends.
Reig. We'll have them then in plenty.
Y. Lio. Caviare, sturgeon, anchoves, pickle-oysters; yes,
And a potato pie ; besides all these,
What thou think'st rare and costly.
Reig. Sir, I know
What's to be done ; the stock that must be spent
Is in my hands, and what I have to do
I will do suddenly.
Y. Lio. No butcher's meat ;
Of that beware in any case.
Reig. I still remember
Your father was no grazier; if he were,
This were a way to eat up all his fields,
Hedges and all.
Y. Lio. You will begone, sir ?

Reig. Yes, and you are i' the way going.   [*Exit.*
Y. Lio. To what may young men best compare them-
selves ?
Better to what, than to a house new built,
The fabric strong, the chambers well contrived,
Polished within, without well beautified ;
When all that gaze upon the edifice
Do not alone commend the workman's craft,
But either make it their fair precedent
By which to build another, or at least
Wish there to inhabit ?   Being set to sale,
In comes a slothful tenant, with a family
As lazy and debauched ; rough tempests rise,
Untile the roof, which by their idleness
Left unrepaired, the stormy showers beat in,
Rot the main posts and rafters, spoil the rooms,
Deface the ceilings, and in little space
Bring it to utter ruin, yet the fault
Not in the architector that first reared it,
But him that should repair it.   So it fares
With us young men ; we are those houses made ;
Our parents raise these structures, the foundation
Laid in our infancy ; and as we grow
In years, they strive to build us by degrees,
Story on story higher ; up at height,
They cover us with counsel, to defend us
From storms without ; they polish us within
With learnings, knowledge, arts and disciplines ;
All that is naught and vicious they sweep from us,
Like dust and cobwebs, and our rooms concealed,
Hang with the costliest hangings, 'bout the walls
Emblems and beauteous symbols pictured round :
But when that lazy tenant, Love, steps in,
And in his train brings sloth and negligence,
Lust, disobedience, and profuse excess,   -
The thrift with which our fathers tiled our roofs
Submits to every storm and winter's blast,

And, yielding place to every riotous sin,
Gives way without to ruin what's within :
Such is the state I stand in.

Enter BLANDA *and* SCAPHA ; Young LIONEL *retires.*

Blan. And how doth this tire become me?
Sca. Rather ask, how your sweet carriage and court
behaviour doth best grace you, for lovers regard not so,
much the outward habit as that which the garment
covers.
Y. Lio. Oh, here's that hail, shower, tempest, storm,
        and gust
That shattered hath this building ; let in lust,
Intemperance, appetite to vice ; withal,
Neglect of every goodness : thus I see
How I am sinking in mine own disease,
Yet can I not abide it.   [*Aside.*
Blan. And how this gown?   I prithee view me
        well,
And speak with thy best judgment.
Sca. What do you talk of gowns and ornaments,
That have a beauty precious in itself,
And becomes anything ?
Y. Lio. Let me not live, but she speaks nought but
        truth,
And I'll for that reward her.   [*Aside.*
Blan. All's one to me, become they me or not,
Or be I fair or foul in others' eyes,
So I appear so to my Lionel ;
He is the glass in whom I judge my face,
By whom in order I will dress these curls,
And place these jewels, only to please him.
Why dost smile?
Sca. To hear a woman that thinks herself so wise
speak so foolishly ; that knows well, and does ill.
Blan. Teach me wherein I err.
Sca. I'll tell thee, daughter : in that thou knowest

thyself to be beloved of so many, and settlest thy
affection only upon one. Doth the mill grind only when
the wind sits in one corner, or ships only sail when it's
in this or that quarter? Is he a cunning fencer that lies
but at one guard, or he a skilful musician that plays
but on one string? Is there but one way to the wood,
and but one bucket that belongs to the well? To affect
one, and despise all other, becomes the precise matron,
not the prostitute; the loyal wife, not the loose wanton.
Such have I been as you are now, and should learn to
sail with all winds, defend all blows, make music with all
strings, know all the ways to the wood, and, like a good
travelling hackney, learn to drink of all waters.

Y. Lio. May I miscarry in my Blanda's love,
If I that old damnation do not send
To hell before her time!   [*Aside.*

Blan. I would not have you, mother, teach me aught
That tends to injure him.

Sca. Well, look to't when 'tis too late, and then repent
at leisure, as I have done. Thou seest, here's nothing
but prodigality and pride, wantoning and wasting, rioting
and revelling, spoiling and spending, gluttony and gor-
mandising—all goes to havoc. And can this hold out?
When he hath nothing left to help himself, how can he
harbour thee? Look at length to drink from a dry
bottle, and feed from an empty knapsack; look to't,
'twill come to that.

Y. Lio. My parsimony shall begin in thee,
And instantly; for from this hour, I vow
That thou no more shalt drink upon my cost,
Nor taste the smallest fragment from my board;
I'll see thee starve i' the street first.   [*Aside.*

Sca. Live to one man! a jest; thou mayst as well tie
thyself to one gown; and what fool but will change with
the fashion? Yes, do, confine thyself to one garment, and
use no variety, and see how soon it will rot, and turn to
rags.

Y. Lio. [*Coming forward.*] Those rags be thy reward !
—Oh, my sweet Blanda,
Only for thee I wish my father dead,
And ne'er to rouse us from our sweet delight ;
But for this hag, this beldam, she whose back
Hath made her items in my mercer's books ;
Whose ravenous guts I have stuffed with delicates,
Nay even to surfeit ; and whose frozen blood
I have warmed with aquavitæ—be this day
My last of bounty to a wretch ingrate ;
But unto thee a new indenture [1] sealed
Of an affection fixed and permanent.
I'll love thee still, be't but to give the lie
To this old cankered worm.
    Blan. Nay, be not angry.
    Y. Lio. With thee my soul shall ever be at peace ;
But with this love-seducer, still at war.
    Sca. Hear me but speak.
    Y. Lio. Ope but thy lips again, it makes a way
To have thy tongue plucked out.

        Enter RIOTER *and two* Gallants.

    Rio. What, all in tempest !
    Y. Lio. Yes, and the storm raised by that witch's
        spells ;
Oh, 'tis a damned enchantress !
    Rio. What's the business ?
    Blan. Only some few words, slipped her unawares :
For my sake make her peace.
    Rio. You charge me deeply.
Come, friend, will you be moved at women's words,
A man of your known judgment ?
    Y. Lio. Had you but heard
The damned erroneous doctrine that she taught,
You would have judged her to the stake.

        [1] Bond.

Blan. But, sweetheart,
She now recants those errors; once more number her
Amongst your household servants.

Rio. Shall she beg,
And be denied aught from you?

Blan. Come, this kiss
Shall end all former quarrels.

Rio. 'Tis not possible
Those lips should move in vain, that two ways plead,—
Both in their speech and silence.

Y. Lio. You have prevailed,
But upon this condition, no way else :
I'll censure her, as she hath sentenced thee,
But with some small inversion.

Rio. Speak, how's that?

Blan. Not too severe, I prithee ; see, poor wretch,
She at the bar stands quaking.

Y. Lio. Now, hold up—

Rio. How, man, how?

Y. Lio. Her hand, I mean.—And now I'll sentence thee,
According to thy counsel given to her :
Sail by one wind ; thou shalt to one tune sing,
Lie at one guard, and play but on one string ;
Henceforth I will confine thee to one garment,
And that shall be a cast one, like thyself,
Just past all wearing, as thou past all use,
And not to be renewed, till't be as ragged
As thou art rotten.

Blan. Nay, sweet—.

Y. Lio. That for her habit.

Sca. A cold suit I have on't.

Y. Lio. To prevent surfeit,
Thy diet shall be to one dish confined,
And that too rifled, with as unclean hands
As e'er were laid on thee.

Sca. What he scants me in victuals, would he but allow
me in drink !

Y. Lio. That shall be the refuse of the flagons, jacks,
And snuffs, such as the nastiest breaths shall leave;
Of wine, and of strong-water, never hope
Henceforth to smell.

Sca. Oh me ! I faint already.

Y. Lio. If I sink in my state, of all the rest
Be thou excused ; what thou proposed to her,
Beldam, is now against thyself decreed :
Drink from dry springs, from empty knapsacks feed.

Sca. No burnt wine,[1] nor hot-waters ! [*She swoons.*

Y. Lio. Take her hence.

Blan. Indeed you are too cruel.

Y. Lio. Yes, to her,
Only of purpose to be kind to thee ;
Are any of my guests come ?

Rio. Fear not, sir,
You will have a full table.

Y. Lio. What, and music ?

Rio. Best consort[2] in the city, for six parts.

Y. Lio. We shall have songs then ?

Rio. By the ear.   [*Whispers.*

Y. Lio. And wenches ?

Rio. Yes, by the eye.

Blan. Ha ! what was that you said ?

Rio. We shall have such to bear you company
As will no doubt content you.

Y. Lio. Ever thine :
In youth there is a fate that sways us still,
To know what's good, and yet pursue what's ill.

                                            [*Exeunt.*

---

[1] Burnt wine, it will be remembered, was much affected by Pepys.
[2] *i.e.*, Concert.

ACT THE SECOND.

SCENE I.—*A Room in* Old WINCOTT'S *House.*

Enter Old WINCOTT *and his* Wife.

IN. And what's this Delavil?
Wife. My apprehension
Can give him no more true expression,
Than that he first appears a gentleman,
And well conditioned.
   Win. That for outward show ;
But what in him have you observèd else,
To make him better known ?
  Wife. I have not eyes
To search into the inward thoughts of men,
Nor ever was I studied in that art
To judge of men's affection by the face ;
But that which makes me best opinioned of him
Is that he's the companion and the friend
Beloved of him whom you so much commend—
The noble Master Geraldine.
  Win. Thou hast spoke
That which not only crowns his true desert,
But now instates him in my better thoughts,
Making his worth unquestioned.
  Wife. He pretends
Love to my sister Pru. I have observed him
Single her out to private conference.
  Win. But I could rather, for her own sake, wish

Young Geraldine would fix his thoughts that way,
And she towards him ; in such affinity,
Trust me, I would not use a sparing hand.
  Wife. But Love in these kinds should not be com-
    pelled,
Forced, nor persuaded ; when it freely springs,
And of itself takes voluntary root,
It grows, it spreads, it ripens, and brings forth
Such an usurious crop of timely fruit
As crowns a plenteous autumn.
  Win. Such a harvest
I should not be the ungladdest man to see,

Enter Clown.

Of all thy sister's friends.—Now, whence come you ?
  Clown. Who, I, sir? from a lodging of largess, a
house of hospitality, and a palace of plenty; where
there's feeding like horses and drinking like fishes ;
where for pints, we're served in pottles; and instead of
pottle-pots, in pails; instead of silver tankards, we drink
out of water-tankards ; claret runs as freely as the cocks,
and canary like the conduits of a coronation day;
where there's nothing but feeding and frolicking, carving
in kissing, drinking and dancing, music and madding,
fiddling and feasting.
  Win. And where, I pray thee, are all these revels kept?
  Clown. They may be rather called reaks[1] than revels ;
as I came along by the door I was called up amongst
them—he-gallants and she-gallants. I no sooner looked
out, but saw them out with their knives, slashing of
shoulders, mangling of legs, and lanching[2] of loins, till
there was scarce a whole limb left amongst them.
  Win. A fearful massacre !
  Clown. One was hacking to cut off a neck ; this was
mangling a breast; his knife slipped from the shoulder,
and only cut off a wing ; one was picking the brains out

----

[1] Pranks.   [2] *i.e.*, Lancing.

of a head, another was knuckle-deep in a belly; one was groping for a liver, another searching for the kidneys. I saw one pluck the soul[1] from the body—goose that she was to suffer't!; another pricked into the breast with his own bill—woodcock to endure it!

Wife. How fell they out at first?

Clown. I know not that, but it seems one had a stomach, and another had a stomach; but there was such biting and tearing with their teeths, that I am sure I saw some of their poor carcasses pay for't.

Win. Did they not send for surgeons?

Clown. Alas, no! surgeons' help was too late; there was no stitching up of those wounds, where limb was plucked from limb; nor any salve for those scars, which all the plaster of Paris cannot cure.

Win. Where grew the quarrel first?

Clown. It seems it was first broached in the kitchen, certain creatures being brought in thither by some of the house. The cook, being a choleric fellow, did so towse them and toss them, so pluck them and pull them, till he left them as naked as my nail; pinioned some of them like felons; cut the spurs from others off their heels; then down went his spits, some of them he ran in at the throat, and out at the backside: about went his basting-ladle, where he did so besauce them that many a shrewd[2] turn they had amongst them.

Wife. But, in all this, how did the women scape?

Clown. They fared best, and did the least hurt that I saw, but for quietness-sake were forced to swallow what is not yet digested; yet every one had their share, and she that had least, I am sure, by this time hath her belly-ful.

Win. And where was all this havoc kept?

Clown. Marry, sir, at your next neighbour's, Young Master Lionel, where there is nothing but drinking out

[1] The dark spongy substance inside a fowl's back.—*Halliwell.*
[2] Sharp or bitter.

of dry-vats, and healthing in half-tubs ; his guests are fed
by the belly, and beggars served at his gate in baskets.
He's the adamant of this age, the daffodil of these days,
the prince of prodigality, and the very Cæsar of all
young citizens.

Win. Belike, then, 'twas a massacre of meat,
Not as I apprehended?

Clown. Your gravity hath guessed aright : the chiefest
that fell in this battle were wild fowl and tame fowl ;
pheasants were wounded instead of alfarez,[1] and capons
for captains ; anchoves stood for ancients, and caviare
for corporals ; dishes were assaulted instead of ditches,
and rabbits were cut to pieces upon the rebellings ;[2] some
lost their legs, whilst other of their wings were forced to
fly; the pioner undermined nothing but pie crust,
and—

Win. Enough, enough ! your wit hath played too long
Upon our patience.—Wife, it grieves me much
Both for the young and old man : the one graces
His head with care, endures the parching heat
And biting cold, the terrors of the lands,
And fears at sea, in travel, only to gain
Some competent estate to leave his son ;
Whiles all that merchandise, through gulfs, cross-tides,
Pirates, and storms, he brings so far, the other
Here shipwrecks in the harbour.

Wife. 'Tis the care
Of fathers ; and the weakness incident
To youth, that wants experience.

Enter Young GERALDINE, DELAVIL, *and* PRUDENTILLA,
laughing.

Clown. I was at the beginning of the battle ; but here
comes some, that it seems were at the rifling of the dead
carcases ; for by their mirth they have had part of the spoil.

---

[1] Ensigns (Spanish).   [2] *i.e.* Ravelins (Sp. *rebellin*).

Win. You are pleasant, gentlemen; what, I entreat,
Might be the subject of your pleasant sport?
It promiseth some pleasure.
    Pru. If their recreation
Be, as I make no question, on truth grounded,
'Twill beget sudden laughter.
    Wife. What's the project?
    Del. Who shall relate it?
    Win. Master Geraldine,
If there be anything can please my ear
With pleasant sounds, your tongue must be the instru-
    ment
On which the string must strike.
    Del. Be it his, then.
    Pru. Nay, hear it, 'tis a good one.
    Wife. Wee'ntreat you,
Possess [1] us o' the novel.[2]
    Win. Speak, good sir.
    Y. Ger. I shall, then, with a kind of barbarism,
Shadow a jest that asks a smoother tongue,
For in my poor discourse, I do protest,
It will but lose its lustre.
    Wife. You are modest.
    Win. However, speak, I pray; for my sake do't.
    Clown. This is like a hasty pudding, longer in eating
than it was in making.
    Y. Ger. Then thus it was: this gentleman and I
Passed but just now by your next neighbour's house,
Where, as they say, dwells one young Lionel.
    Clown. Where I was to-night at supper.
    Win. An unthrift youth, his father now at sea.
    Y. Ger. Why, that's the very subject upon which
It seems this jest is grounded; there this night
Was a great feast.
    Clown. Why, so I told you, sir.
    Win. Be thou still dumb; 'tis he that I would hear.

---

[1] Inform.   [2] *i.e.* Novelty.

Y. Ger. In the height of their carousing, all their
    brains
Warmed with the heat of wine, discourse was offered
Of ships, and storms at sea;[1] when suddenly,
Out of his giddy wildness, one conceives
The room wherein they quaffed to be a pinnace,
Moving and floating; and the confused noise
To be the murmuring winds, gusts, mariners;
That their unsteadfast footing did proceed
From rocking of the vessel: this conceived,
Each one begins to apprehend the danger,
And to look out for safety. " Fly," saith one,
" Up to the main-top, and discover;" he
Climbs by the bed-post to the tester, there
Reports a turbulent sea and tempest towards,
And wills them, if they'll save their ship and lives,
To cast their lading overboard; at this
All fall to work, and hoist into the street,
As to the sea, what next come to their hand—
Stools, tables, trestles, trenchers, bedsteads, cups,
Pots, plate, and glasses; here a fellow whistles,
They take him for the boatswain; one lies struggling
Upon the floor, as if he swum for life;
A third takes the bass-viol for the cockboat,
Sits in the belly on't, labours and rows,
His oar the stick with which the fiddler played;
A fourth bestrides his fellows, thinking to scape
As did Arion on the dolphin's back,
Still fumbling on a gittern.
    Clown. Excellent sport!
    Win. But what was the conclusion?
    Y. Ger. The rude multitude,
Watching without, and gaping for the spoil
Cast from the windows, went by the ears about it;

[1] "This piece of pleasant exaggeration gave rise to the title of
Cowley's Latin play, *Naufragium Joculare,* and furnished the idea
of the best scene in it."—*Charles Lamb.*

The constable is called to atone[1] the broil,
Which done, and hearing such a noise within
Of imminent shipwreck, enters the house, and finds them
In this confusion.   They adore his staff,
And think it Neptune's trident, and that he
Comes with his Tritons (so they called his watch)
To calm the tempest, and appease the waves ;
And at this point we left them.

    Clown. Come what will, I'll steal out of doors, and see
the end of it, that's certain.   [*Exit.*

    Win. Thanks, Master Geraldine, for this discourse ;
In troth it hath much pleased me ; but the night
Begins to grow fast on us : for your parts
You are all young, and you may sit up late ;
My eyes begin to summon me to sleep,
And nothing's more offensive unto age
Than to watch long and late.   [*Exit.*

    Y. Ger. Now good rest with you !

    Del. What says fair Prudentilla ?   Maids and widows,
And we young bachelors, such as indeed
Are forced to lie in solitary beds,
And sleep without disturbance—we, methinks,
Should desire later hours than married wives,
That in their amorous arms hug their delights !
To often wakings subject, their more haste
May better be excused.

    Pru. How can you,
That are, as you confess, a single man,
Enter so far into these mystical secrets
Of marriage, which as yet you never proved?

    Del. There's, lady, an instinct innate in man,
Which prompts us to the apprehensions
Of the uses we were born to ; such we are
Aptest to learn, ambitious most to know,
Of which our chief is marriage.

              [1] Make up, appease.

Pru. What you men
Most meditate, we women seldom dream of.
  Del. When dream maids most?
  Pru. When, think you?
  Del. When you lie upon your backs.   [TILLA.
Come, come; your ear. [*Exeunt* DELAVIL *and* PRUDEN-
  Y. Ger. We now are left alone.
  Wife. Why, say we be, who should be jealous of
      us?
This is not first of many hundred nights
That we two have been private : from the first
Of our acquaintance, when our tongues but clipped
Our mother's-tongue, and could not speak it plain,
We knew each other; as in stature, so
Increased our sweet society ; since your travel,
And my late marriage, through my husband's love,
Midnight hath béen as mid-day, and my bed-chamber
As free to you as your own father's house,
And you aś welcome to't.
  Y. Ger. I must confess
It is in you your noble courtesy,
In him a more than common confidence,
And in this age can scarce find precedent.
  Wife. Most true; it is withal an argument
That both our virtues are so deep impressed
In his good thoughts, he knows we cannot err.
  Y. Ger. A villain were he to deceive such trust,
Or, were there one, a much worse character.
  Wife. And she no less, whom either beauty, youth,
Time, place, or opportunity could tempt
To injure such a husband.
  Y. Ger. You deserve,
Even for his sake, to be for ever young ;
And he, for yours, to have his youth renewed,
So mutual is your true conjugal love ;
Yet, had the Fates so pleased—
  Wife. .I know your meaning.

It was once voiced that we two should have matched ;
The world so thought, and many tongues so spake ;
But Heaven hath now disposed us otherways ;
And being as it is, (a thing in me
Which, I protest, was never wished nor sought),
Now done, I not repent it.

Y. Ger. In those times,
Of all the treasures of my hopes and love,
You were the exchequer, they were stored in you ;
And, had not my unfortunate travel crossed them,
They had been here reserved still.

Wife. Troth, they had ;
I should have been your trusty treasurer.

Y. Ger. However, let us love still, I entreat :
That, neighbourhood and breeding will allow ;
So much the laws divine and human both
'Twixt brother and a sister will approve ;
Heaven then forbid that they should limit us
Wish well to one another !

Wife. If they should not,
We might proclaim they were not charitable,
Which were a deadly sin but to conceive.

Y. Ger. Will you resolve me one thing ?

Wife. As to one
That in my bosom hath a second place,
Next my dear husband.

Y. Ger. That's the thing I crave,
And only that—to have a place next him.

Wife. Presume on that already; but perhaps
You mean to stretch it further.

Y. Ger. Only thus far :
Your husband's old, to whom my soul doth wish
A Nestor's age, so much he merits from me ;
Yet if (as proof and Nature daily teach
Men cannot always live, especially
Such as are old and crazed) he be' call'd hence,
Fairly, in full maturity of time,

And we two be reserved to after-life,
Will you confer your widowhood on me?
   Wife. You ask the thing I was about to beg;
Your tongue hath spake mine own thoughts.
   Y. Ger. Vow to that.
   Wife. As I hope mercy.
   Y. Ger. 'Tis enough; that word
Alone instates me happy.   Now, so please you,
We will divide, you to your private chamber,
I to find out my friend.
   Wife. Nay, Master Geraldine,
One ceremony rests yet unperformed:
My vow is past, your oath must next proceed;
And as you covet to be sure of me,
Of you I would be certain.
   Y. Ger. Make ye doubt?
   Wife. No doubt; but Love's still jealous, and in that
To be excused; you then shall swear by Heaven,
And as in all your future acts you hope
To thrive and prosper;¯as the day may yield
Comfort, or the night rest; as you would keep
Entire the honour of your father's house,
And free your name from scandal and reproach;
By all the goodness that you hope to enjoy,
Or ill to shun—
   Y. Ger. You charge me deeply, lady.
   Wife. Till that day come, you shall reserve yourself
A single man; converse nor company
With any woman, contract nor combine
With maid or widow; which expected hour,
As I do wish not haste, so when it happens
It shall not come unwelcome.   You hear all;
Vow this.
   Y. Ger. By all that you have said, I swear,
And by this kiss confirm.
   Wife. You're now my brother;
But then, my second husband.   *[Exeunt.*

Enter, from the House, Young LIONEL, RIOTER, BLANDA, SCAPHA, *two* Gallants, *and two* Wenches, *as newly waked from sleep.*

Y. Lio. We had a stormy night on't.

Blan. The wine still works,
And, with the little rest they have took to-night,
They are scarce come to themselves.

Y. Lio. Now 'tis a calm,
Thanks to those gentle sea-gods, that have brought us
To this safe harbour : can you tell their names?

Sca.· He with the painted staff I heard you call Neptune.

Y. Lio. The dreadful god of seas,
Upon whose back ne'er stuck March fleas.

1st Gal. One with the bill [1] keeps Neptune's porpoises,
So Ovid says in's Metamorphoses.

2nd Gal. A third the learned poets write on,
And, as they say, his name is Triton.

Y. Lio. These are the marine gods, to whom my father
In his long voyage prays to ; cannot they,
That brought us to our haven, bury him
In their abyss? For if he safe arrive,
I, with these sailors, sirens, and what not,
Am sure here to be shipwrecked.

1st Wench [*to* RIOTER]. Stand up stiff.

Rio. But that the ship so totters—I shall fall.

1st Wench. If thou fall, I'll fall with thee.

Rio. Now I sink,
And, as I dive and drown, thus by degrees
I'll pluck thee to the bottom. [*They fall.*

Enter REIGNALD.

Y. Lio. Amain for England! See, see,
The Spaniard now strikes sail.

[1] A kind of halbert. carried by the watchmen of the period.

Reig. So must you all.

1st Gal. Whence is your ship—from the Bermoothes?[1]

Reig. Worse, I think from Hell :

We are all lost, split, shipwrecked, and undone.

This place is a mere quicksands.

2nd Gal. So we feared.

Reig. Where's my young master?

Y. Lio. Here, man ; speak, the news?

Reig. The news is, I, and you—

Y. Lio. What?

Reig. She, and all these—

Blan. I !

Reig. We, and all ours, are in one turbulent sea

Of fear, despair, disaster, and mischance

Swallowed.   Your father, sir—

Y. Lio. Why, what of him?

Reig. He is—

Oh I want breath.

Y. Lio. Where?

Reig. Landed, and at hand.

Y. Lio. Upon what coast?   Who saw him?

Reig. I—these eyes.

Y. Lio. O Heaven ! what shall I do then?

Reig. Ask ye me

What shall become of you, that have not yet

Had time of study to dispose myself?

I say again, I was upon the quay,

I saw him land, and this way bend his course.

What drunkard's this, that can outsleep a storm

Which threatens all our ruins?   Wake him.

Blan. Ho, Rioter, awake !

Rio. Yes, I am 'wake ;

How dry hath this salt-water made me !   Boy,

Give me the other glass.

Y. Lio. Arise, I say :

My father's come from sea.

---

[1] "Bermoothes" is the usual form of "Bermudas" in the old dramatists.

Rio. If he be come,
Bid him be gone again.
Reig. Can you trifle
At such a time, when your inventions, brains,
Wits, plots, devices, stratagems, and all
Should be at one in action ? Each of you
That love your safeties, lend your helping hands,
Women and all, to take this drunkard hence,
And to bestow him elsewhere.
Blan. Lift, for Heaven's sake.
                              [*They carry* RIOTER *in.*
Reig. But what am I the nearer, were all these
Conveyed to sundry places and unseen ?
The stain of our disorders still remains,
Of which the house will witness, and the old man
Must find it when he enters ; and for these

Re-enter Young LIONEL *and others.*

I am here left to answer.—What, is he gone ?
Y. Lio. But whither ? But into the selfsame house
That harbours him ; my father's, where we all
Attend from him surprisal.
Reig. I will make
That prison of your fears your sanctuary ;
Go, get you in together.
Y. Lio. To this house ?
Reig. Your father's, with your sweetheart, these and all ;
Nay, no more words, but do it.
Blan. That were to
Betray us to his fury.
Reig. I have't here
To bail you hence at pleasure ; and in the interim
I'll make this supposed gaol, to you as safe
From the injured old man's just-incensèd spleen,
As were you now together i' the Low-Countries,
Virginia, or i' the Indies.
Blan. Present fear

Bids us to yield unto the faint belief
Of the least hopèd safety.
  Reig. Will you in ?
  All. By thee we will be counselled.
  Reig. Shut them fast.
  Y. Lio. And thou and I to leave them ?
  Reig. No such thing;
For you shall bear your sweetheart company,
And help to cheer the rest.
  Y. Lio. And so thou meanest to escape alone ?
  Reig. Rather without,
I'll stand a champion for you all within.
Will you be swayed ?   One thing in any case
I must advise : the gates bolted and locked,
See that 'mongst you no living voice be heard ;
No, not so much as but a dog to howl,
Or cat to mew—all silence, that I charge ;
As if this were a mere forsaken house,
And none did there inhabit.
  Y. Lio. Nothing else ?
  Reig. And, though the old man thunder at the gates
As if he meant to. ruin what he had reared,
None on their lives to answer.
  Y. Lio. 'Tis my charge :
Remains there nothing else ?
  Reig. Only the key ;
For I must play the gaoler for your durance,[1]
To be the Mercury in your release.
  Y. Lio. Me, and my hope, I in this key deliver
To thy safe trust.
  Reig. When you are fast you are safe,
And with this turn 'tis done.
       [Exeunt all except REIGNALD *who locks the door.*
What fools are these,
To trust their ruined fortunes to his hands

---

[1] Confinement.

That hath betrayed his own, and make themselves
Prisoner to one deserves to lie for all,
As being cause of all ! And yet something prompts
,   me—
I'll stand it at all dangers ; and, to recompense
The many wrongs unto the young man done,
Now, if I can doubly delude the old—
My brain, about it, then.   All's hushed within ;
The noise that shall be, I must make without,
And he that, part for gain and part for wit,
So far hath travelled, strive to fool at home :
Which to effect, art must with knavery join,
And smooth dissembling meet with impudence.
I'll do my best, and howsoe'er it prove,
My praise or shame, 'tis but a servant's love.   [*Retires.*

Enter Old LIONEL, *with* Watermen, *and two* Servants
with burdens and caskets.

 O. Lio. Discharge these honest sailors that have
      brought
Our chests ashore, and pray them have a care
Those merchandise be safe we left aboard.
As Heaven hath blessed us with a fortunate voyage,
In which we bring home riches with our healths,
So let not us prove niggards in our store ;
See them paid well, and to their full content.
 1st Ser. I shall, sir.
 O. Lio. Then return : these special things,
And of most value, we'll not trust aboard ;
Methinks they are not safe till they see home,
And there repose, where we will rest ourselves,
And bid farewell to travel ; for I vow
After this hour no more to trust the seas,
Nor throw me to such danger.
 Reig. I could wish
You had took your leave o' the land too.   [*Aside.*
 O. Lio. And now it much rejoiceth me to think

What a most sudden welcome I shall bring
Both to my friends and private family.
   Reig. Oh, but how much more welcome had he
been
That had brought certain tidings of thy death !   [*Aside.*
   O. Lio. But soft, what's this? my own gates shut upon
me,   .
And bar their master entrance !   Who's within there?
How, no man speak ! are all asleep or dead,
That no soul stirs to open?   [*Knocks loudly.*
   Reig. What madman's that who, weary of his life,
Dares once lay hand on these accursèd gates?
   O. Lio. Who's that? my servant Reignald !
   Reig. My old master !
Most glad I am to see you ; are you well, sir?
   O. Lio. Thou seest I am.
   Reig. But are you sure you are?
Feel you no change about you?   Pray you stand off.
   O. Lio. What strange and unexpected greeting's this,
That thus a man may knock at his own gates,
Beat with his hands and feet, and call thus loud,
And no man give him entrance?
   Reig. Said you, sir—
Did your hand touch that hammer?
   O. Lio. Why, whose else?
   Reig. But are you sure you touched it?
   O. Lio. How else, I prithee,
Could I have made this noise?
   Reig. You touched it then?
   O. Lio. I tell thee yet I did.
   Reig. Oh, for the love I bear you—
O me most miserable ! you, for your own sake,
Of all alive most wretched !—did you touch it?
   O. Lio. Why, say I did?
   Reig. You have then a sin committed,
No sacrifice can expiate, to the dead ;
But yet I hope you did not.

O. Lio. 'Tis past hope ;
The deed is done, and I repent it not.
Reig. You and all yours will do't.   In this one rash-
     ness,
You have undone us all : pray be not desperate,
But first thank Heaven that you have escaped thus well.
Come from the gate—yet further, further yet—
And tempt your fate no more ; command your servants
Give off and come no nearer ; they are ignorant,
And do not know the danger, therefore pity
That they should perish in't.   'Tis full seven months
Since any of your house durst once set foot
Over that threshold.
     O. Lio. Prithee speak the cause?
     Reig. First look about ; beware that no man hear ;
Command these to remove.
     O. Lio. Begone.—[*Exeunt* Servants *and* Watermen].—
     Now speak.
     Reig. Oh, sir, this house is grown prodigious,[1]
Fatal, disastrous unto you and yours.
     O. Lio. What fatal? what disastrous ?
     Reig. Some host, that hath been owner of this house,
In it his guest hath slain ; and we suspect
'Twas he of whom you bought it.
     O. Lio. How came this
Discovered to you first?
     Reig. I'll tell you, sir ;
But further from the gate.   Your son one night
Supped late abroad, I within—oh, that night
I never shall forget !   Being safe got home,
I saw him in his chamber laid to rest ;
And after went to mine, and, being drowsy,
Forgot by chance to put the candle out :
Being dead asleep, your son, affrighted, calls
So loud that I soon wakened, brought in light,
And found him almost drowned in fearful sweat :

[1] *i.e.* Portentous.

Amazed to see't, I did demand the cause,
Who told me that this murdered ghost appeared,
His body gashed, and all o'er-stuck with wounds,
And spake to him as follows.   ·

O. Lio. Oh, proceed ;
'Tis that I long to hear.

Reig. " I am," quoth he,
" A transmarine by birth, who came well stored
With gold and jewels to this fatal house,
Where, seeking safety, I encountered death :
The covetous merchant, landlord of this rent,
To whom I gave my life and wealth in charge,
Freely to enjoy the one, robbed me of both :
Here was my body buried, here my ghost
Must ever walk, till that have Christian right ;
Till when, my habitation must be here.
Then fly, young man ; remove thy family,
And seek some safer dwelling ; for my death
This mansion is accursed ; 'tis my possession,
Bought at the dear rate of my life and blood :
None enter here, that aims at his own good."
And with this charge he vanished.

O. Lio. O my fear !
Whither wilt thou transport me ?

Reig. I entreat
Keep further from the gate, and fly.

O. Lio. Fly whither ?
Why dos't not thou fly too ?

Reig. What need I fear ?
The ghost and I am friends.

O. Lio. But Reignald——

Reig. [*Turning round.*] Tush !
I nothing have deserved, nor aught transgressed :
I came not near the gate.

O. Lio. To whom was that thou spakest ?

Reig. Was't you, sir, named me ?
Now as I live, I thought the dead man called,

To inquire for him that thundered at the gate
Which he so dearly paid for.   Are you mad,
To stand a foreseen danger?
   O. Lio. What shall I do?
   Reig. Cover your head and fly, lest, looking back,
You spy your own confusion.
   O. Lio. Why dost thou not fly too?
   Reig. I tell you, sir,
The ghost and I am friends.
   O. Lio. Why didst thou quake then?
   Reig. In fear lest some mischance may fall on you,
That have the dead offended; for my part,
The ghost and I am friends.   Why fly you not,
Since here you are not safe?
   O. Lio. Some blest powers guard me!
   Reig. Nay, sir,
I'll not forsake you.—[*Exit* Old LIONEL.]—I have got the
      start;
But ere the goal, 'twill ask both brain and art.   [*Exit.*

ACT THE THIRD.

SCENE I.—*The Dining Hall in* Old GERALDINE'S *House.*

Enter Old GERALDINE, Young GERALDINE, WINCOTT *and his* Wife, DELAVIL, *and* PRUDENTILLA.

IN.   We are bound to you, kind Master Geraldine,
For this great entertainment; troth, your cost
Hath much exceeded common neigh-
    bourhood;
You have feasted us like princes.
    O. Ger. This, and more
Many degrees, can never countervail [1]
The oft and frequent welcomes given my son:
You have took him from me quite, and have, I think,
Adopted him into your family,
He stays with me so seldom.
    Win. And in this,
By trusting him to me, of whom yourself
May have both use and pleasure, you're as kind
As moneyed men, that might make benefit
Of what they are possessed, yet to their friends
In need will lend it gratis.
    Wife. And, like such
As are indebted more than they can pay,

---

[1] Counterbalance.

Heywood.   O

We more and more confess ourselves engaged
To you for your forbearance.

Pru. Yet you see,
Like debtors, such as would not break their day,[1]
The treasure late received we tender back,
The which, the longer you can spare, you still
The more shall bind us to you.

O. Ger. Most kind ladies,
Worthy you are to borrow, that return
The principal with such large use[2] of thanks.

Del. [*Aside.*] What strange felicity these rich men take
To talk of borrowing, lending, and of use !
The usurer's language right.

Win. You've, Master Geraldine,
Fair walks and gardens; I have praisèd them
Both to my wife and sister.

O. Ger. You would see them?
There is no pleasure that the house can yield
That can be debarred from you.—Prithee, son,
Be thou the usher to those mounts and prospects
May one day call thee master.

Y. Ger. Sir, I shall.—
Please you to walk ?

Pru. What, Master Delavil,
Will you not bear us company ?

Del. 'Tis not fit
That we should leave our noble host alone.
Be you my friend's charge, and this old man mine.

Pru. Well, be't then at your pleasure.
                    [*Exeunt all but* DELAVIL *and* Old GERALDINE.

Del. You to your prospects, but there's project here
That's of another nature.—Worthy sir,
I cannot but approve your happiness
To be the father of so brave a son,
So every way accomplished and made up,
In which my voice is least ; for I, alas !

---

[1] Fail to pay at the appointed time.   [2] Interest.

Bear but a mean part in the common choir,
When with much louder accents of his praise
So all the world reports him.

O. Ger. Thank my stars,
They have lent me one who, as he always was
And is my present joy, if their aspéct
Be no ways to our goods malevolent,
May be my future comfort.

Del. Yet must I hold him happy above others,
As one that solely to himself enjoys
What many others aim at, but in vain.

O. Ger. How mean yóu that?

Del. So beautiful a mistress.

O. Ger. A mistress, said you?

Del. Yes, sir, or a friend,
Whether you please to style her.

O. Ger. Mistress! friend!
Pray be more open-languaged.

Del. And indeed
Who can blame him to absent himself from home,
And make his father's house but as a grange [1]
For a beauty so attractive? or blame her,
Hugging so weak an old man in her arms,
To make a new choice of an equal youth,
Being in him so perfect? Yet, in troth,
I think they both are honest.

O. Ger. You have, sir,
Possessed me with such strange fancies—

Del. For my part,
How can I love the person of your son,
And not his reputation? His repair
So often to the house is voiced by all,
And frequent in the mouths of the whole country:
Some, equally addicted, praise his happiness, [2]
But others, more censorious and austere,

---

[1] The word seems to have implied "loneliness."
[2] Good fortune.

Blame and reprove a course so dissolute ;
Each one in general pity the good man,
As one unfriendly dealt with, yet in my conscience
I think them truly honest.

 O. Ger. 'Tis suspicious.

 Del. True, sir, at best ; but what when scandalous
  tongues

Will make the worst, and what's good in itself,
Sully and stain by fabulous misreport ?
For let men live as chary as they can,
Their lives are often questioned ; then no wonder
If such as give occasion of suspicion
Be subject to this scandal.   What I speak
Is as a noble friend unto your son ;
And therefore, as I glory in his fame,
I suffer in his wrong ; for, as I live,
I think they both are honest.

 O. Ger. Howsoever,
I wish them so.

 Del. Some course might be devised
'To stop this clamour ere it grow too rank,
Lest that which yet but inconvenience seems
May turn to greater mischief: this I speak
In zeal to both,—in sovereign care of him
As of a friend, and tender of her honour
As one to whom I hope to be allied
By marriage with her sister.

 O. Ger. I much thank you,
For you have clearly given me light of that
Till now I never dreamt on.

 Del. 'Tis my love,
And therefore I entreat you make not me
To be the first reporter.

 O. Ger. You have done
The office of a noble gentleman,
And shall not be so injured.

Re-enter WINCOTT *and his* WIFE, Young GERALDINE,
and PRUDENTILLA ; *the* ladies *wearing flowers.*

Win. See, Master Geraldine,
How bold we are ; especially these ladies
Play little better than the thieves with you,
For they have robbed your garden.

Wife. You might, sir,
Better have termed it sauciness than theft ;
You see we blush not what we took in private
To wear in public view.

Prud. Besides, these cannot
Be missed out of so many ; in full fields
The gleanings are allowed.

O. Ger. These and the rest
Are, ladies, at your service.

Win. Now to horse :
But one thing, ere we part, I must entreat,
In which my wife will be joint suitor with me,
My sister too.

O. Ger. In what, I pray ?

Win. That he
Which brought us hither may but bring us home ;
Your much-respected son.

O. Ger. How men are born
To woo their own disasters !   [*Aside.*

Wife. But to see us
From whence he brought us, sir, that's all.

O. Ger. This second motion [1] makes it palpable.
To note a woman's cunning !   Make her husband
Bawd to her own lascivious appetite,
And to solicit his own shame !   [*Aside.*

Prud. Nay, sir ;
When all of us join in so small a suit,
It were some injury to be denied.

O. Ger. And work her sister too ! What will not woman

---

[1] Proposal.

To accomplish her own ends?   But this disease
I'll seek to physic ere it grow too far.—   [*Aside.*
I am most sorry to be urged, sweet friends,
In what at this time I can no ways grant ;
Most, that these ladies should be aught denied,
To whom I owe all service ; but occasions
Of weighty and important consequence,
Such as concern the best of my estate,
Call him aside.   Excuse us both this once ;
Presume this business is no sooner over,
But he's at his own freedom.
     Win. 'Twere no manners
In us to urge it further.—We will leave you,
With promise, sir, that he shall in my will
Not be the last remembered.
     O. Ger. We are bound to you.—
See them to horse, and instantly return ;
We have employments for you.
  . *Y. Ger.* Sir, I shall.
     Del. Remember your last promise.
          [*Exeunt* DELAVIL, WINCOTT *and his* Wife,
               PRUDENTILLA, *and* Young GERALDINE.
     O. Ger. Not to do't
I should forget myself.—If I find him false
To such a friend, be sure he forfeits me ;
In which to be more punctually resolved,
I have a project how to sift his soul,
How 'tis inclined,—whether to yonder place,

          Re-enter Young GERALDINE.

The clear bright palace, or black dungeon.   See,
They are onward on the way, and he returned.
     Y. Ger. I now attend your pleasure.
     O. Ger. You are grown perfect man, and now you
          float,
Like to a well-built vessel, 'tween two currents,
Virtue and vice : take this, you steer to harbour ;

Take that, to imminent shipwreck.

Y. Ger. Pray, your meaning?

O. Ger. What fathers' cares are, you shall never know,
Till you yourself have children.   Now my study
Is how to make you such, that you in them
May have a feeling of my love to you.

Y. Ger. Pray, sir, expound yourself; for I protest,
Of all the languages I yet have learned,
This is to me most foreign.

O. Ger. Then I shall ;
I have lived to see you in your prime of youth
And height of fortune, so you will but take
Occasion by the forehead ; to be brief,
And cut off all superfluous circumstance,
All the ambition that I aim at now
Is but to see you married.

Y. Ger. Married, sir !

O. Ger. And, to that purpose, I have found out one
Whose youth and beauty may not only please
A curious eye, but her immediate means
Able to strengthen a state competent,
Or raise a ruined fortune.

Y. Ger. Of all which
I have, believe me, neither need nor use ;
My competence best pleasing as it is,
And this my singularity[1] of life
Most to my mind contenting.

O. Ger. I suspect,
But yet must prove him further.—   [*Aside.*
Say to my care I add a father's charge,
And couple with my counsel my command—
To that how can you answer ?

Y. Ger. That I hope
My duty and obedience, still unblamed,
Did never merit such austerity,
And from a father never yet displeased.

---

[1] Singleness.

O. Ger. Nay, then, to come more near unto the point :
Either you must resolve for present marriage,
Or forfeit all your interest in my love.

Y. Ger. Unsay that language, I entreat you, sir,
And do not so oppress me ; or, if needs
Your heavy imposition stand in force,
Resolve me by your counsel.   With more safety
May I infringe a sacred vow to Heaven,
Or to oppose me to your strict command ?—
Since one of these I must.

O. Ger. Now, Delavil,
I find thy words too true.   [*Aside.*

Y. Ger. For marry, sir,
I neither may nor can.

O. Ger. Yet whore you may,
And that's no breach of any vow to Heaven :
Pollute the nuptial bed with mechal[1] sin ;
Asperse the honour of a noble friend ;
Forfeit thy reputation here below,
And the interest that thy soul might claim above
In yon blest city !   These you may, and can,
With untouched conscience.   Oh that I should live
To see the hopes that I have stored so long
Thus in a moment ruined, and the staff
On which my old decrepit age should lean
Before my face thus broken ; on which trusting,
I thus abortively, before my time,
Fall headlong to my grave.   [*Falls on the ground.*

Y. Ger. It yet stands strong,
Both to support you unto future life
And fairer comfort.

O. Ger. Never, never, son ;
For till thou canst acquit thyself of scandal,
And me of my suspicion, here, even here,
Where I have measured out my length of earth,
I shall expire my last.

[1] Adulterous.

Y. Ger. Both these I can :
Then rise, sir, I entreat you ; and that innocency,
Which poisoned by the breath of calumny
Cast you thus low, shall, these few stains wiped off,
With better thoughts erect you.

    O. Ger. Well, say on.　　　　　　　　　　[*Rises.*

    Y. Ger. There's but one fire from which this smoke
       may grow,
Namely, the unmatched yoke of youth and age,
In which, if ever I occasion was
Of the smallest breach, the greatest implacable mischief
Adultery can threaten fall on me !
Of you may I be disavowed a son,
And unto Heaven a servant ! For that lady,
As she is beauty's mirror, so I hold her
For chastity's example : from her tongue
Never came language that arrived my ear
That even censorious Cato, lived he now,
Could misinterpret ; never from her lips
Came unchaste kiss, or from her constant eye
Look savouring of the least immodesty :
Further—

    O. Ger. Enough ! One only thing remains,
Which, on thy part performed, assures firm credit
To these thy protestations.

    Y. Ger. Name it then.

    O. Ger. Take hence the occasion of this common fame,
Which hath already spread itself so far
To her dishonour and thy prejudice :
From this day forward to forbear the house ;
This do upon my blessing.

    Y. Ger. As I hope it,
I will not fail your charge.

    O. Ger. I am satisfied.　　　　　　　　　[*Exeunt.*

SCENE II.—*Before* Old LIONEL'S *House.*

Enter at one side Usurer *and his* Man ; *at the other,* Old
LIONEL *and his* Servant ; *behind,* REIGNALD.

   Reig. [*Aside.*] To which hand shall I turn me?
   Here's my master
Hath been to inquire of him that sold the house,
Touching the murder ; here's an usuring rascal,
Of whom we have borrowed money to supply
Our prodigal expenses, broke our day,
And owe him still the principal and use.
Were I to meet them single, I have brain
To oppose both, and to come off unscarred ;
But if they do assault me, and at once,
Not Hercules himself could stand that odds :
Therefore I must encounter them by turns,
And to my master first.—Oh, sir, well met.
   O. Lio. What, Reignald ! I but now met with the man
Of whom I bought yon house.
   Reig. What, did you, sir ?
But did you speak of aught concerning that
Which I last told you ?
   O. Lio. Yes, I told him all.
   Reig. Then am I cast ! [*Aside.*]—But I pray tell me,
Did he confess the murder ?   [sir,
   O. Lio. No such thing ;
Most stiffly he denies it.
   Reig. Impudent wretch !
Then serve him with a warrant ; let the officer
Bring him before a justice, you shall hear
What I can say against him ! 'Sfoot ! deny't !
But I pray, sir, excuse me ; yonder's one
With whom I have some business ; stay you here,
And but determine what's best course to take,
And note how I will follow't.
   O. Lio. Be brief, then.
   Reig. Now, if I can as well put off my use-man,
This day I shall be master of the field.   [*Aside.*

Usu. That should be Lionel's man.

Man. The same, I know him.

Usu. After so many frivolous delays,
There's now some hope. He that was wont to shun us,
And to absent himself, accosts us freely,
And with a pleasant countenance.— Well met, Reignald,
What, is this money ready?

Reig. Never could you
Have come in better time.

Usu. Where is your master,
Young Lionel? it something troubles me
That he should break his day.

Reig. A word in private.

Usu. Tush, private me no privates;[1] in a word,
Speak, are my moneys ready?

Reig. Not so loud.

Usu. I will be louder yet. Give me my moneys;
Come, tender me my moneys.

Reig. We know you have a throat wide as your conscience;
You need not use it now. Come, get you home.

Usu. Home!

Reig. Yes, home, I say; return by three o'clock,
And I will see all cancelled.

Usu. 'Tis now past two, and I can stay till three;
I'll make that now my business; otherways,
With these loud clamours I will haunt thee still:
Give me my use, give me my principal.

Reig. This burr will still cleave to me; what, no means
To shake him off! I ne'er was caught till now.—[*Aside.*
Come, come, you're troublesome.

Usu. Prevent that trouble,
And, without trifling, pay me down my cash;
I will be fooled no longer.

Reig. So, so, so.

Usu. I have been still put off, from time to time,

---

[1] Like Shakespeare's "but me no buts."

And day to day ; these are but cheating tricks,
And this is the last minute I'll forbear
Thee, or thy master : once again, I say,
Give me my use, give me my principal.
    Reig. Pox o' this use, that hath undone so many,
And now will confound me !   *[Aside.*
    O. Lio. Hast thou heard this ?
    Ser. Yes, sir, and to my grief.
    O. Lio. Come hither, Reignald.
    Reig. Here, sir. *[Aside.]* Nay, now I am gone.
    O. Lio. What use is this,
What principal he talks of, in which language
He names my son, and thus upbraideth thee ?
What is't you owe this man ?
    Reig. A trifle, sir :
Pray stop his mouth, and pay't him.
    O. Lio. I pay !—what ?
    Reig. If I say pay't him, pay't him.
    O. Lio. What's the sum ?
    Reig. A toy, the main about five hundred pounds ;
And the use fifty.
    O. Lio. Call you that a toy ?
To what use was it borrowed ?   At my departure
I left my son sufficient in his charge,
With surplus, to defray a large expense,
Without this need of borrowing.
    Reig. 'Tis confessed ;
Yet stop his clamorous mouth, and only say
That you will pay't to-morrow.
    O. Lio. I pass my word !
    Reig. Sir, if I bid you, do't ; nay, no more words,
But say you'll pay't to-morrow.
    O. Lio. Jest indeed !
But tell me how these moneys were bestowed ?
    Reig. Safe, sir, I warrant you.
    O. Lio. The sum still safe ?
Why do you not then tender it yourselves ?

Reig. Your ear, sir.   With this sum, joined to the rest,
Your son hath purchased land and houses.

O. Lio. Land, dost thou say?

Reig. A goodly house, and gardens.

O. Lio. Now joy on him,
That whilst his father merchandised abroad,
Had care to add to his estate at home !
But, Reignald, wherefore houses?

Reig. Now, Lord, sir,
How dull you are !   This house possessed with spirits,
And there no longer stay, would you have had
Him, us, and all your other family,
To live and lie i' the streets ?   It had not, sir,
Been for your reputation.

O. Lio. Blessing on him,
That he is grown so thrifty !

Usu. 'Tis struck three ;
My money's not yet tendered.

Reig. Pox upon him !
See him discharged, I pray, sir.

O. Lio. Call upon me
To-morrow, friend, as early as thou wilt ;
I'll see thy debt defrayed.

Usu. It is enough, I have a true man's word.
                        [*Exeunt* Usurer *and* Man.

O. Lio. Now tell me, Reignald,
For thou hast made me proud of my son's thrift,
Where, in what country, doth this fair house stand ?

Reig. [*aside*]   Never in all my time so much to seek ;
I know not what to answer.

O. Lio. Wherefore studiest thou?
Use men to purchase lands at a dear rate,
And know not where they lie ?

Reig. 'Tis not for that ;
I only had forgot his name that sold them.
'Twas, let me see—see—

O. Lio. Call thyself to mind.

Reig. Non-plussed or never now; where are thou,
   brain ?—
O sir, where was my memory ?   'Tis this house
That next adjoins to yours. -

O. Lio. My neighbour Ricott's ?

Reig. The same, the same, sir ; we had pennyworths
   in't ;
And I can tell you, have been offered well
Since, to forsake our bargain.

O. Lio. As I live,
I much commend your choice.

Reig. Nay, 'tis well seated,
Rough-cast without, but bravely lined within ;
You have met with few such bargains.

O. Lio. Prithee knock,
And call the master or the servant on't,
To let me take free view on't.

Reig. [*aside*] Puzzle again on puzzle !—One word, sir :
The house is full of women ; no man knows
How on the instant they may be employed ;
The rooms may lie unhandsome, and maids stand
Much on their cleanliness and huswifery ;
To take them unprovided were disgrace ;
'Twere fit they had some warning.   Now, do you
Fetch but a warrant from the justice, sir ;—
You understand me ?

O. Lio. Yes, I do.

Reig. To attach [1]
Him of suspected murder ; I'll see't served,
Did he deny't ; and in the interim, I
Will give them notice you are now arrived,
And long to see your purchase.

O. Lio. Counselled well ;
And meet some half-hour hence.

Reig. This plunge well passed,
All things fall even, to crown my brain at last. [*Exeunt.*

[1] Charge with.

SCENE III.—*Barnet. A Street.*

Enter DELAVIL *and a* Gentleman.

Gent. Where shall we dine to-day?

Del. At the ordinary.

I see, sir, you are but a stranger here.
This Barnet is a place of great resort,
And commonly, upon the market days,
Here all the country gentlemen appoint
A friendly meeting; some about affairs
Of consequence and profit—bargain, sale,
And to confer with chapmen; some for pleasure,
To match their horses, wager on their dogs,
Or try their hawks; some to no other end
But only meet good company, discourse,
Dine, drink, and spend their money.

Gent. That's the market
We have to make this day.

Del. 'Tis a commodity
That will be easily vented.—What, my worthy friend!

Enter Old GERALDINE *and* Young GERALDINE.

You are happily encountered.   Oh, you're grown strange
To one that much respects you.   Troth, the house
Hath all this time seemed naked without you;
The good old man doth never sit to meat,
But next his giving thanks he speaks of you;
There's scarce a bit that he at table tastes,
That can digest without a Geraldine,
You are in his mouth so frequent.   He and she
Both wondering what distaste from one, or either,
So suddenly should alienate a guest
To them so dearly welcome.

O. Ger. Master Delavil,
Thus much let me for him apologise:
Divers designs have thronged upon us late
My weakness was not able to support
Without his help; he hath been much abroad,

At London, or elsewhere; besides, 'tis term,
And lawyers must be followed; seldom at home, .
And scarcely then at leisure.

    Del. I am satisfied,
And I would they were so too; but I hope, sir,
In this restraint you have not used my name.

    O. Ger. Not as I live.

    Del. You're noble.—Who had thought
To have met with such good company? You are, it seems,
But new alighted. Father and son, ere part,
I vow we'll drink a cup of sack together;
Physicians say it doth prepare the appetite
And stomach against dinner.

    O. Ger. We old men
Are apt to take these courtesies.

    Del. What say you, friend?

    Y. Ger. I'll but inquire for one at the next inn,
And instantly return.

    Del. It is enough.   [*Exeunt.*

SCENE IV.—*Inside a Tavern.*

Enter BESS *and* Young GERALDINE, *meeting.*

    Y. Ger. Bess! How dost thou, girl?

    Bess. Faith, we may do how we list for you, you are grown
So great a stranger: we are more beholding
To Master Delavil; he's a constant guest:
And howsoe'er to some, that shall be nameless,
His presence may be graceful, yet to others—
I could say somewhat.

    Y. Ger. He's a noble fellow,
And my choice friend.

    Bess. Come, come, he is what he is;
And that the end will prove.

    Y. Ger. And how's all at home?

Nay, we'll not part without a glass of wine,
And meet so seldom.—Boy !

Enter Drawer.

Draw. Anon, anon, sir.   [sit down :
Y. Ger. A pint of claret, quickly. [*Exit* Drawer.] Nay,
The news, the news, I pray thee ; I am sure,
I have been much inquired of thy old master,
And thy young mistress too.
Bess. Ever your name
Is in my master's mouth, and sometimes too
In hers, when she hath nothing else to think of.
Well, well, I could say somewhat.

Re-enter Drawer.

Draw. Here's your wine, sir.
Y. Ger. Fill, boy.   Here, Bess, this glass to both their
    healths.   [*Exit* Drawer.
Why dost thou weep, my wench?
Bess. Nay, nothing, sir.
Y. Ger. Come, I must know.
Bess. In troth, I love you, sir,
And ever wished you well ; you are a gentleman
Whom always I respected ; know the passages
And private whisperings of the secret love
Betwixt you and my mistress—I dare swear,
On your part well intended, but—
Y. Ger. But what?
Bess. You bear the name of landlord, but another
Enjoys the rent ; you dote upon the shadow,
But another he bears away the substance.
Y. Ger. Be more plain.
Bess. You hope to enjoy a virtuous widowhood ;
But Delavil, whom you esteem your friend,
He keeps the wife in common.
Y. Ger. You're to blame,
And, Bess, you make me angry : he's my friend,

And she my second self; in all their meetings
I never saw so much as cast of eye
Once entertained betwixt them.
    Bess. That's their cunning.
· *Y. Ger.* For her, I have been with her at all hours,
Both late and early; in her bed-chamber,
And often singly ushered her abroad :
Now, would she have been any man's alive,
She had been mine. You wrong a worthy friend
And a chaste mistress; you're not a good girl.
Drink that, speak better of her; I could chide you,
But I'll forbear. What you have rashly spoke,
Shall ever here be buried.
    Bess. I am sorry
My freeness should offend you, but yet know
I am her chamber-maid.
    Y. Ger. Play now the market-maid,
And prithee 'bout thy business.
    Bess. Well, I shall.—
That man should be so foolèd !   *[Exit.*
    Y. Ger. She a prostitute !
Nay, and to him, my troth-plight, and my friend
As possible it is that Heaven and earth
Should be in love together, meet and kiss,
And so cut off all distance. What strange frenzy
Came in this wench's brain, so to surmise ?
Were she so base, his nobleness is such
He would not entertain it for my sake ;
Or he so bent, his hot and lust-burnt appetite
Would be so quenched at the mere contemplation
Of her most pious and religious life.
The girl was much to blame; perhaps her mistress
Hath stirred her anger by some word or blow,
Which she would thus revenge—not apprehending
At what a high price honour's to be rated ;
Or else some one that envies her rare virtue
Might hire her thus to brand it ; or, who knows

But the young wench may fix a thought on me,
And to divert me from her mistress' love,
May raise this false aspersion? Howsoever,
My thoughts on these two columns fixèd are,
She's good as fresh, and purely chaste as fair.

Enter Clown *with a letter.*

Clown. Oh, sir, you are the needle, and if the whole county of Middlesex had been turned to a mere bottle[1] of hay, I had been enjoined to have found you out, or never more returned back to my old master: there's a letter, sir.

Y. Ger. I know the hand that superscribed it well ;
Stay but till I peruse it, and from me
Thou shalt return an answer. *[Reads letter.*

Clown. I shall, sir. This is market-day, and here acquaintance commonly meet; and whom have I encountered? my gossip Pint-pot, and brim-full; nay, I mean to drink with you before I part. And how doth all your worshipful kindred? your sister Quart, your pater Pottle (who was ever a gentleman's fellow), and your old grandsire Gallon; they cannot choose but be all in health, since so many healths have been drunk out of them : I could wish them all here, and in no worse state than I see you are in at this present. Howsoever, gossip, since I have met you hand to hand, I'll make bold to drink to you— nay, either you must pledge me, or get one to do't for you, Do you open your mouth towards me? well, I know what you would say: "Here, Roger, to your master and mistress, and all our good friends at home. Gramercy, gossip, if I should not pledge thee, I were worthy to be turned out to grass, and stand no more at livery." And now, in requital of this courtesy, I'll begin one health to you and all your society in the cellar—to Peter Pipe,

---

[1] Bundle ; Cotgrave has : "*boteler*, to botle or bundle up, to make into botles or bundles."

Harry Hogshead, Bartholomew Butt, and little Master
Randal Rundlet, to Timothy Taster, and all your other
great and small friends.

Y. Ger. He writes me here
That at my discontinuance he's much grieved ;
Desiring me, as I have ever tendered ·
Or him or his, to give him satisfaction
Touching my discontent ; and that in person,
By any private meeting.

Clown. Ay, sir, 'tis very true ; the letter speaks no more
than he wished me to tell you by word of mouth.

Y. Ger. Thou art then of his counsel ?

Clown. His Privy,[1] an't please you.　　　　　[charge,

Y. Ger. Though ne'er so strict hath been my father's
A little I'll dispense with't, for his love.
Commend me to thy master, tell him from me,
On Monday night (then will my leisure serve)
I will by Heaven's assistance visit him.

Clown. On Monday, sir? that's, as I remember, just
the day before Tuesday.

Y. Ger. But 'twill be midnight first, at which late hour
Please him to let the garden door stand ope ;
At that I'll enter, but conditionally
That neither wife, friend, servant, no third soul
Save him, and thee to whom he trusts this message,
Know of my coming in, or passing out ;
When, tell him, I will fully satisfy him
Concerning my forced absence.

Clown. I am something oblivious; your message
would be the trulier delivered if it were set down in
black and white.

Y. Ger. I'll call for pen and ink,
And instantly despatch it.　　　　　　　　[*Exeunt.*

---

[1] *i.e.* Privy Council.

ACT THE FOURTH.

SCENE I.—*Outside* RICOTT'S *House.*

Enter REIGNALD.

REIG. Now, impudence, but steel my face
. this once,
Although I ne'er blush after!   Here's
the house.
Ho ! who's within ?   What, no man to
defend
These innocent gates from knocking?

Enter Master RICOTT.

Ric. Who's without there ?

Reig. One, sir, that ever wished your worship's health;
And those few hours I can find time to pray in,
I still remember it.

Ric. Gramercy, Reignald,
I love all those that wish it : you are the men
Lead merry lives, feast, revel, and carouse ;
You feel no tedious hours ; Time plays with you—
This is your golden age.

Reig. It was ; but now, sir,
That gold is turned to worse than alchemy ;
It will not stand the test.   Those days are past,
And now our nights come on.

Ric. Tell me, Reignald, is he returned from sea ?

Reig. Yes, to our grief already, but we fear
Hereafter it may prove to all our costs.

Ric. Suspects thy master anything ?

Reig. Not yet, sir.

Now my request is, that your worship being
So near a neighbour, therefore most disturbed,
Would not be first to peach us.
　　Ric. Take my word ;
With other neighbours make what peace you can,
I'll not be your accuser.
　　Reig. Worshipful sir ;
I shall be still your beadsman.　Now the business
That I was sent about : the old man my master
Claiming some interest in acquaintance past,
Desires (might it be no way troublesome)
To take free view of all your house within.
　　Ric. View of my house !　.Why, 'tis not set to sale,
Nor bill upon the door.　Look well upon't ;
View of my house !
　　Reig. Nay, be not angry, sir ;
He no way doth disable ¹ your estate ;
As far to buy, as you are loath to sell.
Some alterations in his own he'd make,
And hearing yours by workmen much commended,
He would make that his precedent.
　　Ric. What fancies
.Should at this age possess him, knowing the cost,
That he should dream of building !·
　　Reig. 'Tis supposed,
He hath late found a wife out for his son ;
Now, sir, to have him near him, and that nearness
Too without trouble, though beneath one roof,
Yet parted in two families, he would build,
And make what's picked ² a perfect quadrangle,
Proportioned just with yours, were you so pleased
To make it his example.
　　Ric. Willingly.
I will but order some few things within,
And then attend his coming.　　　　　　　　　[*Exit.*
　　Reig. Most kind coxcomb !
Great Alexander and Agathocles,

---

¹ Disparage.　　　　　　　² Pitched.

Cæsar, and others, have been famed, they say,
And magnified for high facinorous deeds ;
Why claim not I an equal place with them—
Or rather a precedent ?   These commanded
Their subjects, and their servants ; I my master,
And every way his equals, where I please,
Lead by the nose along : they placed their burdens .
On horses, mules, and camels ; I, old men
Of strength and wit, load with my knavery,
Till both their backs and brains ache ; yet, poor animals,

Enter Old LIONEL.

They ne'er complain of weight.—Oh, are you come, sir ?
  O. Lio. I made what haste I could.
  Reig. And brought the warrant ?
  O. Lio. See here, I have't.
  Reig. 'Tis well done ; but speak, runs it
Both without bail and mainprize ¹ ?
  O. Lio. Nay, it carries
Both form and power.
  Reig. Then I shall warrant him.
I have been yonder, sir.
  O. Lio. And what says he ?
  Reig. Like one that offers you
Free ingress, view, and regress, at your pleasure,
As to his worthy landlord.
  O. Lio. Was that all ?
  Reig. He spake to me, that I would speak to you,
To speak unto your son ; and then again,
To speak to him, that he would speak to you,
You would release his bargain.
  O. Lio. By no means :
Men must advise before they part with land,
Not after to repent it : 'tis most just
That such as hazard ánd disburse their stocks,
Should take all gains and profits that accrue,

¹ A technical term : a writ of mainprize was sent to the sheriff,
directing him to take sureties for a prisoner.

As well in sale of houses as in barter,
And traffic of all other merchandise.

Re-enter RICOTT ; *he walks before the gate.*

Reig. See, in acknowledgment of a tenant's duty,
He attends you at the gate ; salute him, sir.

O. Lio. My worthy friend !

Ric. Now, as I live, all my best thoughts and wishes
Impart with yours, in your so safe return ;
Your servant tells me you have great desire
To take surview of this my house within.

O. Lio. Be't, sir, no trouble to you.

Ric. None ; enter boldly,
With as much freedom as it were your own.

O. Lio. As it were mine ! Why, Reignald, is it not ?

Reig. Lord, sir, that in extremity of grief
'You'll add unto vexation ! See you not
How sad he's on the sudden ?

O. Lio. I observe it.

Reig. To part with that which he hath kept so long,
Especially his inheritance : now, as you love
Goodness and honesty, torment him not
With the least word of purchase.

O. Lio. Counselled well ;
Thou teachest me humanity.

Ric. Will you enter ?
Or shall I call a servant, to conduct you
Through every room and chamber ?

O. Lio. By no means ;
I fear we are too much troublesome of ourselves.

Reig. See what a goodly gate !

O. Lio. It likes me well.

Reig. What brave carved posts ! who knows but here,
In time, sir, you may keep your shrievalty ; [1]
And I be one o' the serjeants !

---

[1] It was customary for the sheriff to have posts in front of his house, to which notices were affixed.

O. Lio. They are well carved.

Ric. And cost me a good price, sir : take your pleasure ;
I have business in the town.   [*Exit.*

Reig. Poor man, I pity him ;
H'ath not the heart to stay and see you come,
As 'twere, to take possession. Look that way, sir,
What goodly fair bay windows.

O. Lio. Wondrous stately.

Reig. And what a gallery, how costly ceiled ;
What painting round about.

O. Lio. Every fresh object
To good adds betterness.

Reig. Terracèd above,
And how below supported.   Do they please you ?

O. Lio. All things beyond opinion. Trust me, Reignald,
I'll not forego the bargain, for more gain
Than half the price it cost me.

Reig. If you would,
I should not suffer you ; was not the money
Due to the usurer, took upon good ground,
That proved well built upon?   We were no fools
That knew not what we did.

O. Lio. It shall be satisfied.   [charged.

Reig. Please you to trust me with't, I'll see't dis-

O. Lio. He hath my promise, and I'll do't myself.
Never could son have better pleased a father
Than in this purchase ! Hie thee instantly
Unto my house i' the country, give him notice
Of my arrive, and bid him with all speed
Post hither.

Reig. Ere I see the warrant served?

O. Lio. It shall be thy first business ; for my soul
Is not at peace, till face to face I approve
His husbandry, and much commend his thrift ;
Nay, without pause, begone.

Reig. But a short journey ;
For he's not far that I am sent to seek :

I have got the start; the best part of the race
Is run already; what remains is small,
And, tire now, I should but forfeit all.
  O. Lio. Make haste, I do entreat thee.   [*Exeunt.*

SCENE II.—*The Garden of* Old WINCOTT'S *House.*

Enter the Clown.

Clown. This is the garden gate; and here am I set to
stand sentinel, and to attend the coming of young master
Geraldine. Master Delavil's gone to his chamber, my
mistress to hers. 'Tis now about midnight; a banquet
prepared, bottles of wine in readiness, all the whole
household at their rest, and no creature by this honestly
stirring, saving I and my old master; he in a bye-chamber,
prepared of purpose for their private meeting, and I
here to play the watchman against my will!

Enter Young GERALDINE.

Chavelah?[1] Stand! Who goes there?
  Y. Ger. A friend.
  Clown. The word?
  Y. Ger. Honest Roger.
  Clown. That's the word indeed; you have leave to
pass freely without calling my corporal.
  Y. Ger. How go the affairs within?
  Clown. According to promise: the business is composed, and the servants disposed; my young mistress re-
posed; my old master, according as you proposed,
attends you, if you be exposed, to give him meeting;
nothing in the way being interposed, to transpose you to
the least danger: and this I dare be deposed, if you will
not take my word, as I am honest Roger.

---

[1] The clown's form of the French phrase *qui va là?*

Y. Ger. Thy word shall be my warrant, but secured
Most in thy master's promise, on which building,
By this known way I enter.

Clown. Nay, by your leave, I that was late but a plain
sentinel will now be your captain conductor : follow me.

[*Exeunt.*

SCENE III.—*A Room in* Old WINCOTT'S *House.   Table
and stools set out, lights, a banquet,*[1] *wine.*

Enter Old WINCOTT.

Win. I wonder whence this strangeness should proceed,
Or wherein I, or any of my house,
Should be the occasion of the least distaste :
Now, as I wish him well, it troubles me ;
But now the time grows on from his own mouth
To be resolved, and I hope satisfied.

· *Enter* Clown *and* Young GERALDINE.

Sir, as I live, of all my friends, to me
Most wishedly you are welcome : take that chair,
I this : nay, I entreat, no compliment.—
Attend ; fill wine.

Clown. Till the mouths of the bottles yawn directly
upon the floor, and the bottoms turn their tails up to the
ceiling ; whilst there's any blood in their bellies I'll not
leave them.

Win. I first salute you thus.

Y. Ger. It could not come
From one whom I more honour ; sir, I thank you.

Clo. Nay, since my master begun it, I'll see't go round
to all three.

Win. Now give us leave.

Clown. Talk you by yourselves, whilst I find some-

¹ *i.e.* A dessert.

thing to say to this :[1] I have a tale to tell him shall make
his stony heart relent.   [*Exit.*

Y. Ger. Now, first, sir, your attention I entreat :
Next, your belief that what I speak is just,
Maugre all contradiction.

Win. Both are granted.

Y. Ger. Then I proceed ; with due acknowledgment
Of all your more than many courtesies :
You've been my second father, and your wife
My noble and chaste mistress ; all your servants
At my command ; and this your bounteous table
As free and common as my father's house :
Neither 'gainst any, or the least of these,
Can I commence just quarrel.

Win. What might then be
The cause of this constraint, in thus absenting
Yourself from such as love you ?

Y. Ger. Out of many,
I will propose some few : the care I have
Of your as yet unblemishèd renown,
The untouched honour of your virtuous wife,
And (which I value least, yet dearly too)
My own fair reputation.

Win. How can these
In any way be questioned ?

Y. Ger. Oh, dear sir,
Bad tongues have been too busy with us all ;
Of which I never yet had time to think,
But with sad thoughts and griefs unspeakable.
It hath been whispered by some wicked ones,
But loudly thundered in my father's ears,
By some that have maligned our happiness,
(Heaven, if it can brook slander, pardon them !)
That this my customary coming hither
Hath been to base and sordid purposes :
To wrong your bed, injure her chastity,

            ·   [1] He refers to the bottle.

And be mine own undoer, which, how false !
Win. As Heaven is true, I know't.
Y. Ger. Now, this calumny
Arriving first unto my father's ears,
His easy nature was induced to think
That these things might perhaps be possible :
I answered him as I would do to Heaven,
And cleared myself in his suspicious thoughts
As truly as the high all-knowing Judge
Shall of these stains acquit me, which are merely
Aspersions and untruths.   The good old man,
Possessed with my sincerity, and yet careful
Of your renown, her honour, and my fame,
To stop the worst that scandal could inflict,
And to prevent false rumours, charges me,
The cause removed, to take away the effect ;
Which only could be to forbear your house—
And this upon his blessing.   You hear all.
Win. And I of all acquit you : this your absence,
With which my love most cavilled, orators [1]
In your behalf.   Had such things passed betwixt you,
Not threats nor chidings could have driven you hence.
It pleads in your behalf, and speaks in hers,
And arms me with a double confidence,
Both of your friendship and her loyalty :
I am happy in you both, and only doubtful
Which of you two doth most impart my love.
You shall not hence to-night.
Y. Ger. Pray, pardon, sir.
Win. You are in your lodging.
Y. Ger. But my father's charge ?
Win. My conjuration shall dispense with that.
You may be up as early as you please,
But hence to-night you shall not.
Y. Ger. You are powerful.
Win. This night, of purpose, I have parted beds,

---

[1] This must be taken as a verb.

Feigning myself not well, to give you meeting ;
Nor can be aught suspected by my wife,
I have kept all so private : now 'tis late,
I'll steal up to my rest.   But, howsoever,
Let's not be strange in our writing ; that way daily
We may confer without the least suspect,
In spite of all such base calumnious tongues.
So now good-night, sweet friend.   [*Exit.*

    Y. Ger. May He that made you
So just and good still guard you !—Not to bed ;
So I perhaps might oversleep myself,
And then my tardy waking might betray me
To the more early household ; thus as I am,
I'll rest me on this pallet.—But in vain :
I find no sleep can fasten on mine eyes,
There are in this disturbèd brain of mine
So many mutinous fancies.   This to me
Will be a tedious night ; how shall I spend it ?
No book that I can spy ? no company ?
A little let me recollect myself.
Oh, what more wishèd company can I find,
Suiting the apt occasion, time, and place,
Than the sweet contemplation of her beauty ;
And the fruition too, time may produce,
Of what is yet lent out ?   'Tis a sweet lady,
And every way accomplished : hath mere accident
Brought me thus near, and I not visit her ?
Should it arrive her ear, perhaps might breed
Our lasting separation ; for, 'twixt lovers,
No quarrels to unkindness.[1]   Sweet opportunity
Offers prevention, and invites me to't :
The house is known to me, the stairs and rooms ;
The way into her chamber frequently
Trodden by me at midnight, and all hours :
How joyful to her would a meeting be,
So strange and unexpected—shadowed too
Beneath the veil of night !   I am resolved

---

[1] No quarrels are so bitter as those caused by unkindness.

To give her visitation in that place
Where we have passed deep vows—her bed-chamber :
My fiery love this darkness makes seem bright,
And this the path that leads to my delight,
          [*Goes in at one door, and comes out at another.*[1]
And this the gate unto't.—I'll listen first,
Before too rudely I disturb her rest
And gentle breathing.   Ha ! she's sure awake,
For in the bed two whisper, and their voices
Appear to me unequal ;—one a woman's—
And hers !   The other should be no maid's tongue,
It bears too big a tone.   And hark, they laugh—
Damnation !   But list further ; t'other sounds
Like—'tis the same false perjured Delavil, traitor
To friend and goodness.   Unchaste, impious woman,
False to all faith and true conjugal love ;
There's met a serpent and a crocodile,
A Sinon and a Circe.   Oh, to what
May I compare you ?——Out, my sword !
I'll act a noble execution
On two unmatched for sordid villany.—
I left it in my chamber, and thank Heaven
That I did so ! it hath prevented me
From playing a base hangman.   Sin securely,
Whilst I, although for many yet less faults,
Strive hourly to repent me !   I once loved her,
And was to him entire.   Although I pardon,
Heaven will find time to punish : I'll not stretch
My just revenge so far as once by blabbing
To make your brazen impudence to blush—
Damn on—revenge too great ; and, to suppress
Your souls yet lower, without hope to rise,
Heap Ossa upon Pelion.   You have made me
To hate my very country, because here bred
Near two such monsters.   First I'll leave this house,

[1] The old stage was wanting in moveable scenery.   The audience
had to suppose that when Young Geraldine re-entered, he was out
side Mistress Wincott's chamber.

And then my father's ; next I'll take my leave,
Both of this clime and nation, travel till
Age snow upon this head.   My passions now
Are unexpressible; I'll end them thus :
Ill man, bad woman, your unheard-of treachery
This unjust censure on a just man give,—
To seek out place where no two such can live.   [*Exit.*

SCENE IV.—*Another Room in the House.*

Enter DELAVIL *in a nightgown, and* Wife *in night attire.*

Del. A happy morning now betide you, lady,
To equal the content of a sweet night.

Wife. It hath been to my wish, and your desire ;
And this your coming by pretended love
Unto my sister Prue cuts off suspicion
Of any such converse 'twixt you and me.

Del. It hath been wisely carried.

Wife. One thing troubles me.

Del. What's that, my dearest ?

Wife. Why, your friend Geraldine
Should on the sudden thus absent himself :
Has he had, think you, no intelligence
Of these our private meetings ?

Del. No, on my soul,
For therein hath my brain exceeded yours :
I, studying to engross you to myself,
Of his continued absence have been cause ;
Yet he of your affection no way jealous,
Or of my friendship.   How the plot was cast,
You at our better leisure shall partake :
The air grows cold, have care unto your health ;
Suspicious eyes are o'er us, that yet sleep,
But with the dawn will open. Sweet, retire you
To your warm sheets ; I now to fill my own,
That have this night been empty.

Wife. You advise well :
Oh, might this kiss dwell ever on thy lips
In my remembrance !
  Del. Doubt it not, I pray,
Whilst day frights night, and night pursues the day.
Good-morrow.   [*Exeunt.*

SCENE V.—*A Room in* Old LIONEL'S *House.*

Enter REIGNALD *with a key in his hand,* Young LIONEL,
  BLANDA, SCAPHA, RIOTER, *and two* Gallants.

  Reig. Now is the gaol delivery ; through this back ga'e
Shift for yourselves ; I here unprison all.
  Y. Lio. But tell me, how shall we dispose ourselves ?
We are as far to seek now as at the first ;
What is it to reprieve us for few hours,
And now to suffer ? better had it been
At first to have stood the trial, so by this
We might have passed our penance.
  Blan. Sweet Reignald !
  Y. Lio. Honest rogue !
  Rio. If now thou fail'st us, then we are lost for ever.
  Reig. This same sweet Reignald, and this honest rogue,
Hath been the burgess under whose protection
You all this while have lived, free from arrests ;
But now the sessions of my power's broke up,
And you exposed to actions, warrants, writs ;
For all the hellish rabble are broke loose,
Of serjeants, sheriffs, and bailiffs.
  All. Guard us, Heaven !
  Reig. I tell you as it is ; nay, I myself
That have been your protector, now as subject
To every varlet's pestle, for you know
How I am engaged with you——At whose suit, sir ?
  Heywood.   Q

All. Why didst thou start ?   [*They all start.*
Reig. I was afraid some catchpole stood behind me,
To clap me on the shoulder.
Rio. No such thing ;
Yet I protest thy fear did fright us all.
Reig. I knew your guilty consciences.
Y. Lio. No brain left ?
Blan. No crotchet for my sake ?
Reig. One kiss then, sweet ;
Thus shall my crotchets and your kisses meet.
Y. Lio. Nay, tell us what to trust to.
Reig. Lodge yourselves
In the next tavern ; there's the cash that's left
Go, health it freely for my good success :
Nay, drown it all, let not a tester¹ scape
To be consumed in rot-gut :² I have begun,
And I will stand the period.
Y. Lio. Bravely spoke.
Reig. Or perish in the conflict.
Rio. Worthy Reignald—
Reig. Will, if he now come off well, fox you all ;³
Go, call for wine ; for singly of myself
I will oppose all danger ; but I charge you,
When I shall faint or find myself distressed,
If I, like brave Orlando,⁴ wind my horn,
Make haste unto my rescue.
Y. Lio. And die in't.
Reig. Well hast thou spoke, my noble Charlemain
With these thy peers about thee.
Y. Lio. May good speed
Attend thee still !
Reig. The end still crowns the deed.   [*Exeunt.*

¹ A sixpence.   ² Cheap ale.
³ Make you all drunk.   ⁴ Alluding to " Orlando Furioso."

SCENE VI.—*Outside* Old LIONEL'S *House.*

Enter Old LIONEL, *and the former* Owner *of the House.*

Owner. Sir, sir, your threats nor warrants can fright me ;
My honesty and innocency's known
Always to have been unblemished ; would you could
As well approve your own integrity
As I shall doubtless acquit myself
Of this surmisèd murder.

O. Lio. Rather surrender
The price I paid, and take into thy hands
This haunted mansion, or I'll prosecute
My wrong, even to the utmost of the law,
Which is no less than death.

Owner. I'll answer all,
Old Lionel, both to thy shame and scorn ;
This [*Snapping his fingers*] for thy menaces !

Enter Clown.

Clown. This is the house, but where's the noise that
was wont to be in't ?   I am sent hither to deliver a note
to two young gentlemen that here keep revel-rout ; I
remember it, since the last massacre of meat that was
made in't; but it seems that the great storm that was
raised then is chased now.   I have other notes to deliver,
one to Master Ricott—and—I shall think on them
all in order.   My old master makes a great feast for the
parting of young Master Geraldine, who is presently upon
his departure for travel, and, the better to grace it, hath
invited many of his neighbours and friends, where will
be old Master Geraldine, his son, and I cannot tell
how many.   But this is strange ; the gates shut up at
this time o' day ! belike they are all drunk and laid to
sleep; if they be, I'll wake them, with a murrain !

[*Knocks.*

O. Lio. What desperate fellow's this, that, ignorant
Of his own danger, thunders at these gates ?

Clown. Ho, Reignald! riotous Reignald, revelling
Reignald!

O. Lio. What madness doth possess thee, honest friend,
To touch that hammer's handle?

Clown. What madness doth possess thee, honest
friend,
To ask me such a question?

O. Lio. [*To* Owner.] Nay, stir not you.

Owner. Not I.   The game begins.

O. Lio. How dost thou? art thou well?

Clown. Yes, very well, I thank you; how do you, sir?

O. Lio. No alteration: what change about thee?

Clown. Not so much change about me at this time as
to change you a shilling into two testers.

O. Lio. Yet I advise thee, fellow, for thy good,
Stand further from the gate.

Clown. And I advise thee, friend, for thine own good,
stand not betwixt me and the gate, but give me leave to
deliver my errand.   Ho! Reignald, you mad rascal!

O. Lio. In vain thou thunder'st at these silent doors,
Where no man dwells to answer, saving ghosts,
Furies, and sprites.

Clown. Ghosts! indeed there has been much walking
in and about the house after midnight.

O. Lio. Strange noise oft heard?

Clown. Yes, terrible noise, that none of the neighbours could take any rest for it.   I have heard it myself.

O. Lio. You hear this? Here's more witness.

Owner. Very well, sir.

O. Lio. Which you shall dearly answer.—Whooping?

Clown. And hollooing.

O. Lio. And shouting?

Clown. And crying out, till the whole house rung again.

O. Lio. Which thou hast heard?

Clown. Oftener than I have toes and fingers.

O. Lio. Thou wilt be deposed of this?

Clown. I'll be sworn to't, and that's as good.

O. Lio. Very good still ;—yet you are innocent.
Shall I entreat thee, friend, to avouch as much
Hereby to the next justice?

Clown. I'll take my soldier's oath on't.

O. Lio. A soldier's oath—what's that?

Clown. My corporal oath; and you know, sir, a
corporal is an office belonging to a soldier.

O. Lio. Yet you are clear? Murder will come to light.

Owner. So will your gullery [1] too.

Enter ROBIN.

Rob. They say my old master's come home ; I'll see if
he will turn me out of doors, as the young man has done.
I have laid rods in piss for somebody; scape Reignald
as he can ; and with more freedom than I durst late, I
boldly now dare knock.   [*Knocks.*

O. Lio. More madmen yet ! I think since my last voyage
Half of the world's turned frantic.   What dost mean?
Or long'st thou to be blasted?

Rob. Oh, sir, you are welcome home ; 'twas time to
    come,
Ere all was gone to havoc.

O. Lio. My old servant !
Before I shall demand of further business,
Resolve me why thou thunder'st at these doors,
Where thou know'st none inhabits?

Rob. Are they gone, sir?
'Twas well they have left the house behind ;
For all the furniture, to a bare bench,
I am sure is spent and wasted.

O. Lio. Where's my son,
That Reignald, posting for him with such speed,
Brings him not from the country?

Rob. Country, sir !
'Tis a thing they know not : here they feast,
Dice, drink, and drab; the company they keep,

---

[1] Trickery.

Cheaters and roaring-lads, and these attended
By bawds and queans; your son hath got a strumpet
On whom he spends all that your sparing left;
And here they keep court, to whose damned abuses
Reignald gives all encouragement.

O. Lio. But stay, stay:
No living soul hath for these six months' space
Here entered, but the house stood desolate.

Rob. Last week I am sure, so late, and the other day,
Such revels were here kept.

O. Lio. And by my son?

Rob. Yes, and his servant Reignald.

O. Lio. And this house
At all not haunted?

Rob. Save, sir, with such sprites.

Owner. This murder will come out.

Enter RICOTT.

O. Lio. But see, in happy time here comes my
neighbour
Of whom he bought this mansion; he, I am sure,
More amply can resolve me.—I pray, sir,
What sums of moneys have you late received
Of my young son?

Ric. Of him? None, I assure you.

O. Lio. What of my servant Reignald?

Ric. But devise
What to call less than nothing, and that sum
I will confess received.

O. Lio. Pray, sir, be serious:
I do confess myself indebted to you
A hundred pound.

Ric. You may do well to pay't then, for here's witness
Sufficient of your words.

O. Lio. I speak no more
Than what I purpose; just so much I owe you,
And ere I sleep will tender.

Ric. I shall be
As ready to receive it, and as willing
As you can be to pay it.
  O. Lio. But provided
You will confess seven hundred pounds received
Beforehand of my son.

Ric. But, by your favour,
Why should I yield seven hundred pounds received
Of them I never dealt with ?   Why ?   For what ?
What reason ?   What condition ?   Where or when
Should such a sum be paid me ?
  O. Lio. Why ? for this bargain.   And for what ? this
    house.
Reason ? because you sold it.   The conditions ?
Such as were agreed between you.   Where and when ?
That only hath escaped me.
  Ric. Madness all.
  O. Lio. Was I not brought to take free view thereof,
As of mine own possession ?
  Ric. I confess
Your servant told me you had found out a wife ·
Fit for your son, and that you meant to build ;
Desired to take a friendly view of mine,
To make it your example : but for selling,
I tell you, sir, my wants be not so great
To change my house to coin.
  O. Lio. Spare, sir, your anger,
And turn it into pity.   Neighbours and friends,
I am quite lost ; was never man so fooled,
And by a wicked servant !   Shame and blushing
Will not permit to tell the manner how,
Lest I be made ridiculous to all :
My fears are, to inherit what's yet left,
He hath made my son away.
  Rob. That's my fear too.
  O. Lio. Friends, as you would commiserate a man
Deprived at once both of his wealth and son,

And in his age, by one I ever tendered
More like a son than servant, by imagining
My case were yours, have feeling of my griefs
And help to apprehend him : furnish me
With cords and fetters; I will lay him safe
In prison within prison.
    Ric. We'll assist you.
    Rob. And I.
    Clown. And all.—But not to do the least hurt to my
old friend Reignald.   [*Aside.*
    O. Lio. His legs will be as nimble as his brain,
And 'twill be difficult to seize the slave,
Yet your endeavours, pray. Peace ! here he comes.

    Enter REIGNALD *with a horn in his pocket; the
        rest withdraw,*[1] *excepting* Old LIONEL.

    Reig. My heart misgives, for 'tis not possible
But that in all these windings and indents [2]
I shall be found at last : I'll take that course
That men both troubled and affrighted do,—
Heap doubt on doubt, and, as combustions rise,
Try if from many I can make my peace,
And work mine own atonement.
    O. Lio. [*Aside.*] Stand you close,
Be not yet seen, but at your best advantage
Hand him, and bind him fast ; whilst I dissemble
As if I yet knew nothing.
    Reig. I suspect
And find there's trouble in my master's looks ;
Therefore I must not trust myself too far
Within his fingers.
    O. Lio. Reignald !
    Reig. Worshipful sir.
    O. Lio. What says my son i' the country?
    Reig. That to-morrow,
Early i' the morning, he'll attend your pleasure,

---

[1] The old edition adds "behind the arras."   [2] Schemes, shifts.

And do as all such duteous children ought—
Demand your blessing, sir.

   O. Lio. Well, 'tis well.

   Reig. I do not like his countenance.   [*Aside.*

   O. Lio. But, Reignald, I suspect the honesty
And the good meaning of my neighbour here,
Old Master Ricott. Meeting him but now,
And having some discourse about the house,
He makes all strange, and tells me in plain terms
He knows of no such matter.

   Reig. Tell me that, sir!

   O. Lio. I tell thee as it is : nor that such moneys,
Took up at use, were ever tendered him
On any such conditions.

   Reig. I cannot blame
Your worship to be pleasant, knowing at what
An under-rate we bought it ; but you ever
Were a most merry gentleman.

   O. Lio. Impudent slave !   [*Aside.*
But, Reignald, he not only doth deny it,
But offers to depose himself and servants
No such thing ever was.

   Reig. Now, Heaven to see
To what this world is grown to ! I will make him—

   O. Lio. Nay more, this man will not confess the
    murder.

   Reig. Which both shall dearly answer ; you have
    warrant
For him already ; but for the other, sir,
If he deny it, he had better—

   O. Lio. Appear, gentlemen ;   [*Softly.*
'Tis a fit time to take him.

   Reig. [*Aside.*] I discover
The ambush that's laid for me.

   O. Lio. Come nearer, Reignald.

   Reig. First, sir,
Resolve me one thing : amongst other merchandize

Bought in your absence by your son and me,
We engrossed a great commodity of combs,
And how many sorts, think you ?

O. Lio. You might buy
Some of the bones of fishes, some of beasts,
Box-combs, and ivory-combs.

Reig. But, besides these, we have for horses, sir,
Mane-combs and curry-combs ; now, sir, for men
We have head-combs, beard-combs, ay, and cox-combs
    too ;
Take view of them at your pleasure, whilst for my part
I thus bestow myself.

    [*Whilst he climbs to the balcony, they come for-*
    ward with cords and shackles.

Clown. Well said, Reignald ; nobly put off, Reignald ;
look to thyself, Reignald.

O. Lio. Why dost thou climb thus?

Reig. Only to practise the nimbleness of my arms and
legs, ere they prove your cords and fetters.

O. Lio. Why to that place ?

Reig. Why ! because, sir, 'tis your own house.   It hath
    been
My harbour long, and now it must be my sanctuary ;
Dispute now, and I'll answer.

Owner. Villain, what devilish meaning hadst thou in't,
To challenge me of murder ?

Reig. Oh, sir, the man you killed is alive at this
present to justify it :
" I am," quoth he, " a trans-marine by birth "—

Ric. Why challenge me
Receipt of moneys, and to give abroad
That I had sold my house ?

Reig. Why ! because, sir,
Could I have purchased houses at that rate,
I had meant to have bought all London.

Clown. Yes, and Middlesex too ; and I would have
been thy half, Reignald.

O. Lio. Yours are great,
My wrongs insufferable.   As first, to fright me
From mine own dwelling, till they had consumed
The whole remainder of the little left ;
Besides, out of my late stock got at sea,
Discharge the clamorous usurer ; make me accuse
This man of murder ; be at charge of warrants ;
And challenging this my worthy neighbour of
Forswearing sums he never yet received ;
Fool me, to think my son, that had spent all,
Had by his thrift bought land ; ay, and him too,
To open all the secrets of his house
To me, a stranger !   O thou insolent villain,
What to all these canst answer ?

Reig. Guilty, guilty.

O. Lio. But to my son's death, what, thou slave ?

Reig. Not guilty.

O. Lio. Produce him then ; i' the meantime, and—
Honest friends, get ladders.

Reig. Yes, and come down in your own ropes.

Owner. I'll fetch a piece,[1] and shoot him.

Reig. So the warrant in my master's pocket will serve for
my murder ; and ever after shall my ghost haunt this house.

Clown. And I will say, like Reignald, " this ghost and
I am friends."

O. Lio. Bring faggots; I'll set fire upon the house
Rather than this endure.

Reig. To burn houses is felony, and I'll not out till I
be fired out ; but, since I am besieged thus, I'll summon
supplies unto my rescue.   [*He winds the horn.*

Enter Young LIONEL, RIOTER, *two* Gallants, BLANDA,
SCAPHA, *and others.*

Y. Lio. Before you chide, first hear me ; next your
        blessing,
That on my knees I beg.   I have but done

---
[1] Gun.

Like misspent youth, which, after wit dear-bought,
Turns his eyes inward, sorry and ashamed.
These things in which I have offended most,
Had I not proved, I should have thought them still
Essential things, delights perdurable;
Which now I find mere shadows, toys and dreams,
Now hated more than erst I doted on.
Best natures are soon'st wrought on ; such was mine ;
As I the offences, so the offenders throw
Here at your feet, to punish as you please ;
You have but paid so much as I have wasted,
To purchase to yourself a thrifty son,
Which I from henceforth vow.

 O. Lio. See what fathers are,
That can three years' offences, foul ones too,
Thus in a minute pardon ; and thy faults
Upon myself chastise, in these my tears.
Ere this submission, I had cast thee off ;
Rise in my new adoption.   But for these—

 Clown. The one you have nothing to do withal ; here's
his ticket for his discharge : another for you, sir, to
summon you to my master's feast,—for you, and you,—
where I charge you all to appear, upon his displeasure
and your own apperils.

 Y. Lio. This is my friend, the other one I loved ;
Only because they have been dear to him
That now will strive to be more dear to you,
Vouchsafe their pardon.

 O. Lio. All dear to me indeed,
For I have paid for't soundly, yet for thy sake
I am atoned with all ; only that wanton,
Her and her company, abandon quite ;
So doing, we are friends.

 Y. Lio. A just condition, and willingly subscribed to.

 O. Lio. But for that villain ; I am now devising
What shame, what punishment remarkable
To inflict on him.

Reig. Why, master ! have I laboured,
Plotted, contrived, and all this while for you,
And will you leave me to the whip and stocks ;
Not mediate my peace ?

O. Lio. Sirrah, come down.

Reig. Not till my pardon's sealed; I'll rather stand
  here
Like a statue, in the fore-front of your house,
For ever, like the picture of Dame Fortune
Before the Fortune play-house.[1]

Y. Lio. If I have here
But any friend amongst you, join with me
In this petition.

Clown. Good sir, for my sake ! I resolved you truly
concerning whooping, the noise, the walking, and the
sprites, and for a need can show you a ticket for him
too.

Owner. I impute my wrongs rather to knavish
  cunning
Than least pretended malice.

Ric. What he did
Was but for his young master ; I allow it
Rather as sports of wit than injuries ;
No other, pray, esteem them.

O. Lio. Even as freely
As you forget my quarrels made with you,
Raised from the errors first begot by him,
I here remit all free. I now am calm,
But had I seized upon him in my spleen—

Reig. I knew that, therefore this was my invention,
For policy's the art still of prevention.

Clown. Come down, then, Reignald,—first on your
hands and feet, and then on your knees to your master.—

[1] The first theatre of this name, built by Henslowe and Alleyn,
was burnt down in 1621 : another theatre was erected on the site in
1622, and in old views of the latter a rudely carved figure, presum-
ably of Fortune, is noticeable on the front of the house.—(See
frontispiece to Dekker's Plays in this series.)

Now, gentlemen, what do you say to your inviting to my
master's feast ?

Ric. We will attend him.

O. Lio. Nor do I love to break good company,
For Master Wincott is my worthy friend
And old acquaintance—

REIGNALD *descends.*

Oh, thou crafty wag-string !
And couldst thou thus delude me ? But we are friends.—
Nor, gentlemen, let not what's hereto past,
In your least thoughts disable my estate :
This my last voyage hath made all things good,
With surplus too.; be that your comfort, son.
Well, Reignald——But no more.

Reig. I was the fox,
But I from henceforth will no more the cox—
Comb put upon your pate.

O. Lio. Let's walk, gentlemen.   [*Exeunt.*

ACT THE FIFTH.

SCENE I.—*Outside* Old WINCOTT'S *House*.

Enter Old GERALDINE *and* Young GERALDINE.

LD GER.   Son, let me tell you, you are
    ill advised,
And doubly to be blamed, by under-
    taking
Unnecessary travel, grounding   no
    reason
For such a rash and giddy enterprise.
What profit aim you at, you have not reaped ?
What novelty affords the Christian world,
Of which your view hath not participated
In a full measure ?   Can you either better
Your language or experience ?   Your self-will
Hath only purpose to deprive a father
Of a loved son, and many noble friends
Of your much-wished acquaintance.
    Y. Ger. Oh, dear sir,
Do not, I do entreat you, now repent you
Of your free grant, which with such care and study
I have so long, so often laboured for.
    O. Ger. Say that may be dispensed with, show me reason
Why you desire to steal out of your country,
Like some malefactor that had forfeited
His life and freedom.   Here's a worthy gentleman

Hath for your sake invited many guests,
To his great charge, only to take of you
A parting leave : you send him word you cannot—
After, you may not come. Had not my urgence,
Almost compulsion, driven you to his house,
The unkindness might have forfeited your love,
And razed you from his will ; in which he hath given you
A fair and large estate ; yet you of all this strangeness
Show no sufficient ground.

 Y. Ger. Then understand
The ground thereof took his first birth from you ;
'Twas you first charged me to forbear the house,
And that upon your blessing. Let it not then
Offend you, sir, if I so great a charge
Have strived to keep so strictly.

 O. Ger. Me perhaps
You may appease, and with small difficulty,
Because a father ; but how satisfy
Their dear and, on your part, unmerited love ?
But this your last obedience may salve all.
We now grow near the house.

 Y. Ger. Whose doors, to me,
Appear as horrid as the gates of Hell.
Where shall I borrow patience, or from whence,
To give a meeting to this viperous brood
Of friend and mistress?   [*They enter the house.*

  SCENE II.—*A Room in* Old WINCOTT'S *House.*

Enter WINCOTT, *his Wife, the two* LIONELS, Owner,
 DELAVIL, PRUDENTILLA, REIGNALD, *and* RIOTER.

 Win. You've entertained me with a strange discourse
Of your man's knavish wit ; but I rejoice
That in your safe return all ends so well.
Most welcome you, and you, and indeed all ;

To whom I am bound, that at so short a warning,
Thus friendly, you will deign to visit me. .
 O. Lio. It seems my absence hath begot some
  sport ;
Thank my kind servant here.
 Reig. Not so much worth, sir.
 O. Lio. But, though their riots tripped at my estate,
They have not quite o'erthrown it.

   Enter Old *and* Young GERALDINE.

 Win. But see, gentlemen,
These whom we most expected come at length.
This I proclaim the master of the feast,
In which, to express the bounty of my love,
I'll show myself no niggard. .
 Y. Ger. Your choice favours
I still taste in abundance.
 Wife. Methinks it would not misbecome me, sir,
To chide your absence, that have made yourself
To us so long a stranger.
    [Young GERALDINE *turns sadly away.*
 Y. Ger. Pardon me, sir,
That have not yet, since your return from sea,
Voted [1] the least fit opportunity
To entertain you with a kind salute.
 O. Lio. Most kindly, sir, I thank you.
 Del. Methinks, friend,
You should expect green rushes [2] to be strowed
After such discontinuance.
 Y. Ger. Mistress Prue,
I have not seen you long, but greet you thus :
May you be lady of a better husband
Than I expect a wife !
 Win. I like that greeting.
Nay, enter, gentlemen ; dinner perhaps

---

 [1] *i. e.* Chosen.
 [2] With which floors were usually covered by way of carpet.
Heywood.   K

Is not yet ready, but the time we stay,
We'll find some fresh discourse to spend away.

                 [Exeunt all but DELAVIL.

Del. Not speak to me, nor once vouchsafe an answer,
But slight me with a poor and base neglect !
No, nor so much as cast an eye on her,
Or least regard, though in a seeming show
She courted a reply ! 'Twixt him and her,
Nay, him and me, this was not wont to be ;
If she have brain to apprehend as much
As I have done, she'll quickly find it out.—

       Re-enter Young GERALDINE *and* Wife.

Now, as I live, as our affections meet,
So our conceits, and she hath singled him
To some such purpose.   I'll retire myself,
Not interrupt their conference.   *[Exit.*

    Wife. You are sad, sir.

    Y. Ger. I know no cause.

    Wife. Then can I show you some.
Who could be otherways, to leave a father
So careful, and each way so provident ?
To leave so many and such worthy friends ?
To abandon your own country ?   These are some ;
Nor do I think you can be much the merrier
For my sake.

    Y. Ger. Now your tongue speaks oracles ;
For all the rest are nothing : 'tis for you—
Only for you I cannot.

    Wife. So I thought ;
Why, then, have you been all this while so strange ?
Why will you travel, suing a divorce
Betwixt us of a love inseparable ;
For here shall I be left as desolate
Unto a frozen, almost widowed bed,
Warmed only in that future stored in you ;
For who can in your absence comfort me ?

Y. Ger. [*Aside.*] Shall my oppressèd sufferance yet
    break forth
Into impatience, or endure her more ?
    Wife. But since by no persuasion, no entreats,
Your settled obstinacy can be swayed,
Though you seem desperate of your own dear life,
Have care of mine, for it exists in you.
Oh, sir, should you miscarry I were lost,
Lost and forsaken ! Then, by our past vows,
And by this hand once given me, by these tears
Which are but springs begetting greater floods,
I do beseech thee, my dear Geraldine,
Look to thy safety, and preserve thy health ;
Have care into what company you fall ;
Travel not late, and cross no dangerous seas ;
For till Heavens bless me in thy safe return,
How will this poor heart suffer !
    Y. Ger. [*Aside.*] I had thought
Long since the sirens had been all destroyed ;
But one of them I find survives in her :
She almost makes me question what I know,
A heretic unto my own belief :—
O thou mankind's seducer !
    Wife. What, no answer !
    Y. Ger. Yes, thou hast spoke to me in showers ; I will
Reply in thunder : thou adulteress,
That hast more poison in thee than the serpent
Who was the first that did corrupt thy sex,
The devil !
    Wife. To whom speaks the man ?
    Y. Ger. To thee,
Falsest of all that ever man termed fair.
Hath impudence so steeled thy smooth soft skin,
It cannot blush ? Or sin so obdured thy heart,
It doth not quake and tremble ? Search thy conscience ;
There thou shalt find a thousand clamorous tongues
To speak as loud as mine doth.

Wife. Save from yours,
I hear no noise at all.
  Y. Ger. I'll play the doctor
To open thy deaf ears.   Monday the ninth
Of the last month—canst thou remember that,
That night more black in thy abhorrèd sin
Than in the gloomy darkness ?—that the time.
  Wife. Monday !
  Y. Ger. Wouldst thou the place know ?—thy polluted
      chamber,
So often witness of my sinless vows.
Wouldst thou the person ?—one not worthy name,
Yet, to torment thy guilty soul the more,
I'll tell him thee—that monster Delavil.
Wouldst thou your bawd know ?—midnight, that the hour.
The very words thou spake ?—" Now what would
      Geraldine
Say, if he saw us here ? "—to which was answered,
" Tush, he's a coxcomb, fit to be so fooled ! "
No blush !   What, no faint fever on thee yet !
How hath thy black sins changed thee !   Thou Medusa !
Those hairs that late appeared like golden wires
Now crawl with snakes and adders.   Thou art ugly.
  Wife. And yet my glass, till now, ne'er told me so.
Who gave you this intelligence ?
  Y. Ger. Only He
That, pitying such an innocency as mine
Should by two such delinquents be betrayed,—
He brought me to that place by miracle,
And made me an ear-witness of all this.
  Wife. I am undone !
  Y. Ger. But think what thou hast lost
To forfeit me ! I, notwithstanding these,
(So fixèd was my love and unalterable,)
I kept this from thy husband, nay, all ears,
With thy transgressions smothering mine own wrongs,
In hope of thy repentance.

Wife. Which begins
Thus low upon my knees—
Y. Ger. Tush ! bow to Heaven,
Which thou hast most offended ; I, alas !
Save in such scarce unheard-of treachery,
Most sinful, like thyself.   Wherein, oh, wherein
Hath my unspotted and unbounded love
Deserved the least of these?   Sworn to be made a
.   stale
For term of life, and all this for my goodness !
Die, and die soon ; acquit me of my oath,
But prithee die repentant.   Farewell ever :
'Tis thou, and only thou, hast banished me
Both from my friends and country.
    Wife. Oh, I am lost !   [*Sinks down.*

Re-enter DELAVIL, *meeting* Young GERALDINE *going out.*

    Del. Why, how now, what's the business?
    Y. Ger. Go, take her up, whom thou hast oft thrown
        down.
Villain !   .   [*Exit.*
    Del. That was no language from a friend,
It had too harsh an accent.   But how's this ?
My mistress thus low cast upon the earth,
Grovelling and breathless !   Mistress, lady, sweet—
    Wife. Oh, tell me if thy name be Geraldine :
Thy very looks will kill me :
    Del. View me well ;
I am no such man ; see, I am Delavil.
    Wife. Thou'rt then a devil, that presents before me
My horrid sins, persuades me to despair,
When he, like a good angel sent from Heaven,
Besought me of repentance.   Swell, sick heart,
Even till thou burst the ribs that bound thee in !
So, there's one string cracked.   Flow, and flow high,
Even till thy blood distil out of mine eyes,
To witness my great sorrow.

Del. Faint again !
Some help within there !   No attendant near ?
Thus to expire !   In this I am more wretched
Than all the sweet fruition of her love
Before could make me happy.

Re-enter WINCOTT, Old GERALDINE, Young GERALDINE,
   the two LIONELS, RICOTT, Owner, PRUDENTILLA,
   and REIGNALD ; *also enter* Clown.

Win. What was he
Clamoured so loud, to mingle with our mirth
This terror and affright ?
   Del. See, sir, your wife
In these my arms expiring.
   Win. How !
   Prud. My sister !
   Win. Support her, and by all means possible
Provide for her dear safety.
   O. Ger. Sèe, she recovers.
   Win. Woman, look up.
   Wife. Oh, sir, your pardon !
Convey me to my chamber ; I am sick,
Sick even to death.   Away, thou sycophant,
Out of my sight ! I have, besides thyself,
Too many sins about me.
   Clown. My sweet mistress !
             [PRUDENTILLA *and* Clown *lead* Wife *off.*
   Del. The storm is coming ; I must provide for harbour.
                                              [*Exit.*
   O. Lio. What strange and sudden alteration's this !
How quickly is this clear day overcast !
But such and so uncertain are all things
That dwell beneath the moon.
   Y. Lio. A woman's qualm,
Frailties that are inherent to her sex—
Soon sick, and soon recovered.
   Win. If she misfare,

I am a man more wretched in her loss
Than had I forfeited life and estate ;
She was so good a creature.
    O. Ger. I the like
Suffered, when I my wife brought to her grave ;
So you, when you were first a widower :
Come, arm yourself with patience.
    Ric. These are casualties
That are not new, but common.
    Reig. Burying of wives !—
As stale as shifting shirts, or for some servants
To flout and gull their masters.
    Owner. Best to send
And see how her fit holds her.

              Re-enter PRUDENTILLA *and* Clown.

    Pru. Sir, my sister
In these few lines commends her last to you,
For she is now no more.   What's therein writ;
Save Heaven and you, none knows : this she desired.
You would take view of, and with these words expired.
    Win. Dead !
    Y. Ger. She hath made me then a free release
Of all the debts I owed her.
    Win [*Aside, reading*] "My fear[1] is beyond pardon.
        Delavil
Hath played the villain ; but for Geraldine,
He hath been each way noble ; love him still.
My peace already I have made with Heaven ;
Oh, be not you at war with me ! my honour
Is in your hands to punish, or preserve ;
I am now confessed, and only Geraldine
Hath wrought on me this unexpected good.
The ink I write with, I wish had been my blood,
To witness my repentance."—Delavil !
Where's he ? go seek him out.

                   [1] ? Sin.

Clown. I shall, I shall, sir.   [*Exit.*

Win. The wills of dead folk should be still obeyed :
However false to me, I'll not reveal't ;
Where Heaven forgives, I pardon.—Gentlemen,
I know you all commiserate my loss ;
I little thought this feast should have been turned
Into a funeral.—

Re-enter Clown.

                        What's the news of him ?
Clown. He went presently[1] to the stable, put the saddle
upon his horse, put his foot into the stirrup, clapped his
spurs into his sides, and away he's galloped, as if he were
to ride a race for a wager.

Win. All our ill lucks go with him !   Farewell he !
But all my best of wishes wait on you,
                              [*To* Young GERALDINE.
As my chief friend ! This meeting, that was made
Only to take of you a parting leave,
Shall now be made a marriage of our love,
Which none save only death shall separate.

Y. Ger. It calls me from all travel, and from hence-
            forth
With my country I am friends.

Win. The lands that I have left,
You lend me for the short space of my life ;
As soon as Heaven calls me, they call you lord.—
First feast, and after mourn ; we'll, like some gallants
That bury thrifty fathers, think't no sin
To wear blacks without, but other thoughts within.
                                        [*Exeunt.*

¹ Immediately

THE WISE-WOMAN OF

HOGSDON.

 *HE WISE-WOMAN OF HOGSDON*
was printed in 1638. Of its history
nothing is known ; that it was popular is
implied by the statement on the title-
page—"As it hath been sundry times
acted with great applause." The technical
cleverness of the last Act is noticeable.
In the original editions the play is divided into acts but not
into scenes. These are now indicated for the first time.

Hogsdon, *i.e.* Hoxton, in the parish of St. Leonard's,
Shoreditch, was described by Stow, in 1598, as "a large
street with houses on both sides." It was in the adjacent
fields that the duel was fought between Ben Jonson and
Gabriel Spenser, a player belonging to Henslowe's company, which resulted in the death of the latter and put
Jonson in peril of his life.

DRAMATIS PERSONÆ.

Young CHARTLEY, a wild-headed Gentleman.
BOYSTER, a blunt Fellow.
SENCER, a conceited Gentleman.
HARINGFIELD, a civil Gentleman.
LUCE's Father, a Goldsmith.
JOSEPH, his Apprentice.
Old Master CHARTLEY.
Sir HARRY, a Knight, who is no Scholar.
Sir BONIFACE, an ignorant Schoolmaster.
Young CHARTLEY's Man.
Old CHARTLEY's Men.
TABER, Sir HARRY's Man.
A Countryman, Client to the Wise-Woman.
A Serving-man.

LUCE, a Goldsmith's Daughter.
The second LUCE.
GRATIANA, Sir HARRY's Daughter.
The Wise-Woman of Hogsdon.
A Kitchen-maid.
Two Citizens' Wives.

SCENE—LONDON and HOGSDON.

THE WISE-WOMAN OF HOGSDON.

— ··♦♪·♪·——

ACT THE FIRST.

SCENE I.—*A Room in a Tavern.*

Enter, as newly come from play, Young CHARTLEY,
SENCER, BOYSTER, *and* HARINGFIELD.

HART. Price of my life! now, if the devil
have bones,
These dice are made of his. Was ever
such
A cast seen in this age? Could any gull
In Europe, saving myself, fling such a cast?

Boys. Ay.

Y. Chart. No.

Boys. Yes.

Y. Chart. But I say no : I have lost an hundred pound,
And I will have my saying.

Boys. I have lost another hundred, I'll have mine.
Ay, yes, I flung a worse,—a worse by odds.

Y. Chart. I cry you mercy, sir ; losers may speak ;
I'll not except 'gainst you : but let me see
Which of these two that pocket up our cash
Dares contradict me?

Sen. Sir, not I :
I say you have had bad casting.

Har. So say I.

Y. Chart. I say this hat's not made of wool :
Which of you all dares say the contrary ?

Sen. It may be 'tis a beaver.

Har. Very likely so : 'tis not wool, but a plain beaver.

Y. Chart. 'Tis wool, but which of you dares say so ?—
[*Aside.*] I would fain pick a quarrel with them, to get
some of my money again ; but the slaves now they have
got it, are too wise to part with it.   I say it is not black.

Har. So say we too.

Boys. 'Tis false : his cap's of wool ; 'tis black and
wool, and wool and black.

Y. Chart. I have nought to say to losers.   Have I
nothing left to set at a cast ?   Ay, finger, must you be
set in gold, and not a jot of silver in my purse ?   A bale [1]
of fresh dice !   Ho, come at this ring !

Sen. Fie, Master Chartley !   'tis time to give over.

Y. Chart. That's the winner's phrase.   Hold me play,
or he that hath uncrowned me, I'll take a speedy order
with him.

Boys. Fresh dice !   This jewel I will venture more :
Take this and all.   I'll play in spite of luck.

Har. Since you will needs, trip for the dice.   I see it
is hard to go a winner from this company.

Y. Chart. The dice are mine.   This diamond I value
at twenty marks : [2]   I'll venture it at a throw.

Har. 'Tis set you.

Y. Chart. Then at all.   All's mine.   Nay, Master Boyster,
I bar you : let us work upon the winners.   Gramercy,
cinques !   Nay, though I owe you no quarrel, yet you
must give me leave to draw.

Har. I had rather you should draw your sword
Than draw my money thus.

Y. Chart. Again, sweet dice.   Nay, I bar swearing :

[1] Pair.   [2] A mark was worth 13*s*. 4*d*.

gentlemen, let's play patiently.   Well, this at the candle-
stick, so—   [*He throws out.*

Boys. Now, dice, at all.   Todo, quoth the Spaniard.

Sen. Here's precious luck.

Boys. Why, *via*!   I think 'tis quicksilver; it goes and
comes so fast: there's life in this.

Har. He passes all with treys.

Y. Chart. With treys, how say by that?   Oh, he's old
dog at bowls and treys!

Sen. Lend me some money : be my half one cast.
I'll once out-brave this gamester with a throw.
So, now the dice are mine, wilt be my half?

Har. I will.

Sen. Then once I'll play the frank gamester.
Let me but see how much you both can make,
And I'll cast at all, all, every cross.[1]

Y. Chart. Now, bless us all, what will you every
          cross?

Sen. I will not leave myself one cross to bless me.

Boys. I set.

Y. Chart. And so do I.

Sen. Why, then, at all.   How!   [*He flings out.*

Y. Chart. Nay, swear not ; let's play patiently.

Sen. Damned dice !   did ever gamester see the like?

Boys. Never, never.

Sen. Was ever known such casting?

Y. Chart. Drunk nor sober, I ne'er saw a man cast
worse.

Sen. I'll prove this hat of mine an helmet.   Which of
you here dares say the contrary?

Y. Chart. As fair an helmet as any man in Europe
needs to wear.

Sen. Chartley, thy hat is black.

Y. Chart. Upon better recollection, 'tis so indeed.

Sen. I say 'tis made of wool.

Y. Chart. True, my losing had took away my senses,

---

[1] Coins bearing a cross on the reverse, hence various quibbles.

Both of seeing and feeling ; but better luck
Hath brought them to their right temper.
But come—a pox of dice ! 'tis time to give over.

Sen. All times are times for winners to give over,
But not for them that lose. I'll play till midnight,
But I will change my luck.

Har. Come, come, you shall not.
Give over; tush, give over ; do, I pray,
And choose the fortune of some other hour :
Let's not, like debauched fellows, play our clothes,
Belts, rapiers, nor our needful ornaments :
'Tis childish, not becoming gentlemen.
Play was at first ordained to pass the time ;
And, sir, you but abuse the use of play
To employ it otherwise.

Sen. You may persuade me.
For once I'll leave a loser.

Y. Chart. Then come, put on your helmet ; let's leave
this abominable game, and find out some better exercise.
I cannot endure this chafing when men lose.

Sen. And there's not a more testy waspish companion
than thyself when thou art a loser, and yet thou must be
vexing others with " Play patiently, gentlemen, and let's
have no swearing."

Y. Chart. A sign that I can give good counsel better
than take it : but say, where be the prettiest wenches,
my hearts ?

Sen. Well remembered ; this puts me in mind of an
appointment I had with a gentlewoman of some respect.

Y. Chart. I have you, sir, I have you ; but I think
you will never have her : 'tis Gratiana, the knight's
daughter in Gracious Street.[1] Have I touched you ?

Sen. You have come somewhat near me, but touched
me not. Master Haringfield, will you bear me company
thither? Have you seen the gentlewoman, Master
Chartley?

[1] *i. e.* Gracechurch Street.

Y. Chart. Never, sir.

Sen. How have you heard of her?

Y. Chart. That she hath as other women have; that she goes for a maid, as others do, &c.[1]

Sen. I can assure you she is a proper gentlewoman. .

Y. Chart. Then, if she have you, she is like to have a proper gentleman.

Sen. You should tell them so that know it not. Adieu, gentlemen. [*Exeunt* SENCER *and* HARINGFIELD.

Boys. I am glad yet they go so lightly away. '

Y. Chart. What will you do, Master Boyster?

Boys. Somewhat.

Y. Chart. You will not acquaint me with your business?

Boys. No. I am in love; my head is full of proclamations. There is a thing called a virgin. Nature hath showed her art in making her. Court her I cannot, but I'll do as I may.

Y. Chart. Do you go or stay, sir?

Boys. Go.   [*Exit.*

Y. Chart. You before, I'll follow.—He thinks, with his blunt humour, to enter as far as I with my sharp. No, my true Trojan, no: there is a fair, sweet, modest rogue, her name is Luce; with this dandiprat, this pretty little ape's face, is yon blunt fellow in love; and no marvel, for she hath a brow bewitching, eyes ravishing, and a tongue enchanting; and, indeed, she hath no fault in the world but one, and that is, she is honest; and were it not for that, she were the only sweet rogue in Christendom. As I live, I love her extremely, and to enjoy her would give anything; but the fool stands in her own light, and will do nothing without marriage. But what should I do marrying? I can better endure gyves than bands of matrimony. But in this meditation, I am· glad I have won my money again. Nay, and she may be

---

1 " &c.," here and elsewhere, means that the actor may add more to the same effect, if he please.

Heywood.   S

glad of it too ; for the girl is but poor, and in my pocket
I have laid up a stock for her,—'tis put to use already.
And if I meet not with a dice-house or an ordinary by
the way, no question but I may increase it to a sum.
Well, I'll unto the Exchange to buy her some pretty
novelty : that done, I'll visit my little rascal, and solicit
instantly.   [*Exit.*

SCENE II.—*Before the* Goldsmith's *Shop.*

Enter LUCE *at work upon a laced handkerchief, and*
JOSEPH.

Luce. Where is my father, Joseph ?

Jos. Mistress, above,
And prays you to attend below a little.

Luce. I do not love to sit thus publicly ;
And yet upon the traffic of our wares
Our provident eyes and presence must still wait.
Do you attend the shop, I'll ply my work.
I see my father is not jealous of me,
That trusts me to the open view of all.
The reason is, he knows my thoughts are chaste,
And my care such, as that it needs the awe
Of no strict overseer.

Enter BOYSTER.

Boys. Yonder's Luce.—Save thee !

Luce. And you too, sir; you're welcome; want you
      aught,
I pray, in which our trade may furnish you ?

Boys. Yes.

Luce. Joseph, show the gentleman—

Boys. 'Tis here that I would buy.

Luce. What do you mean, sir ? speak, what is't you
      lack ?

I pray you wherefore do you fix your eyes
So firmly in my face ?   What would you have ?
  Boys. Thee.
  Luce. Me !
  Boys. Yes, thee.
  Luce. Your pleasure is to jest, and so I take it.
Pray give me leave, sir, to intend [1] my work.
  Boys. You are fair.
  Luce. You flout me.
  Boys. You are, go to, you are ;
I'd vex him that should say the contrary.
  Luce. Well, you may say your pleasure.
  Boys. I love thee.
  Luce. Oh, sir !
  Boys. As I live, I do.
  Luce. Now, as I am a true maid,
The most religious oath that I dare swear,
I hold myself indebted to your love ;
And I am sorry there remains in me
No power how to requite it.
  Boys. Love me ; prithee now, do, if thou canst.
  Luce. I cannot.
  Boys. Prithee, if thou canst.
  Luce. Indeed I cannot.
  Boys. Yet ask thine heart, and see what may be done.
  Luce. In troth, I am sorry you should spend a sigh
For my sake unrequited, or a tear,—
Ay, or a word.
  Boys. 'Tis no matter for my words, they are not many
and those not very wise ones neither.
  Luce. Yet I beseech you spend no more in vain.
I scorn you not ; disdain's as far from me
As are the two poles distant : therefore, sir,
Because I would not hold you in suspense,
But tell you what at first to trust unto,
Thus in a word, I must not fancy [2] you.

---

[1] *i.e.* Attend to.   [2] Love.

Boys. Must not!

Luce. I cannot, nor I may not.

Boys. I am gone:
Thou hast given me, Luce, a bone to gnaw upon. [*Exit.*

Luce. Alas, that beauty should be sought of more
Than can enjoy it!   Might I have my wish,
I would seem fair but only in his eye   .
That should possess me in a nuptial tie.

Enter Young CHARTLEY, *with gloves, ring, purse, &c.*

Y. Chart. Morrow, Luce; in exchange of this kiss,
see what I have brought thee from the Exchange.

Luce. What mean you, sir, by this?

Y. Chart. Guess that by the circumstance: here's a
ring, wear't for my sake; twenty angels, pocket them,
you fool.   Come, come, I know thou art a maid: say nay,
and take them.[1]

Luce. Sweet Master Chartley, do not fasten on me
More than with ease I can shake off: your gift
I reverence, yet refuse; and I pray tell me,
Why do you make so many errands hither,
Send me so many letters, fasten on me
So many favours?   What's your meaning in't?

Y. Chart. Hark in thine ear, I'll tell thee;—nay, hear
me out.   Is't possible so soft a body should have so hard
a soul?   Nay, now I know my penance; you will be angry,
and school me for tempting your modesty: a fig for this
modesty! it hinders many a good man from many a good
turn, and that's all the good it doth.   If thou but knew'st,
Luce, how I love thee, thou wouldst be far more
tractable.   Nay, I bar chiding when you speak; I'll stop thy
lips if thou dost but offer an angry word—by this hand,
I'll do't, and with this hand too.   Go to now, what
say you?

Luce. Sir, if you love me, as you say you do,
Show me the fruits thereof.

---

[1] " Maids say nay, and take it," was a proverbial saying.

Y. Chart. The stock I can ; thou mayst see the fruits hereafter.

Luce. Can I believe you love me, when you seek
The shipwreck of mine honour?

Y. Chart. Honour ! there's another word to flap in a man's mouth ! Honour ! what shouldst thou and I stand upon our honour, that were neither of us yet Right Worshipful?

Luce. I am sorry, sir, I have lent so large an ear
To such a bad discourse ; and I protest
After this hour never to do the like.
I must confess, of all the gentlemen
That ever courted me, you have possessed
The best part in my thoughts : but this coarse language
Exiles you quite from thence. Sir, had you come,
Instead of changing this mine honest name
Into a strumpet's, to have honoured me
With the chaste title of a modest wife,
I had reserved an ear for all your suits ;
But since I see your rudeness finds no limit,
I leave you to your lust.

Y. Chart. You shall not, Luce.

Luce. Then keep your tongue within more moderate
    bounds.

Y. Chart. I will,—as I am virtuous, I will.—[*Aside.*]
I told you the second word would be marriage. It makes a man forfeit his freedom, and makes him walk ever after with a chain at his heels, or a jackanapes hanging at his elbow. Marriage is like Dædalus's labyrinth, and, being once in, there's no finding the way out. Well, I love this little property most intolerably, and I must set her on the last, though it cost me all the shoes in my shop.—Well, Luce, thou seest my stomach is come down : thou hast my heart already ; there's my hand.

Luce. But in what way?

Y. Chart. Nay, I know not the way yet, but I hope to find it hereafter, by your good direction.

Luce. I mean, in what manner? in what way?

Y. Chart. In the way of marriage, in the way of honesty, in the way that was never gone yet. I hope thou art a maid, Luce?

Luce. Yes, sir; and I accept it : in exchange Of this your hand, you shall receive my heart.

Y. Chart. A bargain, and there's earnest on thy lips.

Luce. I'll call my father, sir, to witness it. See, here he comes.

Enter LUCE's Father, *a plain* Citizen.

Y. Chart. Father, save you! You have happened of an untoward son-in-law; here I am, how do you like me?

Luce's Fa. Sir, I was nearer than you were aware, And overheard both sum and circumstance.

Y. Chart. [*Aside.*] Then I perceive you are an old eavesdropper.—But what do you think of it, father?

Luce's Fa. I entertain the motion with all love, And I rejoice my daughter is preferred And raised to such a match ; I heard the contract, And will confirm it gladly : but pray, sir, When shall the merry day be?

Y. Chart. Marry, even to-morrow by that we can see : nay, we'll lose no more time ; I'll take order for that.

Luce. Stay but a month.

Y. Chart. A month! thou canst not hire me to't. Why, Luce, if thou beest hungry, canst thou stay a month from meat? Nay, if I see my diet before me, I love to fall to when I have a stomach. Here, buy thee a new smock ; let's have a new bed too, and look it be strong ; there's a box of rings and jewels, lay them up. Ha, sirrah! methinks the very name of wedlock hath brought me to a night-cap already, and I am grown civil on the sudden. There's more money for dishes, platters, ladles, candlesticks, &c., as I shall find them set down in the inventory.

Luce's Fa. But whom shall we invite unto the wedding?

Enter 2nd LUCE *in the habit of a* Page ; *she retires.*

Y. Chart. Ay, thereby hangs a tale. We will have no more at our marriage but myself, to say, "I take thee, Luce;" thou to say, "I, Luce, take thee, Robin;" the vicar to put us together; and you, father, to play the clerk, and cry "Amen."

Luce's Fa. Your reason for that?

Y. Chart. I would not for a world it should be known to my friends, or come to my father's ear. It may be ten thousand pounds out of my way. For the present, therefore, this is my conceit:[1] let us be married privately, and Luce shall live like a maid still, and bear the name. 'Tis nothing, Luce : it is a common thing in this age to go for a maid, and be none. I'll frequent the house secretly. Fear not, girl ; though I revel abroad o' days, I'll be with thee to bring[2] o' nights, my little whiting-mop.[3]

Luce. But so I may incur a public scandal, By your so oft frequenting to my chamber.

Y. Chart. Scandal! what scandal? Why, to stop the mouth of all scandal, after some few days do I appear in my likeness, married man and honest housekeeper, and then what becomes of your scandal? Come, send for Master Vicar; and what we do, let's do suddenly.

2nd Luce. Cold comfort for me.   [*Aside.*

Luce. If you purpose to be so privately married, I know one excellent at such an exploit. Are you not acquainted with the Wise-woman of Hogsdon?

Y. Chart. Oh, the witch, the beldam, the hag of Hogsdon?

Luce. The same, but I hold her to be of no such condition. I will anon make a step thither, and punctually acquaint her with all our proceedings : she is never without a Sir John[4] at her elbow, ready for such a stratagem.

---

[1] Idea.
[2] In this phrase—of which Dyce says that no satisfactory explanation has been given—"to bring," has apparently the force of "wholly" or "thoroughly."
[3] Young whiting.   [4] A priest.

Y. Chart. Well, be't so, then.

[Exeunt all except 2nd LUCE.

2nd Luce. Heigh-ho ! have I disguised myself, and stolen out of the country thus far, and can light of no better news to entertain me ? Oh, this wild-headed, wicked Chartley, whom nothing will tame ! To this gallant was I, poor gentlewoman, betrothed, and the marriage day appointed ; but he, out of a fantastic and giddy humour, before the time prefixed, posts up to London. After him come I thus habited, and you see my welcome—to be an ear-witness of his second contracting. Modesty would not suffer me to discover myself, otherwise I should have gone near to have marred the match. I heard them talk of Hogsdon, and a wise-woman, where these aims shall be brought to action. I'll see if I can insinuate myself into her service ; that's my next project : and now good luck of my side ! *[Exit.*

ACT THE SECOND.

SCENE I.—*Before the* Wise-woman's *House.*

Enter the Wise-woman, *a* Countryman *with a urinal,* *two* Citizens' Wives, TABER, *and a* Kitchen-maid.

ISE-WO. Fie, fie ! what a toil and a moil it is
For a woman to be wiser than all her neighbours !
I pray, good people, press not too fast upon me ;
Though I have two ears, I can hear but one at once.
You with the urine.

Enter 2nd LUCE *in Boy's clothes ; she s'ands aside.*

Coun. Here, forsooth, mistress.
Wise-wo. And who distilled this water?
Coun. My wife's limbeck, if it please you.
Wise-wo. And where doth the pain hold her most ?
Coun. Marry, at her heart, forsooth.
Wise-wo. Ay, at her heart, she hath a griping at her heart ?
Coun. You have hit it right.
Wise-wo. Nay, I can see so much in the urine.
2nd Luce. Just so much as is told her.   [*Aside.*
Wise-wo. She hath no pain in her head, hath she ?
Coun. No, indeed, I never heard her complain of her head.

Wise-wo. I told you so, her pain lies all at her heart;
Alas, good heart! but how feels she her stomach?

Coun. Oh, queasy[1] and sick at stomach.

Wise-wo. Ay, I warrant you, I think I can see as far
into a mill-stone as another.   You have heard of Mother
Nottingham, who for her time was prettily well skilled in
casting of waters; and after her, Mother Bomby; and
then there is one Hatfield in Pepper Alley, he doth
pretty well for a thing that's lost.   There's another in
Coleharbour, that's skilled in the planets.   Mother Sturton,
in Golden Lane, is for fore-speaking;[2] Mother Phillips,
of the Bankside, for the weakness of the back; and then
there's a very reverend matron on Clerkenwell Green,
good at many things.   Mistress Mary on the Bankside is
for 'recting a figure;[3] and one (what do you call her?) in
Westminster, that practiseth the book and the key, and
the sieve and the shears: and all do well, according to
their talent.   For myself, let the world speak.   Hark you,
my friend, you shall take—   [*She whispers.*

2nd Luce. 'Tis strange the ignorant should be thus
          fooled!
What can this witch, this wizard, or old trot, |
Do by enchantment, or by magic spell?
Such as profess that art should be deep scholars.
What reading can this simple woman have?
'Tis palpable gross foolery.   [*Exit* Countryman.

Wise-wo. Now, friend, your business?

Taber. I have stolen out of my master's house,
forsooth, with the kitchen-maid, and I am come to know
of you whether it be my fortune to have her or no.

Wise-wo. And what's your suit, lady?

Kitchen-m. Forsooth, I come to know whether I be a
maid or no.

Wise-wo. Why, art thou in doubt of that?

---

[1] Squeamish.
[2] Bewitching; or, possibly, prophesying.—*Halliwell.*
[3] The practice of astrology.

Kitchen-m. It may be I have more reason than all the world knows.

Taber. Nay, if thou comest to know whether thou be'st a maid or no, I had best ask to know whether I be with child or no.

Wise-wo. Withdraw into the parlour there; I'll but talk with this other gentlewoman, and I'll resolve you presently.

Taber. Come, Cicely, if she cannot resolve thee, I can; and in the case of a maidenhead do more than she, I warrant thee. [*Exeunt* TABER *and* Kitchen-maid.

1st Cit. Wife. Forsooth, I am bold, as they say——

Wise-wo. You are welcome, gentlewoman.

1st Cit. Wife. I would not have it known to my neighbours that I come to a wise-woman for any thing, by my truly.

Wise-wo. For should your husband come and find you here—

1st Cit. Wife. My husband, woman! I am a widow.

Wise-wo. Where are my brains? 'Tis true, you are a widow; and you dwell—let me see, I can never remember that place.

1st Cit. Wife. In Kent-street.

Wise-wo. Kent-street, Kent-street! and I can tell you wherefore you come.

1st Cit. Wife. Why, and say true?

Wise-wo. You are a wag, you are a wag: why, what do you think now I would say?

1st Cit. Wife. Perhaps to know how many husbands I should have.

Wise-wo. And if I should say so, should I say amiss?

1st Cit. Wife. I think you are a witch.

Wise-wo. In, in: I'll but read a little of Ptolemy and Erra Pater [1]; and when I have cast a figure, I'll come to you presently. [*Exeunt* Citizens' Wives.] Now, wag, what wouldst thou have?

---

[1] Usually the name of a certain mythical astrologer of the "Wandering Jew" type; sometimes, however, as here, applied to an almanac.

2nd Luce. [*Aside.*] If this were a wise-woman, she could
tell that without asking. Now methinks I should come
to know whether I were a boy or a girl.—Forsooth, I lack
a service.

Wise-wo. By my fidelity, and I want a good trusty lad.

2nd Luce. [*Aside.*] Now could I sigh, and say "Alas!
this is some bawd trade-fallen, and out of her wicked
experience is come to be reputed wise." I'll serve her,
be't but to pry into the mystery of her science.

Wise-wo. A proper stripling, and a wise, I warrant
him.—Here's a penny for thee, I'll hire thee for a year by
the Statute of Winchester;[1] prove true and honest, and
thou shalt want nothing that a good boy—

2nd Luce. Here, wise-woman, you are out again : I
shall want what a good boy should have, whilst I live.—
Well, here I shall live both unknown, and my sex unsus-
pected. But whom have we here?

Enter HARINGFIELD, *and* Young CHARTLEY *half drunk.*

Y. Chart. Come, Haringfield, now we have been
drinking of Mother Red-cap's ale, let us now go make
some sport with the wise-woman.

Har. We shall be thought very wise men of all such
as shall see us go in to the wise-woman's.

Y. Chart. See, here she is. How now, witch! How
now, hag! How now, beldam! You are the wise-
woman, are you? and have wit to keep yourself warm
enough, I warrant you.

Wise-wo. Out, thou knave!

2nd Luce. And will these wild oats never be sown?
[*Aside.*

Y. Chart. You enchantress, sorceress, she-devil! you
Madam Hecate, Lady Proserpine! you are too old, you
hag, now, for conjuring up spirits yourself; but you keep
pretty young witches under your roof, that can do that.

[1] The celebrated Statute passed in 1285 : to what clause in the
Statute reference is made is not clear.

Wise-wo. I or my family conjure up any spirits! I defy thee, thou young hare-brained—

Har. Forbear him till he have his senses about him, and I shall then hold thee for a wise-woman indeed: otherwise, I shall doubt thou hast thy name for nothing. Come, friend, away, if thou lovest me.

Y. Chart. Away, you old dromedary! I'll come one of these nights, and make a racket amongst your she-caterwaulers.

Har. I prithee let's be civil.

Y. Chart. Out of my sight, thou she-mastiff!

[*Exeunt* Young CHARTLEY *and* HARINGFIELD.

2nd Luce. Patience, sweet mistress.

Wise-wo. Now, bless me, he hath put me into such a fear, as makes all my bones to dance and rattle in my skin: I'll be revenged on that swaggering companion.

2nd Luce. Mistress, I wish you would; he's a mere mad-cap, and all his delight is in misusing such reverend matrons as yourself.

Wise-wo. Well, what's thy name, boy?

2nd Luce. I am even little better than a turnbroach, for my name is Jack.

Wise-wo. Honest Jack, if thou couldst but devise how I might cry quittance with this cutting Dick[1] I will go near to adopt thee my son and heir.

2nd Luce. Mistress, there is a way, and this it is:
To-morrow morning doth this gentleman
Intend to marry with one Mistress Luce,
A goldsmith's daughter; do you know the maid?

Wise-wo. My daughter, and a pretty smug-faced girl. I had a note but late from her, and she means to be with me in the evening: for I have bespoke Sir Boniface to marry her in the morning.

2nd Luce. Do but prevent this gallant of his wife, And then your wrongs shall be revenged at full.

---

[1] A bully of the time: "cutting" often has the sense of "swaggering."

Wise-wo. I'll do't, as I am matron ; ay, and show him
a new trick for his learning.

Enter BOYSTER.

Boys. Morrow.

Wise-wo. You're welcome, sir.

Boys. Art wise ?

2nd Luce. He should be wise, because he speaks few
words.

Wise-wo. I am as I am, and there's an end.

Boys. Canst conjure ?

Wise-wo. Oh, that's a foul word! but I can tell you
your fortune, as they say ; I have some little skill in
palmistry, but never had to do with the devil.

Boys. And had the devil never anything to do with
thee ? thou look'st somewhat like his dam. Look on me :
canst tell what I ail?

Wise-wo. Can you tell yourself ? I should guess you
be mad, or not well in your wits.

Boys. Thou'rt wise, I am so: men being in love are
mad, and I being in love am so.

Wise-wo. Nay, if I see your complexion once, I think
I can guess as near as another.

Boys. One Mistress Luce I love; know'st thou her,
grannam ?

Wise-wo. As well as the beggar knows his dish. Why,
she is one of my daughters.

Boys. Make her my wife, I'll give thee forty pieces.

2nd Luce. Take them, mistress, to be revenged on
Chartley.

Wise-wo. A bargain ; strike me luck. Cease all your
        sorrow ;
Fair Luce shall be your bride betimes to-morrow.

Boys. Thou'rt a good grannam ; and, but that thy teeth
stand like hedge-stakes in thy head, I'd kiss thee. [*Exit.*

Wise-wo. Pray will you in ? Come hither, Jack ; I have
a new trick come into my head : wilt thou assist me in't ?

2nd Luce. If it concern the crossing of the marriage with Mistress Luce, I'll do't, whate'er it be.

Wise-wo. Thou shalt be tired like a woman. Can you make a curtsey, take small strides, simper, and seem modest? methinks thou hast a woman's voice already.

2nd Luce. Doubt not of me, I'll act them naturally.

Wise-wo. I have conceited to have Luce married to this blunt gentleman, she mistaking him for Chartley; and Chartley shall marry thee, being a boy, and take thee for Luce. Will't not be excellent?

2nd Luce. Oh, super, super-excellent!

Wise-wo. Play but thy part as I'll act mine. I'll fit him with a wife, I warrant him.

2nd Luce. And a wife I'll warrant him. [*Exeunt.*

SCENE II.—*A Room in* Sir HARRY'S *House.*

· *Enter* Sir HARRY *and* TABER.

Sir Harry. Ha, then thou sawest them whispering with my daughter?

Taber. I saw them, if it shall please you, not whisper, but—

Sir Harry. How then, thou knave!

Taber. Marry, sir knight, I saw them in sad[1] talk; but to say they were directly whispering, I am not able.

Sir Harry. Why, Taber, that sad talk was whispering.

Taber. Nay, they did not greatly whisper, for I heard what was said, and what was said I have the wit to keep to myself.

Sir Harry. What said the unthrift, Taber? tell me, knave;

Tell me, good knave, what did the unthrift say?

Taber. I am loth to be called in question about men

---

[1] Serious.

and women's matters, but as soon as ever he saw your
daughter I heard what was spoke.

Sir Harry. Here, sirrah, take thy quarter's wages
afore-hand,
And tell me all their words, and what their greeting
Was at their first encounter ; hold thine hand.

Taber. Thanks, noble sir; and now I'll tell you.
Your daughter being walking to take the air of the fields,
and I before her, whom should we meet just in the
nick—

Sir Harry. Just in the nick, man !

Taber. In the highway I meant, sir.

Sir Harry. Ha, and what conference passed betwixt
them, Taber?

Taber. As well as my pipe can utter, you' shall know,
sir. This gentleman meeting with my young mistress
full butt—imagine you were she, and I young Master
Sencer; now there you come, and here I meet you ; he
comes in this manner, and puts off his hat in this fashion.

Sir Harry. Ay, but what said he?

Taber. "Be with you,[1] fair gentlewoman ; " and so goes
quite away, and scarce so much as once looked back :
and if this were language to offer to a young lady, judge
you.

Sir Harry. But spake he nothing else?

Taber. Nothing, as I am true.

Sir Harry. Why, man, all this was nothing.

Taber. Yes, sir, it was as much as my quarter's wages
afore-hand.

Enter SENCER, HARINGFIELD, *and* GRATIANA.

Grat. Here are two gentlemen, with great desire,
Crave conference with my father. Here he is :
Now, gallants, you may freely speak your minds.

Sen. Save you, sir ! my name is Sencer; I am a
Northamptonshire gentleman, born to a thousand pound

[1] *i.e.* God be with you.

land by the year : I love your daughter, and I am come
to crave your good-will.

Sir Harry. Have you my daughter's, that you covet
mine ?

Sen. No, sir, but I hope in time I shall have.

Sir Harry. So hope not I, sir. Sir, my daughter's
young,

And you a gentleman unknown. Sencer! ha, Sencer?
Oh, sir, your name I now remember well ;
"Tis ranked 'mongst unthrifts, dicers, swaggerers, and
drunkards :
Were not you brought before me, some month since,
For beating of the watch ? by the same token,
I sent you to the Counter.[1]

Sen. I confess myself to have been in that action, but
note the cause, sir: you could not have pleasured me
so much, in giving me a piece of gold, as at the same
time to help me to that Counter.

Sir Harry. Why, sir, what cause had you to beat
the watch,
And raise a midnight tumult in the streets ?

Sen. Nay, but hear me, sweet Sir Harry. Being somewhat late at supper at the Mitre, the doors were shut at
my lodging; I knocked at three or four places more; all
were a-bed, and fast ; inns, taverns, none would give me
entertainment. Now, would you have had me despaired,
and lain in the streets ? No, I bethought me of a trick
worth two of that, and presently devised, having at that
time a charge of money about me, to be lodged, and
safely too.

Sir Harry. As how, I pray you ?

Sen. Marry, thus : I had knocked my heels against the
ground a good while, knew not where to have a bed for
love or money. Now, what did I, but, spying the watch,
went and hit the constable a good souse on the ear, who

---

[1] There were two prisons of this name, one in Wood Street, the
other in the Poultry.

provided me of a lodging presently? and the next day, being brought before your worship, I was then sent thither back again, where I lay three or four days without control.

Sir Harry. Oh, you're a gallant! Is that gentleman
A suitor too?

Har. I am a suitor in my friend's behalf,
No otherwise. I can assure you, sir,
He is a gentleman descended well,
Derived from a good house, well qualified,
And well possessed; but that which most should move
    you,
He loves your daughter.

Grat. [*Aside.*] But were I to choose
Which of these two should please my fancy best,
I sooner should affect this gentleman,
For his mild carriage and his fair discourse,
Than my hot suitor. Ruffians I detest;
A smooth and square behaviour likes me most.

Sen. What say you to me, lady?

Grat. You had best ask my father what I should say.

Sen. Are you angry, sweet lady, that I asked your father's consent?

Grat. No; if you can get his consent to marry him, shall it displease me?

Har. Indeed you therein much forget yourself,
To sound her father ere you tasted her.[1]
You should have first sought means for her goodwill,
And after compassed his.

Sir Harry. He can prevail with neither.—Gentlemen,
If you will come to revel, you are welcome;
If to my table, welcome; if to use me
In any grateful office, welcome too;
But, if you come as suitors, there's the door.

Sen. The door!

Sir Harry. I say the door.

              [1] Tested her disposition.

Sen. Why, sir, tell not me of your door, nor going
out of it. Your company is fair and good, and so is your
daughter's; I'll stay here this twelvemonth, ere I'll offer
to trouble your door.

Sir Harry. Sir, but you shall not.—Taber! where's
that knave?

Sen. Why, sir, I hope you do not mean to make us
dance, that you call for a tabor.

Har. Nay, Master Sencer, do not urge the knight;
He is incensed now; choose a fitter hour,
And tempt his love in that. Old men are testy;
Their rage, if stood against, grows violent,
But, suffered and forborne, confounds itself.

Sir Harry. Where's Taber?

Taber. [*Coming forward.*] At hand, noble master.

Sir Harry. Show them the door.

Taber. That I will,—and take money too, if it please
them.

Sen. Is thy name Taber?

Taber. I am so yclept, sir.

Sen. And, Taber, are you appointed to give us Jack
Drum's entertainment?[1]

Taber. Why, sir, you do not play upon me.

Sen. Though I cannot, yet I have known an hare that
could. But, knight, thou dost not forbid us thine house?

Sir Harry. Yes, and forewarn it too.

Sen. But, by thy favour, we may choose whether we
will take any warning or no. Well, farewell, old knight!
though thou forbid'st me thine house, I'll honour thee,
and extol thee; and, though thou keep'st me from thy
daughter, thou shalt not hinder me to love her and
admire her, and, by thy favour, sometimes to see her.
A cat may look at a king, and so may I at her. Give me
thine hand, knight; the next time I come into··thy

---

[1] "Tom or John Drum's Entertainment, a phrase signifying ill-
treatment, or turning an unwelcome guest out of doors."—*Halliwell.*

company, thou shalt not only bid me welcome, but hire me to stay with thee, and thy daughter.

Sir Harry. When I do that enjoy my full consent
To marry Gratiana.

Sen. 'Tis a match ; strike me luck. Wife that may be, farewell ; father-in-law that must be, adieu. Taber, play before my friend and I will dance after.

[*Exeunt* SENCER, HARINGFIELD *and* TABER.

Sir Harry. When I receive thee gladly to mine house,
And wage thy stay, thou shalt have Gratiana,
Doubt not thou shalt. Here's a strange humourist
To come a-wooing.

Re-enter TABER.

Taber, are they gone ?

Taber. I have played them away, if it please your worship ; and yonder at the door attends a school-master ; you sent for him, if you remember, to teach my little young master and mistress.

Sir Harry. A proper scholar ; pray him to come near.

Enter Sir[1] BONIFACE.

Sir Bon. Eques honoratus, ave salutatus! non video quid est in tergo, sed salve, bona virgo.

Sir Harry. Sir, you may call me nicknames : if you love me,
Speak in your mother-tongue ; or, at the least,
If learning be so much allied unto you,
That Latin unawares flows from your lips,
To make your mind familiar with my knowledge,
Pray utter it in English : what's your name ?

Sir Bon. Sit faustum tibi omen.
I'll tell you my *nomen.*

Sir Harry. Will you tell it to no men ?
I'll entertain none ere I know their names.

[1] "Sir" was applied to all University men who had taken their B.A. degree.

Nay, if you be so dainty of your name,
You are not for my service.

Sir Bon. *Intende, vir nobilis.*

· *Sir Harry.* Not for twenty nobles :
Trust me, I will not buy your name so dear.

Sir Bon. *O ignorantia!* what it is to deal with
stupidity? Sir Henry, Sir Henry, hear me one word : I
see, *Preceptor legit, vos vero negligitis.*

Taber. I think he saith we are a company of fools and
nidgets;[1] but I hope you shall not find us such, Master
Schoolmaster.

Sir Harry. Friend, friend, to cut off all vain cir·
cumstance,
Tell me your name, and answer me directly,
Plainly, and to my understanding too,
Or I shall leave you. Here's a deal of gibberish !

Sir Bon. *Vir bone——*

Sir Harry. Nay, nay, make me no bones,[2] but do't.

· *Sir Bon.* Then, in plain vulgar English, I am called
Sir Boniface Absee.

Sir Harry. Why, this is somewhat like, Sir Boniface !
Give me thine hand ; thou art a proper man,
And in my judgment, a great scholar too.
What shall I give thee by the year?

Sir Bon. I'll trust, sir, to your generosity;
I will not bargain, but account myself,
Mille et mille modis, bound to you.

Sir Harry. I cannot leave my mills; they're farmed
already :
The stipend that I give shall be in money.

Taber. Sure, sir, this is some miller that comes to
undermine you, in the shape of a schoolmaster.

Grat. You both mistake the scholar.

Sir Harry. I understand my English, that I know;
What's more than modern doth surpass my reach.
Sir Boniface, come to me two days hence,

---

[1] Idiots.　　　　[2] *i.e.* No difficulties.

You shall receive an answer; I have now
Matters of some import that trouble me,
Thou shouldst be else despatched.

 Taber. Sir Boniface, if you come to live in our house,
and be a familist amongst us, I shall desire your better
acquaintance; your name and my physiognomy should
have some consanguinity, good Sir Boniface.

 Sir Bon. Quomodo vales, quomodo vales.

 Taber. Go with you to the ale-house? I like the
motion well; I'll make an excuse out of doors and follow
you. I am glad yet, we shall have a good-fellow come
into the house amongst us.

 Sir Bon. Vale, vir magne.

 Sir Harry. You shall not have me at Saint Magnes,
my house is here in Gracious-street.

 Sir Bon. I know it, sweet knight, I know it. Then,
virgo formosa et Domine gratiose valete.

 Sir Harry. Ay, in Gracious-street you shall hear of
me, Sir Boniface.   [*Exit* Sir BONIFACE.
He shall instruct my children; and to thee,
Fair Gratiana, read the Latin tongue.

 Taber. Who shall? Sir Bawdy-face?

 Sir Harry. Sir Boniface, you fool.

 Taber. His name is so hard to hit on.

 Sir Harry. Come, daughter, if things fall out as I intend,
My thoughts shall peace have, and these troubles end.
          [*Exeunt.*

ACT THE THIRD.

SCENE I.—*A Room in the* Wise-woman's *House.*

Enter 2nd LUCE, *in* woman's *apparel, and the* Wise-woman.

ISE-WO. Jack, thou art my boy.

2nd Luce. Mistress !

Wise-wo. I'll be a mother to thee, no mistress. Come, lad, I must have thee sworn to the orders of my house, and the secrets thereof.

2nd Luce. As I am an honest lad, I am yours to command. But, mistress, what mean all these women's pictures, hanged here in your withdrawing-room?

Wise-wo. I'll tell thee, boy—marry, thou must be secret. When any citizens or young gentlemen come hither, under a colour to know their fortunes, they look upon these pictures, and which of them they best like, she is ready with a wet finger.[1] Here they have all the furniture belonging to a private-chamber,—bed, bed-fellow, and all. But mum! thou knowest my meaning, Jack.

2nd Luce. But I see, coming and going, maids, or such as go for maids, some of them as if they were ready to lie down, sometimes two or three delivered in one night ; then suddenly leave their brats behind them, and convey themselves into the city again :—what becomes of their children?

Wise-wo. Those be kitchen-maids, and chamber-maids,

---

[1] *i.e.* With as much ease as any light substance is caught up by oistening one's finger.

and sometimes good men's daughters, who, having
catched a clap,[1] and growing near their time, get leave to
see their friends in the country, for a week or so : then
hither they come, and for a matter of money here they
are delivered. I have a midwife or two belonging to the
house, and one Sir Boniface, a deacon, that makes a
shift to christen the infants ; we have poor, honest, and
secret neighbours, that stand for common gossips.[2] But
dost not thou know this ?

2nd Luce. Yes, now I do; but what after becomes of
the poor infants ?

Wise-wo. Why, in the night we send them abroad,
and lay one at this man's door, and another at that, such
as are able to keep them ; and what after becomes of
them, we inquire not. And this is another string to my
bow.

2nd Luce. [*Aside.*] Most strange, that woman's brain
       should apprehend
Such lawless, indirect, and horrid means
For covetous gain ! How many unknown trades
Women and men are free of, which they never
Had charter for !
But, mistress, are you so cunning as you make yourself?
you can neither write nor read : what do you with those
books you so often turn over ?

Wise-wo. Why, tell[3] the leaves; for to be ignorant, and
seem ignorant, what greater folly !

2nd Luce. [*Aside.*] Believe me, this is a cunning
woman ; neither hath she her name for nothing, who out
of her ignorance can fool so many that think themselves
wise.—But wherefore have you built this little closet close
to the door, where sitting, you may hear every word
spoken by all such as ask for you ?

Wise-wo. True, and therefore I built it. If any knock,
you must to the door and question them, to find what
they come about,—if to this purpose, or to that. Now,

----
[1] Met with a mischance.   [2] Sponsors.   [3] Count over.

they ignorantly telling thee their errand, which I, sitting in my closet, overhear, presently come forth, and tell them the cause of their coming, with every word that hath passed betwixt you in private ; which they admiring, and thinking it to be miraculous, by their report I become thus famous.

2nd Luce. This is no trade, but a mystery ; and, were I a wise-woman, as indeed I am but a foolish boy, I need not live by your service. But, mistress, we lose ourselves in this discourse : is not this the morning in which I should be married ?

Wise-wo. Now, how had I forgot myself ! Mistress Luce promised to be with me half an hour ago, but masked and disguised, and so shalt thou be too : here's a black veil to hide thy face against the rest come.

[*2nd* LUCE *puts on the veil.*

Enter Sir BONIFACE.

Sir Bon. *Sit tibi bona dies, salus et quies.*

Wise-wo. Into the withdrawing-room, Sir Boniface.

Sir Bon. Without any compunction, I will make the conjunction. [*Exit.*

Wise-wo. Now keep thy countenance, boy.

2nd Luce. Fear not me ; I have as good a face in a mask as any lady in the land could wish to have. But to my heart,—he comes, or he comes not—now am I in a pitiful perplexity, until I see the event of all.

Wise-wo. No more Jack now, but Mistress Luce.

2nd Luce. I warrant you, mistress.—That it happens so luckily, that my name should be Luce too, to make the marriage more firm !

Enter Young CHARTLEY *disguised, and in a visard.*

Y. Chart. My honey-sweet hag, where's Luce ?

Wise-wo. Here, sweetheart, but disguised and veiled, as you are visarded.

Y. Chart. But what's the reason we are thus hood-winked ?

· *Wise-wo.* No discovery of yourselves for a million !
There's Sir Boniface within—shall he blab who you are ?
besides, there's a young heir that hath stolen a lord's
daughter from the Court, and would not have their faces
seen for a world.   Cannot you be content to fare well,
and keep your own counsel ?   And see, yonder they
come. ·

Enter, severally, BOYSTER *visarded and* LUCE *masked.*

Y. Chart. Gramercy, my sugar-candy sweet Trot !

Wise-wo. Mum, no more words.

Y. Chart. If the great heir and the young lady be so
dainty of their complexions, they shall see, my sweet
Luce, we can visard it with the best of them.

Luce. [*Looking at* BOYSTER.] That gentleman, by the
wise-woman's description, should be Master Chartley.

Boys. That gallant wench, if my grannam fable not,
should be Luce ; but what be those other ?

Wise-wo. You wrong me but to ask.   Who but a young
heir, and a lady of the Court?   That's Luce; take her, and
keep your promise.

Boys. Pocas palabras.[1]

Wise-wo. That's Chartley ; take him, Luce.

Luce. But who be they ?

Wise-wo. A lord and lady.   Shall Sir Boniface stay?
Rather than so, strive who should lead the way.

[*Exeunt* CHARTLEY *with 2nd* LUCE, BOYSTER *with* LUCE.

Wise-wo. Now, Jack· my boy, keep thine own counsel
and countenance, and I shall cry quittance with my
young gallant.   Well, by this time Sir Boniface is at his
book. But because there is a mistake, known only to my
boy and myself, the marriage shall be no sooner ended
but I'll disturb them by some sudden outcry, and that
too before they have leisure to unmask, and make
known themselves one to another ; for, if the deceit were
known, I should fall into the danger of that young mad

---

[1] " Few words."

rascal. And now this double apprehension of the lord
and the lady shall fetch me off from all. I know it is Sir
Boniface's custom to make short work, and h'ath dis-
patched by this. And now, wise-woman, try if thou
canst bestir thyself like to a mad-woman.—Shift for yourselves ! Warrants and pursuivants ! Away ! warrants and
pursuivants ! shift for yourselves !.

Re-enter, as affrighted and amazed, Young CHARTLEY,
    BOYSTER, Sir BONIFACE, LUCE, *and* 2*nd* LUCE.

Y. Chart. I'll take this way.

Boys. I this. [*Exeunt* Young CHARTLEY *and* BOYSTER.

Sir Bon. *Curro, curris, cucurri :* my cheeks are all
murrey,[1] and I am gone in an hurry.   [*Exit.*

Luce. O Heaven ! what shall become of me ?

2*nd Luce.* I know what shall become of me already.

Wise-wo. O sweet daughter, shift clothes with this
lady. Nay, as thou lovest thy credit and mine, change
habits—[*They change their outer garments.*]—So, if thou
be'st taken in her garments, finding the mistake will let
thee pass; and should they meet her in thine, not
knowing her, would no way question her; and this prove
to both your securities and my safety.

Luce. As fast as I can, good mother. So, madam,
farewell.   [*Exit.*

2*nd Luce.* All happy joys betide you !   [*Exit.*

Wise-wo. Ha, ha! let me hold my sides, and laugh.
Here were even a plot to make a play on, but that
Chartley is so fooled by my boy Jack : well, he'll make a
notable wag, I'll warrant him. All the jest will be, if
Boyster should meet with him in Luce's habit, which he
hath now on, he would think himself merely gulled and
cheated; and should Chartley meet with Luce as she is
now robed, he would be confident he had married her.
Let me see how many trades have I to live by: first, I
am a wise-woman, and a fortune-teller, and under that I

---

[1] A dark red colour.—*Halliwell.*

deal in physic and fore-speaking, in palmistry, and re-
covering of things lost; next, I undertake to cure mad
folks; then I keep gentlewomen lodgers, to furnish
such chambers as I let out by the night; then I am provided for bringing young wenches to bed; and, for a need,
you see I can play the match-maker.
She that is but one, and professeth so many,
May well be termed a wise-woman, if there be any.
[*Exit.*

SCENE II.—*Before the* Wise-woman's *House.*

Enter BOYSTER.

Boys. Why run away, and leave my wench behind?
I'll back. What have warrants and pursuivants to do with
me? with me! why should I budge? why should I wear
mask or visard? If lords or ladies offend, let lords and
ladies answer. Let me better bethink me. Why should I
play at hoodman-blind?[1] Hum: why marry *in tenebris?*
ha! is there no trick in it? If my grannam should make
me a younger brother now, and, instead of Luce, pop me
off with some broken commodity, I were finely served:
most sure I am to be in for better and worse; but with
whom, Heaven and my grannam knows.

Enter 2*nd* LUCE, *half-dressed and masked.*

2nd Luce. I am stolen out of doors, to see if I can
meet my husband, with whom I purpose to make some
sport, ere I suddenly disclose myself. What's he?

Boys. Heyday, what have we here? an hobberdehoy!
Come hither, you.

2nd Luce. 'Tis Mistress Luce's husband, I'll not leave
him thus.

Boys. What art thou?

2nd Luce. Do you not know me?

---

[1] Blind man's buff.

Boys. That mask and robe I know.

2nd Luce. I hope so, or else I were in a woe [1] case.

Boys. That mask, that gown I married.

2nd Luce. Then you have no reason, but to enjoy both them and me too, and so you are like ; I should be loth to divorce man and wife.

Boys. I am fooled. But what cracked ware are you, forsooth ?

2nd Luce. I belong to the old gentlewoman of the house.

Boys. I'll set her house on fire. I am finely bobbed.[2]

2nd Luce. But I hope you will not bob me.

Boys. No, I'se warrant thee. What art thou? girl or boy ?

2nd Luce. Both, and neither ; I was a lad last night, but in the morning I was conjured into a lass ; and, being a girl now, I shall be translated to a boy anon. Here's all I can at this time say for myself. Farewell. [*Exit.*

Boys. Yes, and be hanged withal ! O for some gun-powder to blow up this witch, this she-cat, this damned sorceress ! Oh, I could tear her to fitters [3] with my teeth ! Yet I must be patient, and put up all, lest I be made a jeer to such as know me. Fooled by a boy ! Go to ! of all the rest, the girl Luce must not know it. [*Exit.*

Enter Young CHARTLEY *and his* Man, *and* LUCE, *meeting.*

Y. Chart. So, now am I the same man I was yester-day. Who can say I was disguised ? or who can distin-guish my condition now, or read in my face, whether I be a married man or a bachelor ?

Luce. Who's that ?

Y. Chart. Luce ?

Luce. Sweet husband, is it you ?

Y. Chart. The news ?

Luce. Never so frighted in my days.

Y. Chart. What's become of the lord and the lady ?

---

[1] Sorrowful.   [2] Tricked.   [3] Pieces.

Luce. The lord fled after you ; the lady stayed,
Who, masked and half-unready, ran fast after ·
Her poor affrighted husband.   Now all's quiet.

Y. Chart. This storm is then well past, and now convey yourself home as privately as you can ; and see you
make this known to none but your father.

Luce. I am your wife and servant.   [*Exit.*

Y. Chart. The name of Luce hath been ominous to
me : one Luce I should have married in the country, and,
just the night before, a toy[1] took me in the head, and
mounting my horse, I left capons, ducks, geese, poultry,
wildfowl, father, and bride, and all, and posted up to
London, where I have ever since continued bachelor, till
now.   And now—

Enter GRATIANA *in haste, a* Serving-man *before her, and*
TABER *after her.*

Grat. Nay, on, I prithee, fellow, on ! my father will
wonder where I have been visiting.   Now, what had I
forgot !   Taber, there's money ; go to the goldsmith's,
bid him send me my fan, and make a quick return.   On,
fellow, on.   [*Exeunt* GRATIANA *and* Serving-man.

Taber. Her fan at the goldsmith's ! now had I forgot to ask her his name, or his sign ; but I will after to
know.   [*Exit.*

Y. Chart. Sirrah, go call me back that serving-man,
And ask him what's the gentlewoman's name.

Serv. I shall.   Ho, you, friend, you !

Re-enter TABER.

Taber. Who's that calls ?

Serv. 'Twas I.

Taber. Your business ? You should be one, though not
of my cognisance, yet of my condition,—a serving-
creature, as I take it : pray what's your will with me ?

Serv. Pray, sir, what might I call that gentlewoman,
on whom you were attendant ?

¹ Whim.

Taber. You may call her what you please; but if you call her otherwise than in the way of honesty, you may perchance hear on't.

Serv. Nay, be not offended : I say, what do you call her?

Taber. Why, sir, I call her as it shall best please me; sometimes young lady, sometimes young mistress; and what hath any man to do with that?

Y. Chart. Are you so captious, sirrah? What's her
name?
Speak, and be brief.

Taber. Ay, marry, sir, you speak to purpose, and I can resolve you : her name is Gratiana. But all this while I have forgot my mistress'·fan.   [*Exit.*

Y. Chart. Gratiana ! oft have I heard of her, but saw her not till now : 'tis a pretty wench, a very pretty wench,—nay, a very, very, very pretty wench. But what a rogue am I, of a married man—nay, that have not been married this six hours, and to have my shittle-wits run a wool-gathering already ! What would poor Luce say if she should hear of this? I may very well call her poor Luce, for I cannot presume of five pounds to her portion. What a coxcomb was I, being a gentleman, and well derived, to match into so beggarly a kindred ! What needed I to have grafted in the stock of such a choke-pear, and ·such a goodly popering [1] as this to escape me! Escape me, said I? if she do, she shall do it narrowly. But I am married already, and therefore it ·is not possible, unless I should make away my wife, to compass her. Married ! why, who knows it? I'll out-face the priest, and then there is none but she and her father, and their evidence is not good in law ; and if they put me in suit, the best is, they are poor, and cannot follow it. Ay, marry, sir, a man may have some credit by such a wife as this. I could like this marriage well, if

---

[1] A pear brought from Poperingues in Flanders ; the choke-pear was a coarse variety.

a man might change away his wife, still as he is a-weary
of her, and cope[1] her away like a bad commodity; if
every new moon a man might have a new wife, that's
every year a dozen. But this "Till death us do part"
is tedious. I will go a-wooing to her, I will; but how
shall I do for jewels and tokens? Luce hath mine in
her custody, money and all. Tush, I'll juggle them from
her well enough. See, here she comes.

Enter LUCE *and her* Father.

Luce. Here is my husband; I pray move him in it.

Luce's Fa. It toucheth both our reputations nearly;
For by his oft repair, now whilst the marriage
Is kept from public knowledge, your good name
May be by neighbours hardly censured of.

Y. Chart. Thou'rt sad, thou'rt sad, Luce: what, melancholy already, ere thou hast had good cause to be merry,
and knew'st what sport was!

Luce. I have great reason, when my name is tossed
In every gossip's mouth, and made a bye-word
Unto such people as it least concerns.
Nay, in my hearing, as they pass along,
Some have not spared to brand my modesty,
Saying, "There sits she whom young Chartley keeps:
There hath he entered late, betimes gone forth."
Where I with pride was wont to sit before,
I'm now with shame sent blushing from the door.

Y. Chart. Alas, poor fool! I am sorry for thee, but yet
cannot help thee, as I am a gentleman. Why, say, Luce,
thou losest now forty shillings worth of credit, stay but a
time, and it shall bring thee in a thousand pounds worth
of commodity.

Luce's Fa. Son, son, had I esteemed my profit more
Than I have done my credit, I had now
Been many thousands richer; but you see,
Truth and good dealing bear an humble sail.

---

[1] Chop or exchange.

That little I enjoy, it is with quiet,
Got with good conscience, kept with good report ;
And that I still shall labour to preserve.
    Y. Chart. But do you hear me ?
    Luce's Fa. Nothing I'll hear that tends unto the ruin
Of mine or of my daughter's honesty.
Shall I be held a broker to lewd lust,
Now in my wane of years ?
    Y. Chart. Will you but hear me ?
    Luce's Fa. Not in this case. I that have lived thus
        long,
Reported well, esteemed a welcome guest
At every burthened table, there respected,
Now to be held a pander to my daughter !
That I should live to this !
    Y. Chart. But hark you, father !
    Luce's Fa. A bawd to mine own child !
    Y. Chart. Father !
    Luce's Fa. To my sweet Luce !
    Y. Chart. Father !
    Luce's Fa. Deal with me like a son, then call me
        father.
I that have had the tongues of every man
Ready to crown my reputation;
The hands of all my neighbours to subscribe
To my good life, and such as could not write
Ready with palsied and unlettered fingers
To set their scribbling marks—
    Y. Chart. Why, father-in-law !
    Luce's Fa. Thou hadst a mother, Luce—'tis woe with
        me   .
To say thou hadst, but hast not ; a kind wife,
And a good nurse she was : she, had she lived
To hear my name thus canvassed, and thus tossed,
Seven years before she died, I had been a widower
Seven years before I was.   Heaven rest her soul !
She is in Heaven, I hope.   [*He wipes his eyes.*

   Heywood.   U

Y. Chart. Why, so now, these be good words : I knew these storms would have a shower, and then they would cease. Now, if your anger be over, hear me: *Luce's Fa.* Well, say on, son.

Y. Chart. Stay but a month, 'tis but four weeks—nay, 'tis February, the shortest month of the year—and in that time I shall be at full age; and the land being entailed, my father can disinherit me of nothing. Is your spleen down now? Have I satisfied you? Well, I see you choleric hasty men are the kindest when all is done. Here's such wetting of handkerchiefs ! he weeps to think of his wife; she weeps to see her father cry ! Peace, fool! we shall else have thee claim kindred of the woman killed with kindness.[1]

Luce's Fa. Well, son, my anger's past; yet I must tell you,
It grieves me that you should thus slight it off,
Concerning us in such a dear degree.
In private be it spoke, my daughter tells me
She's both a wife and maid.

Y. Chart. That may be helped.—Now, Luce, your father's pacified, will you be pleased? I would endure a quarter's punishment for thee, and wilt not thou suffer a poor month's penance for me? 'Tis but eight and twenty days, wench; thou shalt fare well all the time, drink well, eat well, lie well : come, one word of comfort at the latter end of the day.

Luce. Yours is my fame, mine honour, and my heart
Linked to your pleasure, and shall never part.

Y. Chart. Gramercy, wench ; thou shalt wear this chain no longer for that word; I'll multiply the links in such order that it shall have light to shine about thy neck oftener than it doth : this jewel—a plain Bristowe[2] stone, a counterfeit. How base was I, that coming to thee in

---

[1] An obvious allusion to Heywood's own masterpiece.
[2] More usually called a " Bristol diamond."

the way of marriage, courted thee with counterfeit
stones! Thou shalt wear right, or none. Thou hast no
money about thee, Luce?

Luce. Yes, sir, I have the hundred pounds that you
gave me to lay up last.

Y. Chart. Fetch it.—[*Exit* LUCE.]—Let me see, how
much branched[1] satin goes to a petticoat? and how
much wrought velvet to a gown? then for a beaver for
the city, and a black bag for the country: I'll promise
her nothing, but if any such trifles be brought home, let
her not thank me for them.

Re-enter LUCE *with the bag.*

Gramercy, Luce.—Nay, go in, Gravity and Modesty;
ten to one but you shall hear of me ere you see me
again.

Luce's Fa. I know you kind; impute my hasty language
Unto my rage, not me.

Y. Chart. Why, do not I know you, and do not I
know her? I doubt you'll wish shortly that I had never
known either of you: now, what sayst thou, my sweet
Luce?

Luce. My words are yours, so is my life: I am now
Part of yourself, so made by nuptial vow.

Y. Chart. What a pagan am I, to practise such villainy
against this honest Christian! If Gratiana did not come
into my thoughts, I should fall into a vein to pity her.
But now that I talk of her, I have a tongue to woo her,
tokens to win her; and that done, if I do not find a
trick both to wear her and weary her, it may prove a
piece of a wonder.—Thou seest, Luce, I have some store
of crowns about me: there are brave things to be bought
in the city; Cheapside and the Exchange afford variety
and rarity. This is all I will say now, but thou mayst
hear more of me hereafter. [*Exit.*

[1] Figured

Luce. Heaven speed you where you go, sir! Shall we in?
Though not from scandal, we live free from sin.
Luce's Fa. I'll in before. [*Exit.*

Enter BOYSTER.

Boys. I am still in love with Luce, and I would know
An answer more directly. Fie, fie! this love
Hangs on me like an ague, makes me turn fool,
Coxcomb, and ass. Why should I love her, why?
A rattle-baby, puppet, a slight toy.
And now I could go to buffets with myself,
And cuff this love away. But see, that's Luce.
Luce. I cannot shun him, but I'll shake him off.
Boys. Morrow.
Luce. As much to you.
Boys. I'll use few words—canst love me?
Luce. 'Deed, sir, no.
Boys. Why, then, farewell; the way I came, I'll go.
[*Exit.*
Luce. This is no tedious courtship; he's soon answered;
So should all suitors else be, were they wise;
For, being repulsed, they do but waste their days
In thankless suits, and superficial praise.

Re-enter BOYSTER.

Boys. Swear that thou wilt not love me.
Luce. Not, sir, for any hate I ever bare you,
Or any foolish pride or vain conceit,
Or that your feature doth not please mine eye,
Or that you are not a brave gentleman,
But for concealèd reasons I am forced
To give you this cold answer, and to swear
I must not: then with patience pray forbear.
Boys. Even farewell then. [*Exit.*
Luce. The like to you; and, save your hopes in me,
Heaven grant you your best wishes! All this strife
Will end itself, when I am known a wife. [*Exit.*

ACT THE FOURTH.

SCENE I.—*A Room in* Sir HARRY'S *House.*

Enter Sir HARRY, HARINGFIELD, GRATIANA, *with others.*

IR HARRY. I am satisfied, good Master
Haringfield,
Touching your friend; and since I see
you have left
His dangerous company, I limit [1] you
To be a welcome guest unto my table.

Har. You have been always noble.

Enter TABER.

Sir Harry. Taber, the news with thee?

Taber. May it please thee, right worshipful, to understand that there are some at the gate who dance a turn
or two without, and desire to be admitted to speak with
you within.

Sir Harry. The scholar, is it not?

Taber. Nay, sir, there are two scholars, and they are
spouting Latin one against the other; and in my simple
judgment the stranger is the better scholar, and is somewhat too hard for Sir Boniface: for he speaks louder,
and that you know is ever the sign of the most learning,
and he also hath a great desire to serve your worship.

Sir Harry. Two scholars! my house hath not place
for two.
Thus it shall be.   Taber, admit them both;
We, though unlearned, will hear them two dispute,

[1] *i.e.* Appoint.

And he that of the two seems the best read
Shall be received, the other quite cashiered.

Har. In that you show but justice : in all persons
Merit should be regarded.

Enter TABER, *ushering in* Sir BONIFACE, *and* SENCER,
disguised like a pedant.

Sir Bon. Venerabiles magistri, absint vobis capistri.

*Sen. Et tu, domine calve, iterum atque iterum salve.
Amo amas amavi.* Sweet lady, Heaven save ye !

Sir Harry. This approves him to be excellent, but I
thank my breeding I understand not a word.
You tongue-men, you whose wealth lies in your brains,
Not in your budgets, hear me.   Be it known,
My house affords room for one schoolmaster,
But not for more ; and I am thus resolved :
Take you that side, gentle Sir Boniface,
And, sir, possess you that.
He of you two in arguing proves the best,
To him will I subscribe.   Are you agreed ?

Sir Bon. Nec animo, nec corde, nec utroque.

Sen. No more of that *nec corde.*   Noble knight, he
wishes you *nec corde;* think of that.

Sir Harry. A cord about my neck, Sir Boniface !
Speak, do you use me well ?

Sir Bon. Domine, cur rogas ?

Sen. Is this to be endured,—to call a knight
Cur, rogue and ass ?

Sir Harry. I find myself abused.

Har. Yet patience, good Sir Harry, and hear more.
Pray, Sir Boniface, of what university were you of?

Sir Bon. I was student in Brazenose.

Har. A man might guess so much by your pimples.
And of what place were you ?

Sen. Petrus dormit securus; I was, sir, of Peterhouse.[1]

---

[1] There is a tradition that Heywood himself was a Fellow of
Peterhouse, Cambridge.

Sir Bon. *Natus eram* in Woxford, and I proceeded[1] in Oxford.

Sen. *Est mihi bene nostrum*, thou wouldst say, in Gotham ; for my part, Sir Harry, I can read service and marry, *Que genus et flexum*, though I go in Genes[2] fustian ; *scalpellum et charta*, I was not brought up at plough and cart ; I can teach *Qui mihi*, and neither laugh nor tee-hee ; *sed as in presenti*, if your worship at this present, *Iste, ista, istud*, will do me any good, to give me *legem pone* in gold or in money, *Piper atque papaver*, I'll deserve it with my labour.

Har. But when go you to dispute?

Sir Bon. *Nominativo hic prediculus*, his words are most ridiculous ; but *tu* thou, *qui* the which, deridest those that be rich, *construe hanc sententiam*, construe me this sentence : *Est modus in rebus, sunt certi denique fines.*

Sen. *Est modus in rebus*, there is mud in the rivers ; *sunt certi denique fines*, and certain little fishes.

Sir Harry. I warrant you he hath his answer ready.

Sir Bon. *Dii boni boni.*

Har. He'll give you more bones than those to gnaw on, Sir Boniface.

Sen. *Kartere Moojotropos poluphiltate phile poetatis Tes Logikes retoon, ouch elachiste sophoon.* That is as much as to say, in our *materna lingua*, I will make you, Sir Boniface, confess yourself an ass in English, speak open and broad words, for want of Latin, and *denique* entreat me to resolve such questions as I shall ask you in our modern tongue.

Sir Harry. Confess himself an ass? speak obscene words?

After entreat thee to resolve thy questions?
Do that ; possess the place.

Sen. *Di do* and *dum:* no more words but *mum:*

---

[1] *i.e.* To his degree, his college, as he tells us, being Brazenose.
[2] Genoese.

Sir Bon. Noble Sir Harry, *numquam sic possit ?*

Sir Harry. Sir Boniface is sick already and calls for a posset ; no marvel, being so threatened.

Sen. You, Boniface, decline me I am a no after the first conjugation, *amo amavi, vocito vocitavi, Titubo Titubavi ?*

Sir Bon. I am not the preceptor to a pupil,
But can decline it ; mark, Sir Timothy.
I am a no.

Sen. Bene bene.

Sir Bon. I am an as.

Sen. Most true, most true, *vos estis, ut ego sum testis,* that what he confessed is as true as the *pestis.*

Sir Harry. This scholar works by magic ; he hath made him confess himself an ass.

Sir Bon. Per has meas manus, vir, tu es insanus.

Sen. I'll make him fret worse yet. Sir Boniface, *quid est grammatica ?*

Sir Bon. Grammatica est ars.

Sir Harry. Fie, fie ! no more of these words, good Sir Boniface.

Sen. Attend again, proceed me with this verse of reverend Cato : *Si deus est animus.*

Sir Bon. Nobis ut carmina dicunt.

Taber. Di—— quotha ! out on him for a beastly man !

Sir Harry. I would not have him teach my children so for more than I am worth.

Sir Bon. O ! but reverend Sir Harry, you must *subaudi.*

Sir Harry. I'll never be so bawdy whilst I live, nor any of mine, I hope.

Sir Bon. O ! *Propria quæ maribus.*

Sir Harry. Ay, Boniface, it is those marrow-bones That make you talk so broadly !

Sir Bon. Venerabilis vir, homo ille est ebrius.

Sir Harry. What doth he mean by that ?

Sen. He saith I can speak Hebrew.

Sir Harry. I believe't :

But if Sir Boniface still con these lessons,
He'll speak the French tongue perfect.

Sen. Now to the last ; I'll task Sir Boniface
But with an easy question.   Tell me, sir,
What's Latin for this earth ?

Sir Bon. Facile and easy, more fit for the pupil than
the preceptor.   What's Latin for this earth?   *Tellus.*

Sen. Tell you ? no, sir, it belongs to you to tell me.

Sir Bon. I say *tellus* is Latin for the earth.

Sen. And I say, I will not tell you what is Latin for
the earth, unless you yield me victor.

Sir Harry. You have no reason : good Sir Timothy,
The place is yours.

Har. He hath deserved it well.

Sen. But I'll deserve it better : why, this fellow
Is frantic ; you shall hear me make him speak
Idly and without sense.   I'll make him say
His nose was husband to a Queen.

> [*He whispers* Sir HARRY.

Sir Harry. Sir Timothy, not possible.

Taber. He will not speak it for shame.

Sen. That you shall hear.   Magister Boniface.

Sir Bon. *Quid ais,* domine Timothy ?

Sen. Who was Pasiphe's husband, Queen of Crete ?

Sir Bon. Who knows not that ?   Why, Minos was her
husband.

Sen. That his nose was ; did I not tell you so ?

Sir Bon. I say that Minos was.

Sen. That his nose was—ha, ha !

Sir Harry. I'll not believe it.—

Sir Boniface, there are a brace of angels ;
You are not for my turn.   Sir Timothy,
You are the man shall read unto my daughter
The Latin tongue, in which I am ignorant.
Confess yourself an ass ; speak bawdy words ;
And after to talk idly !   Hence, away !
You shall have my good word, but not my pay.

Sir Bon. *Opus est usus;* Sir Timothy, you abuse us.
I swear by a noun, had I thy hose down,
Qui, quæ, quod, I would so smoke thee with the rod,
Ille, illa, illud, until I fetched blood.
But, *nobiles vaiete,* remain in *quiete.*
                    [*Exeunt* Sir BONIFACE and TABER.
Sir Harry. Sir Timothy, there is some gold in earnest,
I like you well; take into your tuition
My daughter Gratiana.

Re-enter TABER.

                    The news, Taber?
Taber. Of another gallant, noble sir, that pretends to
have business both with you and my mistress.
Sir Harry. Admit him.

Enter Young CHARTLEY *very galiant, with* GRATIANA.

Taber. Lusty Juventus,[1] will it please you to draw
near?
Y. Chart. Noble knight, whilst you peruse that [*Hands
Sir* HARRY *a letter*], sweet lady, tell me how you like
this?   [*Kisses* GRATIANA.
Grat. You press so suddenly upon me, sir,
I know not what to answer.
Sen. [*Aside*] Mad Chartley! what makes Desperation
        here?
Y. Chart. To the word wooer let me add the name
speeder; my father hath written to your father, and the
cause of his writing at this present is to let you understand that he fears you have lived a maid too long; and
therefore, to prevent all diseases incident to the same, as
the green sickness and others, he sent me, like a skilful
physician, to take order with you against all such mala-
dies. If you will not credit me, list but how fervently
my father writes in my behalf.

---

[1] There is an old interlude entitled *Lusty Juventus*, printed about
the year 1560.

Sir Harry [*Reads*] " He is my only son, and she, I take it, your only daughter. What should hinder then to make a match between them?" Well, 'tis well, 'tis good, I like it. "I will make her jointure three hundred pounds a year."

Y. Chart. How say you by that, sweet lady? three hundred pounds a year, and a proper man to boot?

Sir Harry. All's good, I like it; welcome, Master Chartley.

Thou, Gratiana, art no child of mine
Unless thou bidst him welcome. This I presume
To be your father's hand?

Y. Chart. [*Aside*] But I'll be sworn he never writ it.

Sir Harry. And this his seal at arms?

Y. Chart. Or else I understand it very poorly. But, lady,

In earnest of further acquaintance, receive this chain,
These jewels, hand and heart.

Sir Harry. Refuse no chain nor jewels, heart nor hand,

But in exchange of these bestow thyself,
Thine own dear self, upon him.

Grat. Myself on him, whom I till now ne'er saw?
Well, since I must, your will's to me a law.

Sen. Nay, then, 'tis time to speak. Shall I stand here waiting like a coxcomb, and see her given away before my face? Stay your hand, Sir Harry; and let me claim my promise.

Sir Harry. My promise I'll perform, Sir Timothy;
You shall have all your wages duly paid.

Sen. I claim fair Gratiana by your promise.
No more Sir Timothy, but Sencer now.
You promised me when you received my service,
And with your liberal hand did wage my stay,
To endow me freely with your daughter's love.
That promise now I claim.

Sir Harry. Mere cozenage, knavery:

I tied myself to no conditions
In which such guile is practised.   Come, son Chartley :
To cut off all disasters incident
To these proceedings, we will solemnise
These nuptial rites with all speed possible.

 Y. Chart. Farewell, good Sir Timothy; farewell,
learned Sir Timothy.   [*Exeunt all but* SENCER.

 Sen. Why, and farewell, learned Sir Timothy.
For now Sir Timothy and I am two :
Boast on, brag on, exalt, exalt thyself,
Swim in a sea of pleasure and content
Whilst my bark suffers wreck ! I'll be revenged.
Chartley, I'll cry *vindicta* for this scorn ;
Next time thou gorest, it must be with thy horn.   [*Exit.*

SCENE II.—*The Street outside the Goldsmith's Shop.*

Enter BOYSTER.

 Boys. I am mad, and know not at what ;
I could swagger, but know not with whom ;
I am at odds with myself, and know not why :
I shall be pacified, and cannot tell when ;
I would fain have a wife, but cannot tell where ;
I would fasten on Luce, but cannot tell how.
How ; where ; when ; why ; whom ; what.
Feeding sure makes me lean, and fasting fat.

Enter LUCE *and* JOSEPH.

 Luce. Not all this while once see me !
 Jos. His occasions
Perhaps enforce his absence.
 Luce. His occasions !
Unless he find occasion of new love,
What could enforce such absence from his spouse ?

Am I grown foul and black since my espousals?
It should not seem so; for the shop is daily
Customed with store of chapmen, such as come
To cheapen love. O no, I am myself!
But Chartley he is changed.

Jos. You know that gentleman.

Luce. Escape him if thou canst.   ·

Boys. He cannot. I arrest you.

Luce. At whose suit?

Boys. Not at mine own, that's dashed; I love thee not.
Thou art a Spaniard, gipsy, a mere· blackamoor:
Again I say I love thee not.

Luce. A blackamoor, a gipsy!
Sure I am changed indeed, and that's the cause
My husband left me so; this gentleman
Once termed me beautiful. How look I, Joseph?

Jos. As well as e'er you did—fat, fresh, and fair.

Boys. You lie, boy; pocket that, and now ,be gone.

Jos. And what shall then become of my mistress?

Boys. I'll wait upon your mistress.

Luce. I know you will not wait on such a gipsy.

Boys. Yes, Luce, on such a gipsy. Boy, *abi, abi.*

Jos. Abide, sir! you need not fear that; I have no purpose to leave her.

Boys. Now you are going to the wedding-house.
You are bid to be a bridemaid, are you not?

Luce. What wedding, sir, or whose?

Boys. Why, Chartley's. Luce, hath he been thy friend
     so long,
And would not bid thee to wait on his bride?
Why look'st thou red and pale, and both, and neither?

Luce. To Master Chartley's bridals? Why, to whom
Should he be married?

Boys. To Grace of Gracious-street.

Luce. To Gratiana!
Beshrew you, sir, you do not use me well,
To buzz into mine ears these strange untruths:

I tell you, sir, 'tis as impossible
They two should match, as Earth and Heaven to
    meet.
    Boys. You'll not believe it? Pray then hark within
The nuptial music echoing to their joys.
But you give credit to no certainties :
I told you but a tale, a lie, a fable,
A monstrous, a notorious idle untruth—
That you were black, and that I loved you not—
And you could credit that !

Enter Sir HARRY, HARINGFIELD, Young CHARTLEY
    leading GRATIANA *by the arm,* TABER, *and* Atten-
    dants.
                        Who's tell-troth now?
Know you that man, or know you that fine virgin
Whom by the arm he leads ?
    Luce. I'll not endure't.—Heaven give you joy, sir !
    Y. Chart. I thank you. Luce !   [*She faints.*
    Sir Harry. Look to the maid ; she faints.
       | [BOYSTER *holds her up.*
    Y. Chart. Grace, come not near her, Grace.
Father, keep off ; on, gentlemen, apace.
She's troubled with the falling sickness, for
Oft hath she fallen before me.
    Sir Harry. Nay, if it be no otherwise, on, gentlemen,
Let those with her strive to recover her.
Keep off ; the disease is infectious.
    Y. Chart. If it were in a man, it were nothing, but the
falling sickness in a woman is dangerous.

                  Enter LUCE's Father.

My tother father-in-law ! Now shall I be utterly shamed.
If he assure to know me, I'll outface him.
    Luce's Fa. Son, you're well met.
    Y. Chart. How, fellow !
    Luce's Fa. I cry you mercy, sir.

Y. Chart. No harm done, friend, no harm done.

[*Exeunt* Sir HARRY, HARINGFIELD, Young
CHARTLEY, *and* GRATIANA.

Luce's Fa. If he, he could not but have known me there,
Yet he was wondrous like him.

Boys. How cheér you, Luce? whence grew this
passion?

Luce. Pardon me, sir, I do not know myself:
I am apt to swound, and now the fit is passed me.
1 thank you for your help. Is Master Chartley
Vanished so soon?

Boys. Yes; and to supply his place, see where thy
father comes.

Luce's Fa. He hath not such a suit; besides, this
gallant
Led by the arm a bride, a lusty bride!
How much might 1 have wronged the gentleman
By craving his acquaintance! This it is
To have dim eyes. Why looks my daughter sad?—
1 cry you mercy, sir; I saw not you.

Boys. I would I had not seen you at this time neither.
Farewell.   [*Exit.*

Luce. If he be gone, then let me vent my grief.
Father, I am undone!

Luce's Fa. Forbid it, Heaven!

Luce. Disgraced, despised, discarded, and cast off.

Luce's Fa. How, mine own child?

Luce. My husband, O my husband!

Luce's Fa. What of him?

Luce. Shall I the shower of all my grief at once
Pour out before you? Chartley, once my husband,
Hath left me to my shame. Him and his bride
I met within few minutes.

Luce's Fa. Sure 'twas they;
I met them too: 'twas he; base villain, Jew!
I'll to the wedding board, and tell him so:
I'll do't as I am a man.

Luce. Be not so rash.

Luce's Fa. I'll live and die upon him;
He's a base fellow, so I'll prove him too.
Joseph, my sword !

Luce. This rashness will undo us.

Luce's Fa. I'll have my sword ;
It hath been twice in France, and once in Spain,
With John-a-Gaunt; when I was young like him
I had my wards, and foins, and quarter-blows,
And knew the way into St. George's Fields [1]
Twice in a morning. Tuttle, Finsbury,
I knew them all. I'll to him : where's my sword ?

Luce. Or leave this spleen, or you will overthrow
Our fortunes quite ; let us consult together
What we were best to do.

Luce's Fa. I'll make him play at leap-frog ! Well, I hear
thee.

Luce. I cannot prove our marriage ; it was secret,
And he may find some cavil in the law.

Luce's Fa. I'll to him with no law, but Stafford law.[2]
I'll ferret the false boy—nay, on, good Luce.

Luce. Part of your spleen if you would change to
counsel,
We might revenge us better.

Luce's Fa. Well, I hear thee,

Luce. To claim a public marriage at his hands
We want sufficient proof, and then the world
Will but deride our folly, and so add
Double disgrace unto my former wrong.
To law with him—he hath a greater purse,
And nobler friends. How then to make it known ?

Luce's Fa. Is this his damasked kirtle fringed with gold,
His black bag, and his beaver ? 'Tis well yet
I have a sword.

---

[1] He mentions three well-known duelling resorts.
[2] "He has had a trial in Stafford Court" was a way of saying
"he has been beaten or ill-treated," *Cotgrave*. Florio uses the
expression "Stafford-law" = *braccesca licenza*.

Luce. And I have a project in my brain begot,
To make his own mouth witness to the world
My innocence, and his incontinence.
Leave it to me, I'll clear myself from blame,
Though I the wrong, yet he shall reap the shame.
[*Exeunt.*

SCENE III.—*Outside the* Wise-woman's *House.*

Enter SENCER *like a* Serving-man.

Sen. Now or never, look about thee, Sencer : to-morrow is the marriage day, which to prevent lies not within the compass of my apprehension ; therefore I have thus disguised myself, to go to the looming woman's, the fortune-teller's, the anything, the nothing. This over-against Mother Redcap's is her house ; I'll knock.

Enter 2nd LUCE *in* Boy's *clothes.*

2nd Luce. Who's there ? What would you have ?

Sen. I would speak with the wise gentlewoman of the house.

2nd Luce. Oh, belike you have lost somewhat.

Sen. You are in the wrong, sweet youth.

2nd Luce. I am somewhat thick of hearing ; pray speak out.

Sen. I say I have not lost anything, but wit and time, and neither of those she can help me to.

2nd Luce. Then you belike are crossed in love, and come to know what success you shall have.

Sen. Thou hast hit it, sweet lad ; thou hast hit it.

2nd Luce. What is it you say, sir ?

Sen. Thou hast hit it.

2nd Luce. I pray come in ; I'll bring you to my mistress.
[*Exeunt.*

Heywood.   X

Enter LUCE *and* JOSEPH.

Luce. This is the house; knock, Joseph; my business craves dispatch.

Jos. Now am I as angry as thou art timorous; and now to vent on the next thing I meet—Oh, 'tis the door.
[*Knocks.*

Re-enter 2*nd* LUCE.

2*nd Luce.* Who's there? What are you?

Luce. A maid and a wife.

2*nd Luce.* And that would grieve any wench to be so; I know that by myself, not Luce.

Luce. Boy, where's your mistress?

2*nd Luce.* In some private talk with a gentleman. I'll fetch her to you presently. [*Exit.*

Luce. If she and you see me not, I am but dead;
I shall be made a by-word to the world,
The scorn of women, and my father's shame.

Enter the Wise-woman *and* SENCER, *followed by*
2*nd* LUCE.

Wise-wo. You tell me your name is Sence; I knew it before : and that Chartley is to be married, I could have told it you.

2*nd Luce.* Married to-morrow,—O me!

Sen. Ay, but you tell me that Chartley before to-morrow shall be disappointed of his wife; make that good, thou shalt have twenty angels.

Wise-wo. I'll do't : stand aside; I'll have but a word or two with this gentlewoman, and I am for you presently.

Luce. O mother, mother! [*They whisper.*

2*nd Luce.* My husband marry another wife to-morrow! O changeable destiny! no sooner married to him, but instantly to lose him! Nor doth it grieve me so much that I am a wife, but that I am a maid too; to carry one of them well is as much as any is bound to do, but to be tied to both is more than flesh and blood can endure.

Wise-wo. Well, trust to me, and I will set all things straight.

Enter BOYSTER.

· *Boys.* Where's this witch, this hag, this beldam, this wizard? And have I found thee!—thus then will I tear, mumble, and maul thee!

Wise-wo. Help, help!—an if you be a gentleman!

Sen. Forbear this rudeness; he that touches her, Draws against me.

Boys. Against you, sir! apply thou;[1] that shall be tried.

All. Help, help! part them, help!

Sen. With patience hear her speak.

Boys. Now, trot, now, grannam, what canst thou say for thyself?—What, Luce here! Be patient, and put up thou; she must not see the end.

Sen. Then truce of all sides; if we come for counsel, Let us with patience hear it.

Luce. Then first to me.

Wise-wo. You would prevent young Chartley's marriage? you shall : hark in your ear.   [*Whispers.*

Luce. It pleaseth me.

Wise-wo. You forestall Gratiana's wedding? 'tis but thus.   [*Whispers.*

Sen. I'll do't.

Wise-wo. You would enjoy Luce as your wife, and lie with her to-morrow night? Hark in your ear. [*Whispers.*

Boys. Fiat!

Wise-wo. Away! you shall enjoy him, you are married, Luce, away! you shall see Chartley discarded from Gratiana. Sencer, begone! And if I fail in any of these or the rest, I lay myself open to all your displeasures.

Boys. Farewell till soon!

Wise-wo. You know your meeting-place.

All. We do.

---

[1] Defend yourself.

Wise-wo. You shall report me wise and cunning too.
　　　　　　　　　　　[*Exeunt all except* 2nd LUCE.
2nd Luce. I'll add one night more to the time I have said ;
I have not many, I hope, to live a maid.　　　　[*Exit.*

SCENE IV.—*A Room in* Sir HARRY's *House.*

Enter Sir BONIFACE, *and* TABER *carrying a trencher of broken meat and a napkin.*

Taber. Fie, fie, what a time of trouble is this ! To-morrow is my mistress to be married, and we serving-men are so puzzled.

Sir Bon. The dinner's half done, and before I say grace,
And bid the old knight and his guest proface.[1]
A medicine from your trencher, good Master Taber,
As good a man as e'er was Sir Saber :
Well, think it no shame : men of learning and wit
Say study gets a stomach ; friend Taber, a bit.

Taber. Lick clean, good Sir Boniface, and save the scraper a labour.

Enter SENCER *like a* Serving-man.

Sir Bon. But soft, let me ponder :
Know you him that comes yonder ?

Taber. Most heartily welcome ; would you speak with any here ?

Sen. Pray is the young gentleman of the house at leisure?

Taber. Mean you the bridegroom, Master Chartley ? .

Sen. I have a letter for him. You seem to be a gentleman yourself; acquaint him with my attendance, and I shall rest yours in all good offices.

Taber. Sir Boniface, pray keep the gentleman company. I will first acquaint your lips with the virtue of the cellar.
　　　　　　　　　　　　　　　　　　[*Exit.*

[1] *i.e.* Much good may it do you !

Sir Bon. *Adesdem,* come near, and taste of our beer. Welcome, *sine dole,* for *puntis te vole.*

Sen. When I taste of your liquor, Gramercy, Master Vicar.

Re-enter TABER *with a bowl of beer and a napkin.*

Taber. Most heartily welcome : your courtesy, I beseech you ; ply it off, I entreat you. Pray, Sir Boniface, keep the gentleman company, till I acquaint my young master with his business. [*Exit.*

Sir Bon. Taber, I shall *beso las manus.*[1]

[*They dissemble one to another.*

Sen. *A vostre servitor.*

Enter HARINGFIELD.

Har. Hey ! what art thou ?

Sen. A hanger-on, if it please you.

Har. And I a shaker-off.: I'll not bear your gallows ; You shall not hang on me.

Enter Young CHARTLEY *with his napkin as from dinner.*

Oh, Master Bridegroom !

Y. Chart. Gentlemen, the ladies call upon you to dance ; they will be out of measure displeased, if, dinner being done, you be not ready to lead them a measure.

Har. .Indeed, women love not to be scanted of their measure.

Y. Chart. Fie, Sir Boniface ! have you forgot yourself? Whilst you are in the hall, there's never a whetstone for their wits in the parlour.

Sir Bon. I will enter and set an edge upon their ingenies. [*Exeunt* Sir BONIFACE *and* HARINGFIELD.

Y. Chart. [*To* SENCER, *who hands him a letter.*] To me, sir ! from whom ? A letter ! To her "most dear, most loving, most kind friend Master Chartley, these be delivered." Sure from some wench or other. I long to know the content.

[1] Kiss the hands.

Sen. [*Aside.*] Now to cry quittance with you for my
" farewell, learned Sir Timothy."

Y. Chart. Good news, as I live ! there's for thy pains,
my good Sir Pandarus.[1] Hadst thou brought me word
my father had turned up his heels, thou couldst scarcely
have pleased me better. [*Reads.*] " Though I disclaim
the name of wife, of which I account myself altogether
unworthy, yet let me claim some small interest in your
love. This night I lie at the house where we were married
—the Wise-Woman's I mean—where my maidenhead is
to be rifled : bid fair for it, and enjoy it; see me this night
or never. So may you, marrying Gratiana, and loving me,
have a sweet wife and a true friend. This night or never.
Your *quondam* wife, hereafter your poor sweetheart, no
other, Luce." So, when I am tired with Gratiana, that is
when I am past grace with her, I can make my rendezvous.
I'll not slip this occasion, nor sleep till I see her. Thou art
an honest lad, and mayst prove a good pimp in time.
Canst thou advise me what colour[2] I may have to compass this commodity ?

Sen. Sir, she this night expects you, and prepares a
costly banquet for you.

Y. Chart. I'll go, although the devil and mischance
look big.

Sen. Feign some news that such a piece of land is
fallen to you, and you must instantly ride to take possession of it ; or, which is more probable, cannot you persuade
them you have received a letter that your father lies a-
dying ?

Y. Chart. You rogue, I would he did ; but the name
of that news is called " too good to be true."

Sen. And that if ever you will see him alive, you must
ride post into the country ?

Y. Chart. Enough : if ever I prove knight-errant thou
shalt be mine own proper squire. For this, thou hast fitted

---

[1] Pandarus was the prince of go-betweens ; hence the word
"pander."   [2] Excuse.

me with a plot. Do but wait here; note how I will
manage it.—Taber, my horse, for I must ride to-night.

Re-enter TABER.

Taber. To-night, sir!

Y. Chart. So tell my bride and father: I have news
that quite confounds my senses.   [*Exit* TABER.

Enter Sir HARRY, GRATIANA, *and* HARINGFIELD.

Grat. How, ride to-night! the marriage day to-
And all things well provided for the feast!   [morrow,
Oh, tell me, sweet, why do you look so pale?

Y. Chart. My father, O my father!

Grat. What of him?

Sir Harry. What of your father, son?

Y. Chart. If ever I will hear his agèd tongue
Preach to me counsel, or his palsy hand
Stroke my wild head and bless me, or his eyes
Drop tear by tear, which they have often done
At my misgoverned rioting youth—
What should I more?—if ever I would see
That good old man alive—Oh, oh!

Sen. [*Aside.*] Go thy ways, for thou shalt ha't.

Grat. But do you mean to ride?

Y. Chart. Ay, Grace, all this night.

Sen. [*Aside.*] Not all the night without alighting, sure:
You'll find more in't than to get up and ride.

Har. The gentleman's riding-boots and spurs. Why,
    Taber!

Y. Chart. Nay, Grace, now's no time to stand on
scrupulous parting. Knewest thou my business—

Sen. [*Aside.*] As she shall know it.

Y. Chart. And how I mean this night to toil myself—

Sen. [*Aside.*] Marry hang, you brock¹!

Y. Chart. Thou wouldst bemoan my travel.

Sen. [*Aside.*] I know 'twould grieve her.

---

¹ A term of contempt; a brock is a badger.

Y. Chart. You, father, Grace, good Master Haringfield,
You, sir, and all, pray for me, gentlemen,
That in this dark night's journey I may find
Smooth way, sweet speed, and all things to my mind.

Sir Harry. We'll see my son take horse.

Grat. But I will stay :
I want the heart to see him post away.

> [*Exeunt* Young CHARTLEY, Sir HARRY *and*
> HARINGFIELD.

Sen. Save you, gentlewoman ! I have a message to
deliver to one Mistress Gratiana ; this should be the
knight's house, her father.

Grat. It is : the message that you have to her
You may acquaint me with, for I am one
That knows the inside of her thoughts.

Sen. Are you the lady ?

Grat. Sir, I am the poor gentlewoman.

Sen. There is a cunning woman dwells not far,
At Hogsdon, lady, famous for her skill.
Besides some private talk that much concerns
Your fortunes in your love, she hath to show you,
This night, if it shall please you walk so far
As to her house, an admirable suit
Of costly needlework, which if you please
You may buy under-rate for half the value
It cost the making ; about six o'clock
You may have view thereof, but otherwise,
A lady that hath craved the sight thereof
Must have the first refusal.

Grat. I'll not fail her.
My husband being this day rid from home,
My leisure fitly serves me.

Sen. Thank you, mistress. At six o'clock.

Grat. I will not fail the hour.   [*Exit.*

Sen. Now to Sir Harry ; his is the next place,
To meet at Hogsdon his fair daughter Grace.   [*Exit.*

ACT THE FIFTH.

SCENE I.—*A Street near* Sir HARRY'S *House.*

Enter Old Master CHARTLEY *and three or four* Serving-men.

 CHART. Good Heaven! this London is a stranger grown,
And out of my acquaintance ; this seven years
I have not seen Paul's steeple, or Cheap Cross.[1]

1st Serv. Sir—

O. Chart. Hast thou not made inquiry for my son?

1st Serv. Yes, sir, I have asked about everywhere for him, but cannot hear of him.

O. Chart. Disperse yourselves ; inquire about the taverns, ordinaries, bowl-alleys, tennis-courts, gaming-houses ; for there, I fear, he will be found.

1st Serv. But where shall we hear of your worship again?

O. Chart. At Grace Church by the Conduit, near Sir Harry.

But stay, leave off a while your bootless search.
Had e'er man such a wild brain to his sorrow,
Of such small hope, who, when he should have married
A fair, a modest, and a virtuous maid,

---

[1] At Cheapside, with a statue of the Virgin on it. It was removed in 1643, by Puritan influence, on account of the reverence which it received from Catholics.

Rich and revenued well, and even the night
Before the marriage day took horse, rode thence,
Whither Heaven knows? Since the distracted virgin
Hath left her father's house, but neither found,
Yet in their search we have measured out much ground.

Enter Sir HARRY *and* SENCER.

Sen. Your worship will be there?

Sir Harry. Yes, not to fail,
At half an hour past six, or before seven.

Sen. You shall not find us at six and at seven, I'll
warrant you: good health to your worship.

Sir Harry. Farewell, good fellow;
At the Wise-woman's house (I know it well:
Perhaps she knows some danger touching me).
I'll keep mine hour.   [*Exit* SENCER.

O. Chart. Sir Harry,
A hand, a hand; to baulk you it were sin.
I shall be bold to make your house mine inn.

Sir Harry. Brother Chartley, I am glad to see you.

O. Chart. Methinks, Sir Harry, you look strangely
     on me.
And do not bid me welcome with an heart.

Sir Harry. And blame me not to look amazedly
To see you here.

O. Chart. Why me?

Sir Harry. Come, come, you're welcome.
And now I'll turn my strangeness to true joy.
I am glad to see you well, and safe recovered
Of your late grievous sickness.

O. Chart. The strange amazèd looks that you cast
     off
You put on me; and blame me not to wonder
That you should talk of sickness to sound men.
I thank my stars I did not taste the grief
Of inward pain or outward malady
This seven years day.

Sir Harry. But by your favour, brother,
Then let me have my wonder back again.

O. Chart. Before I quite part with it, let me know
Why you the name of brother put upon me
In every clause—a name as strange to me
As my recovered sickness.

Sir Harry. You are pleasant,
And it becomes you well : welcome again,
The rather you are come just to the wedding.

O. Chart. What wedding, sir ?

Sir Harry. That you should ask that question !
Why, of my daughter Grace.

O. Chart. Is Grace bestowed ?   Of whom, I pray ?

Sir Harry. Of whom but of your son.
I wonder, brother Chartley, and my friend,
You should thus play on me.

O. Chart. But by your favour,
Were you ten knights, Sir Harry—take me with you [1]—
My son match with your daughter ! my consent
Not worthy to be craved !

Sir Harry. Nay, then I see
You'll stir my patience ; know this forward match
Took its first birth from you.

O. Chart. From me ?

Sir Harry. From you.
Peruse this letter : know you your own hand ?
'Twas well that I reserved your hand a witness
Against your tongue.   You had best deny the jointure
Of the three hundred pounds made to my daughter ;
'Tis that I know you aim at ; but your seal—
                              [*Shows him letter.*

O. Chart. Shall not make me approve it : I deny ·
This seal for mine, nor do I vouch that hand.
Your daughter and the dower, letter and all,
I quite disclaim.   Sir Harry, you much wrong me.

[1] *i.e.* Let me understand.

Sir Harry. I can bear more than this ; heap wrong on
    wrong,
And I'll support it all ; I for this time
Will cast my spleen behind me.   And yet hear me :
This letter your son Chartley, as from you,
Delivered me.   I like the motion well.
    O. Chart. My spleen is further thrown aside than yours,
And I am full as patient, and yet hear me ;
My son's contracted to another maid.
Nay, I am patient still—yet that I writ
This letter, sealed this impress, I deny.
    Sir Harry. Why, then, the jack[1] your hand did coun-
    terfeit ?
    O. Chart. Why, then, he did so.   Where's that un-
    thrift, speak?
    Sir Harry. Some hour ago, he mounted and rid post
To give you visit, whom he said lay sick
Upon your death-bed.
    O. Chart. You amaze me, sir.
It is an ill presage ; hereon I see
Your former salutation took its ground,
To see me safe recovered of my sickness.
    Sir Harry. Indeed it did.   Your welcome is a subject
I cannot use too oft ; welcome again.
I am sorry you this night must sup alone,
For I am elsewhere called about some business,
Concerning what I know not.   Hours run on—
I must to Hogsdon ; high time I were gone.   [*Exit.*
    O. Chart. Perhaps to the Wise-woman's ; she may tell
    me
The fortunes of my son.   This accident
Hath bred in me suspicion and strange fears.
I will not sup alone, but I protest,
'Mongst some this night I'll play the intruding guest.
                    [*Exit with* Serving-men.

---

[1] Crafty fellow.

SCENE II.—*The Principal Room in the* Wise-woman's *House, leading to several small rooms, all of which look into it.*

Enter the Wise-woman, SENCER *as a* Serving-man, LUCE *and her* Father, *and 2nd* LUCE *in* Boy's *clothes.*

Wise-wo. But will Sir Harry come?

Sen. Presume he will,
And Chartley too.

Luce's Fa. I'll have the knave by the ears.

Luce. Nay, patience, sir; leave your revenge to me.

Enter BOYSTER.

Boys. Grannam, I am come according to promise.

Wise-wo. And welcome to the best hole that I have in Hogsdon.

Boys. Good even.

Luce. 'Thanks, sir, a good even may it prove,
That each may reap the fruits of their own love!

2nd Luce. That shall be my prayer too.

Boys. Come, what shall's do?

Wise-wo. Withdraw; I'll place you all in several rooms,
Where sit, see, but say nothing.

[*They withdraw. Exeunt* Wise-woman *and 2nd* LUCE.

Enter TABER, *ushering* GRATIANA.

Taber. Here, sweet mistress; I know the place well ever since I was here to know my fortune.

Grat. Call me some half an hour hence.

[*Exit* TABER.

Re-enter the Wise-woman *and 2nd* LUCE.

Wise-wo. Your ladyship is most lovingly welcome. A low stool for the gentlewoman, boy. I made bold to send to you to take view of such a piece of work as I presume you have seldom seen the like.

Grat. Of whose doing, I pray?

Wise-wo. A friend of yours and mine.   Please you withdraw,

I'll bring you to't.

2nd Luce. Mistress!

Wise-wo. One calls, sweet lady; I shall do you wrong,

But pray you think my little stay not long.

[GRATIANA *withdraws, exeunt the others.*

SCENE III.—*An Inner Room in the same.*

Enter SENCER, Sir HARRY, *and* LUCE.

Sen. Here, sir, in this retiring chamber.

Sir Harry. Gramercy, friend.   How now? what's here to do?

A pretty wench and a close chamber too!

Luce. That you have so much graced my mother's house

With your desirèd presence, worthy knight,

Receive a poor maid's thanks.   Who's there? a chair

And cushion for Sir Harry.

Sir Harry. Thanks, most fair.

Luce. Please you but a few minutes here to stay,

Till my return, I'll not be long away.

Sen. The gentlewoman will wait on you by and by,

sir.   [*Exeunt* LUCE *and* SENCER.

Sir Harry. And I'll attend her, friend.

Of all those doubts I long to know the end.

SCENE IV.—*The Principal Room in the same.*

Enter the Wise-woman, SENCER *and* LUCE. *To them
enter 2nd* LUCE *and* Old CHARTLEY.

2nd Luce. The knight you seek was here, or will be
' straight,
And, if you be the man you name yourself,
You are most welcome, and you shall not back
Till you have seen Sir Harry.
    O. Chart. Gentle youth,
I saw him enter here, and under privilege
Of his acquaintance made I bold to stay.
    2nd Luce. And you are welcome, sir; sit down, I pray.
            [*Takes him into one of the inner rooms.*
Wise-wo. Now they are placed in several rooms, that
look into this one. Were Chartley come we had all our
company.
    Sen. Hark, there's one knocks; 'tis Chartley, on my
        life.
    Luce. One of you let him in, whilst I prepare me
To entertain his coming.
                [*Exeunt* SENCER *and* Wise-woman.

Enter Young CHARTLEY, *ushered in by* SENCER, *who
retires.*

    Y. Chart. What, old acquaintance Luce! Not a
word? yet some lip-labour if thou lovest me.
    Grat. [*In an inner room.*] My husband![1]
    Sir Harry. [*In another inner room.*] What, young
Chartley!
    O. Chart. [*Also in an inner room.*] How! my son!
    Y. Chart. Come, come away with this wailing in woe;

---

[1] It is to be understood that the occupants of the various inner
rooms see and hear all that transpires between Young Chartley and
Luce without being themselves seen or heard.

if thou put'st finger in the eye a little longer, I shall
plunge in pain too presently.

Luce. O husband, husband !

Grat. Husband !

Y. Chart. What say'st thou, my sweet wife ?

Grat. Wife ! O my heart !

2nd Luce. [*Aside.*] In that name wife I claim a poor
child's part.

Luce. O husband, how have you used me !

Y. Chart. Nay, how do' I mean to use thee, but as a
man should use his wife ?

Grat. I hope he doth not mean to use her so.

2nd Luce. [*Aside.*] I hope so too.

Boys. [*In an inner room.*] My grannam is a witch.

Y. Chart. Nay, Luce, sweet wife, leave weeping if thou
lovest me.

Luce. Oh, can you blame me, knowing that the
    fountain
Of all these springs took their first head from you ?
You know, you too well know, not three days
    since
Are past since we were married.

Grat. Married ! I can endure no longer.

Sir Harry. It cannot be.

O. Chart. It is not possible.

Boys. I'll be even with' thee for this, old grannam.

Luce. And though we wanted witness upon earth,
Yet Heaven bears record of our nuptial tie.

Y. Chart. Tush, when we meet in Heaven let's talk of
    that.
Nay, come, you ass, you fool, what's past is past ;
Though man and wife, yet I must marry now
Another gallant ; here's thy letter, Luce,
And this night I intend to lodge with thee.

2nd Luce. [*Aside.*] I'll scratch her eyes out first,
although I love her.

Y. Chart. Prithee be merry.

I have made a gull of Grace, and old Sir Harry
Thinks me a great way off.   I told the knight
My father lay a-dying, took post-horse,
Rid out of Holborn, turned by Islington,
So hither, wench, to lodge all night with thee.

2nd Luce. [*Aside.*] Here's one saith nay to that.

O. Chart. Was that your journey?

Y. Chart. Why,[1] I have too much Grace already.

Boys. Thou hast no grace at all.

Y. Chart. Nay, let's to bed; if thou couldst but imagine how I love thee, Luce!

Luce. How is it possible you can love me, and go about to marry another?

Y. Chart. Dost thou not know she's rich? Why, you fool, as soon as I have got her dower, it is but giving her a dram, or a pill to purge melancholy, to make her turn up her heels, and then with all that wealth come I to live with thee, my sweet rascal.

Grat. [*Coming from the inner room.*] She thanks you,
    and is much beholding to you.

Y. Chart. I am betrayed!

Grat. Art thou my suitor? wouldst thou marry me,
And thy first wife alive? then poison me,
To purchase my poor dower?

Y. Chart. What shall I say, or think, or do? I am at a nonplus.

Grat. Hast thou the face, thou brazen impudence,
To look upon me?—past grace!

Y. Chart. Thou canst not properly call me past Grace, for I never enjoyed thee yet.   I cannot tell whether I blush or no, but I have now at this time more Grace than I can tell what to do with.

Grat. Who drew thee to this folly?

Y. Chart. Who but the old dotard thy father, who when I was honestly married to a civil maid, he persuaded me to leave her?   I was loth at first, but after

---

[1] Is not a speech lost here?

entreating, urging, and offering me large proffers, I must confess I was seduced to come a-wooing to thee.

Grat. My father, villain !

Y. Chart. Ay, thy father, Grace. And were he here would justify it to the old dotard's face.

Enter Sir HARRY.

Sir Harry. Vile boy, thou dar'st not be so impudent ! When did I meet thee, seek or sue to thee ? When ? Name the day, the month, the hour, the year.

Y. Chart. Plots, plots ! I can but cry you mercy both. Say that I have done you wrong, I can be but sorry for it. But, indeed, to clear you, and lay the fault where it ought to be, all this comes from mine own father in the country, who hearing I had married with Luce, sends me word, of his blessing,[1] to be divorced from her, and to come a suitor to your daughter. I think you have his hand and seal to show.

Enter Old CHARTLEY.

O. Chart. My hand and seal ! When was that letter writ ?

Y. Chart. Heyday, if you get one word more of me to-night but scurvy looks, I'll give you leave to hang me.

Sir Harry. Vile boy !

O. Chart. Ungracious villain !

Grat. Treacherous youth !

Sir Harry. No grace at all !

Y. Chart. No Grace.   · [thee !

O. Chart. This is bad company who hath seduced Speak, on my blessing, who hath thus misled thee ? But no more lies, I charge thee.

Y. Chart. Bad company hath been the shame of me. I was as virtuously given as any youth in Europe, till I fell into one Boyster's company ; 'tis he that hath done all the harm upon me.

---

[1] *i.e.* On pain of losing his blessing.

Boys. [*Aside.*] I !
O. Chart. And if he should deny it ?

Enter BOYSTER.

Boys. What then ? you'd cry him mercy.
Y. Chart. I had best bite out my tongue, and speak
no more. What shall I do, or what shall I say ? There is
no outfacing them all. Gentlemen, fathers, wives, or
what else, I have wronged you all. I confess it that I
have—what would you more ? Will any of you rail of
me ? I'll bear it. Will any of you beat me ? So they
strike not too hard, I'll suffer it. Will any of you
challenge me ? I'll answer it. What would you have
me say or do ? One of these I have married, the other
I have betrothed, yet both maids for me. Will you have
me take one, and leave the tother ? I will. Will you
have me keep them both ? I will.

Enter LUCE's Father.

Luce's Fa. Perjured ! not mine.
Y. Chart. What, you here too ? Nay, then, I see all
my good friends are met together. Wilt thou have me,
Luce ? I am thy husband, and had I not loved thee
better than Grace, I had not disappointed the marriage
day to-morrow.
Luce. Lascivious ! no.
Y. Chart. Wilt thou have me, Grace ?—for had I not
loved thee better than Luce, I would never after I had
married her been contracted to thee.
Grat. Inconstant ! no.
Y. Chart. Then, neither married man, widower, nor
bachelor, what's to be done ? Here's even the proverb
verified—between two stools, the tail goes to ground.
Sir Harry. Now I bethink me, this our meeting here
is wondrous strange. Call in the gentlewoman that owns
this house.

Enter SENCER *no longer disguised, and the* Wise-woman.

Boys. Old trot, I'll trounce thee.

Here is the marriage proved 'twixt Luce and Chartley:
Witch, this was not your promise.

Wise-wo. Have patience, and in the end we'll pay you
all. Your worships are most heartily welcome. I made
bold to send for you, and you may see to what end,
which was to discover unto you the wild vagaries of this
wanton wag-pasty—a wild oats I warrant him—and, Sir
Harry, that your daughter hath scaped this scouring,
thank this gentleman, and then make of him as he
deserves.

Sir Harry. Oh, I remember him.

Grat. He never pleased mine eye so well as now.
I know his love, and he in Chartley's place
My favour shall possess.

Sen. Thanks, my sweet Grace.

Sir Harry. Ay, and the more the inconstant youth to
      spite,
Sencer, I give her thee in Chartley's sight.

Y. Chart. There's one gone already; but this is my
wife, and her I'll keep in spite both of the devil and his
dam.

Wise-wo. Not from her lawful husband!

Y. Chart. That am I.

Wise-wo. That is the gentleman [*pointing to* BOYSTER],
—accept him, Luce; and you the like of her—nay, I'll make
it good. This gentleman married you visarded, you him
disguised, mistaking him for Chartley, which none but
my boy Jack was privy to: after she changed her habit
with him, as you with Jack; and you in Mistress Luce's
habit—

Luce. May I believe you, mother?

Wise-wo. This be your token.

Boys. Her that I married, I wrung twice by the finger.

Luce. Of that token, my hand was sensible.

Boys. And ere the clamorous and loud noise begun,
I whispered to her thus—   [*Whispers.*
Luce. You are the man.
Boys. Thanks, grannam; what thou promised thou hast
done.
Luce's Fa. And, leaving him, I take you for my son.
Y. Chart. Two gone! then where's the third? This
makes me mad.
Where is my wife, then? for a wife I had.
Wise-wo. Not see thy wife? Come hither, Jack, my
boy.
Nay, take him to thee, and with him all joy.
O. Chart. Well art thou served to be a general scorn
To all thy blood: and, if not for our sakes,
For thy soul's health and credit of the world,
Have some regard to me—to me thy father.
Y. Chart. Enough, sir: if I should say I would
become a new man, you would not take my word; if I
should swear I would amend my life, you would not
take mine oath; if I should bind myself to become an
honest man, you would scarce take my bond.
O. Chart. I should do none of these.
Y. Chart. Then see, sir: when to all your judgments
I see me past grace, do I lay hold of grace, and here
begin to retire myself. This woman hath lent me a glass,
in which I see all my imperfections, at which my conscience doth more blush inwardly than my face out-
wardly; and now I dare confidently undertake for myself
I am honest.
2nd Luce. Then I dare confidently undertake to help
you to a wife who desires to have an honest man or none.
Look on me well: simple though I stand here, I am your
wife. Blush not at your folly, man. Perhaps I have
more in me than you expect from me.
Y. Chart. Knavery and riot, both which are now to
me foreign.
2nd Luce. You and I have been better acquainted, and

yet search me not too far, lest you shame me ; look on
me well—nay better, better yet ;—I'll assure you I left off
a petticoat when I put on these breeches.   What say you
now ?   [*She scatters her hair.*

Y. Chart. First love, and best beloved !

2nd Luce. Let me be both or neither.

Wise-wo. [*Aside*] My boy turned girl ! I hope she'll keep
my counsel.   From henceforth I'll never entertain any
servant but I'll have her searched.

O. Chart. Her love hath drawn her hither after him.—
My loving daughter, welcome ! thou hast run
A happy course to see my son thus changed.

Y. Chart. Father, call me once again your son, and,
Sir Harry, me your friend ; Sencer, a hand, and Mistress
Grace, a heart, in honourable love.   Where I have
wronged you, Luce, forgive ; impute my errors to my
youth, not me.   With Grace I interchange an embrace ;
with you, Luce, a parting buss.   I wish you all joy.
Divide my heart amongst you—thou my soul !
Nay, Mother Midnight, there's some love for you ;
Out of thy folly, being reputed wise,
We, self-conceited, have our follies found :
Bear thou the name of all these comical acts.
Luce, Luce, and Grace —O covetous man ! I see
I sought to engross what now sufficeth three,
Yet each one wife enough.   One nuptial feast
. Shall serve three bridals, where be thou chief guest !

                                                  [*Exeunt.*

THE RAPE OF LUCRECE.

 N edition of *The Rape of Lucrece* was published in 1608 ; two other editions followed in 1609, and others again in 1630 and 1638. It was acted at the Red Bull in Clerkenwell. In the old copies neither the acts nor the scenes, excepting in the case of the senate scenes, are marked ; in the present reprint the divisions are given, it is hoped, with approximate correctness.

To the READER.

T hath been no custom in me of all other men (courteous readers) to commit my plays to the press ; the reason though some may attribute to my own insufficiency, I had rather subscribe, in that, to their severe censure, than by seeking to avoid the imputation of weakness, to incur greater suspicion of honesty : for, though some have used a double sale of their labours, first to the stage, and after to the press, for my own part I here proclaim myself ever faithful in the first, and never guilty of the last. Yet since some of my plays have (unknown to me, and without any of my direction) accidentally come into the printer's hands, and therefore so corrupt and mangled (copied only by the ear) that I have been as unable to know them as ashamed to challenge them, this therefore I was the willinger to furnish out in his native habit : first being by consent ; next because.the rest have been so wronged, in being published in such savage and ragged ornaments. Accept it, courteous gentlemen, and prove as favourable readers as we have found you gracious auditors.

Yours, T. H.

DRAMATIS PERSONÆ.

SERVIUS, King of Rome.

TARQUIN the Proud.

ARUNS,
SEXTUS, } the two Sons of TARQUIN.

BRUTUS JUNIOR.

COLLATINUS, otherwise COLLATINE.

HORATIUS COCLES.

MUTIUS SCEVOLA.

LUCRETIUS.

VALERIUS.

POPLICOLA.

PORSENNA, King of the Tuscans.

PORSENNA's Secretary.

The Priest of Apollo.

Two Sentinels.

Senators.

Serving-man.

Clown.

LUCRECE, Wife of COLLATINUS.

TULLIA, Wife of TARQUIN.

MIRABLE, LUCRECE's Maid.

SCENE.—ROME and its outskirts, DELPHI, and ARDEA.

THE RAPE OF LUCRECE.

ACT THE FIRST.

SCENE I.—*The Senate-house.*

Enter TARQUIN, TULLIA, SEXTUS, ARUNS, LUCRETIUS, VALERIUS, POPLICOLA, *and* Senators *before them.*

UL. Withdraw ; we must have private conference
With our dear husband.
   [*Exeunt all except* TARQUIN *and*
    TULLIA.
  Tar. What wouldst thou, wife ?
  Tul. Be what I am not ; make thee
greater far
Than thou canst aim to be.
  Tar. Why, I am Tarquin.
  Tul. And I am Tullia—what of that ?
What diapason's more in Tarquin's name
Than in a subject's ? or what's Tullia
More in the sound than to become the name
Of a poor maid or waiting gentlewoman ?
I am a princess both by birth and thoughts,
Yet all's but Tullia. There's no resonance
In a bare style ; my title bears no breadth,
Nor hath it any state. O me, I'm sick !
  Tar. Sick, lady !
  Tul. Sick at heart.

Tar. Why, my sweet Tullia ?

Tul. To be a queen I long, long, and am sick ;
With ardency my hot appetite's a-fire,
Till my swollen fervour be deliverèd   .
Of that great title queen.   My heart's all royal,
Not to be circumscribed in servile bounds.   ,
While there's a king that rules the peers of Rome,
Tarquin makes legs,[1] and Tullia curtsies low, ˙
Bows at each nod, and must not near the state
Without obeisance.   Oh! I ·hate this awe ;
My proud heart cannot brook it.

Tar. Hear me, wife.

Tul. I am no wife of Tarquin's if not king :
Oh, had Jove made me man, I would have mounted
Above the base tribunals of the earth,
Up to the clouds, for pompous sovereignty.
Thou art a man : oh, bear my royal mind,
Mount heaven, and see if Tullia lag behind:
There is no earth in me, I am all fire ;
Were Tarquin so, then should we both aspire.

Tar. O Tullia, though my body taste of dulness,
My soul is winged to soar as high as thine ;
But note what flags our wings,—forty-five years
The king thy father hath protected Rome.

Tul. That makes for us : the people covet change ;
Even the best things in time grow tedious.

Tar. 'Twould seem unnatural in thee, my Tullia,
The reverend king thy father to depose.

Tul. A kingdom's quest makes sons and fathers foes.

Tar. And but by Servius' fall we cannot climb;
The balm[2] that must anoint us is his blood.

Tul. Let's lave our brows then in that crimson flood ;
We must be bold and dreadless : who aspires,
Mounts by the lives of fathers, sons, and sires.

---

[1] Bows.
[2] The consecrated oil used at coronations.   Shakespeare has the expression : "'Tis not the balm, the sceptre and the ball."

Tar. And so must I, since, for a kingdom's love,
Thou canst despise a father for a crown.
Tarquin shall mount, Servius be tumbled down,
For he usurps my state, and first deposed
My father in my swathèd infancy,
For which he shall be countant :[1] to this end
I have sounded all the peers and senators,
And, though unknown to thee, my Tullia,
They all embrace my faction ; and so they
 Love change of state, a new king to obey.
  Tul. Now is my Tarquin worthy Tullia's grace,
Since in my arms I thus a king embrace.
  Tar. The king should meet this day in parliament
With all the Senate and Estates[2] of Rome.
His place will I assume, and there proclaim
All our decrees in royal Tarquin's name.   [*Flourish.*

Re-enter SEXTUS, ARUNS, LUCRETIUS, VALERIUS, COLLA-
        TINE, *and* Senators.

  Luc. May it please thee, noble Tarquin, to attend
The king this day in the high Capitol?
  Tul. Attend !
  Tar. We intend this day to see the Capitol.
You knew our father, good Lucretius ?
  Luc. I did, my lord.
  Tar. Was not I his son ?
The queen my mother was of royal thoughts,
And heart pure as unblemished innocence.
  Luc. What asks my lord ?
  Tar. Sons should succeed their fathers : but anon
You shall hear more ; high time that we were gone.
        [*Flourish. Exeunt all but* COLLATINE *and*
                VALERIUS.
  Col. There's moral sure in this, Valerius :
Here's model, yea, and matter too to breed
Strange meditations in the provident brains

----

[1] *i.e.* Held accountant.   [2] Nobles.

Of our grave fathers : some strange project lives
This day in cradle that's but newly born.

Val. No doubt, Collatine, no doubt, here's a giddy
and drunken world ; it reels ; it hath got the staggers ; the
commonwealth is sick of an ague, of which nothing can
cure her but some violent and sudden affrightment.

Col. The wife of Tarquin would be a queen—nay, on
my life, she is with child till she be so.

Val. And longs to be brought to bed of a kingdom. I
divine we shall see scuffling to-day in the Capitol.

Col. If there be any difference among the princes and
Senate, whose faction will Valerius follow ?

Val. Oh, Collatine, I am a true citizen, and in this I
will best show myself to be one, to take part with the
strongest. If Servius o'ercome, I am liegeman to
Servius ; and if Tarquin subdue, I am for *vive* Tarquinius.

Col. Valerius, no more, this talk does but keep us
from the sight of this solemnity : by this the princes are
entering the Capitol : come, we must attend.   [*Exeunt.*

SCENE II.—*The same.*

Enter TARQUIN, TULLIA, SEXTUS, ARUNS, LUCRETIUS
on one side : BRUTUS *meeting them on the other very
humorously.*[1]

Tar. This place is not for fools, this parliament
Assembles not the strains of idiotism,
Only the grave and wisest of the land :
Important are the affairs we have in hand.
Hence with that mome.[2]

Luc. Brutus, forbear the presence.

Bru. Forbear the presence ! why, pray ?

---

[1] Oddly.   [2] Blockhead.

Sex. None are admitted to this grave concourse 1
But wise men. Nay, good Brutus.

Bru. You'll have an empty parliament then.

Aruns. Here is no room for fools.

Bru. Then what makest thou here, or he, or he ? O
Jupiter ! if this command be kept strictly, we shall have
empty benches : get you home, you that are here, for here
will be nothing to do this day. A general concourse of
wise men ! 'twas never seen since the first chaos. Tarquin, if the general rule have no exceptions, thou wilt
have an empty consistory.

Tul. Brutus, you trouble us.

Bru. How powerful am I, you Roman deities, that
am able to trouble her that troubles a whole empire !
Fools exempted, and women admitted ! laugh, Democritus.[1] But have you nothing to say to madmen ?

Tar. Madmen have here no place.

Bru. Then out of doors with Tarquin. What's he
that may sit in a calm valley, and will choose to repose
in a tempestuous mountain, but a madman ? that may
live in tranquillous pleasures, and will seek out a kingdom's care, but a madman ? who would seek innovation
in a commonwealth in public, or be overruled by a
curst[2] wife in private, but a fool or a madman ? Give me
thy hand, Tarquin ; shall we two be dismissed together
from the Capitol ?

Tar. Restrain his folly.

Tul. Drive the frantic hence.

Aruns. Nay, Brutus.

Sex. Good Brutus.

Bru. Nay, soft, soft, good blood of the Tarquins, let's
have a few cold words first, and I am gone in an instant.
I claim the privilege of the nobility of Rome, and by that
privilege my seat in the Capitol. I am a lord by birth,

---

[1] The laughing philosopher of Abdera :   [2] Shrewish.
  Perpetuo risu pulmonem agitare solebat
  Democritus.—*Juvenal*, x., 33-4.

my place is as free in the Capitol as Horatius, thine ; or
thine, Lucretius; thine, Sextus; Aruns, thine; or any here :
I am a lord, and you banish all the lord fools from the
presence.   You'll have few to wait upon the king, but
gentlemen.   Nay, I am easily persuaded then—hands off!
since you will not have my company, you shall have my
room.

[*Aside.*] My room indeed ; for what I seem to be
Brutus is not, but born great Rome[1] to free.
The state is full of dropsy, and swollen big
With windy vapours, which my sword must pierce,
To purge the infected blood bred by the pride
Of these infested bloods.   Nay, now I go ;
Behold, I vanish, since 'tis Tarquin's mind :
One small fool goes, but great fools leaves behind. [*Exit.*

Luc. 'Tis pity one so generously [2] derived
Should be deprived his best induements thus,
And want the true directions of the soul.

Tar. To leave these dilatory trifles, lords,
Now to the public business of the land.
Lords, take your several places.

Luc. Not, great Tarquin,
Before the king assume his regal throne,
Whose coming we attend.

Tul. He's come already.

Luc. The king ?

Tar. The king.

Col. Servius ?

Tar. Tarquinius.

Luc. Servius is king.

Tar. He was : by power divine [3]
The throne that long since he usurped is mine.
Here we enthrone ourselves, cathedral state,
Long since detained us, justly we resume;

---

[1] "Rome" was pronounced like "room."   [2] Of such noble blood.
[3] The old editions miss the point by reading " he was by power
divine."

Then let our friends and such as love us cry,
Live Tarquin, and enjoy this sovereignty!
All. Live Tarquin and enjoy this sovereignty !

[*Flourish.*

Enter VALERIUS.

Val. The king himself, with such confederate peers
As stoutly embrace his faction, being informed
Of Tarquin's usurpation, armèd comes
Near to the entrance of the Capitol.
　Tar. No man give place ; he that dares to arise
And do him reverence, we his love despise.

Enter SERVIUS, HORATIUS, SCEVOLA, *and* Soldiers.

　Ser. Traitor !
　Tar. Usurper !
　Ser. Descend.
　Tul. Sit still.
　Ser. In Servius' name, Rome's great imperial monarch,
I charge thee, Tarquin, disenthrone thyself,
And throw thee at our feet, prostrate for mercy.
　Hor. Spoke like a king.
　Tar. In Tarquin's name, now Rome's imperial mon-
　　arch,
We charge thee, Servius, make free resignation
Of that arched wreath thou hast usurped so long.
　Tul. Words worth an empire.
　Hor. Shall this be brooked, my sovereign ?
Dismount the traitor.
　Sex. Touch him he that dares.
　Hor. Dares !
　Tul. Dares.
　Ser. Strumpet, no child of mine !
　Tul. Dotard, and not my father !
　Ser. Kneel to thy king.
　Tul. Submit thou to thy queen.
　Ser. Insufferable treason ! with bright steel

Heywood　　　　　　　　　　　　　　　　　z

Lop down these interponents that withstand
The passage to our throne.
Hor. That Cocles dares.
Sex. We with our steel guard Tarquin and his chair.
Sce. A Servius !
Aruns. A Tarquin !   [*They fight ;* SERVIUS *is slain.*
Tar. Now are we king indeed ; our awe is builded
Upon this royal base, the slaughtered body
Of a dead king ; we by his ruin rise
To a monarchal throne.
Tul. We have our longing ;
My father's death gives me a second life
Much better than the first; my birth was servile,
But this new breath of reign is large and free :
Welcome, my second life of sovereignty !
Luc. I have a daughter, but, I hope, of mettle
Subject to better temperature ; should my Lucrece
Be of this pride, these hands should sacrifice
Her blood unto the gods that dwell below ;
The abortive brat should not out-live my spleen.
But Lucrece is my daughter, this my queen.
Tul. Tear off the crown that yet empales the temples
Of our usurping father—quickly, lords—
And in the face of his yet bleeding wounds
Let us receive our honours.
Tar. The same breath
Gives our state life, that was the usurper's death.
Tul. Here then by Heaven's hand we invest ourselves :
Music, whose loftiest tones grace princes crowned,
Unto our novel coronation sound.
      [*Flourish.* VALERIUS *leads forward* HORATIUS *and*
      SCEVOLA.
Tar. Whom doth Valerius to our state present ?
Val. Two valiant Romans ; this Horatius Cocles,
This gentleman called Mutius Scevola,
Who, whilst King Servius wore the diadem,
Upheld his sway and princedom by their loves ;

But he being fallen, since all the peers of Rome
Applaud King Tarquin in his sovereignty,
They with like suffrage greet your coronation.
  Hor. This hand, allied unto the Roman crown,
Whom never fear dejected or cast low,
Lays his victorious sword at Tarquin's feet,
And prostrates with that sword allegiance.
King Servius' life we loved, but, he expired,
Great Tarquin's life is in our hearts desired.
  See. Who, whilst he rules with justice and integrity,
Shall with our dreadless hands our hearts command,
Even with the best employments of our lives.
Since fortune lifts thee, we submit to fate :
Ourselves are vassals to the Roman state.
  Tar. Your rooms were empty in our train of friends,
Which we rejoice to see so well supplied :
Receive our grace, live in our clement favours,
In whose submission our young glory grows
To his ripe height : fall in our friendly train,
And strengthen with your loves our infant reign.
  Hor. We live for Tarquin.
  See. And to thee alone,
Whilst Justice keeps thy sword and thou thy throne.
  Tar. Then are you ours. And now conduct us straight
In triumph through the populous streets of Rome
To the king's palace, our majestic seat.
Your hearts, though freely proffered, we entreat. [*Music.*

As they march, TULLIA *treads on* SERVIUS'S *dead body*
and pauses.

  Tul. What block is that we tread on ?
  Luc. 'Tis the body
Of your deceasèd father, madam queen ;
Your shoe is crimsoned with his vital blood.
  Tul. No matter ; let his mangled body lie,
And with his base confederates strew the streets,
That, in disgrace of his usurpèd pride,

We o'er his trunk may in our chariot ride;
For, mounted like a queen, 'twould do me good
To wash my coach-naves [1] in my father's blood.
    Luc. Here's a good child !
    Tar. Remove it, we command,
And bear his carcase to the funeral pile,
Where, after this dejection, let it have
His solemn and due obsequies.   Fair Tullia,
Thy hate to him grows from thy love to us;
Thou show'st thyself in this unnatural strife
An unkind daughter, but a loving wife.
But on unto our palace : this blest day,
A king's increase grows by a king's decay.   [*Exeunt.*

SCENE III.—*A Public Place in Rome.*

Enter BRUTUS.

    Bru. Murder the king ! a high and capital treason.
Those giants that waged war against the gods,
For which the o'erwhelmed mountains hurled by Jove
To scatter them, and give them timeless [2] graves,
Was not more cruel than this butchery,
This slaughter made by Tarquin.   But the queen !
A woman—fie, fie ! did not this she-parricide
Add to her father's wounds ? and when his body
Lay all besmeared and stained in the blood royal,
Did not this monster, this infernal hag,
Make her unwilling charioter drive on,
And with his shod wheels crush her father's bones,
Break his crazed skull, and dash his sparkled [3] brains
Upon the pavements, whilst she held the reins ?
The affrighted sun at this abhorrèd object

---

[1] Wheels, properly part of the axle.
[2] Untimely.   This passage is corrupt.   [3] Scattered.

Put on a mask of blood, and yet she blushed not.
Jove, art thou just ? hast thou reward for piety,
And for offence no vengeance ? or canst punish
Felons, and pardon traitors ? chastise murderers,
And wink at parricides ? if thou be worthy,
As well we know thou art, to fill the throne
Of all eternity, then with that hand
That flings the trifurk [1] thunder, let the pride
Of these our irreligious monarchisers
Be crowned in blood.   This makes poor Brutus mad,—
To see sin frolic, and the virtuous sad.

Enter SEXTUS *and* ARUNS.

Aruns. Soft, here's Brutus ; let us acquaint him with
the news.

Sex. Content.   Now, cousin Brutus.

Bru. Who, I your kinsman ! though I be of the blood
of the Tarquins, yet no cousin, gentle prince.

Aruns. And why so, Brutus ? scorn you our alliance ?

Bru. No ; I was cousin to the Tarquins when they
were subjects, but dare claim no kindred as they are
sovereigns ; Brutus is not so mad, though he be merry,
but he hath wit enough to keep his head on his
shoulders.

Aruns. Why do you, my lord, thus lose your hours,
and neither profess war nor domestic profit ? the first
might beget you love, the other riches.

Bru. Because I would live.   Have I not answered you ?
because I would live.   Fools and madmen are no rubs [2] in
the way of usurpers; the firmament can brook but one
sun, and for my part I must not shine : I had rather live
an obscure black than appear a fair white to be shot at.
The end of all is, I would live.   Had Servius been a shrub,
the wind had not shook him ; or a madman, he had not

[1] Three-forked.
[2] Obstacles : originally a term used at the game of bowls.

perished. I covet no more wit nor employment than as much as will keep life and soul together—I would but live.

Aruns. You are satirical, cousin Brutus: but to the purpose. The king dreamt a strange and ominous dream last night, and, to be resolved of the event, my brother Sextus and I must to the oracle.

Sex. And, because we would be well accompanied, we have got leave of the king that you, Brutus, shall associate us, for our purpose is to make a merry journey on't.

Bru. So you'll carry me along with you to be your fool, and make you merry.

Sex. Not our fool, but—

Bru. To make you merry : I shall, nay, I would make you merry, or tickle you till you laugh. The oracle ! I'll go to be resolved of some doubts private to myself : nay, princes, I am so much endeared both to your loves and companies, that you shall not have the power to be rid of me. What limits have we for our journey ?

Sex. Five days, no more.

Bru. I shall fit me to your preparations. But one thing more : goes Collatine along ?

Sex. Collatine is troubled with the common disease of all new-married men ; he's sick of the wife : his excuse is, forsooth, that Lucrece will not let him go : but you, having neither wife nor wit to hold you, I hope will not disappoint us.

Bru. Had I both, yet should you prevail with me above either.

Aruns. We shall expect you.

Bru. Horatius Cocles and Mutius Scevola are not engaged in this expedition?

Aruns. No, they attend the king. Farewell.

Bru. Lucretius stays at home too, and Valerius ?

Sex. The palace cannot spare them.

Bru. None but we three ?

Sex. We three.

Bru. We three; well, five days hence.

Sex. You have the time, farewell.

[*Exeunt* SEXTUS *and* ARUNS.

Bru. The time I hope cannot be circumscribed
Within so short a limit ; Rome and I
Are not so happy.   What's the reason then,
Heaven spares his rod so long?   Mercury, tell me.
I have't, the fruit of pride is yet but green,
Not mellow; though it grows apace, it comes not
To his full height : Jove oft delays his vengeance,
That when it haps 't may prove more terrible.
Despair not, Brutus, then, but let thy country
And thee take this last comfort after all :
Pride, when thy fruit is ripe 't must rot and fall.
But to the oracle.   [*Exit.*

ACT THE SECOND.

SCENE I.—*A Street in Rome.*

Enter HORATIUS COCLES *and* MUTIUS SCEVOLA.

OR. I would I were no Roman.

Sce. Cocles, why?

Hor. I am discontented, and dare not speak my thoughts.

Sce. What, shall I speak them for you?

Hor. Mutius, do.

Sce. Tarquin is proud.

Hor. Thou hast them.

Sce. Tyrannous.

Hor. True.

Sce. Insufferably lofty.

Hor. Thou hast hit me.

Sce. And shall I tell thee what I prophesy
Of his succeeding rule?

Hor. No, I'll do't for thee:
Tarquin's ability will in the weal
Beget a weak unable impotence;
His strength make Rome and our dominions weak,
His soaring high make us to flag our wings,
And fly close by the earth; his golden feathers
Are of such vastness, that they spread like sails,
And so becalm us that we have not air
Able to raise our plumes, to taste the pleasures
Of our own elements.

Sce. We are one heart ;
Our thoughts and our desires are suitable.
Hor. Since he was king he bears him like a god,
His wife like Pallas, or the wife of Jove ;
Will not be spoke to without sacrifice,
And homage sole due to the deities.

Enter LUCRETIUS.

Sce. What haste with good Lucretius ?
Luc. Haste, but small speed.
I had an earnest suit unto the king,
About some business that concerns the weal
Of Rome and us ; 'twill not be listened to.
He has took upon him such ambitious state
That he abandons conference with his peers,
Or, if he chance to endure our tongues so much
As but to hear their sonance, he despises
The intent of all our speeches, our advices,
And counsel, thinking his own judgment only
To be approved in matters military,
And in affairs domestic ; we are but mutes,
And fellows of no parts, viols unstrung,
Our notes too harsh to strike in princes' ears.
Great Jove amend it !
Hor. Whither will you, my lord ?
Luc. No matter where,
If from the court.   I'll home to Collatine
And to my daughter Lucrece : home breeds safety,
Danger's begot in court ; a life retired
Must please me now perforce : then, noble Scevola,
And you my dear Horatius, farewell both.
Where industry is scorned let's welcome sloth.

Enter COLLATINE.

Hor. Nay, good Lucretius, do not leave us thus.
See, here comes Collatine ; but where's Valerius ?
How does he taste these times?
Col. Not giddily like Brutus, passionately

Like old Lucretius with his tear-swollen eyes;
Not laughingly like Mutius Scevola,
Nor bluntly like Horatius Cocles here;
He has usurped a stranger garb of humour,
Distinct from these in nature every way.

Luc. How is he relished? can his eyes forbear
In this strange state to shed a passionate tear?

Sce. Can he forbear to laugh with Scevola,
At that which passionate weeping cannot mend?

Hor. Nay, can his thought shape aught but melancholy
To see these dangerous passages of state?
How is he tempered, noble Collatine?

Col. Strangely; he is all song, he's ditty all,
Note that: Valerius hath given up the court,
And weaned himself from the king's consistory,
In which his sweet harmonious tongue grew harsh.
Whether it be that he is discontent,
Yet would not so appear before the king,
Or whether in applause of these new edicts,
Which so distaste the people, or what cause
I know not, but now he's all musical.
Unto the council chamber he goes singing,
And whilst the king his wilful edicts makes,
In which none's tongue is powerful save the king's,
He's in a corner, relishing strange airs.
Conclusively, he's from a toward hopeful gentleman,
Transhaped to a mere ballater,[1] none knowing
Whence should proceed this transmutation.

Enter VALERIUS.

Hor. See where he comes.   Morrow, Valerius.

Luc. Morrow, my lord.

Val. [*Sings.*] When Tarquin first in court began,
        And was approvèd king,
    Some men for sudden joy 'gan weep,
        But I for sorrow sing.

---
[1] Maker of ballads

Sce. Ha, ha ! how long has my Valerius
Put on this strain of mirth, or what's the cause?
    Val. [*Sings.*] Let humour change and spare not ;
        Since 'Tarquin's proud, I care not ;
        His fair words so bewitchèd my delight,
        That I doted on his sight :
        Now he is changed, cruel thoughts embracing,
        And my deserts disgracing.

    Hor. Upon my life he's either mad or love-sick.
Oh, can Valerius, but so late a statesman,
Of whom the public weal deserved so well,
Tune out his age in songs and canzonets,
Whose voice should thunder counsel in the ears
Of Tarquin and proud Tullia? Think, Valerius,
What that proud woman Tullia is ; 'twill put thee
Quite out of tune.
    Val. [*Sings.*] Now what is love I will thee tell :
        It is the fountain and the well,
        Where pleasure and repentance dwell ;
        It is perhaps the sansing [1] bell,
        That rings all in to heaven or hell ;
    And this is love, and this ıs love, as I hear tell.

        Now what is love I will you show :
        A thing that creeps and cannot go,
        A prize that passeth to and fro,
        A thing for me, a thing for moe,[2]
        And he that proves shall find it so ;
    And this is love, and this is love, sweet friend, I trow.

    Luc. Valerius, I shall quickly change thy cheer,
And make thy passionate eyes lament with mine.
Think how that worthy prince, our kinsman king,
Was butchered in the marble Capitol :
Shall Servius Tullius unregarded die
Alone of thee, whom all the Roman ladies,

    [1] *i.e.* Sanctus bell.   [2] More ; *i.e.* others.

Even yet with tear-swollen eyes, and sorrowful souls,
Compassionate, as well he merited?
To these lamenting dames what canst thou sing,
Whose grief through all the Roman temples ring?   ,
    Val. [*Sings.*] Lament, ladies, lament!
        Lament the Roman land!
        The king is fra thee hent
        Was doughty on his hand.

        We'll gang into the kirk,
          His dead corpse we'll embrace,
        And when we see him dead,
          We aye will cry alas!—Fa la!

    Hor. This music mads me; I all mirth despise.
    Luc. To hear him sing draws rivers from mine eyes.
    Sce. It pleaseth me; for since the court is harsh,
And looks askance on soldiers, let's be merry,
Court ladies, sing, drink, dance, and every man
Get him a mistress, coach it in the country,
And taste the sweets of it.   What thinks Valerius
Of Scevola's last counsel?
    Val. [*Sings.*] Why, since we soldiers cannot prove,
        And grief it is to us therefore,
        Let every man get him a love,
          To trim her well, and fight no more;
          That we may taste of lovers' bliss,
          Be merry and blithe, embrace and kiss,
          That ladies may say, Some more of this;
          That ladies may say, Some more of this.

        Since court and city both grow proud,
          And safety you delight to hear,
        We in the country will us shroud,
          Where lives to please both eye and ear:
          The nightingale sings jug, jug, jug,
          The little lamb leaps after his dug,

And the pretty milk-maids they look so smug,
And the pretty milk-maids, &c.

Come, Scevola, shall we go and be idle?

Luc. I'll in to weep.

Hor. But I my gall to grate.

Sce. I'll laugh at time, till it will change our fate.

[*Exeunt all but* COLLATINE.

Col. Thou art not what thou seem'st, Lord Scevola;
Thy heart mourns in thee, though thy visage smile;
And so does thy soul weep, Valerius,
Although thy habit sing; for these new humours
Are but put on for safety, and to arm them
Against the pride of Tarquin, from whose danger,
None great in love, in counsel, or opinion,
Can be kept safe : this makes me lose [1] my hours
At home with Lucrece, and abandon court.

Enter Clown.

Clown. Fortune, I embrace thee, that thou hast assisted me in finding my master; the gods of good Rome keep my lord and master out of all bad company !

Col. Sirrah, the news with you?

Clown. Would you ha' court news, camp news, city news, or country news, or would you know what's the news at home?

Col. Let me know all the news.

Clown. The news at court is, that a small leg and a silk stocking is in the fashion for your lord, and the water that God Mercury makes [2] is in request, with your lady. The heaviness of the king's wine makes many a light head, and the emptiness of his dishes many full bellies; eating and drinking was never more in use; you shall find the baddest legs in boots, and the worst faces in masks. They keep their old stomachs still : the king's good cook hath the most wrong; for that which was wont to be private only to him is now usurped among all

---

[1] Waste.   [2] *i.e.* A cosmetic lotion containing mercury.

the other officers ; for now every man in his place, to the prejudice of the master cook, makes bold to lick his own

Col. The news in the camp?   [fingers.

Clown. The greatest news in the camp is that there is no news at all ; for being no camp at all, how can there be any tidings from it ?

Col. Then for the city?

Clown. The senators are rich, their wives fair, credit grows cheap, and traffic dear, for you have many that are broke ; the poorest man that is may take up what he will, so he will be but bound—to a post till he pay the debt. There was one courtier lay with twelve men's wives in the suburbs, and pressing farther to make one more cuckold within the walls, and being taken with the manner,[1] had nothing to say for himself but this—he that made twelve made thirteen.

Col. Now, sir, for the country ?

Clown. There is no news there but at the ale-house ; there's the most receipt. And is it not strange, my lord, that so many men love ale that know not what ale is ?

Col. Why, what is ale?

Clown. Why, ale is a kind of juice made of the precious grain called malt ; and what is malt? Malt's M A L T ; and what is M A L T ? M much, A ale, L little, T thrift ; that is, much ale, little thrift.

Col. Only the news at home, and I have done?

Clown. My lady must needs speak with you about earnest business, that concerns her nearly, and I was sent in all haste to entreat your lordship to come away.

Col. And couldst thou not have told me ? Lucrece And I stand trifling here ! Follow, away !   [stay,

Clown. Ay, marry, sir, the way into her were a way worth following, and that's the reason that so many serving-men that are familiar with their mistresses have lost the name of servitors, and are now called their masters' followers. Rest you merry !   [*Music.*

---

[1] Caught in the act. Cowel says, "manner or mainour denotes the thing that a thief taketh or stealeth."

SCENE II.—*The Temple at Delphi.*

Enter APOLLO'S Priests, *with tapers ; after them,* ARUNS,
SEXTUS, *and* BRUTUS, *with their oblations, all kneel-
ing before the Oracle.*

Priest. O thou Delphian god, inspire
Thy priests, and with celestial fire
Shot from thy beams crown our desire,
   That we may follow,
In these thy true and hallowed measures,
The utmost of thy heavenly treasures,
According to the thoughts and pleasures
   Of great Apollo.

Our hearts with inflammations burn,
Great Tarquin and his people mourn,
Till from thy temple we return,
   With some glad tiding.
Then tell us, shall great Rome be blest,
And royal Tarquin live in rest,
That gives his high-ennobled breast
   To thy safe guiding?

Oracle. Then Rome her ancient honours wins,
When she is purged from Tullia's sins.
Bru. Gramercies, Phœbus, for these spells !
Phœbus alone, alone excels.
Sex. Tullia perhaps sinned in our grandsire's death,
And hath not yet by reconcilement made
Atone with Phœbus, at whose shrine we kneel ;
Yet, gentle priest, let us thus far prevail,
To know if Tarquin's seed shall govern Rome,
And by succession claim the royal wreath ?
Behold me, younger of the Tarquins' race,
This elder Aruns, both the sons of Tullia ;
This Junius Brutus, though a madman, yet
Of the high blood of the Tarquins.

Priest. Sextus, peace.
 Tell us, O thou that shin'st so bright,
 From whom the world receives his light,
 Whose absence is perpetual night,
   Whose praises ring :
 Is it with Heaven's applause decreed,
 When Tarquin's soul from earth is freed,
 That noble Sextus shall succeed
   In Rome as king?

Bru. Ay, oracle, hast thou lost thy tongue ?
Aruns. Tempt him again, fair priest.
Sex. If not as king, let Delphian Phœbus yet
Thus much resolve us : who shall govern Rome,
Or of us three bear great'st pre-eminence?
Priest. Sextus, I will.
 Yet, sacred Phœbus, we entreat,
 Which of these three shall be great
 With largest power and state replete,
   By the Heaven's doom?[1]
 Phœbus, thy thoughts no longer smother.
Oracle. He that first shall kiss his mother
 Shall be powerful, and no other
   Of you three in Rome.

Sex. Shall kiss his mother !   [BRUTUS *falls.*
Bru. Mother Earth, to thee
An humble kiss I tender.
Aruns. What means Brutus ?
Bru. The blood of the slaughtered sacrifice made this
floor as slippery as the place where Tarquin treads; 'tis
glassy and as smooth as ice : I was proud to hear the
oracle so gracious to the blood of the Tarquins, and so
I fell.
Sex. Nothing but so ? then to the oracle.
I charge thee, Aruns,—Junius Brutus, thee,—
To keep the sacred doom of the oracle

    [1] Decree.

From all our train, lest when the younger lad
Our brother, now at home, sits dandled
Upon fair Tullia's lap, this understanding,
May kiss our beauteous mother, and succeed.

Bru. Let the charge go round.
It shall go hard but I'll prevent[1] you, Sextus.

Sex. I fear not the madman Brutus ; and for Aruns, let
me alone to buckle[2] with him : I'll be the first at my
mother's lips for a kingdom.

Bru. If the madman have not been before you, Sextus.
If oracles be oracles, their phrases are mystical ; they
speak still in clouds.   Had he meant a natural mother he
would not ha' spoke it by circumstance.

Sex. Tullia, if ever thy lips were pleasing to me, let it
be at my return from the oracle.

Aruns. If a kiss will make me a king, Tullia, I will
spring to thee, though through the blood of Sextus.

Bru. Earth, I acknowledge no mother but thee ;
accept me as thy son, and I shall shine as bright in
Rome as Apollo himself in his temple at Delphos.

Sex. Our superstitions ended, sacred priest,
Since we have had free answer from the gods,
To whose fair altars we have done due right,
And hallowed them with presents acceptable,
Let's now return, treading these holy measures
With which we entered great Apollo's temple.
Now, Phœbus, let thy sweet-tuned organs sound,
Whose sphere-like music must direct our feet
Upon the marble pavement.   After this
We'll gain a kingdom by a mother's kiss.   [*Exeunt.*

[1] Forestall.   [2] Contend.

SCENE III.—*The Senate-house.*

Enter TARQUIN, TULLIA, *and* COLLATINE, SCEVOLA, HORATIUS, LUCRETIUS, VALERIUS, Nobles.

Tar. Attend us with your persons, but your ears
Be deaf unto our counsels.
        [*The* Lords *fall off on either side and attend.*
Tul. Farther yet.
Tar. Now, Tullia, what must be concluded next?
Tul. The kingdom you have got by policy
You must maintain by pride.
Tar. Good.
Tul. Those that were late of the king's faction
Cut off, for fear they prove rebellious.
Tar. Better.
Tul. Since you gain nothing by the popular love,
Maintain by fear your princedom.
Tar. Excellent;
Thou art our oracle, and, save from thee,
We will admit no counsel. We obtained
Our state by cunning; it must be kept by strength;
And such as cannot love we'll teach to fear:
To encourage which, upon our better judgment,
And to strike greater terror to the world,
I have forbid thy father's funeral.
Tul. No matter.
Tar. All capital causes are by us discussed,
Traversed,[1] and executed without counsel:
We challenge too, by our prerogative,
The goods of such as strive against our state;
The freest citizens, without attaint,[2]
Arraign, or judgment, we to exile doom;
The poorer are our drudges, rich our prey,
And such as dare not strive our rule obey.
Tul. Kings are as gods, and divine sceptres bear;

---

[1] Thoroughly examined.   [2] Accusation.

The gods command, for mortal tribute, fear ;
But, royal lord, we that despise their love,
Must seek some means how to maintain this awe.

    Tar. By foreign leagues, and by our strength abroad.
Shall we, that are degreed above our people,
Whom Heaven hath made our vassals, reign with them?
No ; kings, above the rest tribunaled high,
Should with no meaner than with kings ally :
For this we to Mamilius Tusculan,
The Latin king, ha' given in marriage
Our royal daughter ; now his people's ours :
The neighbour princes are subdued by arms ;
And whom we could not conquer by constraint,
Them we have sought to win by courtesy.
Kings that are proud, yet would secure their own,
By love abroad shall purchase fear at home.

    Tul. We are secure, and yet our greatest strength
Is in our children : how dare treason look
Us in the face, having issue ? Barren princes
Breed danger in their singularity ;
Having none to succeed, their claim dies in them.
But when, in topping [1] one, three Tarquins more,
Like hydras' heads, grow to revenge his death,
It terrifies black treason.

    Tar. Tullia's wise
And apprehensive ! Were our princely sons
Sextus and Aruns back returnèd safe,
With an applausive answer of the gods
From the oracle, our state were able then,
Being gods ourselves, to scorn the hate of men.

       Enter SEXTUS, ARUNS, *and* BRUTUS.

    Sex. Where's Tullia ?
    Aruns. Where's our mother?
    Hor. Yonder, princes,
At council with the king.

---

[1] Lopping off.

Tul. Our sons returned!

Sex. Royal mother!

Aruns. Renowned queen!

Sex. I love her best,
Therefore will Sextus do his duty first.

Aruns. Being eldest in my birth, I'll not be youngest
In zeal to Tullia.

Bru. To't, lads!

Aruns. Mother, a kiss.

Sex. Though last in birth, let me be first in love.
A kiss, fair mother.

Aruns. Shall I lose my right?

Sex. Aruns shall down, were Aruns twice my brother,
If he presume 'fore me to kiss my mother.

Aruns. Ay, Sextus, think this kiss to be a crown, thus
would we tug for't.

Sex. Aruns, thou must down.

Tar. Restrain them, lords.

Bru. Nay, to't, boys! Oh, 'tis brave!
They tug for shadows, I the substance have.

Aruns. Through armèd gates, and thousand swords
To show my duty : let my valour speak.   [I'll break
                              [*Breaks from the* Nobles *and kisses her.*

Sex. O Heavens! you have dissolved me.

Aruns. Here I stand,
What I ha' done to answer with this hand.

Sex. O all ye Delphian gods, look down and see
How for these wrongs I will revenged be!

Tar. Curb in the proud boys' fury ; let us know
From whence this discord riseth.

Tul. From our love.
How happy are we in our issue now,
Whenas our sons even with their bloods contend
To exceed in duty ! We accept your zeal :
This your superlative degree of kindness
So much prevails with us, that to the king
We engage our own dear love 'twixt his incensement

And your presumption ; you are pardoned both.
And, Sextus, though you failed in your first proffer,
We do not yet esteem you least in love :
Ascend and touch our lips.

Sex. Thank you, no.

Tul. Then to thy knee we will descend thus low.

Sex. Nay, now it shall not need. How great's my
heart !

Aruns. In Tarquin's crown thou now hast lost thy part.

Sex. No kissing now. Tarquin, great queen, adieu !
Aruns, on earth we ha' no foe but you.

Tar. What means this their unnatural enmity ?

Tul. Hate, born from love.

Tar. Resolve us then, how did the gods accept
Our sacrifice ? how are they pleased with us ?
How long will they applaud our sovereignty ?

Bru. Shall I tell the king ?

Tar. Do, cousin, with the process of your journey.

Bru. I will. We went from hither when we went
from hence, arrived thither when we landed there, made
an end of our prayers when we had done our orisons,
when thus quoth Phœbus : " Tarquin shall be happy
whilst he is blest, govern while he reigns, wake when he
sleeps not, sleep when he wakes not, quaff when he
drinks, feed when he eats, gape when his mouth opens,
live till he die, and die when he can live no longer." So
Phœbus commends him to you.

Tar. Mad Brutus still. Son Aruns, what say you ?

Aruns. That the great gods, to whom the potent king
Of this large empire sacrificed by us,
Applaud your reign, commend your sovereignty :
And by a general synod grant to Tarquin
Long days, fair hopes, majestic government.

Bru. Adding withal, that to depose the late king,
which in others had been arch-treason, in Tarquin was
honour ; what in Brutus had been usurpation, in Tarquin
was lawful succession ; and for Tullia, though it be

parricide for a child to kill her father, in Tullia it was
charity by death to rid him of all his calamities.
Phœbus himself said she was a good child—and shall not
I say as he says?—to tread upon her father's skull,
Sparkle his brains upon her chariot-wheel,
And wear the sacred tincture of his blood
Upon her servile shoe.   But more than this,
After his death deny him the due claim
Of all mortality, a funeral,
An earthen sepulchre—this, this, quoth the oracle,
Save Tullia none would do.

   Tul. Brutus, no more,
Lest with the eyes of wrath and fury incensed
We look into thy humour : were not madness
And folly to thy words a privilege,
Even in thy last reproof of our proceedings
Thou hadst pronounced thy death.

   Bru. If Tullia will send Brutus abroad for news, and
after at his return not endure the telling of it, let Tullia
either get closer ears, or get for Brutus a stricter tongue.

   Tul. How, sir !

   Bru. God be wi' ye.   [*Exit.*

   Tar. Alas, 'tis madness—pardon him—not spleen ;
Nor is it hate, but frenzy.   We are pleased
To hear the gods propitious to our prayers.
But whither's Sextus gone ? resolve us, Cocles ;
We saw thee in his parting follow him.

   Hor. I heard him say, he would straight take his horse
And to the warlike Sabines, enemies
To Rome and you.

   Tar. Save them we have no opposites.
Dares the proud boy confederate with our foes ?
Attend us, lords ; we must new battle wage,
And with bright arms confront the proud boy's rage.

       [*Exeunt all but* LUCRETIUS, COLLATINE, HORA-
        TIUS, VALERIUS, *and* SCEVOLA.

   Hor. Had I as many souls as drops of blood

In these branched veins, as many lives as stars
Stuck in yond azure roof, and were to die
More deaths than I have wasted weary minutes
To grow to this, I'd hazard all and more
To purchase freedom to this bondaged Rome.
I'm vexed to see this virgin conqueress
Wear shackles in my sight.

   Luc. Oh, would my tears
Would rid great Rome of these prodigious fears !

Re-enter BRUTUS.

   Bru. What, weeping-ripe, Lucretius ! possible ? Now lords, lads, friends, fellows, young madcaps, gallants, and old courtly ruffians, all subjects under one tyranny, and therefore should be partners of one and the same unanimity, shall we go single ourselves by two and two, and go talk treason? then 'tis but his yea, and my nay, if we be called to question. Or shall's go use some violent bustling to break through this thorny servitude ? or shall we every man go sit like a man in desperation, and with Lucretius weep at Rome's misery. Now am I for all things, anything, or nothing. I can laugh with Scevola, weep with this good old man, sing " Oh hone hone " with Valerius, fret with Horatius Cocles, be mad like myself, or neutrize with Collatine. Say, what shall's do ?

   Hor. Fret.

   Val. Sing.

   Luc. Weep.

   Sce. Laugh.

   Bru. Rather let's all be mad,
That Tarquin he still reigneth, Rome's still sad.

   Col. You are madmen all that yield so much to
     passion ;
You lay yourselves too open to your enemies,
That would be glad to pry into your deeds,
And catch advantage to ensnare our lives ;
The king's fear, like a shadow, dogs you still,

Nor can you walk without it. I commend
Valerius most, and noble Scevola,
That what they cannot mend, seem not to mind.
By my consent let's ail wear out our hours .
In harmless sports : hawk, hunt, game, sing, drink, dance,
So shall we seem offenceless and live safe
In danger's bloody jaws : where [1] being humorous,
Cloudy, and curiously inquisitive
Into the king's proceedings, there armed fear
May search into us, call our deeds to question,
And so prevent all future expectation
Of wished amendment. Let us stay the time,
Till Heaven have made them ripe for just revenge,
When opportunity is offered us,   .
And then strike home ; till then do what you please : ·
No discontented thought my mind shall seize.

Bru. I am of Collatine's mind now. Valerius, sing us
a bawdy song, and make's merry : nay, it shall be so.

Val. Brutus shall pardon me.

Sce. The time that should have been seriously spent in
the state-house, I ha' learnt securely to spend in a
wenching-house, and now I profess myself anything but
a statesman.

Hor. The more thy vanity.

Luc. The less thy honour.

Val. The more his safety, and the less his fear.

[*Sings.*] She that denies me, I would have ;
   Who craves me, I despise :
   Venus hath power to rule mine heart,
    But not to please mine eyes.
   Temptations offered, I still scorn ;
    Denied, I cling them still.
   I'll neither glut mine appetite,
    Nor seek to starve my will.
   Diana, double clothed, offends ;

---

[1] *i.e.* Whereas.

So Venus, naked quite:
The last begets a surfeit, and
The other no delight.
That crafty girl shall please me best
That no, for yea, can say,
And every wanton willing kiss
Can season with a nay.

Bru. We ha' been mad lords long, now let us be merry lords. Horatius, maugre thy melancholy, and Lucretius, in spite of thy sorrow, I'll have a song. A subject for the ditty?

Hor. Great Tarquin's pride and Tullia's cruelty.

Bru. Dangerous ; no.

Luc. The tyrannies of the court, and vassalage of the

Sce. Neither. Shall I give the subject? [city.

Bru. Do, and let it be of all the pretty wenches in Rome.

Sce. It shall : shall it, shall it, Valerius?

Val. Anything according to my poor acquaintance and little conversance.

Bru. Nay, you shall stay, Horatius ; Lucretius, so shall you ; he removes himself from the love of Brutus that shrinks from my side till we have had a song of all the pretty suburbians :[1] sit round. When, Valerius?

Val. [*Sings*] Shall I woo the lovely Molly,
She's so fair, so fat, so jolly?
But she has a trick of folly,
Therefore I'll ha' none of Molly.
    No, no, no, no, no, no ;
I'll have none of Molly, no, no, no.

Oh, the cherry lips of Nelly,
They are red and soft as jelly;
But too well she loves her belly,
Therefore I'll have none of Nelly.
    No, no, &c.

[1] The suburbs of London were formerly the chief resort of loose women.

What say you to bonny Betty?
Ha' you seen a lass so pretty?
But her body is so sweaty,
Therefore I'll ha' none of Betty.
　　No, no, &c.

When I dally with my Dolly,
She is full of melancholy;
Oh, that wench is pestilent holly; [1]
Therefore I'll have none of Dolly.
　　No, no, &c.

I could fancy lovely Nanny,
But she has the loves of many,
Yet herself she loves not any,
Therefore I'll have none of Nanny.
　　No, no, &c.

In a flax shop I spied Rachel,
Where she her flax and tow did hatchel; [2]
But her cheeks hang like a satchel,
Therefore I'll have none of Rachel.
　　No, no, &c.

In a corner I met Biddy,
Her heels were light, her head was giddy;
She fell down, and somewhat did I,
Therefore I'll have none of Biddy.
　　No, no, &c.

Bru. The rest we'll hear within. What offence is there in this, Lucretius? what hurt's in this, Horatius? is it not better to sing with our heads on than to bleed with our heads off? I ne'er took Collatine for a politician till now. Come, Valerius; we'll run over all the wenches in Rome, from the community of lascivious Flora to the chastity of divine Lucrece; come, good Horatius.

　　　　　　　　　　　　　　　　　　　[*Exeunt.*

　　[1] Holy.　　　[2] Heckle or dress.

SCENE IV.—*A Room in the House of* COLLATINE.

Enter LUCRECE, Maid, *and* Clown.

Lucrece. A chair.

Clown. A chair for my lady.   Mistress Mirable, do
you not hear my lady call ?

Lucrece. Come near, sir ; be less officious
In duty, and use more attention. —
Nay, gentlewoman, we exempt not you
From our discourse, you must afford an ear
As well as he to what we ha' to say.

Maid. I still remain your handmaid.

Lucrece. Sirrah, I ha' seen you oft familiar
With this my maid and waiting gentlewoman,
As casting amorous glances, wanton looks,
And privy becks savouring incontinence :
I let you know you are not for my service
Unless you grow more civil.

Clown. Indeed, madam, for my own part I wish
Mistress Mirable well, as one fellow servant ought to
wish to another, but to say that ever I flung any sheep's
eyes in her face—how say you, Mistress Mirable, did I
ever offer it ?

Lucrece. Nay, mistress, I ha' seen you answer him
With gracious looks and some uncivil smiles,
Retorting eyes, and giving his demeanour
Such welcome as becomes not modesty.
Know henceforth there shall no lascivious phrase,
. Suspicious look, or shadow of incontinence,
Be entertained by any that attend
On Roman Lucrece.

Maid. Madam, I !

Lucrece. Excuse it not, for my premeditate thought
Speaks nothing out of rashness nor vain hearsay,
But what my own experience testifies
Against you both ; let then this mild reproof
Forewarn you of the like : my reputation,

Which is held precious in the eyes of Rome,
Shall be no shelter to the least intent
Of looseness ; leave all familiarity,
And quite renounce acquaintance, or I here
Discharge you both my service.

Clown. For my own part, madam, as I am a true
Roman by nature, though no Roman by my nose, I
never spent the least lip-labour on Mistress Mirable,
never so much as glanced, never used any winking or
pinking, never nodded at her—no, not so much as when I
was asleep ; never asked her the question so much as
what's her name : if you can bring any man, woman, or
child, that can say so much behind my back as " For he
did but kiss her, for I did but kiss her, and so let her go,"
let my Lord Collatine, instead of plucking my coat,
pluck my skin over my ears and turn me away naked,
that wheresoever I shall come I may be held a raw
serving-man hereafter.

Lucrece. Sirrah, you know our mind.

Clown. If ever I knew what belongs to these cases, or
yet know what they mean ; if ever I used any plain
dealing, or were ever worth such a jewel, would I might
die like a beggar ! If ever I were so far read in my
grammar as to know what an interjection is, or a
conjunction copulative, would I might never have good
of my *qui quæ quod !* Why, do you think, madam, I have
no more care of myself, being but a stripling, than to go
to it at these years ? Flesh and blood cannot endure it ;
I shall even spoil one of the best faces in Rome with
crying at your unkindness.

Lucrece. I ha' done. See if you can spy your lord
returning from the court, and give me notice what
strangers he brings home with him.

Clown. Yes, I'll go : but see, kind man, he saves me a
labour.   [*Exeunt.*

SCENE V.—*Outside the House of* COLLATINE.

Enter COLLATINE, VALERIUS, HORATIUS, *and* SCEVOLA.

Hor. Come, Valerius, let's hear, in our way to the house of Collatine, that you went late hammering of concerning the taverns in Rome.

Val. Only this, Horatius.

[*Sings*] The gentry to the King's Head,
    The nobles to the Crown,
    The knights unto the Golden Fleece,
    And to the Plough the clown ;
    The churchman to the Mitre,
    The shepherd to the Star,
    The gardener hies him to the Rose,
    To the Drum the man of war ;
    To the Feathers ladies you ; the Globe
    The sea-man doth not scorn ;
    The usurer to the Devil, and
    The townsman to the Horn ;
    The huntsman to the White Hart,
    To the Ship the merchants go ;
    But you that do the Muses love
    The sign called River Po.
    The banquerout to the World's End,
    The fool to the Fortune hie ;
    Unto the Mouth the oyster-wife,
    The fiddler to the Pie,
    The punk unto the Cockatrice,
    The drunkard to the Vine,
    The beggar to the Bush, then meet
    And with Duke Humphrey dine.[1]

Enter LUCRECE *and* Clown.

Col. Fair Lucrece, I ha' brought these lords from court

---

[1] *i.e.* Not dine at all. "This phrase is said to have arisen from part of the public walks in Old St. Paul's called Duke Humphrey's walk, where those who were without the means of defraying their expenses at a tavern were accustomed to walk in hope of procuring an invitation."—*Halliwell.*

To feast with thee. [*To* Clown]   Sirrah, prepare us
    dinner.   [*Exit* Clown.

Lucrece. My lord is welcome, so are all his friends.
The news at court, lords?

   Hor. Madam, strange news :
Prince Sextus by the enemies of Rome
Was nobly used, and made their general;
Twice hath he met his father in the field,
And foiled him by the warlike Sabines' aid :
But how hath he rewarded that brave nation,
That in his great disgrace supported him ?
I'll tell you, madam : he since the last battle
Sent to his father a close messenger
To be received to grace, withal demanding
What he should do with those his enemies.
Great Tarquin from his son receives this news,
Being walking in his garden ; when the messenger
Importuned him for answer, the proud king
Lops with his wand the heads of poppies off,
And says no more ; with this uncertain answer
The messenger to Sextus back returns,
Who questions of his father's words, looks, gesture :
He tells him that the haughty speechless king
Did to the heads of poppies, which bold Sextus
Straight apprehends, cuts off the great men's heads,
And, having left the Sabines without govern,
Flies to his father, and this day is welcomed
For this his traitorous service by the king,
With all due solemn honours to the court.

   Sce. Courtesy strangely requited; this none but the
son of Tarquin would have enterprised.

   Val. I like it, I applaud it ; this will come to somewhat in the end ; when Heaven has cast up his account,
some of them will be called to a hard reckoning.   For
my part, I dreamt last night I went a-fishing.

   [*Sings.*] Though the weather jangles
      With our hooks and our angles,

Our nets be shaken, and no fish taken ;
Though fresh cod and whiting
Are not this day biting,
Gurnet, nor conger, to satisfy hunger,
     Yet look to our draught.
Hale the main bowling ;
The seas have left their rolling,
The waves their huffing, the winds their puffing :
Up to the top-mast, boy,
And bring us news of joy ;
Here's no demurring, no fish is stirring,
     Yet something we have caught.

Col. Leave all to Heaven.

Re-enter Clown.

Clown. My lords, the best plum-porridge in all Rome
cools for your honours ; dinner is piping hot upon the
table, and if you make not the more haste you are like
to have but cold cheer: the cook hath done his
part, and there's not a dish on the dresser but he has
made it smoke for you ; if you have good stomachs, and
come not in while the meat is hot, you'll make hunger
and cold meet together.

Col. My man's a rhetorician, I can tell you,
And his conceit is fluent.   Enter, lords ;
You must be Lucrece' guests, and she is scant
In nothing, for such princes must not want.

[*Exeunt all except* VALERIUS *and* Clown.

Clown. My lord Valerius, I have even a suit to your
honour. I ha' not the power to part from you without
a relish, a note, a tone ; we must get an air betwixt us.

Val. Thy meaning?

Clown. Nothing but this.

[*Sings.*] John for the king has been in many ballads,
    John for the king down dino,
      John for the king has eaten many salads,
    John for the king sings hey ho.[1]

---

[1] A favourite ballad-burden.

Val. Thou wouldst have a song, wouldst thou not?

Clown. And be everlastingly bound to your honour. I am now forsaking the world and the devil, and somewhat leaning towards the flesh; if you could but teach me how to choose a wench fit for my stature and complexion, I should rest yours in all good offices.

Val. I'll do that for thee. What's thy name?

Clown. My name, sir, is Pompey.

Val. Well then, attend.

[*Sings.*] Pompey, I will show thee the way to know
 A dainty dapper wench.
  First see her all bare, let her skin be rare,
And be touched with no part of the French.
  Let her eye be clear, and her brows severe.
Her eye-brows thin and fine;
  But if she be a punk, and love to be drunk,
Then keep her still from the wine.
  Let her stature be mean, and her body clean,
Thou canst not choose but like her;
  But see she ha' good clothes, with a fair Roman
For that's the sign of a striker.   [nose,
  Let her legs be small, but not used to sprawl,
Her tongue not too loud nor cocket.[1]
  Let her arms be strong, and her fingers long,
But not used to dive in pocket.
  Let her body be long, and her back be strong,
With a soft lip that entangles,
  With an ivory breast, and her hair well dressed
Without gold lace or spangles.
  Let her foot be small, clean-legged withal,
Her apparel not too gaudy;
  And one that hath not been in any house of sin,
Nor place that hath been bawdy.

Clown. But, God's me! am I trifling here with you, and dinner cools o' the table, and I am called to my attendance! O my sweet Lord Valerius! [*Exeunt.*

---

[1] Pert.

ACT THE THIRD.

SCENE I.—*The Senate-house.*

Enter TARQUIN, PORSENNA, TULLIA, SEXTUS, *and* ARUNS.

AR. Next King Porsenna, whom we
tender dearly,
Welcome, young Sextus! thou hast to
our yoke
Suppressed the neck of a proud nation,
The warlike Sabines, enemies to Rome.
Sex. It was my duty, royal emperor,
The duty of a subject and a son.
We at our mother's intercession likewise
Are now atoned with Aruns, whom we here
Receive into our bosom.
Tul. This is done
Like a kind brother and a natural son.
Aruns. We interchange a royal heart with Sextus,
And graft us in your love.
Tar. Now, King Porsenna,
Welcome once more to Tarquin and to Rome.
Por. We are proud of your alliance : Rome is ours,
And we are Rome's ; this our religious league
Shall be carved firm in characters of brass,
And live for ever to succeeding times.
Tar. It shall, Porsenna. Now this league's established,
We will proceed in our determined wars,
To bring the neighbour nations under us.
Our purpose is to make young Sextus general
Of all our army; who hath proved his fortunes,
And found them full of favour. We'll begin

Heywood.   B B

With strong Ardea;—ha' you given in charge
To assemble all our captains, and take muster
Of our strong army?
    Aruns. That business is dispatched.
    Sex. We have likewise sent
For all our best commanders, to take charge
According to their merit,—Lord Valerius,
Lord Brutus, Cocles, Mutius Scevola,
And Collatine,—to make due preparation
For such a gallant siege.
    Tar. This day you shall set forward. Sextus, go,
And let us see your army march along
Before this king and us, that we may view
The puissance of our host prepared already
To lay high-reared Ardea waste and low.
    Sex. I shall, my liege.
    Tul. Aruns, associate him.
    Aruns. A rival with my brother in his honours.
                  [*Exeunt* ARUNS *and* SEXTUS.
    Tar. Porsenna shall behold the strength of Rome,
And body of the camp, under the charge
Of two brave princes, to lay hostile siege
Against the strongest city that withstands
The all-commanding Tarquin.
    Por. 'Tis an object
To please Porsenna's eye.   [*Soft march.*
    Luc. The host is now
Upon their march. You from this place may see
The pride of all the Roman chivalry.

Enter SEXTUS, ARUNS, BRUTUS, COLLATINE, VALERIUS,
    SCEVOLA, COCLES, *with* Soldiers, *drum and colours.*
    They march over the stage, and congee to the King
    and Queen.

    Por. This sight's more pleasing to Porsenna's eye
Than all our rich Attalia's [1] pompous feasts

---

[1] Heywood was probably thinking of Horace's *Attalicæ condiciones.*

Or sumptuous revels : we are born a soldier,
And in our nonage sucked the milk of war.
Should any strange fate lour upon this army,
Or thàt the merciless gulf of confusion
Should swallow them, we, at our proper charge,
And from our native confines, vow supply
Of men and arms to make these numbers full.

 Tar. You are our royal brother, and in you
Tarquin is powerful and maintains his awe.

 Tul. The like Porsenna may command of Rome.

 Por. But we have in your fresh varieties
Feasted too much, and kept ourself too long
From our own seat : our prosperous return
Hath been expected by our lords and peers.

 Tar. The business of our wars thus forwarded,
We ha' best leisure for your entertainment,
Which now shall want no due solemnity.

 Por. It hath been beyond both expectation
And merit ; but in sight of Heaven I swear,
If ever royal Tarquin shall demand
Use of our love, 'tis ready stored for you
Even in our kingly breast.

 Tar. The like we vow
To King Porsenna.   We will yet a little
Enlarge your royal welcome with rarities,
Such as Rome yields : that done, before we part,
Of two remote dominions make one heart.
Set forward then.   Our sons wage war abroad,
To make us peace at home : we are of ourself,
Without supportance ; we all fate defy :
Aidless, and of ourself, we stand thus high.   [*Exeunt.*

SCENE II.—*The Camp before Ardea.*

Enter two Soldiers *meeting as in the watch.*

1st Sol. Stand, who goes there ?

2nd Sol. A friend.

1st Sol. Stir not, for if thou dost I'll broach thee straight
upon this pike.   The word?

2nd Sol. Porsenna.

1st Sol. Pass ;—stay, who walks the round to-night?
the general, or any of his captains ?

2nd Sol. Horatius hath the charge ; the other chieftains
Rest in the general's tent ; there's no commander
Of any note, but revel with the prince :
And I amongst the rest am charged to attend
Upon their rouse.

1st Sol. Pass freely ; I this night must stand 'twixt
them and danger.   The time of night ?

2nd Sol. The clock last told eleven.

1st Sol. The powers celestial
That have took Rome in charge, protect it still !
Again good-night.   [*Exit 2nd* Soldier.]   Thus must poor
    soldiers do ;
Whilst their commanders are with dainties fed,
And sleep on down, the earth must be our bed.   [*Exit.*

SCENE III.—*Inside* SEXTUS'S *Tent.   A banquet prepared.*

Enter SEXTUS, ARUNS, BRUTUS, VALERIUS, HORATIUS,
    SCÉVOLA, *and* COLLATINE.

Sex. Sit round : the enemy is pounded[1] fast
In their own folds ; the walls made to oppugn
Hostile incursions become a prison,
To keep them fast for execution ;
There's no eruption to be feared.

[1] *i.e.* Penned up.

Bru. What shall's do? Come, a health to the general's health; and Valerius, that sits the most civilly, shall begin it; I cannot talk till my blood be mingled with this blood of grapes. Fill for Valerius. Thou shouldst drink well, for thou hast been in the German wars; if thou lovest me, drink *upse freeze.*[1]

Sex. Nay, since Brutus has spoke the word, the first health shall be imposed on you, Valerius; and if ever you have been Germanized, let it be after the Dutch fashion.

Val. The general may command.

Bru. He may; why else is he called the commander?

Sex. We will entreat Valerius.

Val. Since you will needs enforce a high-German health, look well to your heads, for I come upon you with this Dutch tassaker[2]: if you were of a more noble science than you are, it will go near to break your heads round.

[*Sings a Dutch song.*]

O mork giff men ein man,
Skerry merry vip,
O mork giff men ein man
Skerry merry vap.
O mork giff men ein man,
That tik die ten long o drievan can,
Skerry merry vip, and skerry merry vap,
And skerry merry runke ede bunk,
Ede hoore was a hai dedle downe
Dedle drunke a :
Skeery merry runke ede bunk, ede hoor was drunk a.

O daughter yeis ein alto kleene,
Skerry merry vip,
O daughter yeis ein alto kleene,
Skerry merry vap.
O daughter yeis ein alto kleene,

---

[1] Strong beer, imported from Friesland: hence to drink *upse freeze* was to drink hard.
[2] From *tasse?* Hence a cup or goblet.

Ye molten slop, ein yert aleene
Skeery merry vip, and skerry merry vap ,
And skerry merry runk ede bunk,
Ede hoore was a hey dedle downe
Dedle drunke a :
Skeery merry, runk ede bunk, ede hoor was drunk a.

Sex. Gramercies, Valerius; came this high-German health as double as his double ruff, I'd pledge it.

Bru. Were it in Lubeck or double-double beer, their own natural liquor, I'd pledge it were it as deep as his ruff: let the health go round about the board, as his band goes round about his neck. I am no more afraid of this Dutch fashion than I should be of the heathenish invention.

Col. I must entreat you spare me, for my brain brooks not the fumes of wine; their vaporous strength offends me much.

Hor. I would have none spare me, for I'll spare none. Collatine will pledge no health unless it be to his Lucrece.

Sex. What's Lucrece but a woman? and what are women
But tortures and disturbance unto men?
If they be foul they're odious, and if fair,
They're like rich vessels full of poisonous drugs,
Or like black serpents armed with golden scales :
For my own part, they shall not trouble me.

Bru. Sextus, sit fast; for I proclaim myself a woman's champion, and shall unhorse thee else.

Val. For my own part, I'm a married man, and I'll speak to my wife to thank thee, Brutus.

Aruns. I have a wife too, and I think the most virtuous lady in the world.

Sce. I cannot say but that I have a good wife too, and I love her : but if she were in heaven, beshrew me if I would wish her so much hurt as to desire her com-

pany upon earth again; yet, upon my honour, though
she be not very fair, she is exceeding honest.

Bru. Nay, the less beauty, the less temptation to despoil her honesty.

Sce. I should be angry with him that should make
question of her honour.

Bru. And I angry with thee if thou shouldst not maintain her honour.

Aruns. If you compare the virtues of your wives, let
me step in for mine.

Col. I should wrong my Lucrece not to stand for her.

Sex. Ha, ha! all captains, and stand upon the honesty
of your wives ! Is't possible, think you,
That women of young spirit and full age,
Of fluent wit, that can both sing and dance,
Read, write, such as feed well and taste choice cates.
That straight dissolve to purity of blood,
That keep the veins full, and inflame the appetite,
Making the spirit able, strong, and prone,—
Can such as these, their husbands being away
Employed in foreign sieges or elsewhere,
Deny such as importune them at home ?
Tell me that flax will not be touched with fire,
Nor they be won to what they most desire !

Bru. Shall I end this controversy in a word ?

Sex. Do, good Brutus.

Bru. I hold some holy, but some apt to sin ;
Some tractable, but some that none can win;
Such as are virtuous, gold nor wealth can move ;
Some vicious of themselves are prone to love ;
Some grapes are sweet and in the garden grow,
Others unpruned turn wild neglected so ;
The purest ore contains both gold and dross,
The one all gain, the other nought but loss ;
The one disgrace, reproach, and scandal taints,
The other angels and sweet-featured saints.

Col. Such is my virtuous Lucrece.

Aruns. Yet she for virtue is not comparable to the wife of Aruns.

Sce. And why may not mine be ranked with the most virtuous?

Hor. I would put in for a lot, but a thousand to one I shall draw but a blank.

Val. I should not show I loved my wife, not .to take her part in her absence : I hold her inferior to none.

Aruns. Save mine.

Val. No, not to her.

Bru. Oh, this were a brave controversy for a jury of women to arbitrate !

Col. I'll hazard all my fortunes on the virtues
Of divine Lucrece. Shall we try them thus ?
It is now dead of night; let's mount our steeds ;
Within this two hours we may reach to Rome,
And to our houses all come unprepared,
And unexpected by our high-praised wives.
She of them all that we find best employed,
Devoted, and most huswife-exercised,
Let her be held most virtuous, and her husband
Win by the wager a rich horse and armour.

Aruns. A hand on that.

Val. Here's a helping hand to that bargain.

Hor. But shall we to horse without circumstance?

Sce. Scevola will be mounted with the first.

Sex. Then mount cheval ! Brutus, this night take you the charge of the army. I'll see the trial of this wager : 'twould do me good to see some of them find their wives in the arms of their lovers, they are so confident in their virtues. Brutus, we'll interchange goodnight ; be thou but as provident o'er the army as we (if our horses fail not) expeditious in our journey. To horse, to horse !

All. Farewell, good Brutus.   [*Exeunt.*

SCENE IV.—*A Room in the House of* COLLATINE.

Enter LUCRECE *and her two* Maids.

Lucrece. But one hour more, and you shall all to rest.
Now that your lord is absent from this house,
And that the master's eye is from his charge,
We must be careful, and with providence
Guide his domestic business; we ha' now
Given o'er all feasting and left revelling,
Which ill becomes the house whose lord is absent ;
We banish all excess till his return,
In fear of whom my soul doth daily mourn.

1st Maid. Madam, so please you to repose yourself
Within your chamber; leave us to our tasks ;
We will not loiter, though you take your rest.

Lucrece. Not so ; you shall not overwatch yourselves
Longer than I wake with you ; for it fits
Good huswives, when their husbands are from home,
To eye their servants' labours, and in care
And the true manage [1] of his household state,
Earliest to rise, and to be up most late.
Since all his business he commits to me,
I'll be his faithful steward till the camp
Dissolve, and he return ; thus wives should do,
In absence of their lords be husbands too.

2nd Maid. Madam, the Lord Turnus his man was
thrice for you here, to have entreated you home to
supper ; he says his lord takes it unkindly he could not
have your company.

Lucrece. To please a loving husband, I'll offend
The love and patience of my dearest friend.
Methinks his purpose was unreasonable,
To draw me in my husband's absence forth
To feast and banquet ; 'twould have ill become me
To have left the charge of such a spacious house
Without both lord and mistress.

[1] Management.

I am opinioned thus : wives should not stray
Out of their doors, their husbands being away.
Lord Turnus shall excuse me.

    1st Maid. Pray, madam, set me right into my work.

    Lucrece. Being abroad, I may forget the charge
Imposed me by my lord, or be compelled
To stay out late, which, were my husband here,
Might be without distaste, but he from hence,
With late abroad, there can no excuse dispense.
Here, take your work again, a while proceed,
And then to bed; for whilst you sew I'll read. [*They retire.*

    Enter SEXTUS, ARUNS, VALERIUS, COLLATINE, HORATIUS,
        and SCEVOLA.

    Aruns. I would have hazarded all my hopes, my wife
had not been so late a-revelling.

    Val. Nor mine at this time of night a-gambolling.

    Hor. They wear so much cork under their heels, they
cannot choose but love to caper.

    Sce. Nothing does me good, but that if my wife were
watching, all theirs were wantoning, and if I ha' lost,
none can brag of their winnings.

    Sex. Now, Collatine, to yours ; either Lucrece must be
better employed than the rest, or you content to have her
virtues rank with the rest.

    Col. I am pleased.

    Hor. Soft, soft, let's steal upon her as upon the rest,
lest having some watch-word at our arrival, we may give
her notice to be better prepared : nay, by your leave,
Collatine, we'll limit you no advantage.

    Col. See, lords, thus Lucrece revels with her maids : -
Instead of riot, quaffing, and the practice
Of high lavoltoes [1] to the ravishing sound
Of chambering music, she, like a good huswife,

---

[1] A dance in the course of which the woman, after being turned
round several times, sprang up as high as she could with her partner's
assistance.

Is teaching of her servants sundry chares.—
Lucrece !

Lucrece. [*Coming forward.*] My lord and husband,
  welcome, ten times welcome.
Is it to see your Lucrece you thus late
Ha' with your person's hazard left the camp,
And trusted to the danger of a night
So dark, and full of horror?

Aruns. Lords, all's lost.

Hor. By Jove, I'll buy my wife a wheel,[1] and make her
spin for this trick.

Sex. If I make not mine learn to live by the prick of
her needle for this, I'm no Roman.

Col. Sweet wife, salute these lords; thy continence
Hath won thy husband a Barbarian horse
And a rich coat of arms.

Lucrece. Oh, pardon me; the joy to see my lord
Took from me all respect of their degrees.
The richest entertainment lives with us,
According to the hour, and the provision
Of a poor wife in the absence of her husband,
We prostrate to you; howsoever mean,
We thus excuse't,—Lord Collatine away,
We neither feast, dance, quaff, riot, nor play.

Sex. If one woman among so many bad may be found
good, if a white wench may prove a black swan, it is
Lucrece ; her beauty hath relation to her virtue, and her
virtue correspondent to her beauty, and in both she is
matchless.

Col. Lords, will you yield the wager?

Aruns. Stay, the wager was as well which of our wives
was fairest too; it stretched as well to their beauty as to
their continence.   Who shall judge that?

Hor. That can none of us, because we are all parties.
Let Prince Sextus determine it, who hath been with us,
and been an eye-witness of their beauties.

---

[1] *i.e.* A spinning-wheel.

Val. Agreed.

Sce. I am pleased with the censure of Prince Sextus.

Aruns. So are we all.

Col. I commit my Lucrece wholly to the dispose of Sextus.

Sex. And Sextus commits him wholly to the dispose of
I love the lady and her grace desire, 　　　　　[Lucrece.
Nor can my love wrong what my thoughts admire.
Aruns, no question but your wife is chaste
And thrifty, but this lady knows no waste.
Valerius, yours is modest, something fair;
Her grace and beauty are without compare.
Thine, Mutius, well disposed, and of good feature,
But the world yields not so divine a creature.
Horatius, thine a smug lass and graced well,
But amongst all, fair Lucrece doth excel.
Then our impartial heart and judging eyes
This verdict gives,—fair Lucrece wins the prize.

Col. Then, lords, you are indebted to me a horse and

All. We yield it. 　　　　　　　　　　　　[armour.

Lucrece. Will you taste such welcome, lords, as a poor unprovided house can yield?

Sex. Gramercy, Lucrece, no; we must this night sleep by Ardea walls.

Lucrece. But, my lords, I hope my Collatine will not so leave his Lucrece.

Sex. He must: we have but idled from the camp, to try a merry wager about their wives, and this at the hazard of the King's displeasure, should any man be missing from his charge. The powers that govern Rome make divine Lucrece for ever happy! Good-night.

Sce. But, Valerius, what thinkest thou of the country girls from whence we came, compared with our city wives whom we this night have tried?

Val. Scevola, thou shalt hear.

[*Sings.*] 　O yes, room for the crier,
　　　　　Who never yet was found a liar!

O ye fine smug country lasses,
That would for brooks change crystal glasses,
And be transhaped from foot to crown,
And straw-beds change for beds of down ;
Your partlets turn into rebatoes,[1]
.And 'stead of carrots eat potatoes ;
Your frontlets[2] lay by, and your rails,[3]
And fringe with gold your daggled tails :
Now your hawk-noses shall have hoods
And billements[4] with golden studs ;
Straw-hats shall be no more bongraces[5]
From the bright sun to hide your faces ;
For hempen smocks to help the itch,
Have linen, sewed with silver stitch ;
And wheresoe'er they chance to stride,
One bare before to be their guide. ·
    O yes, room for the crier,
    Who never yet was found a liar !

Lucrece. Will not my husband repose this night with me ?

Hor. Lucrece shall pardon him : we ha' took our leaves of our wives, nor shall Collatine be before us, though our ladies in other things come behind you.

Col. I must be swayed : the joys and the delights
Of many thousand nights meet all in one,
To make my Lucrece happy !   [night.

Lucrece. I am bound to your strict will. To each good- ·,

Sex. To horse, to horse! [*Aside.*] Lucrece, we cannot rest
Till our hot lust embosom in thy breast.
               [*Exeunt all but* LUCRECE.

Lucrece. With no unkindness we should our lords
    upbraid ;
Husbands and kings must always be obeyed.
Nothing save the high business of the state,
And the charge given him at Ardea's siege,

---

[1] *i.e.* Turn your ruffs into loose collars.   [2] Forehead-bands.
[3] Short mantles.   [4] Head and neck ornaments.
[5] Shades to preserve the complexion.

Could ha' made Collatine so much digress
From the affection that he bears his wife ;
But subjects must excuse when kings claim power.
But, leaving this, before the charm of sleep
Seize with his downy wings upon my eyes,
I must go take account among my servants
Of their day's task ; we must not cherish sloth.
No covetous thought makes me thus provident,
But to shun idleness, which, wise men say,
Begets rank lust, and virtue beats away.   [*Exit.*

SCENE V.—*The Road to Ardea.*

Enter SEXTUS, ARUNS, HORATIUS, BRUTUS, SCEVOLA,
and VALERIUS.

Hor. Return to Rome now we are in the midway to
the camp !
Sex. My lords, 'tis business that concerns my life :
To-morrow, if we live, we'll visit thee.
Val. Will Sextus enjoin me to accompany him?
Sce. Or me ?
Sex. Nor you, nor any : 'tis important business
And serious occurrences that call me.
Perhaps, lords, I'll commend you to your wives.
Collatine, shall I do you any service to your Lucrece ?
Col. Only commend me.
Sex. What, no private token to purchase our kind
          welcome ?
Col. Would royal Sextus would but honour me
To bear her a slight token.
Sex. What ?
Col. This ring.
Sex. As I am royal I will see't delivered.
[*Aside.*] This ring to Lucrece shall my love convey,
And in this gift thou dost thy bed betray.

To-morrow we shall meet.—This night, sweet fate,
May I prove welcome, though a guest ingrate !   [*Exit.*
    Aruns. He's for the city, we for the camp.   The night
makes the way tedious and melancholy; prithee a merry
song to beguile it.
    Val. [*Sings.*]   There was a young man and a maid fell
        in love,
Terry derry ding, terry derry ding, terry derry dino.
To get her good will he often did ———[1]
Terry derry ding, terry derry ding, langtido dille.
There's many will say, and most will allow,
Terry derry ding, terry derry ding, &c.,
There's nothing so good as a terry derry ding, &c.
I would wish all maids before they be sick, ·
Terry, derry, &c.
To inquire for a young man that has a good ———[1]
Terry derry, &c.

    Sce. Nay, my lord, I heard them all have a conceit of
an Englishman—a strange people, in the western islands
—one that for his variety in habit, humour, and gesture, puts down all other nations whatsoever; a little
of that, if you love me.
    Val. Well, Scevola, you shall.

    [*Sings.*[2]]   The Spaniard loves his ancient slop,
        The Lombard his Venetian,
        And some like breechless women go —
        The Russ, Turk, Jew, and Grecian ;
        The thrifty Frenchman wears small waist,
        The Dutch his belly boasteth ;
        The Englishman is for them all,
        And for each fashion coasteth.
        The Turk in linen wraps his head,
        The Persian his in lawn too ;

----

[1] There is no dash in the original ; the singer evidently sub-
stituted the refrain for the omitted word.
[2] This song also occurs in Heywood's *Challenge for Beauty.*

The Russ with sables furs his cap,
　And change will not be drawn to ;.
The Spaniard's constant to his block ;
　The French, inconstant ever ;
But, of all felts that can be felt,
　Give me your English beaver.

The German loves his cony-wool,[1]
　The Irishman his shag [2] too ;
The Welsh his monmouth [3] loves to wear,
　And of the same will brag too ;
Some love the rough, and some the smooth,
　Some great, and others small things ;
But oh, your lecherous Englishman,
　He loves to deal in all things.

The Russ drinks quass ; Dutch, Lubeck beer,
　And that is strong and mighty ;
The Briton, he metheglin quaffs ;
　The Irish, aquavitæ ;
The French affects the Orleans grape,
　The Spaniard tastes his sherry ;
The English none of these can scape,
　But he with all makes merry.

The Italian in her high chapine,[4]
　Scotch lass, and lovely frau too,
The Spanish donna, French madame,
　He will not fear to go to ;
Nothing so full of hazard dread,
　Nought lives above the centre,
No fashion, health, no wine, nor wench,
　On which he dare not venture.

Hor. Good Valerius, this has brought us even to the
skirts of the camp. Enter, lords. *[Exeunt.*

---

[1] Rabbit skin. 　[2] Rough hair. 　[3] A kind of flat cap.
[4] Chapines were shoes with very high soles, worn by ladies to
make them look tall.

ACT THE FOURTH.

SCENE I.—*A Room in the House of* COLLATINE.

Enter SEXTUS, LUCRECE *and* Attendants.

LUCRECE. This ring, my lord, hath
      oped the gates to you ;
      For, though I know you for a royal
      prince,
      My sovereign's son, and friend to Col-
      latine,
Without that key you had not entered here.—
More lights, and see a banquet straight provided.
My love to my dear husband shall appear
In the kind welcome that I give his friend.
    Sex. [*Aside.*] Not love-sick, but love-lunatic, love-mad:
I am all fire, impatience, and my blood
Boils in my heart, with loose and sensual thoughts.
              [*Enter* Servants, *who set out a banquet.*
    Lucrece. A chair for the prince.
May't please your highness sit ?
    Sex. Madam, with you.
    Lucrece. It will become the wife of Collatine
To wait upon your trencher.
    Sex. You shall sit :
Behind us at the camp we left our state ;
We are but your guest—indeed, you shall not wait.
[*Aside.*] Her modesty hath such strong power o'er me,
And such a reverence hath fate given her brow,
That it appears a kind of blasphemy

Heywood.   C C

To have any wanton word harsh in her ears.
I cannot woo, and yet I love 'bove measure ;
'Tis force, not suit, must purchase this rich treasure.

   Lucrece. Your highness cannot taste such homely cates ?

   Sex. Indeed, I cannot feed. [*Aside.*] But on thy face :
Thou art the banquet that my thoughts embrace.

   Lucrece. Knew you, my lord, what free and zealous
      welcome
We tender you, your highness would presume
Upon your entertainment.   Oft, and many times,
I have heard my husband speak of Sextus' valour,
Extol your worth, praise your perfection,
Ay, dote upon your valour, and your friendship
Prize next his Lucrece.

   Sex. [*Aside.*] O impious lust,
In all things base, respectless, and unjust !
Thy virtue, grace, and fame I must enjoy,
Though in the purchase I all Rome destroy.—
Madam, if I be welcome as your virtue
Bids me presume I am, carouse to me
A health unto your husband.

   Lucrece. A woman's draught, my lord, to Collatine !

   Sex. Nay, you must drink off all.

   Lucrece. Your grace must pardon
The tender weakness of a woman's brain.

   Sex. It is to Collatine.

   Lucrece. Methinks 'twould ill become the modesty
Of any Roman lady to carouse,
And drown her virtues in the juice of grapes.
How can I show my love unto my husband
To do his wife such wrong?   By too much wine
I might neglect the charge of this great house
Left solely to my keep ; else my example
Might in my servants breed encouragement
So to offend, both which were pardonless ;
Else to your grace I might neglect my duty,
And slack obeisance to so great a guest ;

All which being accidental unto wine,
Oh, let me not so wrong my Collatine !
   Sex. We excuse you.   [*Aside.*] Her perfections, like a
      torrent
With violence breaks upon me, and at once
Inverts and swallows all that's good in me.
Preposterous Fates, what mischiefs you involve
Upon a caitiff prince, left to the fury
Of all grand mischief ! hath the grandame world
Yet mothered such a strange abortive wonder,
That from her virtues should arise my sin ?
I am worse than what's most ill, deprived all reason,
My heart all fiery lust, my soul all treason.
   Lucrece. My lord, I fear your health, your changing
      brow
Hath shown so much disturbance.   Noble Sextus,
Hath not your venturous travel from the camp,
Nor the moist rawness of this humorous [1] night
Impaired your health ?
   Sex. Divinest Lucrece, no.   I cannot eat.
   Lucrece. To rest then.—
A rank of torches, there, attend the prince !
   Sex. Madam, I doubt I am a guest this night
Too troublesome, and I offend your rest.
   Lucrece. This ring speaks for me, that next Collatine
You are to me most welcome ; yet, my lord,
Thus much presume,—without this from his hand,
Sextus this night could not have entered here ;
No, not the king himself.
My doors the daytime to my friends are free,
But in the night the obdure gates are less kind ;
Without this ring they can no entrance find.—
Lights for the prince !
   Sex. A kiss, and so good-night—nay, for your ring's
sake, deny not that.
   Lucrece. Jove give your highness soft and sweet repose !

            [1] Damp.

Sex. And thee the like, with soft and sweet content !—
My vows are fixed, my thoughts on mischief bent. [*Exit.*

Lucrece. 'Tis late ; so many stars [1] shine in this room,
By reason of this great and princely guest,   /
The world might call our modesty in question,
To revel thus, our husband at the camp.
Haste, and to rest ; save in the prince's chamber,
Let not a light appear.—My heart's all sadness.
Jove, unto thy protection I commit
My chastity and honour; to thy keep
My waking soul I give, whilst my thoughts sleep.
                                        [*Exeunt.*

SCENE II.—*Another Room in the same.*

Enter Clown *and a* Serving-man.

Clown. Soft, soft ; not too loud ; imagine we were now
going on the ropes with eggs at our heels ; he that hath
but a creaking shoe I would he had a crick in his neck ;
tread not too hard for disturbing [2] Prince Sextus.

Ser. I wonder the prince would ha' none of us stay in
his chamber and help him to bed.

Clown. What an ass art thou to wonder ! there may
be many causes : thou know'st the prince is a soldier,
and soldiers many times want shift : who can say whether
he have a clean shirt on or no ? for any thing that we
know he hath used staves-acre [3] o' late, or hath ta'en a
medicine to kill the itch. What's that to us ? we did
our duty to proffer our service.

Ser. And what should we enter farther into his
thoughts? Come, shall's to bed? I am as drowsy as a
dormouse, and my head is as heavy as though I had a
night-cap of lead on.

[1] *i.e.* Candles.   [2] *i.e.* Lest you should disturb.
[3] A kind of larkspur used to kill lice.

Clown. And my eyes begin to glue themselves together. I was till supper was done altogether for your repast, and now after supper I am only for your repose : I think, for the two virtues of eating and sleeping, there's never a Roman spirit under the cope of Heaven can put me down.

Enter MIRABLE.

Mir. For shame ! what a conjuring and caterwauling keep you here, that my lady cannot sleep ! you shall have her call by and by, and send you all to bed with a witness.

Clown. Sweet Mistress Mirable, we are going.

Mir. You are too loud ; come, every man dispose him to his rest, and I'll to mine.

Ser. Out with your torches.

Clown. Come, then, and every man sneak into his kennel.   [*Exeunt.*

SCENE III.—LUCRECE'S *Bedchamber.*

Enter SEXTUS, *with a drawn sword and a lighted taper.*

Sex. Night, be as secret as thou art close, as close
As thou art black and dark ! thou ominous queen
Of tenebrous silence, make this fatal hour
As true to rape as thou hast made it kind
To murder and harsh mischief ! Cynthia, mask thy cheek,
And, all you sparkling elemental fires,
Choke up your beauties in prodigious fogs,
Or be extinct in some thick vaporous clouds,
Lest you behold my practice ! I am bound
Upon a black adventure, on a deed
That must wound virtue, and make beauty bleed.
Pause, Sextus, and, before thou runn'st thyself
Into this violent danger, weigh thy sin.

Thou art yet free, beloved, graced in the camp,
Of great opinion [1] and undoubted hope,
Rome's darling, in the universal grace
Both of the field and Senate, where these fortunes
Do make thee great in both.   Back! yet thy fame
Is free from hazard, and thy style from shame.
O Fate! thou hast usurped such power o'er man
That where thou plead'st thy will no mortal can
On then, black mischief! hurry me the way;
Myself I must destroy, her life betray;
The hate of king and subject, the displeasure
Of prince and people, the revenge of noble,
And the contempt of base, the incurred vengeance
Of my wronged kinsman Collatine, the treason
Against divinest Lucrece—all these total curses,
Foreseen not feared, upon one Sextus meet,
To make my days harsh—so this night be sweet!
No jar of clock, no ominous hateful howl
Of any starting hound, no horse-cough breathed from the
        entrails
Of any drowsy groom, wakes this charmed silence
And starts this general slumber.   Forward still:
To make thy lust live, all thy virtues kill.

  [He draws a curtain; LUCRECE *is discovered in bed.*
Here, here, behold! beneath these curtains lies
That bright enchantress that hath dazed my eyes.
Oh, who but Sextus could commit such waste
On one so fair, so kind, so truly chaste?
Or like a ravisher thus rudely stand,
To offend this face, this brow, this lip, this hand?
Or at such fatal hours these revels keep,
With thought once to defile thy innocent sleep?
Save in this breast, such thoughts could find no place,
Or pay with treason her kind hospitable grace';
But I am lust-burnt all, bent on what's bad,

---

[1] Reputation.

That which should calm good thought makes Tarquin
    mad.—
Madam! Lucrece!
  Lucrece. Who's that? O me! beshrew you!
  Sex. Sweet, 'tis I.
  Lucrece. What I?
  Sex. Make room.
  Lucrece. My husband Collatine?
  Sex. Thy husband's at the camp.
  Lucrece. Here is no place for any man save him.
  Sex. Grant me that grace.
  Lucrece. What are you?
  Sex. Tarquin, and thy friend, and must enjoy thee.
  Lucrece. Heaven such sins defend![1]
  Sex. Why do you tremble, lady? cease this fear:
I am alone; there's no suspicious ear
That can betray this deed: nay, start not, sweet.
  Lucrece. Dream I, or am I full awake? oh, no!
I know I dream to see Prince Sextus so.
Sweet lord, awake me, rid me from this terror.
I know you for a prince, a gentleman,
Royal and honest, one that loves my lord,
And would not wreck a woman's chastity
For Rome's imperial diadem. Oh, then,
Pardon this dream; for, being awake, I know
Prince Sextus, Rome's great hope, would not for shame
Havoc his own worth, or despoil my fame.
  Sex. I'm bent on both; my thoughts are all on fire:
Choose thee; thou must embrace death or desire.
Yet do I love thee. Wilt thou accept it?
  Lucrece. No.
  Sex. If not thy love, thou must enjoy thy foe.
Where fair means cannot, force shall make my way:
By Jove, I must enjoy thee!
  Lucrece. Sweet lord, stay.
  Sex. I'm all impatience, violence and rage,

---

[1] Forbid.

And, save thy bed, nought can this fire assuage.
Wilt love me?

Lucrece. No, I cannot.

Sex. Tell me why?

Lucrece. Hate me, and in that hate first let me die.

Sex. By Jove, I'll force thee!

Lucrece. By a god you swear
To do a devil's deed. Sweet lord, forbear.
By the same Jove I swear, that made this soul,
Never to yield unto an act so foul.
Help, help!

Sex. These pillows first shall stop thy breath,
If thou but shriekest: hark how I'll frame thy death—

Lucrece. For death I care not, so I keep unstained
The uncrazed[1] honour I have yet maintained.

Sex. Thou canst keep neither, for if thou but squeakest
Or lett'st the least harsh noise jar in my ear, ✿
I'll broach thee on my steel; that done, straight murder
One of thy basest grooms, and lay you both,
Grasped arm in arm, on thy adulterate bed,
Then call in witness of that mechal[2] sin.
So shalt thou die, thy death be scandalous,
Thy name be odious, thy suspected body
Denied all funeral rites, and loving Collatine
Shall hate thee even in death: then save all this,
And to thy fortunes add another friend,
Give thy fears comfort, and these torments end.

Lucrece. I'll die first; and yet hear me. As you're noble,
If all your goodness and best generous thoughts
Be not exiled your heart, pity, oh, pity
The virtues of a woman; mar not that
Cannot be made again; this once defiled,
Not all the ocean waves can purify
Or wash my stain away: you seek to soil
That which the radiant splendour of the sun

---

[1] Unbroken.   [2] Adulterous.

Cannot make bright again. Behold my tears ;
Oh, think them pearlèd drops, distilled from the heart
Of soul-chaste Lucrece ; think them orators,
.To plead the cause of absent Collatine,
Your friend and kinsman.

    Sex. Tush, I am obdure.

    Lucrece. Then make my name foul, keep my body
        pure.
Oh, prince of princes, do but weigh your sin ;
Think how much I shall lose, how small you win.
I lose the honour of my name and blood,
Loss Rome's imperial crown cannot make good ;
You win the world's shame and all good men's hate—
Oh, who would pleasure buy at such dear rate ?
Nor can you term it pleasure, for what's sweet
Where force and hate, jar and contention meet ?
Weigh but for what 'tis that you urge me still :
To gain a woman's love against her will.
You'll but repent such wrong done a chaste wife,
And think that labour's not worth all your strife,
Curse your hot lust, and say you have wronged your
        friends ;
But all the world cannot make me amends.
I took you for a friend ; wrong not my trust,
But let these chaste tears quench your fiery lust.

    Sex. No ; those moist tears, contending with my fire
Quench not my heat, but make it climb much higher :
I'll drag thee hence.

    Lucrece. Oh !

    Sex. If thou raise these cries,
Lodged in thy slaughtered arms some base groom dies.
And Rome, that hath admired thy name so long,
Shall blot thy death with scandal from my tongue.

    Lucrece. Jove guard my innocence !

    Sex. Lucrece, thou'rt mine,
In spite of Jove and all the powers divine.

                   [He bears her out.

SCENE IV.—*An Anteroom in* COLLATINE'S *House.*

Enter a Serving-man.

Ser. What's o'clock, trow? my lord bade me be early ready with my gelding, for he would ride betimes in the morning : now had I rather be up an hour before my time than a minute after, for my lord will be so infinitely angry if I but oversleep myself a moment that I had better be out of my life than in his displeasure : but soft, some of my Lord Collatine's men lie in the next chamber ; I care not if I call them up, for it grows towards day. What, Pompey, Pompey!

Enter Clown.

Clown. Who is that calls?

Ser. 'Tis I.

Clown. Who's that, my Lord Sextus his man ?—what a pox make you up before day?

Ser. I would have the key of the gate to come at my lord's horse in the stable.

Clown. I would my Lord Sextus and you were both in the hay-loft, for Pompey can take none of his natural rest among you ; here's e'en " Ostler, rise, and give my horse another peck of hay."

Ser. Nay, good Pompey, help me to the key of the stable.

Clown. Well, Pompey was born to do Rome good in being so kind to the young prince's gelding, but if for my kindness in giving him pease and oats he should kick me, I should scarce say " God-a-mercy, horse." But come, I'll go with thee to the stable.   [*Exeunt.*

SCENE V.—SEXTUS's *Chamber in* COLLATINE'S *House.*

SEXTUS *and* LUCRECE *discovered.*

Sex. Nay, weep not, sweet, what's done is past recall.
Call not thy name in question, by this sorrow,
Which is yet without blemish ; what hath passed
Is hid from the world's eye, and only private
'Twixt us. Fair Lucrece, pull not on my head
The wrath of Rome ; if I have done thee wrong,
Love was the cause ; thy fame is without blot,
And thou in Sextus hast a true friend got.
Nay, sweet, look up; thou only hast my heart ;
I must be gone, Lucrece ; a kiss and part.
 Lucrece. Oh !   [*She flings from him and exit.*
 Sex. No ? Peevish dame, farewell ! then be the bruiter
Of thy own shame, which Tarquin would conceal ;
I am armed 'gainst all can come ; let mischief frown,
With all his terror, armed with ominous fate ;
To all their spleens a welcome I'll afford,
With this bold heart, strong hand and my good sword.
          [*Exit.*

SCENE VI.—*The Camp at Ardea.*

Enter BRUTUS, VALERIUS, HORATIUS, ARUNS, SCEVOLA,
and COLLATINE.

 Bru. What, so early, Valerius, and your voice not up
yet ? thou wast wont to be my lark, and raise me with
thy early notes.

 Val. I was never so hard set yet, my lord, but I had
ever a fit of mirth for my friend.

 Bru. Prithee, let's hear it then while we may, for I
divine thy music and my madness are both short-lived ;
we shall have somewhat else to do ere long, we hope,
Valerius.

Hor. Jove send it !

Val. [*Sings.*] Pack, clouds, away, and welcome, day !
    With night we banish sorrow ;
    Sweet air, blow soft ; mount, lark, aloft,
    To give my love good-morrow.
    Wings from the wind, to please her mind,
    Notes from the lark I'll borrow ;
    Bird, prune thy wing, nightingale, sing,
    To give my love good-morrow.
    To give my love good-morrow,
    Notes from them all I'll borrow.

    Wake from thy nest, robin red-breast ;
    Sing, birds, in every furrow,
    And from each bill let music shrill
    Give my fair love good-morrow ;
    Blackbird and thrush, in every bush,
    Stare,[1] linnet, and cock-sparrow,
    You pretty elves, amongst yourselves,
    Sing my fair love good-morrow.
    To give my love good-morrow,
    Sing, birds, in every furrow.

Bru. Methinks our wars go not well forwards,
Horatius : we have greater enemies to bustle with than
the Ardeans, if we durst but front them.

Hor. Would it were come to fronting !

Bru. Then we married men should have the advantage
of the bachelors, Horatius, especially such as have
revelling wives, those that can caper in the city while
their husbands are in the camp.   Collatine, why are you
so sad ? the thought of this should not trouble you,
having a Lucrece to your bedfellow.

Col. My lord, I know no cause of discontent, yet
cannot I be merry.

Sce. Come, come, make him merry ; let's have a song
in praise of his Lucrece.

---

[1] Starling.

Val. Content.

[*Sings.*] On two white columns arched she stands;
　　Some snow would think them, sure,
　　Some crystal, other lilies stripped,
　　　But none of those so pure.

This beauty when I contemplate,
　　What riches I behold !
'Tis roofed within with virtuous thoughts,
　　Without, 'tis thatched with gold.

Two doors there are to enter at :
　　The one I'll not inquire,
Because concealed ; the other seen,
　　Whose sight inflames desire.

Whether the porch be coral clear,
　　Or with rich crimson lined,
Or rose-leaves, lasting all the year,
　　It is not yet divined.

Her eyes not made of purest glass,
　　Or crystal, but transpareth ;
The life of diamonds they surpass,
　　Their very sight ensnareth.

That which without we rough-cast call,
　　To stand 'gainst wind and weather,
For its rare beauty equals all
　　That I have named together.

For, were it not by modest art
　　Kept from the sight of skies,
It would strike dim the sun itself,
　　And daze the gazer's eyes.

The case so rich, how may we praise
　　The jewel lodged within ?
To draw their praise I were unwise,
　　To wrong them it were sin.

Aruns. I should be frolic if my brother were but returned to the camp.

Hor. And, in good time, behold Prince Sextus.

Enter SEXTUS.

All. Health to our general.

Sex. Thank you.

Bru. Will you survey your forces, and give order for a present assault? Your soldiers long to be tugging with the Ardeans.

Sex. No.

Col. Have you seen Lucretia, my lord? how fares she?

Sex. Well; I'll to my tent.

Aruns. Why, how now! what's the matter, brother?

[*Exeunt* ARUNS *and* SEXTUS.

Bru. "Thank you." " No." " Well; I'll to my tent." Get thee to thy tent, and a coward go with thee, if thou hast no more spirit to a speedy encounter.

Val. Shall I go after him, and know the cause of his discontent?

Sce. Or I, my lord?

Bru. Neither; to pursue a fool in his humour is the next way to make him more humorous. I'll not be guilty of his folly; thank you, no! Before I wish him health again when he is sick of the sullens, may I die, not like a Roman, but like a runagate!

Sce. Perhaps he's not well.

Bru. Well, then, let him be ill.

Val. Nay, if he be dying, as I could wish he were, I'll ring out his funeral peal; and this it is.

Come, list and hark;
The bell doth toll,
For some but now
Departing soul.
And was not that
Some ominous fowl,

The bat, the night-
 Crow, or screech-owl ?
'I'o these I hear
 The wild wolf howl
In this black night
 That seems to scowl.
· All these my black-
 Book shall enroll,
For hark ! still, still
 The bell doth toll
For some but now
 Departing soul.

Sce. Excellent, Valerius. But is not that Collatine's man ?

Enter Clown.

Val. The news with this hasty post ?

Clown. Did nobody see my lord Collatine ? Oh ! my lady commends her to you ; here's a letter.

Col. Give it me.

Clown. Fie upon't ! never was poor Pompey so over-laboured as I have been. I think I have spurred my horse such a question, that he is scarce able to wig or wag his tail for an answer ; but my lady bade me spare for no horse-flesh, and I think I have made him run his race.

Bru. Cousin Collatine, the news at Rome ?

Col. Nothing but what you all may well partake.
Read here, my lord,   [BRUTUS *reads the letter.*
" Dear lord, if ever thou wilt see thy Lucrece,
Choose of the friends which thou affectest best,
And, all important business set apart,
Repair to Rome. Commend me to Lord Brutus,
Valerius, Mutius, and Horatius :
Say I entreat their presence, where my father
Lucretius shall attend them. Farewell, sweet !
The affairs are great, then do not fail to meet."

Bru. I'll thither as I live.   [*Exit.*
Col. I though I die.   [*Exit.*
Sce. To Rome with expeditious wings we'll fly. [*Exit.*
Hor. The news, the news? if it have any shape
Of sadness, if some prodigy have chanced
That may beget revenge, I'll cease to chafe,
Vex, martyr, grieve, torture, torment myself,
And tune my humour to strange strains of mirth.
My soul divines some happiness : speak, speak ;
I know thou hast some news that will create me
Merry and musical, for I would laugh,
Be new transhaped.   I prithee sing, Valerius,
That I may air with thee.
  Val. [*Sings.*]—
        I'd think myself as proud in shackles
        As doth the ship in all her tackles ;
        The wise man boasts no more his brains
        Than I'd insult in gyves and chains ;
        As creditors would use their debtors,
        So could I toss and shake my fetters ;
        But not confess : my thoughts should be
        In durance fast as those kept me.
        And could, when spite their hearts environs,
        Then dance to the music of my irons.

Now tell us what's the project of thy message?
  Clown. My lords, the princely Sextus has been at
home, but what he hath done there I may partly mis-
trust, but cannot altogether resolve you : besides, my
lady swore me that whatsoever I suspected I should say
nothing. .
  Val. If thou wilt not say thy mind, I prithee sing thy
mind, and then thou mayst save thine oath.
  Clown. Indeed, I was not sworn to that ; I may either
laugh out my news or sing 'em, and so I may save mine
oath to my lady.
  Hor. How's all at Rome, that with such sad presage
Disturbèd Collatine and noble Brutus

Are hurried from the camp with Scevola,
And we with expedition 'mongst the rest,
Are charged to Rome? ,Speak, what did Sextus there
With thy fair mistress?

Val. Second me, my lord, and we'll urge him to disclose it.

CATCH.[1]

Val. Did he take fair Lucrece by the toe, man?
Hor. Toe, man?
Val. Ay, man.
Clown. Ha ha ha ha ha, man!
Hor. And further did he strive to go, man?
Clown. Go, man?
Hor. Ay, man.
Clown. Ha ha ha ha, man, fa derry derry down, ha fa
 derry dino!
Val. Did he take fair Lucrece by the heel, man?
Clown. Heel, man?
Val. Ay, man.
Clown. Ha ha ha ha, man!
Hor. And did he further strive to feel, man?
Clown. Feel, man?
Hor. Ay, man.
Clown. Ha ha ha ha, man, ha fa derry, &c.
Val. Did he take the lady by the shin, man?
Clown. Shin, man?
Val. Ay, man.
Clown. Ha ha ha ha, man!
Hor. Further too would he have been, man?
Clown. Been, man?
Hor. Ay, man.
Clown. Ha ha ha ha, man, ha fa derry, &c.

[1] This catch, which jokes in such a ribald fashion over Tarquin's
crime, furnishes a pointed example of the way in which the dramatists of the period pandered to the tastes of the less refined among
their audiences.

Heywood.   D D

Val. Did he take the lady by the knee, man?

Clown. Knee, man?

Val. Ay, man.

Clown. Ha ha ha ha, man!

Hor. Farther than that would he be, man?

Clown. Be, man?

Hor. Ay, man.

Clown. Ha ha ha ha, man, hey fa derry, &c.

Val. Did he take the lady by the thigh, man?

Clown. Thigh, man?

Val. Ay, man.

Clown. Ha ha ha ha, man!

Hor. And now he came it somewhat nigh, man.

Clown. Nigh, man?

Hor. Ay, man.

Clown. Ha ha ha ha, man, hey fa derry, &c.

Val. But did he do the tother thing, man?

Clown. Thing, man?

Val. Ay, man.

Clown. Ha ha ha ha, man!

Hor. And at the same had he a fling, man?

Clown. Fling, man?

Hor. Ay, man.

Clown. Ha ha ha ha, man, hey fa derry, &c. [*Exeunt.*

ACT THE FIFTH.

SCENE I.—*A Room in the House of* COLLATINE. *A table and a chair covered with black*

Enter LUCRECE *and her* Maid.

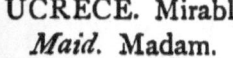UCRECE. Mirable.
    Maid. Madam.
    Lucrece. Is not my father, old Lucre-
    tius, come yet?
    Maid. Not yet.
    Lucrece. Nor any from the camp?
    Maid. Neither, madam.
    Lucrece. Go, begone,
And leave me to the truest grief of heart
That ever entered any matron's breast:
Oh!
    Maid. Why weep you, lady? alas! why do you stain
Your modest cheeks with these offensive tears?
    Lucrece. Nothing, nay, nothing. O you powerful
    gods,
That should have angels guardants on your throne.
To protect innocence and chastity! oh, why
Suffer you such inhuman massacre
On harmless virtue? wherefore take you charge
On sinless souls, to see them wounded thus
With rape or violence? or give white innocence
Armour of proof 'gainst sin, or by oppression
Kill virtue quite, and guerdon base trangression.

Is it my fate above all other women,
Or is my sin more heinous than the rest,
That amongst thousands, millions, infinites,
I, only I, should to this shame be born,
To be a stain to women, nature's scorn?
Oh!

   Maid. What ails you, madam? truth, you make me weep
To see you shed salt tears: what hath oppressed you?
Why is your chamber hung with mourning black,
Your habit sable, and your eyes thus swollen
With ominous tears? Alas! what troubles you?

   Lucrece. I am not sad; thou didst deceive thyself;
I did not weep, there's nothing troubles me;
But wherefore dost thou blush?

   Maid. Madam, not I.

   Lucrece. Indeed thou didst, ·
And in that blush my guilt thou didst betray.
How cam'st thou by the notice of my sin?

   Maid. What sin?

   Lucrece. My blot, my scandal, and my shame.
O Tarquin, thou my honour didst betray;
Disgrace no time, no age can wipe away!
Oh!

   Maid. Sweet lady, cheer yourself; I'll fetch my viol,
And see if I can sing you fast asleep;
A little rest would wear away this passion.

   Lucrece Do what thou wilt, I can command no more.
Being no more a woman, I am now
Devote to death, and an inhabitant
Of the other world: these eyes must ever weep
Till fate hath closed them with eternal sleep.

Enter BRUTUS, COLLATINUS, HORATIUS, SCEVOLA, *and*
   VALERIUS *on one side,* LUCRETIUS *on the other.*

   Luc. Brutus! .

   Bru. Lucretius!

   Lucrece. Father!

Col. Lucrece !

Lucrece. Collatine !

Bru. How cheer you, madam ? how is't with you, cousin ?

Why is your eye deject and drowned in sorrow ?

Why is this funeral black, and ornaments

Of widowhood ? resolve me, cousin Lucrece.

Hor. How fare you, lady ?

Luc. What's the matter, girl ?

Col. Why, how is't with you, Lucrece ? tell me, sweet,

Why dost thou hide thy face, and with thy hand

Darken those eyes that were my suns of joy,

To make my pleasures flourish in the spring ?

Lucrece. O me !

Val. Whence are these sighs and tears ?

Sce. How grows this passion ?

Bru. Speak, lady; you are hemmed in with your friends.

Girt in a pale of safety, and environed

And circled in a fortress of your kindred.

Let not those drops fall fruitless to the ground,

Nor let your sighs add to the senseless wind.

Speak, who hath wronged you?

Lucrece. Ere I speak my woe,

Swear you'll revenge poor Lucrece on her foe.

Bru. Be his head arched with gold.

· *Hor.* Be his hand armed

With an imperial sceptre.

Luc. Be he great

As Tarquin, throned in an imperial seat.

Bru. Be he no more than mortal, he shall feel

The vengeful edge of this victorious steel.

Lucrece. Then seat you, lords, whilst I express my
 wrong.

Father, dear husband, and my kinsmen lords,

Hear me ; I am dishonoured and disgraced,

My reputation mangled, my renown

Disparaged,—but my body, oh, my body !

Col. What, Lucrece ?

Lucrece. Stained, polluted, and defiled.
Strange steps are found in my adulterate bed,
And, though my thoughts be white as innocence,
Yet is my body soiled with lust-burnt sin,
And by a stranger I am strumpeted,
Ravished, enforced, and am no more to rank
Among the Roman matrons.

Bru. Yet cheer you, lady, and restrain these tears.
If you were forced the sin concerns not you ;
A woman's born but with a woman's strength.
Who was the ravisher?

Hor. Ay, name him, lady :
Our love to you shall only thus appear,
In the revenge that we will take on him.

Lucrece. I hope so, lords. 'Twas Sextus, the king's son.

All. How ! Sextus Tarquin !

Lucrece. That unprincely prince,
Who guest-wise entered with my husband's ring.
This ring, O Collatine ! this ring you sent
Is cause of all my woe, your discontent.
I feasted him, then lodged him, and bestowed
My choicest welcome ; but in dead of night
My traitorous guest came armed unto my bed,
Frighted my silent sleep, threatened, and prayed
For entertainment : I despisèd both.
Which hearing, his sharp-pointed scimitar
The tyrant bent against my naked breast.
Alas ! I begged my death ; but note his tyranny :
He brought with him a torment worse than death,
For, having murdered me, he swore to kill
One of my basest grooms, and lodge him dead
In my dead arms, then call in testimony
Of my adultery, to make me hated,
Even in my death, of husband, father, friends,
Of Rome, and all the world. This, this, O princes,
Ravished and killed me at once.

Col. Yet comfort, lady ;
I quit thy guilt, for what could Lucrece do
More than a woman ? hadst thou died polluted
By this base scandal, thou hadst wronged thy fame :
And hindered us of a most just revenge.
   All. What shall we do, lords?
   Bru. Lay your resolute hands
Upon the sword of Brutus : vow and swear,
As you hope meed for merit from the gods,
Or fear reward for sin from devils below,
As you are Romans, and esteem your fame
More than your lives, all humorous toys set off,
Of madding, singing, smiling, and what else,
Revive your native valours, be yourselves,
And join with Brutus in the just revenge
Of this chaste ravished lady ;—swear !
   All. We do.
   Lucrece. Then with your humours here my grief ends
      too :
My stain I thus wipe off, call in my sighs,
And in the hope of this revenge, forbear
Even to my death to fall [1] one passionate tear ;
Yet, lords, that you may crown my innocence
With your best thoughts, that you may henceforth know
We are the same in heart we seem in show,
And though I quit my soul of all such sin,
                              [*The* Lords *whisper.*
I'll not debar my body punishment.
Let all the world learn of a Roman dame,
To prize her life less than her honoured fame.
                              [*Stabs herself.*

   Luc. Lucrece !
   Col. Wife !
   Bru. Lady !
   Sec. She hath slain herself.

---

[1] To let fall, as often to be found in Shakespeare.

Val. Oh, see yet, lords, if there be hope of life.

Bru. She's dead : then turn your funeral tears to fire
And indignation; let us now redeem
Our misspent time, and overtake our sloth
With hostile expedition.   This, great lords,
This bloody knife, on which her chaste blood flowed,
Shall not from Brutus till some strange revenge
Fall on the heads of Tarquins.

Hor. Now's the time
To call their pride to count.   Brutus, lead on ;
We'll follow thee to their confusion.

Val. By Jove, we will ! the sprightful youth of Rome,
Tricked up in plumèd harness, shall attend
The march of Brutus, whom we here create
Our general against the Tarquins.

Sce. Be it so.

Bru. We embrace it.   Now, to stir the wrath of Rome,
You, Collatine and good Lucretius,
With eyes yet drowned in tears, bear that chaste body
Into the market-place ; that horrid object
Shall kindle them with a most just revenge.   (

Hor. To see the father and the husband mourn
O'er this chaste dame, that have so well deserved
Of Rome and them ; then to infer the pride,
The wrongs and the perpetual tyranny
Of all the Tarquins, Servius Tullius' death,
And his unnatural usage by that monster
Tullia, the queen ; all these shall well concur
In a combined revenge.

Bru. Lucrece, thy death we'll mourn in glittering
          arms
And plumèd casques.   Some bear that reverend load
Unto the Forum, where our force shall meet
To set upon the palace, and expel
This viperous brood from Rome : I know the people
Will gladly embrace our fortunes.   Scevola,
Go you and muster powers in Brutus' name.

Valerius, you assist him instantly,
And to the 'mazèd people speak
The cause of this concourse.
  Val. We go.   [*Exeunt* VALERIUS *and* SCEVOLA.
 Bru. And you, dear lords, whose speechless grief is
  boundless,
Turn all your tears, with ours, to wrath and rage.
The hearts of all the Tarquins shall weep blood
Upon the funeral hearse, with whose chaste body
Honour your arms, and to the assembled people
Disclose her innocent wounds. Gramercies, lords !
  [*A great shout and a flourish with drums and
   trumpets within.*
That universal shout tells me their words
Are gracious with the people, and their troops
Are ready embattled, and expect but us
To lead them on. Jove give our fortunes speed !
We'll murder murder, and base rape shall bleed. [*Exeunt.*

   SCENE II.—*The Outskirts of Rome.*

Alarum. Enter TARQUIN *and* TULLIA *flying, pursued by*
BRUTUS *and the* Romans *with drums and colours.*
PORSENNA, ARUNS *and* SEXTUS *meet and join with*
TARQUIN *and* TULLIA. BRUTUS *and the* Romans
advance ; they make a stand.

 Bru. Even thus far, tyrant, have we dogged thy steps,
Frighting thy queen and thee with horrid steel.
 Tar. Lodged in the safety of Porsenna's arms,
Now, traitor Brutus, we dare front thy pride.
 Hor. Porsenna, thou'rt unworthy of a sceptre,
To shelter pride, lust, rape, and tyranny,
In that proud prince and his confederate peers.
 Sex. Traitors to Heaven, to Tarquin, Rome and us !
Treason to kings doth stretch even to the gods,

And those high gods that take great Rome in charge
Shall punish your rebellion.

Col. O devil Sextus, speak not thou of gods,
Nor cast those false and feignèd eyes to Heaven,
Whose rape the furies must torment in hell
Of Lucrece—Lucrece !

See. Her chaste blood still cries
For vengeance to the ethereal deities.

Luc. Oh, 'twas a foul deed, Sextus !

Val. And thy shame
Shall be eternal and outlive her fame.

Aruns. Say Sextus loved her, was she not a woman ?
Ay, and perhaps was willing to be forced.
Must you, being private subjects, dare to ring
War's loud alarum 'gainst your potent king ?

Por. Brutus, therein thou dost forget thyself,
And wrong'st the glory of thine ancestors,
Staining thy blood with treason.

Bru. Tuscan, know
The Consul Brutus is their powerful foe.

Tarquin, Tullia, &c. Consul !

Hor. Ay, Consul ; and the powerful hand of Rome
Grasps his imperial sword : the name of king
The tyrant Tarquins have made odious
Unto this nation, and the general knee
Of this our warlike people now low bends
To royal Brutus, where the king's name ends.

Bru. Now, Sextus, where's the oracle ? when I kissed
My mother earth it plainly did foretell
My noble virtues did thy sin exceed,
Brutus should sway, and lust-burnt Tarquin bleed.

Val. Now shall the blood of Servius fall as heavy
As a huge mountain on your tyrant heads,
O'erwhelming all your glory.

Hor. Tullia's guilt
Shall be by us revenged, that, in her pride,
In blood paternal her rough coach-wheels dyed.

Luc. Your tyrannies—
Sex. Pride—
Col. And my Lucrece' fate,
Shall all be swallowed in this hostile hate.
   Sex. O Romulus! thou that first reared yon walls
In sight of which we stand, in thy soft bosom
Is hanged the nest in which the Tarquins build;
Within the branches of thy lofty spires
Tarquin shall perch, or where he once hath stood
His high built aery shall be drowned in blood.
Alarum then! Brutus, by Heaven I vow
My sword shall prove thou ne'er wast mad till now.
   Bru. Sextus, my madness with your lives expires;
Thy sensual eyes are fixed upon that wall
Thou ne'er shalt enter; Rome confines you all.
   Por. A charge then!
   Tar. Jove and Tarquin!
   Hor. But we cry a Brutus!
   Bru. Lucrece, fame, and victory!   [*Exeunt.*

SCENE III.—*A Bridge across the Tiber.*

Alarum.   The Romans *are beaten off.   Enter*
' BRUTUS, HORATIUS, VALERIUS, SCEVOLA,
        LUCRETIUS *and* COLLATINE.

Bru. Thou Jovial hand, hold up thy sceptre high,
And let not justice be oppressed with pride!   '
O you Penates; leave not Rome and us
Grasped in the purple hands of death and ruin!
The Tarquins have the best.
   Hor. Yet stand; my foot is fixed upon this bridge.
Tiber, thy archèd streams shall be changed crimson
With Roman blood before I budge from hence.
   Sce. Brutus, retire; for if thou enter Rome
We are all lost.   Stand not on valour now,

But save thy people ; let's survive this day,
To try the fortunes of another field.

Val. Break down the bridge, lest the pursuing enemy
Enter with us and take the spoil of Rome.

Hor. Then break behind me ; for, by Heaven, I'll grow
And root my foot as deep as to the centre,
Before I leave this passage !

Luc. Come, you're mad.

Col. The foe comes on, and we in trifling here,
Hazard ourself and people.

Hor. Save them all ;
To make Rome stand, Horatius here will fall.

Bru. We would not lose thee ; do not breast thyself
'Gainst thousands ; if thou front'st them thou art ringed
With million swords and darts, and we behind
Must break the bridge of Tiber to save Rome.
Before thee infinite [1] gaze on thy face
And menace death ; the raging streams of Tiber
Are at thy back to swallow thee.

Hor. Retire ;
To make Rome live, 'tis death that I desire.

Bru. Then farewell, dead Horatius ! think in us
The universal arm of potent Rome
Takes his last leave of thee in this embrace.

                        [All embrace him.

Hor. Farewell !

All. Farewell !

Bru. These arches all must down
To interdict their passage through the town.

                    [Exeunt all except HORATIUS.

Alarum.   *Enter* TARQUIN, PORSENNA, *and* ARUNS,
         with their pikes and targeters.

All. Enter, enter, enter.

         [A noise of knocking down the bridge, within.

Hor. Soft, Tarquin ! see a bulwark to the bridge,

---

        [1] *i.e.* Infinite numbers.

You first must pass ; the man that enters here
Must make his passage through Horatius' breast ;
See, with this target do I buckler[1] Rome,
And with this sword defy the puissant army
Of two great kings.

   Por. One man to face an host !
Charge, soldiers ! of full forty thousand Romans
There's but one daring hand against your host,
To keep you from the sack or spoil of Rome.
Charge, charge !

   Aruns. Upon them, soldiers !   [*Alarum.*

   Enter SEXTUS *and* VALERIUS *above, at opposite sides.*

   Sex. O cowards, slaves, and vassals ! what, not enter !
Was it for this you placed my regiment
Upon a hill, to be the sad spectator
Of such a general cowardice ? Tarquin, Aruns,
Porsenna, soldiers, pass Horatius quickly,
For they behind him will devolve the bridge,
And raging Tiber, that's impassable,
Your host must swim before you conquer Rome.

   Val. Yet stand, Horatius ; bear but one brunt more ;
The archèd bridge shall sink upon his piles,
And in his fall lift thy renown to Heaven.

   Sex. Yet enter !

   Val. Dear Horatius, yet stand,
And save a million by one powerful hand.

                     [*Alarum ; the bridge falls.*

   All. Charge, charge, charge !

   Sex. Degenerate slaves! the bridge is fallen, Rome's lost.

   Val. Horatius, thou art stronger than their host ;
Thy strength is valour, theirs are idle braves,
Now save thyself, and leap into the waves.

   Hor. Porsenna, Tarquin, now wade past your depths
And enter Rome. I feel my body sink

            [1] Defend.

Beneath my ponderous weight; Rome is preserved,
And now farewell ; for he that follows me
Must search the bottom of this raging stream.
Fame, with thy golden wings renown my crest !
And, Tiber, take me on thy silver breast !   [*Exit.*

   Por. He's leapt off from the bridge and drowned
      himself.

   Sex. You are deceived ; his spirit soars too high
To be choked in with the base element
Of water ; lo ! he swims, armed as he is,
Whilst all the army have discharged their arrows,
Of which the shield upon his back sticks full.

                    [*Shout and flourish.*

And hark, the shout of all the multitude
Now welcomes him a-land ! Horatius' fame
Hath checked our armies with a general shame.
But come, to-morrow's fortune must restore
This scandal, which I of the gods implore.

   Por. Then we must find another time, fair prince,
To scourge these people, and revenge your wrongs.
For this night I'll betake me to my tent.   [*Exit.*

   Tar. And we to ours; to-morrow we'll renown
Our army with the spoil of this rich town.   [*Exeunt.*

    SCENE IV.—*Inside* PORSENNA'S *Tent.*

        Enter PORSENNA.

   Por. Our secretary !

        Enter Secretary.

   Secre. My lord.
   Por. Command lights and torches in our tent,

     Enter Soldiers *with Torches.*

And let a guard engirt our safety round,

Whilst we debate of military business.
Come, sit and let's consult.

Enter SCEVOLA, *disguised.*

Sce. [*Aside.*] Horatius famous for defending Rome,
But we ha' done nought worthy Scevola,
Nor of a Roman : I in this disguise
Have passed the army and the puissant guard
Of King Porsenna : this should be his tent ;
And in good time, now fate direct my strength
Against a king, to free great Rome at length.

                  [*Stabs the* Secretary *in mistake for* PORSENNA.

Secre. Oh, I am slain ! treason, treason !
Por. Villain, what hast thou done ?
Sce. Why, slain the king.
Por. What king ?
Sce. Porsenna.
Por. Porsenna lives to see thee tortured,
With plagues more devilish than the pains of hell.
Sce. O too rash Mutius, hast thou missed thy aim !
And thou, base hand, that didst direct my poniard
Against a peasant's breast, behold, thy error
Thus I will punish : I will give thee freely
Unto the fire, nor will I wear a limb
That with such rashness shall offend his lord.

                  [*Thrusts his hand into the fire.*

Por. What will the madman do ?
Sce. Porsenna, so,—
Punish my hand thus, for not killing thee.
Three hundred noble lads beside myself
Have vowed to all the gods that patron Rome
Thy ruin for supporting tyranny ;
And, though I fail, expect yet every hour
When some strange fate thy fortunes will devour.
Por. Stay, Roman ; we admire thy constancy,
And scorn of fortune. Go, return to Rome,—
We give thee life,—and say, the King Porsenna,

Whose life thou seek'st, is in this honourable.
Pass freely ; guard him to the walls of Rome ;
And, were wo not so much engaged to Tarquin,
We would not lift a hand against that nation
That breeds such noble spirits.

    Sce. Well, I go,
And for revenge take life even of my foe.   [*Exit.*

    Por. Conduct him safely.   What, three hundred gallants
Sworn to our death, and all resolved like him !
We must be provident : to-morrow's fortunes
We'll prove for Tarquin ; if they fail our hopes,
Peace shall be made with Rome.   But first our secretary
Shall have his rites of funeral ; then our shield
We must address next for to-morrow's field.   [*Exit.*

SCENE V.—*A Public Place in Rome.*

Enter BRUTUS, HORATIUS, VALERIUS, COLLATINE, *and*
LUCRETIUS, *marching.*

    Bru. By thee we are consul, and still govern Rome,
Which but for thee had been despoiled and ta'en,
Made a confusèd heap of men and stones,
Swimming in blood and slaughter ; dear Horatius,
Thy noble picture shall be carved in brass,
And fixed for thy perpetual memory
In our high Capitol.

    Hor. Great consul, thanks !
But, leaving this, let's march out of the city,
And once more bid them battle on the plains.

    Val. This day my soul divines we shall live free
From all the furious Tarquins.   But where's Scevola ?
We see not him to-day.

Enter SCEVOLA.

    Sce. Here, lords, behold me handless as you see.
The cause—I missed Porsenna in his tent,

And in his stead killed but his secretary.
The 'mazèd king, when he beheld me punish
My rash mistake with loss of my right hand,
Unbegged, and almost scorned, he gave me life,
Which I had then refused, but in desire
To 'venge fair Lucrece' rape.   [*Soft alarum.*

  Hor. Dear Scevola,
Thou hast exceeded us in our resolve :
But will the Tarquins give us present battle ?

  See. That may ye hear ; the skirmish is begun
Already 'twixt the horse.

  Luc. Then, noble consul,
Lead our main battle [1] on.

  Bru. O Jove, this day
Balance our cause, and let the innocent blood
Of rape-stained Lucrece crown with death and horror
The heads of all the Tarquins ! See, this day
In her cause do we consecrate our lives,
And in defence of justice now march on.
I hear their martial music : be our shock
As terrible as are the meeting clouds
That break in thunder ! yet our hopes are fair,
And this rough charge shall all our loss repair.
           [*Exeunt. Alarum, battle within.*

SCENE VI.—*Outside Rome.*

Enter PORSENNA *and* ARUNS.

  Por. Yet grow our lofty plumes unflagged with blood,
And yet sweet pleasure wantons in the air.
How goes the battle, Aruns ?

  Aruns. 'Tis even balanced.
I interchanged with Brutus, hand to hand,
A dangerous encounter ; both are wounded,

              [1] Battalion.

And, had not the rude press divided us,
One had dropped down to earth.
    Por. 'Twas bravely fought.
' I saw the king your father free his person
From thousand Romans that begirt his state,
Where flying arrows thick as atoms sung
About his ears.
    Aruns. I hope a glorious day.
Come, Tuscan king, let's on them.   [*Alarum.*

Enter HORATIUS *and* VALERIUS.

    Hor. Aruns, stay!
That sword, that late did drink the consul's blood,
Must with his keen fang tire upon[1] my flesh,
Or this on thine.
    Aruns. It spared the consul's life
To end thy days in a more glorious strife.
    Val. I stand against thee, Tuscan!
    Por. I for thee!
    Hor. Where'er I find a Tarquin, he's for me.
        [*Alarum. They fight;* ARUNS *is slain,* POR-
        SENNA *driven off.*

Alarum. Enter TARQUIN *with an arrow in his breast,*
    TULLIA *with him, pursued by* COLLATINE, LUCRE-
    TIUS, SCEVOLA.

    Tar. Fair Tullia, leave me; save thy life by flight,
Since mine is desperate; behold, I am wounded
Even to the death. There stays within my tent
A wingèd jennet, mount his back and fly;
Live to revenge my death, since I must die.
    Tul. Had I the heart to tread upon the bulk[2]
Of my dead father, and to see him slaughtered,
Only for love of Tarquin and a crown,
And shall I fear death more than loss of both?

---

    [1] Tear, like a beast or bird of prey.   [2] Body.

No, this is Tullia's fame,—rather than fly
From Tarquin, 'mongst a thousand swords she'll die.

Coll., Luc., and Sce. Hew them to pieces both.

Tar. My Tullia save,
And o'er my caitiff head those meteors wave !

Coll. Let Tullia yield then.

Tul. Yield me, cuckold ! no ;
Mercy I scorn ; let me the danger know.

Sce. Upon them, then !

Val. Let's bring them to their fate,
And let them perish in the people's hate.

Tul. Fear not, I'll back thee, husband.

Tar. But for thee,
Sweet were the hand that this charged soul could free !
Life I despise. Let noble Sextus stand
To avenge our death. Even till these vitals end,
Scorning my own, thy life will I defend.

Tul. And I'll, sweet Tarquin, to my power guard
    thine.
Come on, ye slaves, and make this earth divine !

> [*Alarum.* TARQUIN *and* TULLIA *are slain.*

Enter BRUTUS *all bloody.*

Bru. Aruns, this crimson favour, for thy sake,
I'll wear upon my forehead masked with blood,
Till all the moisture in the Tarquins' veins
Be spilt upon the earth, and leave thy body
As dry as the parched summer, burnt and scorched
With the canicular stars.

Hor. Aruns lies dead
By this bright sword that towered about his head.

Col. And see, great consul, where the pride ·of Rome
Lies sunk and fallen.

Val. Beside him lies the queen,
Mangled and hewn amongst the Roman soldiers.

Hor. Lift up their slaughtered bodies; help to rear
    them

E E 2

Against this hill in view of all the camp:
This sight will be a terror to the foe,
And make them yield or fly.

Bru. But where's the ravisher,
Injurious Sextus, that we see not him?   [*Short alarum.*

Enter SEXTUS.

Sex. Through broken spears, cracked swords, unbow-
elled steeds,
Flawed armours, mangled limbs, and battered casques,
Knee-deep in blood, I ha' pierced the Roman host
To be my father's rescue.

Hor. 'Tis too late;
His mounting pride's sunk in the people's hate.

Sex. My father, mother, brother!   Fortune, now
I do defy thee; I expose myself
To horrid danger; safety I despise:
I dare the worst of peril; I am bound
On till this pile of flesh be all one wound.

Val. Begirt him, lords; this is the ravisher;
There's no revenge for Lucrece till he fall.

Luc. Seize Sextus, then—

Sex. Sextus defies you all!
Yet will you give me language ere I die?

Bru. Say on.

Sex. 'Tis not for mercy, for I scorn that life
That's given by any; and, the more to add
To your immense unmeasurable hate,
I was the spur unto my father's pride;
'Twas I that awed the princes of the land;
That made thee, Brutus, mad, these discontent:
I ravished the chaste Lucrece; Sextus, I,—
Thy daughter,—and thy wife,—Brutus, thy cousin,—
Allied, indeed, to all; 'twas for my rape
Her constant [1] hand ripped up her innocent breast:
'Twas Sextus did all this.

[1] Resolute.

Col. Which I'll revenge.

Hor. Leave that to me.

Luc. Old as I am, I'll do't.

Sce. I have one hand left yet, of strength enough
To kill a ravisher.

Sex. Come all at once—ay, all !
Yet hear me, Brutus; thou art honourable,
And my words tend to thee : my father died
By many hands; what's he 'mongst you can challenge
The least, ay, smallest honour in his death?
If I be killed amongst this hostile throng,
The poorest snaky [1] soldier well may claim
As much renown in royal Sextus' death
As Brutus, thou, or thou, Horatius :
I am to die, and more than die I cannot ;
Rob not yourselves of honour in my death.
When the two mightiest spirits of Greece and Troy
Tugged for the mastery, Hector and Achilles,
Had puissant Hector, by Achilles' hand, .
Died in a single monomachy,[2] Achilles
Had been the worthy ; but, being slain by odds,
The poorest Myrmidon had as much honour
As faint Achilles in the Trojan's death.

Bru. Hadst thou not done a deed so execrable
That gods and men abhor, I'd love thee, Sextus,
And hug thee for this challenge breathed so freely.
Behold, I stand for Rome as general :
Thou of the Tarquins dost alone survive,
The head of all these garboils,[3] the chief actor
Of that black sin, which we chastise by arms.—
Brave Romans, with your bright swords be our lists,
And ring us in ; none dare to offend the prince
By the least touch, lest he incur our wrath :
This honour do your consul, that his hand
May punish this arch-mischief, that the times

---

[1] " Snake " was often used as a term of contempt.
[2] " Single monomachy " is rather an absurd pleonasm.
[3] Tumults.

Succeeding may of Brutus thus much tell,—
By him pride, lust, and all the Tarquins fell.

Sex. To ravish Lucrece, cuckold Collatine,
And spill the chastest blood that ever ran
In any matron's veins, repents me not
So much as to have wronged a gentleman
So noble as the consul in this strife.
Brutus, be bold ! thou fight'st with one scorns [1] life.

Bru. And thou with one that less than his renown,
Prizeth his blood, or Rome's imperial crown.

> [*Alarum ; a fierce fight with sword and target ;
> then a pause.*

Bru. Sextus, stand fair: much honour shall I win
To revenge Lucrece, and chastise thy sin.

Sex. I repent nothing, may I live or die ;
Though my blood fall, my spirit shall mount on high.

> [*Alarum ; they fight with single swords, and,-
> being deadly wounded and panting for breath,
> they strike at each other with their gauntlets
> and fall.*

Hor. Both slain !   O noble Brutus, this thy fame
To after ages shall survive ; thy body
Shall have a fair and gorgeous sepulchre,
For whom the matrons shall in funeral black
Mourn twelve sad moons—thou that first governed Rome,
And swayed the people by a consul's name.
These bodies of the Tarquins we'll commit
Unto the funeral pile.   You, Collatine,
Shall succeed Brutus in the consul's place,
Whom with this laurel-wreath we here create.

> [*Crowning him with laurel.*

Such is the people's voice ; accept it, then.

Col. We do ; and may our power so just appear,
Rome may have peace, both with our love and fear.
But soft, what march is this ?

---

[1] *i.e.* That scorns.

Flourish. Enter PORSENNA, COLLATINE, *and* Soldiers.

Por. The Tuscan King, seeing the Tarquins slain,
Thus armed and battled, offers peace to Rome,
To confirm which, we'll give you present hostage ;
If you deny, we'll stand upon our guard,
And by the force of arms maintain our own.

Val. After so much effusion and large waste
Of Roman blood, the name of peace is welcome :
Since of the Tarquins none remain in Rome,
And Lucrece' rape is now revenged at full,
'Twere good to entertain Porsenna's league.

Col. Porsenna we embrace, whose royal presence
Shall grace the consul to the funeral pile.
March on to. Rome. Jove be our guard and guide,
That hath in us 'venged rape, and punished pride !

[*Exeunt.*

To the Reader.

Because we would not that any man's expectation should be deceived in the ample printing of this book, lo, Gentle Reader, we have inserted these few songs, which were added by the stranger that lately acted Valerius his part, in form following.

The Cries of Rome.

Thus go the cries in Rome's fair town ;
First they go up street, and then they go down.

Round and sound, all of a colour ; buy a very fine marking stone, marking stone ; round and sound, all of a
colour; buy a very fine marking stone, a very very fine !
Thus go the cries in Rome's fair town ;
First they go up street, and then they go down.

Bread and—meat—bread—and meat, for the ten—der—
mercy of God, to the poor pris—ners of Newgate,
four—score and—ten—poor—prisoners !
Thus go the cries in Rome's fair town ;
First they go up street, and then they go down.

Salt—salt—white Wor—stershire salt !
Thus go the cries in Rome's fair town ;
First they go up street, and then they go down.

Buy a very fine mouse-trap, or a tormentor
for your fleas !
Thus go the cries in Rome's fair town ;
First they go up street, and then they go down.

Kitchen-stuff, maids!
  Thus go the cries in Rome's fair town;
  First they go up street, and then they go down.

Ha' you any wood to cleave?
  Thus go the cries in Rome's fair town;
  First they go up street, and then they go down.

I ha' white radish, white hard lettuce, white young
onions!
  Thus go the cries in Rome's fair town;
  First they go up street, and then they go down.

I ha' rock-sampier, rock-sampier![1]
  Thus go the cries in Rome's fair town;
  First they go up street, and then they go down.

Buy a mat, a mil-mat, mat, or a hassock for your pew,
a stopple for your close-stool, or a pesock to thrust
your feet in!
  Thus go the cries in Rome's fair town;
  First they go up street, and then they go down.

Whiting, maids, whiting!
  Thus go the cries in Rome's fair town;
  First they go up street, and then they go down.

Hot fine oat-cakes, hot!
  Thus go the cries in Rome's fair town;
  First they go up street, and then they go down.

Small-coals here!
  Thus go the cries in Rome's fair town;
  First they go up street, and then they go down.

Will you buy any milk to-day?
  Thus go the cries in Rome's fair town;
  First they go up street, and then they go down.

[1] Samphire.

Lanthorn and candle-light here!   Maid, a light here!
   Thus go the cries in Rome's fair town;
     First they go up street, and then they go down.

Here lies a company of very poor women in the dark
   dungeon, hungry, cold, and comfortless night and day!
   Pity the poor women in the dark dungeon!
     Thus go the cries where they do house them;
     First they come to the grate, and then they go louse
     them.

The Second Song.

"Arise, arise, my Juggy, my Puggy,
   Arise, get up, my dear;
The weather is cold, it blows, it snows;
   Oh, let me be lodgèd here.
My Juggy, my Puggy, my honey, my cony,
   My love, my dove, my dear;
Oh, oh, the weather is cold, it blows, it snows,
   Oh, oh, let me be.lodgèd here."

" Begone, begone, my Willy, my Billy,
   Begone, begone, my dear;
The weather is warm, 'twill do thee no harm;
   Thou canst not be lodgèd here.
My Willy, my Billy, my honey, my cony,
   My love, my dove, my dear;
Oh, oh, the weather is warm, 'twill do thee no harm
   Oh oh, thou canst not be lodgèd here."

" Farewell, farewell, my Juggy, my Puggy,
   Farewell, farewell, my dear;
Then will I begone from whence that I came,
   If I cannot be lodgèd here.

My Juggy, my Puggy, my honey, my cony,
　　My love, my dove, my dear ;
'Oh, oh, then will I begone, from whence that I came,
　　Oh, oh, if I cannot be lodgèd here."

" Return, return, my Willy, my Billy,
　　Return, my dove and my dear ;
The weather doth change, then seem not strange ;
　　Thou shalt be lodgèd here.
My Willy, my Billy, my honey, my cony,
　　My love, my dove, my dear ;
Oh, oh, the weather doth change, then seem not strange,
　　Oh, oh, and thou shalt be lodgèd here."

THE MERMAID SERIES.

"I lie and dream of your full MERMAID wine."
Master Francis Beaumont to Ben Jonson.

Now Publishing,

In Half-Crown monthly vols., post 8vo, each volume containing 500 pages and an etched frontispiece, bound in cloth with cut or uncut edges,

AN UNEXPURGATED EDITION OF

THE BEST PLAYS

OF

THE OLD DRAMATISTS;

UNDER THE GENERAL EDITORSHIP OF HAVELOCK ELLIS.

IN the MERMAID SERIES are being issued the best plays of the Elizabethan and later dramatists—plays which, with Shakespeare's works, constitute the chief contribution of the English spirit to the literature of the world. The Editors who have given their assistance to the undertaking include men of literary eminence, who have distinguished themselves in this field, as well as younger writers of ability.

Each volume contains on an average five complete plays, prefaced by an Introductory Notice of the Author. Great care is taken to ensure, by consultation among the Editors, that the Plays selected are in every case the *best* and most representative—and not the most conventional, or those which have lived on a merely accidental and traditional reputation. A feature will be made of plays by little-known writers, which although often so admirable are now almost inaccessible. In every instance the utmost pains is taken to secure the best text, the spelling is modernised, and brief but adequate notes are supplied. In no case do the Plays undergo any process of expurgation. It is believed that, although they may sometimes run counter to what is called modern taste, the free and splendid energy of Elizabethan art, with its extreme realism and its extreme idealism —embodying, as it does, the best traditions of the English Drama—will not suffer from the frankest representation.

16, HENRIETTA STREET, COVENT GARDEN,
APRIL, 1888.

VIZETELLY & CO.'S NEW BOOKS, AND NEW EDITIONS.

RE-ISSUE OF CHOICE ILLUSTRATED BOOKS OF THE EIGHTEENTH CENTURY.

VIZETELLY & Co. beg to announce that they have made arrangements for the early publication of translations of some of the most charming illustrated volumes produced in France at the latter part of the 18th century. These works, so highly prized by amateurs, are distinguished for their numerous graceful designs by EISEN, MARILLIER, COCHIN, MOREAU, LE BARBIER, &c., finely engraved on copper by LE MIRE, LONGUEIL, ALIAMET, BACQUOY, BINET, DELAUNAY, and others. The volumes, which will be printed on handmade paper, with the engravings on India, Japanese, or Dutch paper, will be produced in the most perfect style, and issued in tasteful bindings.

I.

THE KISSES PRECEDED BY THE MONTH OF MAY. By
CLAUDE JOSEPH DORAT, Musketeer of the King. Illustrated with 47 Copper-plate Engravings from designs by Eisen and Marillier.

II.

DELIA BATHING. By the MARQUIS DE PEZAY. FOLLOWED BY
CELIA'S DOVES. By CLAUDE JOSEPH DORAT. Illustrated with 17 Copper-plate Engravings from designs by Eisen.

III.

THE TEMPLE OF GNIDUS. By MONTESQUIEU, with a Preface by
OCTAVE UZANNE. Illustrated with 15 Copper-plate Engravings from designs by Eisen and Le Barbier.

IV.

DAPHNIS AND CHLOE. By LONGUS. Illustrated with numerous
Copper-plate Engravings from designs by Eisen, Gerard, Prudhon, &c.

V.

THE ORIGIN OF THE GRACES. By Mdlle. DIONIS DUSÉJOUR.
Illustrated with Copper-plate Engravings from designs by Cochin.

VI.

BEAUTY'S DAY. By DE FAVRE. Illustrated with 10 Copper-
plate Engravings from designs by Leclerc.

IMPORTANT NEW NOVELS.

In crown 8vo, price 6s.

WILL. (Volonté.) By GEORGES OHNET,
Author of "The Ironmaster."

In crown 8vo, containing about 500 pages, price 7s. 6d.

BABOE DALIMA; OR, THE OPIUM FIEND.
By T. H. PERELAER.

"Is well written, and contains much that is interesting."—*Saturday Review*

In crown 8vo, price 6s.

A GARDEN OF TARES.
By JOHN HILL (Author of "The Corsars," &c.) and CLEMENT HOPKINS

In crown 8vo, with Frontispiece by H. Gray, price 6s.

THE SOIL. (La Terre.) By EMILE ZOLA.

RECENTLY PUBLISHED MASTERPIECES OF FRENCH FICTION.

In large octavo, beautifully printed and bound, and illustrated with 40 charming Etchings by Paul Avril, printed in the text. Price 15s.

MY UNCLE BARBASSOU. By MARIO UCHARD.

In demy 8vo, illustrated with 10 full-page Etchings by C. Courtry, price 7s. 6d.

THE BOHEMIANS OF THE LATIN QUARTER
(Scènes de la Vie de Bohème). By HENRI MURGER.

In crown 8vo, with Page Illustrations by James Tissot, price 6s.

RENÉE MAUPERIN. By E. and J. DE GONCOURT.
"One of the most pathetic romances of our day. Running through almost the whole gamut of human passion, it has the alternatives of sunshine and shade that exist in real life."—*Morning Post.*

In crown 8vo, price 3s. 6d.

FANNY. By ERNEST FEYDEAU.

In crown 8vo, price 3s. 6d. Uniform with "A CRUEL ENIGMA."

A LOVE CRIME. By PAUL BOURGET.
From the 17th French Edition.
"Who could take up such books, by the way, admirably translated, and not be simply and absolutely spellbound?"—*Truth.*

With upwards of 100 Engravings, price 3s. 6d.

THE EMOTIONS OF POLYDORE MARASQUIN.
By LÉON GOZLAN.
"An excellent translation of Léon Gozlan's best work."—*Echo.*

With 17 high-class Etchings after Toudouze, price 10s. 6d., elegantly bound.

MADEMOISELLE DE MAUPIN. By THEOPHILE GAUTIER.

"The golden book of spirit and sense, the Holy Writ of beauty."—A. C. SWINBURNE.
"Gautier is an inimitable model. His manner is so light and true, so really creative, his fancy so alert, his taste so happy, his humour so genial, that he makes illusion almost as contagious as laughter."—MR. HENRY JAMES.

Illustrated with Etchings by French Artists, price 6s., elegantly bound.

MADAME BOVARY: Provincial Manners. By GUSTAVE FLAUBERT.

TRANSLATED BY E. MARX-AVELING. With an Introduction and Notes of the proceedings against the author before the "Tribunal Correctionnel" of Paris.

"'Madame Bovary' grips your very vitals with an invincible power, like some scene you have really witnessed, some event which is actually happening before your eyes."—EMILE ZOLA.

With Six Etchings by Pierre Vidal and a Portrait of the Author, from a drawing by FLAUBERT'S niece, price 6s.

SALAMBO. By GUSTAVE FLAUBERT.

TRANSLATED FROM THE FRENCH "ÉDITION DÉFINITIVE" BY J. S. CHARTRES.

"The Translator has thoroughly understood the original, and has succeeded in putting it into good English. The type, paper, and material execution of the volume, inside and out, leave nothing to be desired."—*Westminster Review.*

Illustrated with highly finished Etchings, price 6s., handsomely bound.

GERMINIE LACERTEUX. By EDMOND and JULES DE GONCOURT.

"For myself, I can say that I could not lay the book down for a moment until I had finished it."—Letters on Books in *Truth.*
"The novelist throws a woman on to the slab of the amphitheatre and patiently dissects her and this suffices to uncover a whole bleeding corner of humanity."—EMILE ZOLA.

In tasteful binding, price 3s. 6d.

A CRUEL ENIGMA. By PAUL BOURGET.

TRANSLATED WITHOUT ABRIDGMENT FROM THE 18TH FRENCH EDITION.

"M. Bourget's most remarkable work, 'A Cruel Enigma,' has placed him above all competitors. The rare qualities of poet and critic which blend with and complete each other in this writer's mind have won him the spontaneous applause of that feminine circle to which his writings seem specially dedicated, as well as the weighty approbation of connoisseurs."—*Athenæum.*

Illustrated with 16 page Engravings, price 3s. 6d., attractively bound.

PAPA, MAMMA, AND BABY. By GUSTAVE DROZ.

TRANSLATED WITHOUT ABRIDGMENT FROM THE 130TH FRENCH EDITION.

"The lover who is a husband and the wife who is in love with the man she has married have never before been so attractively portrayed."—*Pictorial World.*

TWELFTH THOUSAND.

With 32 highly finished page Engravings, cloth gilt, price 3s. 6d.

SAPPHO: Parisian Manners. By ALPHONSE DAUDET.

TRANSLATED WITHOUT ABRIDGMENT FROM THE 100TH FRENCH EDITION

Specimen of the Engravings in DAUDET'S "SAPPHO."

"'SAPPHO' may, without exaggeration, be described as a glowing picture of Parisian life, with all its diversity of characters, with its Bohemian and half-world circles that are to be found nowhere else; with all its special immorality, in short, but also with the touch of poetry that saves it from utter corruption, and with the keen artistic sense that preserves its votaries from absolute degradation."—*Daily Telegraph.*

*** *VIZETELLY & CO.'S Edition of "SAPPHO" contains every line of the original work, and is the only complete version. All others are either expurgated or abridged.*

MISS F. MABEL ROBINSON'S NOVELS.

Second Edition, one vol., price 3s. 6d.

THE PLAN OF CAMPAIGN.

"Is a story of real power."—*Saturday Review.*

Third Edition, one vol., price 3s. 6d.

DISENCHANTMENT.

"Is full of humour and the liveliest and healthiest appreciation of the tender and emotional side of life, and the accuracy—the almost relentless accuracy—with which the depths of life are sounded, is startling in the work of an almost unknown writer."—*Pall Mall Gazette.*

"Some of the scenes are given with remarkably impressive power . . . The book is altogether of exceptional interest as an original study of many sides of actual human nature."—*The Graphic.*

Third Edition, one vol., price 3s. 6d.

MR. BUTLER'S WARD.

"A charming book, worked out with tenderness and insight."—*Athenæum.*

"The heroine is a very happy conception, a beautiful creation whose affecting history is treated with much delicacy, sympathy, and command of all that is touching."—*Illustrated News.*

"All the characters are new to fiction, and the author is to be congratulated on having made so full and original a haul out of the supposed to be exhausted waters of modern society."—*Graphic.*

MR. GEORGE MOORE'S REALISTIC NOVELS.

In one vol., price 3s. 6d.

A MERE ACCIDENT: A Realistic Story.

"The 'MERE ACCIDENT' is treated with a power and pathos which only serve to enhance the painfulness of the affair."—*Times.*

"Mr. Moore is one of our most powerful novelists. His gift of imagination and pathos are especially conspicuous in 'A MERE ACCIDENT.'"—*Morning Post.*

"'A MERE ACCIDENT' is one of the most agonising tragedies that was ever written."—*Society.*

Sixth Edition, price 3s. 6d.

A DRAMA IN MUSLIN.

"Mr. George Moore's work stands on a very much higher plane than the facile fiction of the circulating libraries. The hideous comedy of the marriage-market has been a stock topic with novelists from Thackeray downwards; but Mr. Moore goes deep into the yet more hideous tragedy which forms its afterpiece, the tragedy of enforced stagnant celibacy, with its double catastrophe of disease and vice."—*Pall Mall Gazette.*

Eleventh Edition, carefully Revised, and with a Special Preface, price 2s.

A MUMMER'S WIFE.

"A striking book, different in tone from current English fiction. The woman's character is a very powerful study. —*Athenæum.*

"'A Mummer's Wife' holds at present an unique position among English novels. It is a conspicuous success of its kind."—*Graphic.*

Fourth Edition, price 2s.

A MODERN LOVER.

"Mr. Moore has a real power of drawing character, and some of his descriptive scenes are capital."—*St. James's Gazette.*

"It would be difficult to praise too highly the strength, truth, delicacy, and pathos of the incident of Gwynnie Lloyd, and the admirable treatment of the great sacrifice she makes. The incident is depicted with skill and beauty."—*Spectator.*

CELEBRATED RUSSIAN NOVELS—*continued.*

By FEDOR DOSTOIEFFSKY.

Translated from the original Russian by Fred. Whishaw.

"There are three Russian novelists who, though, with one exception, little known out of their own country, stand head and shoulders above most of their contemporaries. In the opinion of some not indifferent critics, they are superior to all other novelists of this generation. Two of them, Dostoieffsky and Turgenieff, died not long ago, the third, Lyof Tolstoi, still lives. The one with the most marked individuality of character, probably the most highly gifted, was unquestionably Dostoieffsky."—*Spectator.*

In crown 8vo, price 5s.

UNCLE'S DREAM, & THE PERMANENT HUSBAND.

In crown 8vo, containing nearly 500 pages, price 6s.

THE IDIOT.

"Is unquestionably a work of great power and originality. M. Dostoieffsky crowds his canvas with living organisms, depicted with extreme vividness."—*Scotsman.*

In crown 8vo, price 5s.

THE FRIEND OF THE FAMILY; & THE GAMBLER.

" Dostoieffsky is one of the keenest observers of humanity amongst modern novelists. Both stories are very valuable as pictures of a society and a people with whom we are imperfectly acquainted, but who deserve the closest scrutiny."—*Public Opinion.*

Third Edition, in crown 8vo, with Portrait and Memoir, price 5s.

INJURY AND INSULT.

"That 'Injury and Insult' is a powerful novel few will deny. Vania is a marvellous character. Once read, the book can never be forgotten."—*St. Stephen's Review.*
" A masterpiece of fiction. The author has treated with consummate tact the difficult character of Natasha 'the incarnation and the slave of passion.' She lives and breathes in these vivid pages, and the reader is drawn into the vortex of her anguish, and rejoices when she breaks free from her chain."—*Morning Post.*

Third Edition. In crown 8vo, 450 pages, price 6s.

CRIME AND PUNISHMENT.

"Dostoieffsky is one of the most remarkable of modern writers, and his book, 'CRIME AND PUNISHMENT,' is one of the most moving of modern novels. It is the story of a murder and of the punishment which dogs the murderer ; and its effect is unique in fiction. It is realism, but such realism as M. Zola and his followers do not dream of. The reader knows the personages—strange, grotesque, terrible personages they are—more intimately than if he had been years with them in the flesh. He is constrained to live their lives, to suffer their tortures, to scheme and resist with them, exult with them, weep and laugh and despair with them ; he breathes the very breath of their nostrils, and with the madness that comes upon them he is afflicted even as they. This sounds extravagant praise, no doubt; but only to those who have not read the volume. To those who have, we are sure that it will appear rather under the mark than otherwise."—*The Athenæum.*

By M. U. LERMONTOFF.

In crown 8vo, with Frontispiece, price 3s. 6d.

A HERO OF OUR TIME.

" Lermontoff's genius was as wild and erratic as his stormy life and tragic end. But it had the true ring, and his name is enrolled among the literary immortals of his country. 'A Hero of Our Time' is utterly unconventional, possesses a weird interest all its own, and is in every way a remarkable romance."—*Spectator.*

THE MERMAID SERIES.

"I lie and dream of your full MERMAID wine."
Master Francis Beaumont to Ben Jonson.

Now Publishing,

In Half-Crown monthly vols., post 8vo, each volume containing 500 pages and an etched frontispiece, bound in cloth with cut or uncut edges.

AN UNEXPURGATED EDITION OF

THE BEST PLAYS

OF

THE OLD DRAMATISTS,

UNDER THE GENERAL EDITORSHIP OF HAVELOCK ELLIS.

IN the MERMAID SERIES are being issued the best plays of the Elizabethan and later dramatists—plays which, with Shakespeare's works, constitute the chief contribution of the English spirit to the literature of the world. The Editors who have given their assistance to the undertaking include men of literary eminence, who have distinguished themselves in this field, as well as younger writers of ability.

Each volume contains on an average five complete plays, prefaced by an Introductory Notice of the Author. Great care is taken to ensure, by consultation among the Editors, that the Plays selected are in every case the *best* and most representative—and not the most conventional, or those which have lived on a merely accidental and traditional reputation. A feature will be made of plays by little known writers, which although often so admirable are now almost inaccessible. In every instance the utmost pains is taken to secure the best text, the spelling is modernised, and brief but adequate notes are supplied. In no case do the Plays undergo any process of expurgation. It is believed that, although they may sometimes run counter to what is called modern taste, the free and splendid energy of Elizabethan art, with its extreme realism and its extreme idealism—embodying, as it does, the best traditions of the English Drama—will not suffer from the frankest representation.

VOLUMES ALREADY PUBLISHED.

EACH CONTAINING 500 PAGES AND UPWARDS, WITH STEEL ENGRAVED PORTRAITS
OR OTHER FRONTISPIECES.

With Portrait of William Wycherley, from the picture by Sir P. Lely.

THE COMPLETE PLAYS OF WILLIAM WYCHERLEY.
Edited, with an Introduction and Notes, by W. C. WARD.

With an engraved Portrait of Nathaniel Field, from the picture at Dulwich College.

NERO AND OTHER PLAYS. Edited, with Introductory Essays and
Notes, by H. P. HORNE, ARTHUR SYMONS, A. W. VERITY, and H. ELLIS.

With a View of Old London showing the Bankside and its Theatres.

THE BEST PLAYS OF JOHN FORD. Edited by HAVELOCK ELLIS.

With a View of the Globe Theatre.

THE BEST PLAYS OF WEBSTER AND TOURNEUR. With
an Introduction and Notes by JOHN ADDINGTON SYMONDS.

With an engraved portrait of James Shirley, from the picture in the Bodleian Gallery.

THE BEST PLAYS OF JAMES SHIRLEY. With an Introduction
by EDMUND GOSSE.

With a View of the Old Fortune Theatre, forming the Frontispiece.

THE BEST PLAYS OF THOMAS DEKKER. With Introductory Essay and Notes by ERNEST RHYS.

With a Portrait of Congreve, from the picture by Sir Godfrey Kneller.

THE COMPLETE PLAYS OF WILLIAM CONGREVE.
Edited and annotated by ALEX. C. EWALD.

In Two Vols., with Portraits of Beaumont and Fletcher.

THE BEST PLAYS OF BEAUMONT AND FLETCHER.
With an Introduction and Notes by J. ST. LOE STRACHEY.

With a Portrait of Middleton.

THE BEST PLAYS OF THOMAS MIDDLETON. With an
Introduction by ALGERNON CHARLES SWINBURNE.

*With a full-length Portrait of Alleyn, the Actor, from the Picture at
Dulwich College, the Third Edition of*

THE BEST PLAYS OF CHRISTOPHER MARLOWE. Edited,
with Critical Memoir and Notes, by HAVELOCK ELLIS, and containing a General
Introduction to the Series by J. ADDINGTON SYMONDS.

With a Portrait of Massinger, the Second Edition of

THE BEST PLAYS OF PHILIP MASSINGER. With a
Critical and Biographical Essay and Notes by ARTHUR SYMONS.

To be followed by

THE BEST PLAYS OF THOMAS HEYWOOD, Edited by J.
ADDINGTON SYMONDS—of THOMAS OTWAY, Edited by the Hon. RODEN
NOEL—of BEN JONSON, 3 Vols., Edited by BRINSLEY NICHOLSON and C. H.
HERFORD—SHADWELL, Edited by GEORGE SAINTSBURY.

ALSO **ARDEN OF FEVERSHAM,** and other Plays attributed to Shakespeare, Edited by ARTHUR SYMONS; and THE BEST PLAYS OF CHAPMAN,
MARSTON, ROWLEY, and FIELD, DRYDEN, APHRA BEHN, &c.

VIZETELLY'S ONE-VOLUME NOVELS.

"The idea of publishing cheap one-volume novels is a good one, and we wish the series every success."—*Saturday Review.*

3s. 6d. each.

COMPLETE IN HERSELF: A Love Story.

BY FRANCIS FORBES-ROBERTSON. With a Frontispiece.

THIRD EDITION.

DR. PHILLIPS: A Maida Vale Idyll. By FRANK DANBY.

"'Dr. Phillips' will make a sensation second to none that has yet been made in the world of fiction."—*Whitehall Review.*

AN EXILE'S ROMANCE. By ARTHUR KEYSER,

Author of "So English," "Dollars and Sense," &c.

"A very bright and vivacious novel."—*Daily Telegraph.*
"Abounds in exciting incidents."—*Morning Post.*

DOMINIC PENTERNE. By GODFREY BURCHETT.

"The cruel tragedy of the climax is terribly true to nature."—*Morning Post.*
"The curiosity of the reader is kept active until the end."—*Scotsman.*

MY BROTHER YVES. By PIERRE LOTI.

FROM THE 18TH FRENCH EDITION.

"A wonderfully vivid picture."—*Literary World.*
"Pierre Loti may be called the Clark Russell of France. His novels represent the best achievements of contemporary French fiction."—*Academy.*

THE MEADOWSWEET COMEDY. By T. A. PINKERTON

"There is clever smart writing in the book, and Mr. Pinkerton is certainly not tedious."—*Saturday Review.*
"The plot is one of love and intrigue well constructed."—*Scotsman.*

CLOUD AND SUNSHINE. (Noir et Rose.)

BY GEORGES OHNET, AUTHOR OF "THE IRONMASTER."

TRANSLATED FROM THE 60TH FRENCH EDITION BY MRS. HELEN STOTT.

THIRD EDITION.

COUNTESS SARAH. By GEORGES OHNET.

FROM THE 118TH FRENCH EDITION.

"The book contains some very powerful situations and first-rate character studies."—*Whitehall Review.*

THE THREATENING EYE. By E. F. KNIGHT.

"There is a good deal of power about this romance."—*Graphic.*
"Full of extraordinary power and originality. The story is one of quite exceptional force and impressiveness."—*Manchester Examiner.*

THE FORKED TONGUE. By R. L. DE HAVILLAND.

"In many respects the story is a remarkable one. Its men and women are drawn with power and without pity; their follies and their vices are painted in unmistakable colours, and with a skill that fascinates."—*Society.*

"Kiss me, dear," said Athénais.

MR. E. C. GRENVILLE-MURRAY'S WORKS.

Third and Cheaper Edition, in post 8vo, 434 pp., with numerous Page and other Engravings, handsomely bound, price 5s.

IMPRISONED IN A SPANISH CONVENT:

AN ENGLISH GIRL'S EXPERIENCES.

"Intensely fascinating. The *exposé* is a remarkable one, and as readable as remarkable." — *Society.*

"Excellent specimens of their author in his best and brightest mood." — *Athenæum.*

"Highly dramatic." — *Scotsman.*   "Strikingly interesting." — *Literary World.*

"Instead of the meek cooing dove with naked feet and a dusty face who had talked of dying for me, I had now a bright-eyed rosy-cheeked companion who had cambric pocket-handkerchiefs with violet scent on them and smoked cigarettes on the sly." — *Page* 75.

New and Cheaper Edition, Two Vols. large post 8vo, attractively bound, price 15s.

UNDER THE LENS: SOCIAL PHOTOGRAPHS.

ILLUSTRATED WITH ABOUT 300 ENGRAVINGS BY WELL-KNOWN ARTISTS.

CONTENTS: — JILTS — ADVENTURERS AND ADVENTURESSES — HONOURABLE GENTLEMEN (M.P.s) — PUBLIC SCHOOLBOYS AND UNDERGRADUATES — SPENDTHRIFTS — SOME WOMEN I HAVE KNOWN — ROUGHS OF HIGH AND LOW DEGREE.

"Brilliant, highly-coloured sketches. . . . containing beyond doubt some of the best writing that has come from Mr. Grenville-Murray's pen." — *St. James's Gazette.*

"Limned audaciously, unsparingly, and with much ability." — *World.*

"Distinguished by their pitiless fidelity to nature." — *Society.*

At the Eton and Harrow Cricket Match : *from "UNDER THE LENS."*

MR. E. C. GRENVILLE-MURRAY'S WORKS—*continued.*

Seventh Edition, in post 8vo, handsomely bound, price 7s. 6d.

SIDE-LIGHTS ON ENGLISH SOCIETY:

Sketches from Life, Social and Satirical.

ILLUSTRATED WITH NEARLY 300 CHARACTERISTIC ENGRAVINGS.

CONTENTS:—FLIRTS. — ON HER BRITANNIC MAJESTY'S SERVICE. — SEMI-DETACHED WIVES.—NOBLE LORDS.—YOUNG WIDOWS.—OUR SILVERED YOUTH, OR NOBLE OLD BOYS.

"This is a startling book. The volume is expensively and elaborately got up; the writing is bitter, unsparing, and extremely clever."—*Vanity Fair.*

"Mr. Grenville-Murray sparkles very steadily throughout the present volume, and puts to excellent use his incomparable knowledge of life and manners, of men and cities, of appearances and facts. Of his several descants upon English types, I shall only remark that they are brilliantly and dashingly written, curious as to their matter, and admirably readable."—*Truth.*

"No one can question the brilliancy of the sketches, nor affirm that ' Side-Lights' is aught but a fascinating book. . . . . . . The book is destined to make a great noise in the world."—*Whitehall Review.*

Third Edition, with Frontispiece and Vignette, price 2s. 6d.

HIGH LIFE IN FRANCE UNDER THE REPUBLIC:

SOCIAL AND SATIRICAL SKETCHES IN PARIS AND THE PROVINCES.

"Take this book as it stands, with the limitations imposed upon its author by circumstances, and it will be found very enjoyable. . . . . The volume is studded with shrewd observations on French life at the present day."—*Spectator.*

"A very clever and entertaining series of social and satirical sketches, almost French in their point and vivacity."—*Contemporary Review.*

"A most amusing book, and no less instructive if read with allowances and understanding."—*World.*

"Full of the caustic humour and graphic character-painting so characteristic of Mr. Grenville-Murray's work, and dealing trenchantly yet lightly with almost every conceivable phase of social, political, official, journalistic and theatrical life."—*Society.*

MR. E. C. GRENVILLE-MURRAY'S WORKS—*continued.*

Second Edition, in large 8vo, tastefully bound, with gilt edges, price 10s. 6d.

FORMING A HANDSOME VOLUME FOR A PRESENT.

PEOPLE I HAVE MET.

Illustrated with 54 tinted Page Engravings, from Designs by FRED. BARNARD.

THE RICH WIDOW (reduced from the original engraving).

"Mr. Grenville-Murray's pages sparkle with cleverness and with a shrewd wit, caustic or cynical at times, but by no means excluding a due appreciation of the softer virtues of women and the sterner excellences of men. The talent of the artist (Mr. Barnard) is akin to that of the author, and the result of the combination is a book that, once taken up, can hardly be laid down until the last page is perused."—*Spectator.*

"All of Mr. Grenville-Murray's portraits are clever and life-like, and some of them are not unworthy of a model who was more before the author's eyes than Addison—namely, Thackeray."—*Truth.*

"Mr. Grenville-Murray's sketches are genuine studies, and are the best things of the kind that have been published since 'Sketches by Boz,' to which they are superior in the sense in which artistically executed character portraits are superior to caricatures."—*St. James's Gazette.*

"No book of its class can be pointed out so admirably calculated to show another generation the foibles and peculiarities of the men and women of our times."—*Morning Post.*

An Edition of "PEOPLE I HAVE MET" is published in small 8vo, with Frontispiece and other page Engravings, price 2s. 6d.

In post 8vo, 150 engravings, cloth gilt, price 5s.

JILTS AND OTHER SOCIAL PHOTOGRAPHS.

Uniform with the above.

SPENDTHRIFTS AND OTHER SOCIAL PHOTOGRAPHS.

MR. G. A. SALA'S WORKS—*continued.*

In demy 8vo, handsomely printed on hand-made paper, with the Illustrations, on India paper mounted (only 250 copies printed), price 10s. 6d.

UNDER THE SUN:
ESSAYS MAINLY WRITTEN IN HOT COUNTRIES.

A New Edition, containing several Additional Essays, with an Etched Portrait of the Author by BOCOURT, and 12 full-page Engravings.

"There are nearly four hundred pages between the covers of this volume, which means tha contain plenty of excellent reading."—*St. James's Gazette.*

Uniform with the above, with Frontispiece and other Page Engravings.

DUTCH PICTURES, and PICTURES DONE WITH A QUILL.

The Graphic remarks: "We have received a sumptuous new edition of Mr. G. A. Sala's well-known 'Dutch Pictures.' It is printed on rough paper, and is enriched with many admirable illustrations."

"Mr. Sala's best work has in it something of Montaigne, a great deal of Charles Lamb—made deeper and broader—and not a little of Lamb's model, the accomplished and quaint Sir Thomas Brown. These 'Dutch Pictures' and 'Pictures Done with a Quill' should be placed alongside Oliver Wendell Holmes's inimitable budgets of friendly gossip and Thackeray's 'Roundabout Papers.' They display to perfection the quick eye, good taste, and ready hand of the born essayist—they are never tiresome."—*Daily Telegraph.*

UNDER THE SUN, and DUTCH PICTURES AND PICTURES DONE WITH A QUILL *are also published in crown 8vo, price 2s. 6d. each.*

Fourth and Cheaper Edition, in crown 8vo, price 3s. 6d.

A JOURNEY DUE SOUTH;
TRAVELS IN SEARCH OF SUNSHINE,

INCLUDING

MARSEILLES, NICE, BASTIA, AJACCIO, GENOA, PISA, BOLOGNA, VENICE, ROME, NAPLES, POMPEII, &c.

ILLUSTRATED WITH 16 FULL-PAGE ENGRAVINGS BY VARIOUS ARTISTS.

"In 'A Journey due South' Mr. Sala is in his brightest and cheeriest mood, ready with quip and jest and anecdote, brimful of allusion ever happy and pat."—*Saturday Review.*

Tenth Edition, in crown 8vo, containing over 400 pages, attractively bound, price 2s. 6d.

PARIS HERSELF AGAIN.
BY GEORGE AUGUSTUS SALA.

WITH NUMEROUS CHARACTERISTIC ILLUSTRATIONS BY FRENCH ARTISTS.

"On subjects like those in his present work, Mr. Sala is at his best."—*The Times.*

"This book is one of the most readable that has appeared for many a day. Few Englishmen know so much of old and modern Paris as Mr. Sala."—*Truth.*

"'Paris Herself Again' is infinitely more amusing than most novels. There is no style so chatty and so unwearying as that of which Mr. Sala is a master."—*The World.*

A BUCK OF THE REGENCY : *from* "*DUTCH PICTURES.*"

" Mr. Sala's best work has in it something of Montaigne, a great deal of Charles Lamb—made deeper and broader—and not a little of Lamb's model, the accomplished and quaint Sir Thomas Brown.   These ' Dutch Pictures ' and ' Pictures Done With a Quill' should be placed alongside Oliver Wendell Holmes's inimitable budgets of friendly gossip and Thackeray's 'Roundabout Papers.   They display to perfection the quick eye, good taste, and ready hand of the born essayist—they are never tiresome." —*Daily Telegraph*.

a

NEW AND CHEAPER EDITION OF
ZOLA'S POWERFUL REALISTIC NOVELS.

Translated without Abridgment, and Illustrated with all the Original Engravings.

Price 3s. 6d. per volume.

Mr. HENRY JAMES on ZOLA'S NOVELS.

"A novelist with a system, a passionate conviction, a great plan—incontestable attributes of M. Zola—is not now to be easily found in England or the United States, where the story-teller's art is almost exclusively feminine, is mainly in the hands of timid (even when very accomplished) women, whose acquaintance with life is severely restricted, and who are not conspicuous for general views. The novel, moreover, among ourselves, is almost always addressed to young unmarried ladies, or at least always assumes them to be a large part of the novelist's public.

"This fact, to a French story-teller, appears, of course, a damnable restriction, and M. Zola would probably decline to take *au sérieux* any work produced under such unnatural conditions. Half of life is a sealed book to young unmarried ladies, and how can a novel be worth anything that deals only with half of life? These objections are perfectly valid, and it may be said that our English system is a good thing for virgins and boys, and a bad thing for the novel itself, when the novel is regarded as something more than a simple *jeu d'esprit*, and considered as a composition that treats of life at large and helps us to *know*."

NANA. *From the 127th French Edition.*

THE "ASSOMMOIR." (The Prelude to "NANA.")

PIPING HOT! (POT-BOUILLE.)

GERMINAL; OR, MASTER AND MAN.

THE RUSH FOR THE SPOIL. (LA CURÉE.)

THE LADIES' PARADISE. (The Sequel to "PIPING HOT!")

ABBÉ MOURET'S TRANSGRESSION.

THÉRÈSE RAQUIN.

HIS MASTERPIECE? (L'ŒUVRE.) *With a Portrait of* M. EMILE ZOLA, *Etched by* BOCOURT.

THE FORTUNE OF THE ROUGONS.

HOW JOLLY LIFE IS!

A LOVE EPISODE.

VIZETELLY'S HALF-CROWN SERIES.

PARIS HERSELF AGAIN. By George Augustus Sala. Tenth

Edition. Over 400 pages and numerous Engravings.

"On subjects like those in his present work, Mr. Sala is at his best."—*The Times.*

"This book is one of the most readable that has appeared for many a day. Few English-men know so much of old and modern Paris as Mr. Sala."—*Truth.*

UNDER THE SUN. Essays Mainly Written in Hot Countries.

By George Augustus Sala. A New Edition. Illustrated with 12 page Engravings and an etched Portrait of the Author.

"There are nearly four hundred pages between the covers of this volume, which means that they contain plenty of excellent reading."—*St. James's Gazette.*

DUTCH PICTURES and PICTURES DONE WITH A QUILL.

By George Augustus Sala. A New Edition. Illustrated with 8 page Engravings.

"Mr. Sala's best work has in it something of Montaigne, a great deal of Charles Lamb—made deeper and broader—and not a little of Lamb's model, the accomplished and quaint Sir Thomas Brown. These 'Dutch Pictures' and 'Pictures Done with a Quill,' display to perfection the quick eye, good taste, and ready hand of the born essayist—they are never tiresome."—*Daily Telegraph.*

HIGH LIFE IN FRANCE UNDER THE REPUBLIC. Social

AND SATIRICAL SKETCHES IN PARIS AND THE PROVINCES. By E. C. Grenville-Murray. Third Edition, with a Frontispiece.

"A very clever and entertaining series of social and satirical sketches, almost French in their point and vivacity."—*Contemporary Review.*

"A most amusing book, and no less instructive if read with allowances and understanding."—*World.*

PEOPLE I HAVE MET. By E. C. Grenville-Murray. A New

Edition. With 8 page Engravings from Designs by F. Barnard.

"Mr. Grenville-Murray's pages sparkle with cleverness and with a shrewd wit, caustic or cynical at times, but by no means excluding a due appreciation of the softer virtues of women and the sterner excellencies of men."—*Spectator.*

"All of Mr. Grenville-Murray's portraits are clever and life-like, and some of them are not unworthy of a model who was more before the author's eye than Addison—namely, Thackeray."—*Truth.*

A BOOK OF COURT SCANDAL.

CAROLINE BAUER AND THE COBURGS. From the German,

with two carefully engraved Portraits. Second Edition.

"Caroline Bauer's name became in a mysterious and almost tragic manner connected with those of two men highly esteemed and well remembered in England—Prince Leopold of Coburg, and his nephew, Prince Albert's trusty friend and adviser, Baron Stockmar."—*The Times.*

THE STORY OF THE DIAMOND NECKLACE, Told in Detail

FOR THE FIRST TIME. A New Edition. By Henry Vizetelly. Illustrated with an authentic representation of the Diamond Necklace, and a Portrait of the Countess de la Motte, engraved on steel, and other Engravings.

"Had the most daring of our sensational novelists put forth the present plain unvarnished statement of facts as a work of fiction, it would have been denounced as so violating all probabilities as to be a positive insult to the common sense of the reader. Yet strange, startling, incomprehensible as is the narrative which the author has here evolved, every word of it is true."—*Notes and Queries.*

GUZMAN OF ALFARAQUE. A Spanish Novel, translated by

E. Lowdell. Illustrated with highly finished steel Engravings from Designs by Stahl.

"The wit, vivacity and variety of this masterpiece cannot be over-estimated."—*Morning Post.*

In post 8vo, with numerous Page and other Engravings, cloth gilt, price 3s. 6d.,

NO ROSE WITHOUT A THORN,
AND OTHER TALES.

By F. C. BURNAND, H. SAVILE CLARKE, R. E. FRANCILLON, &c.

" By the aid of the chimney with the register up Mrs. Lupscombe's curiosity was, to certain extent, gratified."—*Page* 19.

In post 8vo, with numerous Page and other Engravings, cloth gilt, price 3s. 6d.

THE DOVE'S NEST,
AND OTHER TALES.

By JOSEPH HATTON, RICHARD JEFFERIES, H. SAVILE CLARKE, &c.

A STORY OF THE STAGE.
In crown 8vo, with eight tinted page engravings, price 2s.

SAVED BY A SMILE.
By JAMES SIREE.

Third Edition. In picture boards, crown 8vo, with page engravings, price 2s.

MY FIRST CRIME.

By G. MACÉ, FORMER "CHEF DE LA SÛRETÉ" OF THE PARIS POLICE.

"An account by a real Lecoq of a real crime is a novelty among the mass of criminal novels with which the world has been favoured since the death of the great originator Gaboriau. It is to M. Macé, who has had to deal with real *juges d'instruction*, real *agents de la sûreté*, and real murderers, that we are indebted for this really interesting addition to a species of literature which has of late begun to pall."—*Saturday Review.*

CAPITAL STORIES.

In Shilling Volumes. The Earlier Volumes, shortly to be published, will include :

THE CHAPLAIN'S SECRET. By LÉON DE TINSEAU.

AVATAR; OR, THE DOUBLE TRANSFORMATION. By THÉOPHILE GAUTIER.

COLONEL QUAGG'S CONVERSION; and Other Stories. By GEORGE AUGUSTUS SALA.

THE MARCHIONESS'S TEAM. By LÉON DE TINSEAU.

In scarlet covers, price One Shilling each.

CELEBRATED SENSATIONAL NOVELS.

BEWITCHING IZA. By ALEXIS BOUVIER.

LECOQ THE DETECTIVE'S DAUGHTER. By BUSNACH AND CHABRILLAT.

DISPATCH AND SECRECY. By GEORGES GRISON.

THE MEUDON MYSTERY. By JULES MARY.

A WILY WIDOW. By ALEXIS BOUVIER.

Other Volumes are in preparation.

MISCELLANEOUS SHILLING BOOKS.

SAPPHO: Parisian Manners. By ALPHONSE DAUDET. With 8 Page Engravings. 140th Thousand.

SO ENGLISH! By THE AUTHOR OF "AN EXILE'S ROMANCE."

WRECKED IN LONDON: A Story founded on one of the Great Scandals of the Day. By WALTER FAIRLIE.

A TALE OF MADNESS: Being the Narrative of PAUL STAFFORD. EDITED BY JULIAN CRAY.

IRISH HISTORY FOR ENGLISH READERS. By WILLIAM STEPHENSON GREGG. *Second Edition.* 1s., *or cloth,* 1s. 6d.

In paper cover, 1s.; or in parchment binding, gilt on side, 2s. 6d.

THE PASSER-BY. A Comedy in one Act, suited for Private Representation. By FRANÇOIS COPPÉE, of the French Academy.

LUCIFER IN LONDON, and his Reflections on Life, Manners, and the Prospects of Society. A SATIRICAL POEM. BY A WELL-KNOWN POET.

THE EXCELLENT MYSTERY. A MATRIMONIAL SATIRE. By LORD PIMLICO.

JUVENAL IN PICCADILLY. By OXONIENSIS.

VIZETELLY'S SIXPENNY SERIES OF AMUSING AND ENTERTAINING BOOKS.

KING SOLOMON'S WIVES: Or the Mysterious Mines. By HYDER RAGGED. *With Humorous Illustrations by* LANCELOT SPEED.

THE MANCHESTER MERCHANT. From the German.

TARTARIN OF TARASCON. By ALPHONSE DAUDET.

CECILE'S FORTUNE. By F. DU BOISGOBEY.

THE THREE-CORNERED HAT. By P. A. DE ALARCON.

THE BLACK CROSS MYSTERY. By H. CORKRAN.

THE STEEL NECKLACE. By F. DU BOISGOBEY.

THE GREAT HOGGARTY DIAMOND. By W. M. THACKERAY.

CAPTAIN SPITFIRE, AND THE UNLUCKY TREASURE. By P. A. DE ALARCON.

MATRIMONY BY ADVERTISEMENT; AND OTHER ADVENTURES OF A JOURNALIST. BY C. G. PAYNE. 15 *Engravings.*

VOTE FOR POTTLEBECK! THE STORY OF A POLITICIAN IN LOVE. BY C. G. PAYNE. 20 *Engravings.*

YOUNG WIDOWS. By E. C. GRENVILLE-MURRAY. 50 *Engravings.*

THE DETECTIVE'S EYE. By F. DU BOISGOBEY.

THE STRANGE PHANTASY OF DR. TRINTZIUS. By AUGUSTE VITU.

A SHABBY GENTEEL STORY. By W. M. THACKERAY.

THE RED LOTTERY TICKET. By F. DU BOISGOBEY.

THE FIDDLER AMONG THE BANDITS. By ALEX. DUMAS.

Other Volumes are in Preparation.

In One Volume, large imperial 8vo, price 3s., or single numbers price 6d. each,

THE SOCIAL ZOO;

SATIRICAL, SOCIAL, AND HUMOROUS SKETCHES BY THE BEST WRITERS.
Copiously Illustrated in many Styles by well-known Artists.

OUR GILDED YOUTH. By E. C. GRENVILLE-MURRAY.
NICE GIRLS. By R. MOUNTENEY JEPHSON.
NOBLE LORDS. By E. C. GRENVILLE-MURRAY.
FLIRTS. By E. C. GRENVILLE-MURRAY.
OUR SILVERED YOUTH. By E. C. GRENVILLE-MURRAY.
MILITARY MEN AS THEY WERE. By E. DYNE FENTON.

With over 30 Illustrations, price 6d.

A POPULAR LIFE OF THE RT. HON. W. E. GLADSTONE.

In small 8vo Ornamental Scarlet Covers. 1s. per Volume.

DU BOISGOBEY'S SENSATIONAL NOVELS.

" Ah, friend, how many and many a while
They've made the slow time fleetly flow,
And solaced pain and charmed exile,
BOISGOBEY and GABORIAU !"

Ballade of Railway Novels in " Longman's Magazine."

Lately Published Volumes.

SAVED FROM THE HAREM.
Two Volumes.

WHERE'S ZENOBIA ?
Two Volumes.

THE FATAL LEGACY.

THE RESULTS OF A DUEL.

THE RED CAMELLIA. 2 Vols.

THE RED BAND. 2 Vols.

THE NAMELESS MAN.

THE CONVICT COLONEL.

THE CORAL PIN. 2 Vols.

ANGEL OF THE CHIMES.

THIEVING FINGERS.

THE THUMB STROKE.

FERNANDE'S CHOICE.

PRETTY BABIOLE.

THE GOLDEN TRESS.

A FIGHT FOR A FORTUNE.

HIS GREAT REVENGE. Two Vols.

THE GOLDEN PIG. 2 Vols.

THE MATAPAN AFFAIR.

THE PHANTOM LEG.

THE JAILER'S PRETTY WIFE.

A RAILWAY TRAGEDY.

THE STEEL NECKLACE and
CECILE'S FORTUNE.

THE DETECTIVE'S EYE and
THE RED LOTTERY TICKET

THE OLD AGE OF LECOQ, THE DETECTIVE. Two Vols.

"The romances of Gaboriau and Du Boisgobey picture the marvellous Lecoq and other wonders of shrewdness, who piece together the elaborate details of the most complicated crimes, as Professor Owen with the smallest bone as a foundation could reconstruct the most extraordinary animals."—*Standard.*

IN THE SERPENTS' COILS.

"Its interest never flags. Its terrific excitement continues to the end."—*Oldham Chronicle.*

THE DAY OF RECKONING. Two Vols.

"M. du Boisgobey gives us no tiresome descriptions or laboured analyses of character; under his facile pen plots full of incident are quickly opened and unwound. He does not stop to moralise; all his art consists in creating intricacies which shall keep the reader's curiosity on the stretch, and offer a full scope to his own really wonderful ingenuity for unravelling."—*Times.*

THE SEVERED HAND.

"The plot is a marvel of intricacy and cleverly managed surprises."—*Literary World.*

BERTHA'S SECRET.

"'Bertha's Secret' is a most effective romance. We need not say how the story ends, for this would spoil the reader's pleasure in a novel which depends for all its interest on the skilful weaving and unweaving of mysteries."—*Times.*

WHO DIED LAST? OR THE RIGHTFUL HEIR.

"Travellers will find the time occupied by a long journey pass away rapidly with one of Du Boisgobey's absorbing volumes in their hand."—*London Figaro.*

THE CRIME OF THE OPERA HOUSE. Two Vols.

"We are led breathless from the first page to the last, and close the book with a thorough admiration for the vigorous romancist who has the courage to fulfil the true function of the story-teller, by making reflection subordinate to action."—*Aberdeen Journal.*

GABORIAU & DU BOISGOBEY SENSATIONAL NOVELS.

In double volumes, bound in scarlet cloth, price 2s. 6d. each.

1.—THE MYSTERY OF ORCIVAL, AND THE GILDED CLIQUE.
2.—THE LEROUGE CASE, AND OTHER PEOPLE'S MONEY.
3.—LECOQ, THE DETECTIVE.   4.—THE SLAVES OF PARIS.
5.—IN PERIL OF HIS LIFE, AND INTRIGUES OF A POISONER.
6.—DOSSIER NO. 113, AND THE LITTLE OLD MAN OF BA-
   TIGNOLLES.   7.—THE COUNT'S MILLIONS.
8.—THE OLD AGE OF LECOQ, THE DETECTIVE.
9.—THE CATASTROPHE.   10.—THE DAY OF RECKONING.
11.—THE SEVERED HAND, AND IN THE SERPENTS' COILS.
12.—BERTHA'S SECRET, AND WHO DIED LAST?
13.—THE CRIME OF THE OPERA HOUSE.
14.—THE MATAPAN AFFAIR, AND A FIGHT FOR A FORTUNE.
15.—THE GOLDEN PIG.
16.—THE THUMB STROKE, AND PRETTY BABIOLE.
17.—THE CORAL PIN.   18.—HIS GREAT REVENGE.

In small post 8vo, ornamental covers, 1s. each ; in cloth, 1s. 6d.

VIZETELLY'S POPULAR FRENCH NOVELS.

EXAMPLES OF THE BEST FRENCH FICTION UNOBJECTIONABLE IN CHARACTER.

"*They are books that may be safely left lying about where the ladies of the family can pick them up and read them.*"—SHEFFIELD INDEPENDENT.

FROMONT THE YOUNGER & RISLER THE ELDER. By A. DAUDET.

"The series starts well with M. Alphonse Daudet's masterpiece."—*Athenæum.*
"A terrible story, powerful after a sledge-hammer fashion in some parts, and wonderfully tender, touching, and pathetic in others."—*Illustrated London News.*

SAMUEL BROHL AND PARTNER. By V. CHERBULIEZ.

"A supremely dramatic study of a man who lived two lives at once, even within himself. The reader's discovery of his double nature is one of the most cleverly managed of surprises, and Samuel Brohl's final dissolution of partnership with himself is a remarkable stroke of almost pathetic comedy."—*The Graphic.*

THE DRAMA OF THE RUE DE LA PAIX. By A. Belot.

"A decidedly interesting and thrilling narrative is told with great force and passion, relieved by sprightliness and tenderness."—*Illustrated London News.*

MAUGARS JUNIOR. By A. Theuriet.

"One of the most charming novelettes we have read for a long time."—*Literary World.*

WAYWARD DOSIA, & THE GENEROUS DIPLOMATIST. By Henry Gréville.

"As epigrammatic as anything Lord Beaconsfield has ever written."—*Hampshire Telegraph.*

A NEW LEASE OF LIFE, & SAVING A DAUGHTER'S DOWRY. By E. About.

"The story, as a flight of brilliant and eccentric imagination, is unequalled in its peculiar way."—*The Graphic.*

COLOMBA, & CARMEN. By P. Mérimée.

"The freshness and raciness is quite cheering after the stereotyped three-volume novels with which our circulating libraries are crammed."—*Halifax Times.*

A WOMAN'S DIARY, & THE LITTLE COUNTESS. By O. Feuillet.

"Is wrought out with masterly skill, and although of a slightly sensational kind, cannot be said to be hurtful either mentally or morally."—*Dumbarton Herald.*

BLUE-EYED META HOLDENIS, & A STROKE OF DIPLOMACY. By V. Cherbuliez.

"'Blue-eyed Meta Holdenis' is a delightful tale."—*Civil Service Gazette.*
"'A Stroke of Diplomacy' is a bright vivacious story."—*Hampshire Advertiser.*

THE GODSON OF A MARQUIS. By A. Theuriet.

"From the beginning to the close the interest of the story never flags."—*Life.*

THE TOWER OF PERCEMONT & MARIANNE. By George Sand.

"George Sand has a great name, and the 'Tower of Percemont' is not unworthy of it."—*Illustrated London News.*

THE LOW-BORN LOVER'S REVENGE. By V. Cherbuliez.

"One of M. Cherbuliez's many exquisitely written productions. The studies of human nature under various influences, especially in the cases of the unhappy heroine and her low-born lover, are wonderfully effective."—*Illustrated London News.*

THE NOTARY'S NOSE, AND OTHER AMUSING STORIES. By E. About.

"Crisp and bright, full of movement and interest."—*Brighton Herald.*

DOCTOR CLAUDE; OR, LOVE RENDERED DESPERATE. By H. Malot. Two vols.

"We have to appeal to our very first flight of novelists to find anything so artistic in English romance as these books."—*Dublin Evening Mail.*

THE THREE RED KNIGHTS; OR, THE BROTHERS' VENGEANCE. By P. Féval.

"The one thing that strikes us in these stories is the marvellous dramatic skill of th writers."—*Sheffield Independent.*

Unabridged Edition : in small 8vo, ornamental scarlet covers,

Price 9d. per Volume.

GABORIAU'S SENSATIONAL NOVELS.

IN PERIL OF HIS LIFE.

"A story of thrilling interest, and admirably translated."—*Sunday Times.*

THE LEROUGE CASE.

"M. Gaboriau is a skilful and brilliant writer, capable of so diverting the attention and interest of his readers that not one word or line in his book will be skipped or read carelessly."—*Hampshire Advertiser.*

OTHER PEOPLE'S MONEY.

"The interest is kept up throughout, and the story is told graphically and with a good deal of art."—*London Figaro.*

LECOQ THE DETECTIVE. Two Vols.

"In the art of forging a tangled chain of complicated incidents involved and inexplicable until the last link is reached and the whole made clear, Mr. Wilkie Collins is equalled, if not excelled, by M. Gaboriau."—*Brighton Herald.*

THE GILDED CLIQUE.

"Full of incident, and instinct with life and action. Altogether this is a most fascinating book."—*Hampshire Advertiser.*

THE MYSTERY OF ORCIVAL.

"The Author keeps the interest of the reader at fever heat, and by a succession of unexpected turns and incidents, the drama is ultimately worked out to a very pleasant result. The ability displayed is unquestionable."—*Sheffield Independent.*

DOSSIER NO. 113.

"The plot is worked out with great skill, and from first to last the reader's interest is never allowed to flag."—*Dumbarton Herald.*

THE LITTLE OLD MAN OF BATIGNOLLES.

THE SLAVES OF PARIS. Two Vols.

"Sensational, full of interest, cleverly conceived, and wrought out with consummate skill."—*Oxford and Cambridge Journal.*

THE CATASTROPHE. Two Vols.

"'The Catastrophe' does ample credit to M. Gaboriau's reputation as a novelist of vast resource in incident and of wonderful ingenuity in constructing and unravelling thrilling mysteries."—*Aberdeen Journal.*

THE COUNT'S MILLIONS. Two Vols.

"To those who love the mysterious and the sensational, Gaboriau's stories are irresistibly fascinating. His marvellously clever pages hold the mirror up to nature with absolute fidelity ; and the interest with which he contrives to invest his characters proves that exaggeration is unnecessary to a master."—*Society.*

INTRIGUES OF A POISONER.

"The wonderful Sensational Novels of Emile Gaboriau."—*Globe.*

In demy 4to, handsomely printed and bound, with gilt edges, price 12s.

A HISTORY OF CHAMPAGNE;

WITH NOTES ON THE OTHER SPARKLING WINES OF FRANCE.

By HENRY VIZETELLY.

CHEVALIER OF THE ORDER OF FRANZ-JOSEF.
WINE JUROR FOR GREAT BRITAIN AT THE VIENNA AND PARIS EXHIBITIONS OF 1873 AND 1878.

Illustrated with 350 Engravings,

FROM ORIGINAL SKETCHES AND PHOTOGRAPHS, ANCIENT MSS., EARLY PRINTED
BOOKS, RARE PRINTS, CARICATURES, ETC.

"A very agreeable medley of history, anecdote, geographical description, and such like matter, distinguished by an accuracy not often found in such medleys, and illustrated in the most abundant and pleasingly miscellaneous fashion."—*Daily News.*

"Mr. Henry Vizetelly's handsome book about Champagne and other sparkling wines of France is full of curious information and amusement. It should be widely read and appreciated."—*Saturday Review.*

"Mr. Henry Vizetelly has written a quarto volume on the 'History of Champagne,' in which he has collected a large number of facts, many of them very curious and interesting. Many of the woodcuts are excellent."—*Athenæum.*

"It is probable that this large volume contains such an amount of information touching the subject which it treats as cannot be found elsewhere. How competent the author was for the task he undertook is to be inferred from the functions he has discharged, and from the exceptional opportunities he enjoyed."—*Illustrated London News.*

"A veritable *édition de luxe*, dealing with the history of Champagne from the time of the Romans to the present date. . . . An interesting book, the incidents and details of which are very graphically told with a good deal of wit and humour. The engravings are exceedingly well executed."—*The Wine and Spirit News.*

www.ingramcontent.com/pod-product-compliance
Lightning Source LLC
Chambersburg PA
CBHW032012110726

47901CB00004B/1057